THE SECOND SON

Published by: **Morehead Publishing Inc.**
284 Englewood Drive
Mineral Wells, West Virginia 26150
www.moreheadpublishing.com

Nielsen, Paul W.
The Second Son
Medical Thriller

ISBN 978-0-9903845-3-3 (Paperback)
ISBN 978-0-9903845-4-0 (ePub)
ISBN 978-0-9903845-5-7 (Kindle)

Cover Illustration: **Becky Anderson & Jeff Morehead**
Covers and Book Design: **Morehead Publishing Inc.**

First Edition, February 2015

Printed in the United States of America

MOREHEAD
P U B L I S H I N G
WEST VIRGINIA, USA

ONE

He was unique. "Unique" is an adequate word as any. In reality, it wasn't that Jason himself was distinctive. He felt like any other person in this world — or so he supposed. No, it was more a matter of the things that happened to him or, to be precise, a power he possessed.

When exactly the power started was hard to say. There hadn't been an earthshaking epiphany or something that would even suggest who or what he was. The revelation had been more a matter of a subtle fruition: a premonition here, a foreshadowing there — things that could be rationalized away if one tried hard enough. But at those times, a dim memory teased the interface between what was and what was not. That usually crisp line became blurred; reminiscent of the tidemarks left on a sandy beach.

There had been several glimpses of his power in the past, but none had been so profound they couldn't be tempered with time and reason. Then the undeniable event occurred. It sat in his memory like a lone beacon marking the beginning of his awareness. He didn't know it then, of course; he was only ten years old. But it was a colossal event of a magnitude that shaped the past and will shape the future of mankind.

Jason Corey awoke to the sounds of summer that early June morning, just as he had every morning since summer vacation had started. He glanced out the window of his upstairs bedroom while he peeled off his pajamas and retrieved clean socks and underwear from his dresser drawer. The still chilly morning air raised goose bumps on his bare skin while he dressed. The sun was out, but ominous, distant clouds predicted it might well end up a day to be indoors. That didn't bother him since reading was one of his favorite pastimes. He wanted to be a doctor, just like Doogie Howser. Jason never missed his favorite show, and sometimes he would practice his resolute face in the bathroom mirror. He was a smart kid, the kind his classmates called "teacher's pet." As is often the case with such children, he had learned to pass much of his time alone. The possibility of becoming a physician was within his capacity.

Jason picked up yesterday's jeans and selected a t-shirt from his closet. His mother allowed jeans for more than one day, but he needed fresh underwear, shirts, and socks every day. He shuffled into his sneakers as he headed toward the stairs of the large Victorian home then took the stairs in four enormous bounds, supporting himself as he slid his hands along the railings. He dropped into the kitchen where he knew he would find his mother.

"Good morning, Jason." She greeted him with her usual cheerful words, and he paused and lifted his cheek for her daily morning kiss. "Sit down and I'll make you some breakfast."

Jason gulped the glass of fresh orange juice that waited for him on the kitchen table. "I'll eat something later, Mom. I'm not hungry right now," he answered as he jogged across the kitchen and pushed through the boy-tattered screen door.

"Jason, where are you going honey?" she called after him.

"No place, Mom. Just outside."

His mother called him back to her. "I want you to stay close. There are storm warnings out, and I want you nearby." She tousled his thick blond hair before he broke away.

"Okay, Mom, I won't go far," he shouted back over his shoulder.

He walked outside into the early June Minnesota day. A warm morning breeze moved over him and warmed his newly sunburned face. His sneakers left footprints in the dew-covered grass behind him. The stifling humidity of late summer, which would saturate his clothes in perspiration the moment he stepped outside, had yet to arrive. School had been out for a week, but the feeling of independence that could only come with the season and his age still gripped him. Jason loved summer, but secretly he already missed school.

He trotted across the lawn to his bike, lying on its side near the empty driveway. Jason's father left early for his job at the college, and his car had been gone for hours. Jason missed his dad. It wasn't that his father didn't love him; in fact, he loved him very much. But like so many fathers, he was busy. The distant rumbling sound of thunder briefly quieted a small flock of sparrows in the trees above him and brought his focus to the overcast cerulean sky, which forewarned of a pending storm. He picked up his bike and threw his leg over the crossbar, then paused to finalize his plans.

Next door, the neighbor's 1980 Ford Fairmont pulled into the drive. Jason watched the car stop, and Rachel Hanson climbed out from behind the wheel. The sixteen-year-old Scandinavian beauty had sat with him a few times when his parents were out. Jason loved the way her short blonde hair bounced as she walked. It was part of the reason he had a crush on her.

"Hi Rachel!" he shouted.

He watched her, clad in madras shorts, lean into the car and pull a bag of groceries from the seat beside her. She had only had her driver's license a few weeks and, like most teen drivers, was only too happy to take on any errand that involved driving. He called to her, and she turned toward his voice and answered.

"Hi, Jason. How ya doin'?" She waved her free hand over her head.

He started to return her wave, but her face stopped him. Something had changed in her visage. Her aquamarine eyes and usual smile was there. In fact, all of her features were there, just as they had been for sixteen years, but Jason saw something else. The essence of her life had vanished — had washed away — and been replaced with a patina of mortality. When he tried later to recall her face, he could only remember it as the face of death.

Jason dropped his bike back onto its side and slowly returned to the house.

"What's wrong, Jason, are you all right?" his mother asked.

"Yeah, Mom, fine."

"I thought you were going outside to play."

He didn't respond, but continued to his room, sat down on the edge of his bed, and tried to understand what he had seen. Of course, he had no answer.

The storm hit an hour later. The breeze, which had progressed to a wind, suddenly stopped, and the air became totally still. The sky turned bottle green, and the thunder rolled closer with every flash of lightning. The storm broke suddenly with a deluge of windblown rain, which obscured their view of the nearby houses. The deep-rooted maple trees in their yard bent and threatened to snap as they yielded to the force of the storm. The sound of hail drumming on the roof brought Jason to his bedroom window but only for a few moments.

The storm moved on as suddenly as it had started, leaving a persistent summer rain in its wake. Jason found his favorite book, a tattered copy of *Robinson Crusoe* and curled up on his bed to read. He was still there when his father came home that evening. He heard his mother greet him and exchange a few words, followed by slow footsteps on the stairs.

"You okay, guy?" his father asked as he checked Jason's temperature with a hand to his forehead. "Your mom says you've been in your room all day."

"I'm good, Dad," was his only answer.

"Is something wrong, son? Your mother thinks something's bothering you."

Jason wanted to tell his father, but he knew he could neither explain what had happened nor make his father understand. His father was a scientist and had trouble accepting anything he couldn't quantify. Jason decided once again to remain silent.

Jason remained indoors for three days, trying to understand what he had seen. He might have pushed the memory into acceptance had it not been for the *feeling* growing inside him. It wasn't in his stomach or his chest, or any place else he could identify. It was just there, growing in his soul. It hurt unlike any pain he had experienced before, like an unseen hand pushing him to take some unperceived action. It left him edgy. He tried to deal with it in his ten-year-old mind, but there was no peace. Finally, out of some need to identify, he named it. For lack of a defining word, he called it anger. He had no idea that his young mind had come extremely close to the precise term. Years later, in his medical training he would learn the term *angor animi*, but even then he would not make the connection to the *feeling* he had experienced and named as a child. It would be years before Jason Corey understood the true meaning of the term: fear of impending doom.

The moving reflection of ambulance lights against his bedroom wall awoke Jason late that night. His bare feet padded across the wood floor as he walked to his window and pushed the curtains aside. Through sleep-clouded eyes, he watched two men roll Rachel across the driveway and put her into an ambulance. The misty darkness swallowed the flashing lights and Rachel. Jason returned to bed, but the question he couldn't have read on Rachel's lips filled his dreams. "Why didn't you save me, Jason?" The feeling disappeared.

Jason slept late, perhaps because his subconscious mind was trying to protect him by postponing the inevitable. When he finally awoke, he dressed slowly and walked down the stairs to the kitchen. He already knew what had happened before his mother told him. She was there, sitting at the table with her embroidery lying in front of her, untouched. When she saw him, her eyes filled with tears, and she motioned him to the chair beside her.

"Jason, I need to talk to you. Something terrible has happened," she said as she knelt in front of him. She squeezed his hands together in hers while he listened in silence.

"Rachel Hanson died last night. They think it was meningitis."

He nodded his understanding. "I know, Mom," he stated flatly. His grief was dampened by his guilt. Although he didn't understand, he sensed that his premonition might have been a means to save Rachel's life. Of course, it couldn't have been. Not then.

Other things had happened after that, but none of them had been so profound or changed him as much as Rachel's death. Perhaps it was because he loved her.

It all stopped when Jason's mother died. He came home from school to find her dead and cold on the kitchen floor. He hadn't had a chance to warn her; no chance to save her. There had been no premonition. His nameless power had failed him. Jason knew on some level his mother was dead because of his failure, and the self-blame crushed the boy. His soul emptied with the force of a receding tide.

His father moved them away from their home in Minnesota, away from the memories. There were no more insights into the future — no more warnings of impending death — and his mind eventually succeeded in pushing those memories to a dim secreted place.

The Land of Oz changes with the seasons. Not unlike the other Emerald City, the life energy of Seattle and the Pacific Northwest rises and falls with each equinox.

Spring in the Pacific Northwest is almost a spiritual experience. The air is crisp and fresh, in profound contrast to the oppressive gray mists of fall and winter. The fir trees grow in an indistinct carpet, covering the mountains with a seemingly endless blanket of green. The giant ferns fill in the spaces of the collage, painting the earth a lush emerald. The fragrance of the primordial forest permeates the world, and the unsullied salt air off the Puget Sound washes the countryside, leaving the mountains and valleys renewed. The experience of such a spring day remains in the vault of one's memory, no matter how far they wander from this Eden.

People who are lucky enough to live near the shores of the Puget Sound on such days, find a way to travel to one of its washed pebble beaches. There, the pure breeze from the ocean cleanses and revitalizes their winter-dreary souls. The cold, salty water is brilliantly clear, and explorers can always find something to discover in the pools left isolated by the low tide. Even adults who have probed the tide flats for years become children at the discovery of a starfish or urchin clinging to the crags of one of the exposed rocky sanctuaries. The sound of the gulls is ever present, calling from a faraway place it seems one has been before; a place just beyond the reach of one's memory.

Those who choose the mountains also have a short trip to the windswept ridges of the Olympics or the rugged slopes of the Cascades. Either mountain range offers a seemingly endless series of panoramic views, which can be absorbed from a distance or experienced more intimately while hiking to hidden mountain lakes or through majestic stands of hemlocks and virgin firs. Hikers can rest at the edge of a rushing mountain stream in the lacey moving shadows of ancient evergreen giants and easily forget the rest of the world. The frenzied rush to meet a never-ending string of deadlines vanishes in the quiet.

Even Eden had its turmoil, and likewise, chaos exists in this near-perfect place. Today the ER at Harborline was busy, as it usually was on weekends during these soft early summer days. There was a steady stream of the typical problems seen in a suburban hospital ER, but nothing to give the staff an adrenaline charge — so far. The ER staff went about their routine, but it was obvious, revealed by their frequent glances out the doors and windows that their hearts were, in fact, with everybody else enjoying the mountains and the ocean.

Dr. Jason Corey, M.D. was one of the good guys. Everybody knows or has known someone like him — someone untainted. His only flaw, if you would call it that, was his addiction. Dr. Corey, like so many other emergency physicians, was a stone-cold adrenaline junkie. Despite this flaw, or maybe because of it, he was a gifted doctor.

Doctor Corey was the perfect fit for Harborline. At thirty-six, he had all the appropriate training and necessary experience to work as an ER staff physician at this demanding hospital. He fit the physical image of the young, successful doctor on his way up. Polite and reserved, he projected an aura of professionalism, exuding concern and compassion for his patients. That was the easy part, since he truly cared about those people in his care. The nursing staff adored him. Most people, especially women, considered him handsome. What the people in his life couldn't see was the distinctive secret hidden so deeply in his core that even he didn't recognize its existence.

The routine of the ER ended abruptly when the strobe light over the EMS radio flashed, announcing a level one trauma. All remnants of tranquility vanished while Medic One gave their report over the radio speaker.

"Harborline, this is Medic One. How do you copy?"

The stress in the paramedic's voice was unmistakable. Paramedics were usually a pretty unruffled group, and the strained words caught the attention of every staff member in the department.

"We read you loud and clear, Medic One. Go." Jeff Noles, the head nurse, acknowledged the ambulance call.

"We are on our way to you with a level one trauma. Patient is a four-year-old white female victim of an auto versus pedestrian. Patient is in full arrest with CPR in progress. Patient is intubated, but we are unable to obtain an IV. Patient has multiple injuries, including chest trauma and multiple fractures. Monitor shows asystole. Our ETA is five to seven minutes."

"Medic One, that's a copy. We'll be awaiting your arrival to trauma room one."

All action shifted to the main trauma room. The physician working with Jason today, Larry Todd, was a solid doc, but the staff understood he was not as strong as Jason, especially in trauma cases. Although Dr. Todd was the more senior physician, he made no attempt to supersede when Jason walked toward Trauma One.

Within a few minutes, the swan song of the approaching ambulance reached the ER and abruptly stopped. Jason heard the commotion as the medics rolled the gurney through the ambulance entrance, down the short hall, and finally into the trauma room. The broken body of a little girl, made smaller by the size of the adult gurney, lay at one end of the rolling cot. One of the medics was doing chest compressions, trying to pump blood through her diminutive body. These were not the usual two-handed adult compressions but rather kid-sized, one-handed movements, pushing on the fragile torso.

Jason was ready and started working before they lifted the lifeless body onto the ER table. He knew there was no time to search for the

IV site they desperately needed. Time was a luxury they plainly didn't have with this patient. He already had the spike needle used to start an IV in a bone in his gloved hand. One of the nurses quickly swabbed the child's lower leg with antiseptic, while Jason felt for the landmarks below the tiny girl's knee. He pushed the large interosseous needle through the skin toward the marrow of her shinbone until a telltale pop told him the needle had penetrated the tibia. He removed the obturator and held the needle in place while the nurse plugged an IV of normal saline into the hub of the needle. They watched the fluid run freely through the line while the nurse squeezed the IV bag. Jason heard the medic giving his report behind him while he worked.

"The family was coming back from a picnic at the park. The grandfather was holding the kid's hand, but she yanked away and jumped right in front of the car."

"How fast was the car going?" Jason asked as he moved to the head of the table.

"The police estimate about forty-five. Threw her about forty feet off the shoulder of the road." The medic shook his head, his only other commentary on the tragedy.

Jason moved his stethoscope from one side of the little girl's chest to the other. The medics had already placed an endotracheal tube into her lungs, and the tube seemed to be in the correct place. He heard clear breath sounds on the left side, but there were no sounds on the right. While he listened to the lungs, the nurses cut the little girl's pink playsuit away, leaving her petite body vulnerable and exposed and revealing a large vicious bruise that covered the right side of her chest. Jason's mind registered immediately — pneumothorax, a collapsed lung. In cases such as this, life-and-death decisions had to be made in seconds. There was no time to wait for X-rays or labs and to deliberate over the case. Emergency medicine was not a casual specialty.

"We need a chest tube tray setup now." His voice was urgent but controlled. "And give me a twenty French chest tube."

Jason changed sterile gloves and reached for the chest tube tray already being opened beside him. He turned to his patient, a scalpel in his right hand, and waited briefly while a nurse threw a splash of brown antiseptic over the frail torso. He found the spot for the incision and slid the scalpel blade over the skin. As if by magic, a small incision materialized on the side of the little girl's chest. He picked up a surgical clamp off the tray beside him and pushed it through the chest wall, breaking the remaining resistance with a snapping tear. The nurse standing next to him held the long plastic chest tube ready for him to slide through the hole he had made in the chest.

Jason expected a rush of air, but instead a torrent of warm blood bathed his gloved hand, and at that moment he knew he had lost this battle.

He fed the clear plastic chest tube through the hole, then passed the end of the tube off to the nurse to secure and attach to the Pleur-evac. Dark crimson blood continued to drain from the tube into the Pleur-evac canister — more blood than he believed could come from the elfin body.

He flashed a light into the little girl's eyes, hoping for some sign of life, but only death returned his gaze. The cardiac monitor was silent except for the hum of a single, unvarying line that repeatedly slid across the screen.

Jason stood beside the bed, dropped his shoulders, and exhaled deeply. There was no choice but to accept the inevitable, "Okay, folks, we're done." His voice was matter-of-fact, almost without emotion. He peeled his gloves off and tossed the bloody wad in the direction of a trash can. The wet mass missed the can, clung momentarily, then dropped to the floor, leaving a red smudge on the wall. Jason wanted to scream at something or someone but couldn't allow himself that luxury. "Shit," he murmured.

The clock read 16:15 hours. A few minutes after her arrival in the ER, he pronounced the little girl dead. The room, which seconds earlier had been full of activity, was now still, engulfed in a death shroud of silence. Jason heard quiet crying from somewhere behind him where a student nurse stood alone, shaking. The faces of the rest of the staff revealed little. Their professionalism masked their grief, because they knew they had to maintain control now for the sake of the rest of the patients they would care for today. There would be time later to deal with their emotions when their shifts had ended, and they were alone with their feelings and a cold beer.

Jason stood motionless beside the gurney and, in truth, saw the little girl's face for the first time. Someone dimmed the lights in the room, except for the spotlight over the bed. She was — had been — beautiful. Several ringlets of blonde hair curled into a halo around her cherub face, now serene in death. He reached out and picked up her tiny, still-warm arm and gently rubbed his thumb over the limp hand. The changes of death had not seized her body yet.

This wasn't gracious, sterile funeral home death. This was Death up close and indecent, as it was in reality. He turned to walk away when his foot brushed a small white tennis shoe discarded on the floor. A purple cartoon character he didn't recognize danced on the side of the blood-spattered shoe. He started to reach for it but stopped, realizing she wouldn't need it again. As he walked away, he felt the wet stickiness of fresh blood under his shoes.

Jason picked up the little girl's chart lying on his desk and scanned across the top line: "Barelli, Beth. Female. Age 4."

"Is the family in the quiet room?" he asked.

The ward clerk nodded in response.

The quiet room was a small private waiting room just off the ER for families waiting for news of critical patients. Jason headed down the short hall, running his routine speech through his mind and prepared himself for the parents. He had learned not to think about the reality of what was happening. Talking to the family was just an impersonal part of the case that needed to be done. He had done it before, and he was sure he would do it again. There were only two rules for talking to a family: don't get close enough to care but pretend you do.

Jason opened the door of the tastefully decorated room and found it crowded with people. He had expected a mother and father — these days maybe just one or the other — but today he was met by a crowd. An elderly man sat near the center of the room with his face in his hands, crying. Jason remembered the medic's words, and assumed this was the grandfather who had been holding the little girl's hand.

The room quieted quickly. "I'm Dr. Corey from the Emergency Department."

He introduced himself and shook a few hands that were extended to him.

"Mr. and Mrs. Barelli?" he asked, searching. The crowd opened and turned to a couple seated near the old man.

Someone pushed a chair forward for him, and Jason sat down opposite the parents and grandfather. The father's gaze dropped to Jason's feet, and for the first time he noticed that the lower leg of his scrub suit was saturated with fresh blood. He shifted his weight and crossed his legs under his chair, hiding the grim stain on his leg.

"Can you tell me what happened today?" Jason asked softly.

Mr. Barelli answered. "We were coming back from the park at the lake. We were having a little family reunion. Pop was holding Beth's hand, and she was playing and jumping around like kids do when they're excited." He moved his hand to his father's arm. "All of a sudden she pulled away — out toward traffic — and there was this car right there. It all happened so fast that . . ." His voice broke.

Mrs. Barelli leaned forward in her chair and spoke. "How is she, Doctor? Is she all right?"

Jason felt his jaw muscles tighten. I hate this; he thought. I hate this more than any other part of this job. Why can't they just let me get through this? Nothing I say is going to change anything. Their little girl will still be dead.

Jason's thoughts and a well-planned speech became jumbled in his mind as he realized they didn't know. How could they not know, for Christ's sake? How could they see their daughter thrown through the air by a car, taken away not breathing, and still ask if she were all right? Mrs. Barelli's eyes pleaded, and finally Jason understood. They knew but didn't want to believe it. They wanted it to be like it was on TV or in the movies. They wanted to be surprised and relieved and hear their little girl would be ready to go home soon. All this fuss was over nothing. But that wasn't going to happen today. He was going to have to say it.

Jason started to explain, "When your daughter, Beth, got here she had been hurt very badly. The medics had placed a tube into her lungs to breathe for her. Her heart had stopped, and they were doing CPR. Her injuries were very severe." He paused.

A small child in the room started to cry. Not fussing but already sensing what had happened; it started to mourn.

Jason continued, "I'm afraid we lost her."

The rest of his words were lost in a tempest of anguish and grief. He tried to speak. "We did everything we could." No one heard. "She didn't have any pain." He was floundering, lost in the grief of the people around him. "If there's anything I can do . . . "

Mr. Barelli raised his hand in desperate protest. He kept an arm around his wife and spoke through his sobs. "Please, no more! No more," he pleaded.

It wasn't supposed to be like this. Jason had more lines to say — things that were supposed to make a difference — but the father's eyes stopped him. Those eyes said what the man could not put into words. Simply, their sorrow couldn't endure one more word of explanation or attempted solace. It was what it was, and now they would have to deal with it in their own way.

Jason remained seated in front of them, uncertain what to do or say. He understood that nothing he had to offer now would make a difference, and his role in this scene of their lives was over. The grandfather sat in silence; his face drained of color and the tears gone as the reality of his mistake seized him. This single moment would define his life, and years later when he lay dying, this experience would be the last image in his mind before death took him.

Jason stood and left the room, with the muffled sounds of grief echoing behind him. "Well, that went well," he muttered sarcastically to himself.

Larry Todd was at the desk working on a chart. "You okay?"

"Yeah, fine." Jason tried to sound credible. "I'm going out back for a minute if it's all right in here."

"We're good," Larry answered. "Go ahead."

Jason walked through the department past the doctor's call room and out onto the raised concrete deck behind the ER. He reached into his pocket for a cigarette, lit up, and inhaled deeply as he rested his foot on the lower guardrail. He looked up and watched the cloudless sapphire-blue sky absorb the wisp of exhaled smoke. His eyes traveled to the nearby giant fir trees. "I could be lost in those trees in a few minutes, if I just walk away," he said to himself. He thought about the grieving family he had just left in the quiet room, but he would not let his thoughts go to the tiny broken body in Trauma One.

Jason heard the door open behind him, but he didn't turn. He already knew it was Rooster, the medical director of the ER. Jason heard him light a cigarette and settle into the bar rail pose beside him.

"I was doing some paperwork and heard you were playing without me," Rooster quipped.

"Yeah," Jason answered flatly and cleared his throat. He knew gallows humor was an essential part of every ER in the world.

Rooster exhaled, leaving a cloud of smoke rolling above him. "The kids are never easy."

Jason answered, trying to push the emotion down, "Yeah." The word caught in his throat.

"You've lost kids before, J.C. Something different about this one?" Rooster asked, sensing Jason's mood.

"Just wasn't ready for the family." Jason looked out over the trees and watched another smoke cloud dissolve.

"Unfortunately, it goes with the territory. You'll get used to it or your skin will get thicker."

"I guess my skin is still a little thin, and I'm sure as hell not used to it."

Rooster paused before he continued. "Remember, J.C., we don't get paid for what we do; we get paid for what our job as a physician does to our lives and our souls."

"Rooster, I'm not sure I can do this." The words erupted from a hidden place deep within him. "The price is higher than I thought it was going to be. I knew medicine would drive my life, but I didn't think it would," he paused, searching for the word, "consume me."

"That's why you make the big bucks."

"Can I ask you something, Rooster?"

"Uh-huh." The answer was barely an acknowledgment.

"Why do things like this happen? Why doesn't God just alter things by fifteen seconds one way or another and prevent this? A different colored light down the street?" The kid can't get her shoelace tied? Any one of a thousand things could have stopped this." Jason rubbed his hands through his hair and inhaled deeply on his cigarette.

"You want the official PC religious answer or the truth?"

Jason turned toward him and exhaled.

"Okay, nobody knows. It's all just part of the bullshit of life. And remember, anyone who claims to know the answer, whether it's me, some guru or the Pope, it's all just opinion."

"I assume that was not the official religious answer."

Rooster laughed, "That's the gospel according to Rooster."

He exhaled and flipped his cigarette over the rail. "There's one thing I will tell you, and it's not just an opinion. Thinking about this stuff will drive you out of your fucking mind." He turned back towards the ER.

"I'll be back in a minute," Jason said.

Rooster stopped, "I know you will," he said as if it were a given, then disappeared through the door.

Jason stood alone, savoring the air off the sound and absorbing the warmth of the sun on his face. For a moment, he felt like a kid again standing in the early Minnesota summer before his mind pushed that feeling away. He squinted and looked out over the water where several gulls effortlessly rode the air currents. The cry of a seagull is a peculiar sound, he thought as their laughs drifted past him. What other sound was a laugh and a cry at the same time? He needed a break.

Medicine wasn't supposed to be like this. This isn't what he had signed up for. It wasn't just this case; it was something more. His idealism had left him, beaten to death by the reality of practicing medicine. "God," he whispered. "I can't do this." Deep inside of him something rumbled and stirred like the first movements of a fetus — as if a life was being called into existence by some greater power.

He took a last drag from his cigarette, flipped the butt away over the rail as Rooster had done, and returned to the patients waiting inside. He still had four hours of his shift left.

TWO

Jason survived another day — barely.

Everyone has a potential breaking point; a line in the sand that they cannot or will not cross. On rare occasion, a case can push an ER doctor too far, and he puts his stethoscope into his bag, collects his belongings and walks away forever. More often, he absorbs the insult to his being, limps through his shift, and tries to hold himself together for another day.

Every time Jason walked into the ER for a shift, he tried to prepare himself for what he might have to do or what he might see, that day. Most days he did pretty well. Other days, like today, he was blindsided. Just when he believed he'd seen it all, something came along that sucker punched him and left him struggling.

The double doors to the ambulance bay opened and released him into the evening air, signaling the end of Jason's shift. He heaved a simultaneous physical and mental sigh of relief. Every one of the six hundred and thirty muscles in his body ached — not from physical strain but the crushing stress of the preceding twelve hours. He stretched and tried to rub away the ropes that had formed in the back of his neck. Shifting his bag to the opposite shoulder, he tried to settle its weight to a position that didn't bite into his aching muscles. His body started a winding down process, which could take hours to complete.

The hazy early-summer sun was still visible but setting quickly. Jason looked out over the sound at the orange fireball resting on the surface of the water before its final egress and smiled. He tolerated the wet, dreary Seattle winters, but like most people, he lived for the summers.

Jason had attended undergrad and med school at the University of Washington in Seattle. He called himself a native even though he wasn't. It was part of his attempt to forget anything that had happened before he and his father had moved to the Pacific Northwest. After med school, he headed to southern California for his residency in Emergency Medicine at one of the war-zone hospitals in the inner city.

After residency, he had no doubt as to where he wanted to practice medicine. He had interviewed at every large ER in the Pacific

Northwest and had offers from them all but decided on Harborline Hospital. Harborline was, for the most part, far from the gunshot wounds, drug ODs, stabbings, and rapes of his residency years. The impressive hospital stood on the shores of the Puget Sound in the most affluent suburb of the city; a fact that said something about the hospital, patients, and doctors.

Jason's starting salary package was over three hundred thousand dollars a year, an enormous change from the poverty of his residency. Besides the money, he had selected Harborline because of the ER medical director. Dr. Ian Christianson, known to everyone as Rooster, had made an impression on Jason at their first meeting. Rooster was one of those guys that could be thirty or fifty, but no one knew his age for certain, just as no one seemed to know why he was called Rooster. He was handsome in a way that attracted most women, but few could tolerate his strong personality for long. Rooster was a man's man and ran his life the way he ran his ER. He seemed to like everyone, unless they crossed him. He called his method of management a "benevolent dictatorship." He listened to what others had to say, and then did it his way. Once Rooster made a decision, it was "my way or the highway," as he liked to say. Jason liked the way Rooster ran things, and he seemed to agree with almost everything Rooster did. If he didn't agree with Rooster, he kept his mouth shut. He had heard stories about careers ending in Rooster's ER, and Jason wasn't about to make that mistake.

Mount Rainier appeared as a giant still life painted on a deep cobalt sky of a canvas. The mountain gazed down on the city like a Goliath, its permanent mushroom cloud cap slightly askew, as usual. Across the Sound, the peaks of the Olympic Range, still ridged in white, stood electrified by the setting sun. The view helped temper his spirits and let him begin to expunge the memory of the little girl and her family.

Jason opened the trunk of his BMW Z4 and stuffed his bag inside. He slammed the trunk harder than he meant to and winced at the sound. He slid behind the wheel, threw his stethoscope and hospital ID badge onto the passenger seat, and started the car. He closed his door carefully. The engine responded with a deep, animal growl, and he felt his pulse respond to the small adrenaline fix. ER doctors and nurses are well-known adrenaline junkies, and the sports car was all part of the addiction. The radio was still set to the easy listening station he had chosen on his way to the hospital this morning, and he pushed the second button from the left for his favorite oldies rock station, KZOK. He turned the volume up until he could feel the music rumble through the car.

Jason pushed the power switch that moved the car's ragtop back and watched it collapse and disappear behind him. He pulled on his red BMW cap that matched the cinnamon-red roadster, adjusted his sunglasses, and was ready. He accelerated hard out of the parking lot to the sounds of Jim Morrison and squealing tires.

Jesse claimed he loved the car more than he loved her. The roadster had been a gift he bought for himself when he signed his contract at Harborline. He felt he deserved something for sweating through the agonizing years of college, medical school and residency. Those years had been an ordeal that couldn't be understood by anyone who hadn't experienced them. His undergrad classes had been easy for him, but he had worried over the ever-present push for the grades needed to get into med school. While other students were satisfied with a C, he knew any grade below an A would end his dream. Med school had been the best. The courses were harder than undergrad classes, but he had enjoyed them more. All night study sessions had been the norm. In residency, the main battle had been the sheer physical demand. Over 100-hour workweeks, together with reading and case preparations, had been exhausting. Days blended into months, and the calendar became an abstract entity. This car marked the end of those years, and yes, he loved the car — not more than Jesse but perhaps almost as much.

Jason pulled onto the interstate and accelerated to eighty-five miles per hour. His radar detector blinked on the dash and periodically chirped a false warning. He didn't worry much about speeding. He had learned ER doctors had what amounted to a get-out-of-jail-free card with the police when it came to things like speeding tickets. Rooster had explained it to him one day when they were coming back from a day's sailing on his boat. Rooster was cruising at his usual ninety miles per hour in his Porsche when a young cop named Brady pulled them over. The cop's older partner recognized Rooster and let him drive away without a ticket. Rooster's explanation made sense.

"It can happen, but it's not very likely once they know who you are. It's simple really. First, no cop in the city of Seattle knows when he or she might end up in our ER with something serious like a bullet in the chest. Second, it's a given that sooner or later these guys are going to want a favor. They're going to want to get somebody through the ER quickly. Maybe a quick blood alcohol check, or they just want to get a bad guy cleared so they can get him booked into jail. In any case, they want a friendly ER doc. In the first situation, of course, we wouldn't let a cop die because they gave us a ticket, but they don't know that," he chuckled. "In the second situation, an unfriendly ER doc can keep a cop waiting for hours for a blood alcohol — long after he's scheduled to go off shift and long enough for a blood alcohol to go below the legal limit. We take care of them, and they take care of us." Since then, Jason always left his stethoscope and hospital ID tag lying on the passenger's seat — just in case. He didn't like playing the doctor card for things like restaurant reservations, but this was one perk he gladly accepted.

The feel of the speed and the cool evening air re-energized him. The music pounded through the car and pushed at the events of the day, but the images refused to let go. By the time he neared home, his hands had relaxed on the wheel, and the aching tension had left his shoulders. Unfortunately, the memory of the little girl had entrenched itself permanently in his consciousness. Strangely, the image that attached itself to his memory like a permanent file tag wasn't the little girl's face or even her parents cries, but a small, blood-spattered tennis shoe.

Jason rolled into the parking garage, stopped next to Jesse's Mercedes, and closed up his car. The garage was secure, but Seattle was a big city. Their condo, located on the water near the marina, placed them in a higher mortgage class. The building had been one of the old waterfront monoliths, which were now popular with developers and the young, affluent set. Several million dollars did wonders for the ambiance of one of these hulks. The building had been stripped to its skeleton and totally redone, turning it into a glass and copper nouveau rustic work of art, complete with old bricks and the occasional ancient timber. Jason and Jesse loved this place. They loved sitting on their balcony in the evenings with drinks and watching boats sail across the horizon. Tonight he was counting on that and perhaps more.

Jesse had materialized during his residency at one of the hospital's weekly house-staff beer parties, commonly known as "fluid rounds." She was a nurse on pediatric oncology and, like many of the young nurses, attended the house-staff functions whenever she could. Unlike many of the other nurses, Jesse wasn't there on a hunting expedition.

Jason had spotted her first while she was talking with several other residents who had also noticed her. Jesse was extraordinary. He was attracted to her short blonde hair and enormous deep- sapphire eyes, but it had been her smile that singled her out as someone remarkable. She was intelligent and rarely went unnoticed, especially by men. More important to Jason than Jesse's looks was that she was "good of heart." She was the woman of his dreams, incarnate.

There had been a deep physical attraction between them from the start — something potent and vital. They both said it was love at first sight, and that was true, as long as one recognized lust was an essential part of love.

They were inseparable for the first six months, but it wasn't enough, and Jason had moved in with her before they had been together a year. Despite his love for Jesse, Jason was still reluctant to commit to their future together. Marriage frightened him.

Jesse had burned out on pediatric oncology; her soul had become scarred and she made a change to OB. She had seen enough children die and wanted to see some children coming into the world. She wanted to see parents crying with joy instead of grief. Jason never told stories about the kids in the ER when Jesse was around. She still carried too many memories of her time on pediatric oncology — memories Jason knew would never leave her.

The elevator powered to the top floor, and Jason found their townhouse quiet in the now early night. He opened the sliders onto the deck and stopped briefly to look at the lights already appearing across the bay. The condo was far enough out of the city that the air was untainted. Tonight the breeze off the water was cool, fresh, and sentient with the smells of early summer and the promise of no more than an occasional rain shower for at least a few months. A thin, misty night fog had started to form over the water in the quickly cooling evening air. The rhythm of the waves below him filled the night with a primitive energy that resonated deep within him.

Jason walked through the townhouse and turned on the light, partially illuminating the walls in the main room. In the bedroom, the subdued lights were already on above their bed. Jesse was there, asleep in the near darkness. He stood over her, quietly watching the slow rise and fall of her chest — life in, life out. His love evoked an overwhelming desire to both protect her and possess her forever. Her face appeared faultless in the glow of the subdued light. She slept on her side with the sheet pulled against her, barely covering her breasts. The sheet had ridden up behind her, exposing one smooth cheek. As always, Jesse slept in the nude. Carefully, he sat next to her and stroked her exposed bottom as he inhaled deeply and absorbed her scent. The emotion of the moment and the depth of his love for her enveloped him and numbed his mind like a hypnotic drug. She stirred and, without opening her eyes, moaned, "Is that you, John?"

Jason had learned her tricks a long time ago.

"John, huh. I'll John you."

She tried to escape, but he was too quick for her. His hands were already on her belly, tickling.

"No, no, I've got to pee," she screamed and wiggled away.

He let her slip out of his grasp, and she sprang out of bed, sprinting for the bathroom. The beauty of her naked form in the dim light warmed him. She returned a few moments later, still naked, and launched herself at him. She was now the attacker, laughing and tickling. He easily restrained her and held her in his lap close to him. He gave her a quick slap on her butt, and she squealed through her kiss, then dissolved into his arms.

The kiss waned, but he held her tightly, still captivated by the potency of the love between them. She nestled her head against his chest and purred. "I'm hungry."

He nuzzled her neck. "Me too."

"I mean for dinner," she chided, still holding him.

He feigned a groan. "I knew it — only using me."

She stood and grabbed a pair of panties off the foot of the bed.

"You got it, big guy. Now, where are you taking me for dinner?" she asked as she stepped into the panties.

Jason had trouble changing his train of thought from Jesse to food. "How about if we order a large Garlic Special from Boston Pizza and have a quiet night at home?" he offered.

"Ooor, how about steamed clams and Dungeness crab with a nice bottle of wine at Anthony's on the waterfront?" she countered. She saw his face drop. "And then an even nicer evening at home," she offered.

"How nice?" He continued the game.

"Very nice." She looked up seductively as she reached behind her back and snapped her bra.

Jason decided compromise was sometimes acceptable. "You got it, lady, but no squelching on desert."

She buttoned her jeans and pulled her top over her head, then glanced into the mirror and tousled her hair. It amazed him that she could look so beautiful in just those few seconds. She came to him and wrapped her arms around his neck. She kissed him tenderly then touched his lips with her finger. "No squelching," she whispered.

Before he could answer, she whirled and headed for the door. She grabbed his keys off the hall table and shouted back over her shoulder. "We're taking your car, and I'm driving."

Jason started to protest but stopped, knowing it was useless. He walked after her, shaking his head. "Jesse, Jesse, Jesse," he murmured.

It was true; this woman owned him. On some level, he knew he wanted to spend the rest of his life with her, yet from another obscure place in his soul, a terrorizing image said he would not.

They raced down the highway, Jesse behind the wheel of the Z4, her hair blowing in the wind. Steppenwolf pounded from the stereo as they savored the excitement of life as only two people can do when they are young and in love.

The galaxy of stars in the night sky melded into the lights surrounding the Sound. A waxing gibbous moon silhouetted the mountains and turned the water into a sea of living cold-white jewels. They flew into the feral night, leaving the peaceful city behind them, all thoughts of death and mortality banished — eclipsed by their love.

THREE

The triple shot latte slammed into his brain and kick-started his cold-engine mind. Today was Jason's first shift back in the ER after two days off, and he should have been refreshed, but it was taking him longer than usual to clear his head and shift into ER mode. As usual, he had stopped at a Starbuck's drive-through on his way to the hospital. Caffeine was the lifeblood of Seattle, and Starbuck's was the Holy Grail of coffee. Only the truly desperate or exceptionally brave drank the vile brew that the ER called coffee, but then his latte would probably have been a little chewy too, after simmering for several hours.

Jason was the solo doctor in the ER until eleven o'clock — four hours from now. Mornings in the ER were a crapshoot. Some, like today, were reasonable and allowed Jason time to joke with the nurses while he caught up on paperwork. Other days, it could be brutal for the lone doctor on duty.

Jeff Noles, the charge nurse, moved around the department stirring up trouble wherever he could. His easy-going farm-boy charm bought him some slack from the nursing staff, but ER nurses could be a temperamental group. Many of them had worked in other parts of the hospital before coming to the ER. Once there, they either quickly fled back to the more mundane areas of the hospital or got hooked on the adrenaline, which sometimes seemed to drift through the department like opium. Those select few who stayed would rather leave nursing than leave the ER. As a group, they were typically extroverts — smart, independent, and extremely resilient. An experienced ER nurse, or "warhorse," as Rooster called them, was not someone to be taken lightly.

Jeff eventually gravitated to Bonnie Grady, the team leader, and started with his usual shots about men being better nurses than women. Bonnie countered in her thick Irish brogue, "Don't be givin' me any of yer shite today, Noles."

Jeff decided that harassing Bonnie wasn't worth the risk and retreated. It was a prudent decision. The only thing bigger than Bonnie's heart was her temper.

Jason picked up snippets of conversation around the department:

"I told him if he ever wanted to have sex again, I'd better see a diamond the size of a cantaloupe."

"Then she wanders in two hours after her curfew. I told her she's grounded until she's thirty."

"His mother is driving me out of my frigging mind."

They were the typical things he would probably overhear in any office, but these weren't typical people. Every morning they showered and dressed, then drove to work prepared to deal intimately with life and death. Their routine days consisted of blood, broken bones, pain, and death. Their lunch breaks were either nonexistent or consisted of a few minutes spent inhaling a cold sandwich while they cleaned the blood off their scrub suits. Their shifts were the same on weekends, holidays, birthdays, and anniversaries. There was a camaraderie among the ER staff that crossed the lines of title, gender, age and job description. Over time, they shared emotions and experiences that they couldn't share with anyone else. They were family.

Jason leaned back in his chair and propped his feet on his desk. His latte had cooled, but he was determined to savor every drop of the brew. He had just lifted the cardboard cup to his lips when the EMS radio came to life. The alarm startled him, and he sloshed the last mouthful of his latte down his scrub suit.

"Damn it!" he blurted.

"Harborline, this is Medic 1. Come in."

Jeff smirked as he headed for the radio. "Time to rock and roll, Doc." He picked up the radio mic and responded, "This is Harborline. Go."

"We're en route to you with a fifty-six-year-old white male in full cardiac arrest. Witnessed arrest, with bystander CPR started immediately. Patient is currently intubated with bagged respirations and two IVs running normal saline. Monitor initially showed VF, which converted to asystole after epinephrine and two shocks. CPR is in progress. We have a three-minute ETA. Any questions or orders?"

Jeff looked up and raised his eyebrows, but Jason shook his head in response to the question.

"No orders at this time. We'll be expecting you in Cardiac Room One."

The medic came back. "Harborline, be advised that this patient is conscious and seems to understand what's going on."

"That's a copy. Harborline clear." Jeff ended their transmission. "Conscious with CPR going on? Something's not right there." Jeff shook his head in bewilderment.

"We'll know in about three minutes," Jason answered and shrugged.

Several of the ER nurses had already moved to the first cardiac room and were preparing for the patient in a carefully choreographed ballet. The pace was quick but controlled, as the well-practiced team went through the setup routine. They spiked several IV bags and ran fluid through the lines, then recapped them and laid them over their IV poles. They attached the cardiac defibrillator lead wires to sticky pads to hold them on the patient's chest. In the background, Jason heard the overhead page for "respiratory therapy to the ER stat."

The wait for a critical patient to arrive wired Jason. His body tightened, and his pulse drummed. This was the beginning of the adrenaline rush every ER doctor and nurse recognized and savored. He knew from experience this feeling wouldn't last once the ambulance arrived. It would be obscured by the intensity of the moment when he went into the near fugue state that came from repeating this scenario many times in his training and the ER. He also knew that whether the patient lived or died, he would experience a feeling of power unequal to anything he could imagine — the power of playing God.

Today, however, something was different. The familiar excitement of the adrenaline push surged higher than he had ever experienced. No, that wasn't right. He *had* experienced this somewhere. He remembered it like an old pain — something unpleasantly familiar. He tried to fight it, but it grew out of his control, like a wind-driven fire.

The medics rolled into the cardiac room, still doing chest compressions. The patient was intubated, and one of the medics was breathing for him with an Ambu bag. Jason had seen this many times before. What he hadn't seen was the obvious look of terror on the patient's face. His eyes were open, and it was clear this patient was awake and seemed to know what was happening to him. Patients in cardiac arrest were always unconscious. Jason had never seen this in an arrest and apparently neither had any of the nurses. They each periodically glanced up at the patient's face, then went back to their tasks.

Jason questioned the paramedic with the Ambu bag.

"Whatcha got?"

"This guy was working in his garage at home with his two sons, when he grabbed his chest and collapsed. They started CPR right away and called 911. When we got there, the monitor showed V-fib.

We started ACLS protocol and shocked him once, gave him one round of drugs, and shocked him again — into asystole. From bad to worse." The medic grimaced.

"Any cardiac history?" Jason asked.

"None. Been in good health, according to the family. Name's Carl Simon."

Jeff had already taken control, and they prepared to transfer the patient to the ER gurney. "On three," he directed. Several of the nurses grabbed the sheet under the patient. "One, two, three," he said in rapid succession, and they lifted the patient onto the gurney with seemingly little effort.

The nurses switched the lead wires from the paramedic's equipment to the ER's cardiac monitor. Harborline used state-of-the-art equipment that both read the patient's heart rhythm and could deliver a shock through the same wires and pads. Jason waited in the background, listening and watching. He knew if he forced himself to the bedside and tried to start his care before the nurses were ready for him, he would only slow things down. Patient care was a team project, and while Jason was highly specialized, he was just one element of the team.

At the right moment, Jason slid between two nurses at the side of the gurney. Mr. Simon looked directly into his eyes when he spoke.

"Mr. Simon, blink your eyes twice if you can hear me." He received two deliberate blinks in response.

Jason moved his stethoscope from side to side on Mr. Simon's chest and listened. The ET tube was in good position, moving air well through both lungs.

Jason felt for a pulse on his patient's neck over the carotid artery and felt a strong surge each time the medic compressed the chest. The pulse matched with an electrical complex on the cardiac monitor.

"Come off the chest." Jason held his hand up and motioned to the medic doing CPR to stop chest compressions. The cardiac monitor changed to a flat line, and the pulse under Jason's fingers vanished. Jason watched Mr. Simon's eyes slowly close as the circulation to his brain stopped.

"Back on the chest," he ordered.

The medic started chest compressions again, and the patient's pulse reappeared. Slowly, Mr. Simon's eyes opened and focused.

"Mr. Simon, are you having pain anyplace?" Two blinks.

"Does your chest hurt?" Two blinks.

"My chest would hurt, too, if Bubba was pumping on it," the other paramedic offered.

Jason glanced up but ignored the comment. "Setup the external pacer and give me one milligram per kilogram of Enoxaparin subQ."

Jeff peeled apart two large sticky pads, each the size of his palm. He stuck one on the middle of the patient's chest, then half rolled him and placed the other pad in the middle of his back. He attached the wires to the external cardiac pacer and signaled Jason he was ready.

"Set the rate at eighty and the power at .5 milliamps," Jason directed. "Come off the chest again," he ordered the paramedic.

The patient's chest muscles twitched in rhythmic response to a small electric current running between the two pads through his chest. His eyes slowly closed again as he lost consciousness. Jeff kept his fingers on Mr. Simon's carotid artery, searching for a pulse. The monitor showed the electric impulse from the external pacer but no cardiac beat.

"Move the current up," Jason ordered.

Jeff moved up a click on the pacemaker.

" No change," Jeff responded.

Jason nodded, and the pacer clicked again.

"No change."

"Go to max voltage," Jason shot back.

"No change."

"Okay, pacer off and go back on the chest. Call radiology for a C-arm, and set up for an internal pacer. I'm going to talk to the family."

Jason walked to the quiet room, but the family was the last thing on his mind. The *feeling* twisted and surged inside him. If it didn't stop, he was going to loose his mind.

"Are you with Mr. Simon?"

A middle-aged woman and two young men responded simultaneously.

"I'm Dr. Corey." He introduced himself briefly to the woman seated against the wall. He was in a hurry, and he wanted the family to know it.

"Right now your husband is very sick," he said matter-of-factly. "He has a tube in his lungs, and we're breathing for him. We're still doing CPR — compressing his heart to make it pump. We've tried an external cardiac pacer without success, and in a few minutes, I'm going to slide a pacer wire through a vein directly into his heart.

We've got to get his heart beating again." Jason paused to let the wife and two grown sons absorb the information.

Mrs. Simon cried softly and blotted her eyes with a shredded tissue. One of the sons spoke up. "He's gonna make it though, isn't he? He's never been sick a day in his life."

"We're doing everything we can, and I've got to get back. I've got to tell you now that if we can't get his heart started soon, we'll lose him."

Mrs. Simon spoke through her tears. "We've been together twenty-eight years, Doctor. I can't lose him. I just can't."

Jason paused before he turned back toward the door. "You should know he's awake while we do CPR. He seems to understand what we're doing and what's going on. We must be getting enough blood to his brain with CPR to keep him conscious."

"We've got to see him," Mrs. Simon cried and leaped to her feet.

"Not now. I've got to get his heart started first, and we need all the room we've got." Jason eased her back onto her chair. "I've got to get back in there, but I'll let you know how things are going."

Jason was gone. The whole interaction had lasted less than two minutes. That's all the time he had to tell a family their husband and father might be dying — that their lives might be changing forever. He had learned it was better to have some contact with the family if possible — no matter how brief — instead of just walking in with the ultimate bad news. Jason jogged back to the cardiac room, and the old joke about the little old lady and the singing telegram flashed through his mind. *Your sister Rose is dead. She died this morning right in bed,* sung to the tune of "Hello to Hollywood" flashed through his mind. He let it go. The *feeling* grew in intensity and ferocity as he moved down the hallway back to the ER. It's strength frightened him, but he tried to contain it. He simply didn't have time to deal with it now.

Back in the cardiac room, an X-ray tech rolled the C-arm into place. As its name implied, the large C-shaped machine opened above and below the patient's chest. It would show Jason an X-ray movie of the transvenous pacer wire as he positioned it in his patient's heart. His instrument tray with the pacer wire and other equipment stood ready.

Jason pulled on his sterile gloves. "Any change?"

"Nothing," Jeff answered. "Still asystole."

Jason picked up a small syringe and felt for a spot just below the patient's left collarbone. He could see Mr. Simon's eyes follow him, and he stopped briefly to talk to his patient.

"Mr. Simon, we're going to put a pacemaker wire into your heart. You're going to feel a little stick here." Two blinks.

Jason couldn't imagine what his patient was going through watching his own CPR, and he wondered if Mr. Simon knew he was probably watching his own death. The statistics for cardiac arrests were dismal at best and got worse as the downtime increased. Mr. Simon had been down an awfully long time. This wasn't like it was on TV where most people survived a cardiac arrest. Unfortunately, this was the real deal.

Jason injected a small amount of xylocaine, a local anesthetic, under the skin. He switched to a larger syringe with a much longer needle and slid the needle under the left collarbone, deep into the patient's chest. A stream of blood filled the syringe and told Jason he was in the subclavian vein. He left the needle buried in the patient and removed the syringe from the hub. A flow of dark blood ran from the hub of the needle, as expected, and Jason quickly plugged it with his thumb. He wasn't concerned about the blood loss but wanted to make sure the negative pressure in the chest that came with each bagged inhalation didn't suck air through the needle and into the patient's heart. An air embolus would kill him quickly.

Jason reached to the tray and picked up the thin guide wire held in its reel and carefully fed the floppy end of the wire through the hub of the needle into the patient's chest. With any luck, the wire would end up in the subclavian vein near the vena cava, at the entrance to the heart. He pulled the needle out and off over the wire, leaving the wire protruding from the chest. The nurse handed him a scalpel, and he made a nick in the skin next to the wire. Jason picked up a small blue dilator and slid it over the wire into Mr. Simon's chest to stretch the hole in the blood vessel without making it bigger. He pulled the dilator back off the wire and replaced it with the pencil-sized catheter, then removed the wire. The result was a large IV catheter sticking out of the patient's chest, which led directly into a central vein, just above the heart. The whole process, called the Seldinger technique, had taken ninety seconds.

One of the nurses attached a syringe to the catheter and pulled the plunger back. The syringe filled with dark blood, confirming Jason was on target just outside his patient's heart.

Jeff peeled open the packet that contained the pacer wire and held it out toward Jason's gloved hand. The lights in the room had been dimmed to give him a better view of the TV screen on the C-arm machine. Jason watched the progression of the long plastic-coated pacer wire as he slid it through the subclavian catheter into Mr. Simon's chest. He advanced the lead into the upper part of the heart, the right atrium, then inflated a small balloon near the tip of the wire. The balloon, carried by the blood flowing through the heart with each chest compression, floated the wire through the tricuspid valve into the lower part of the heart, the right ventricle. "Almost home," Jason half whispered. He advanced the wire to the tip of the heart and applied a slight pressure to keep the electrodes against the heart wall so the electric current could pass directly into the cardiac muscle. "And . . . home," he said with finality and started breathing again. The *feeling* had receded slightly while he placed the pacer, but now it rose up with a furor, demanding his full attention.

Jeff hooked the contacts from the pacer wire into the small transvenous pacer pack.

"Start at seventy and four," Jason ordered. "Off the chest." The paramedic stopped CPR and Mr. Simon's eyes slowly closed again.

One of the nurses noticed the sweating bright red face of the medic who had been doing chest compressions and shouldered him away from the patient. The medic, physically spent, didn't object to the nurse's move to replace him.

The monitor again showed the electric pacer spikes but no familiar cardiac beats in response.

"No capture," Jeff said.

"Walk your voltage up," Jason directed.

The pacer box clicked with each increase in voltage output, each followed by Jeff's report, "No capture." Finally, there were no more clicks.

"That's as high as it goes, boss."

"Give me another amp of IV Epi," Jason ordered. "I'll irritate the hell out of his heart cells until they respond."

Jeff looked at him as he processed what Jason had just said. It wasn't ACLS protocol, but in a way, it made sense. The med nurse popped a syringe of epinephrine, slid the needle into the IV line, and pushed the drug in with the heel of her hand.

Suddenly, a pattern appeared on the monitor in response to the pacer spikes, accompanied by a welcomed audible blip with each electric impulse as it crossed the heart. Jason felt a weight lift off his shoulders. "Check for a pulse," he ordered.

Jeff checked for a carotid pulse again. "No pulse, Doc. Must be in EMD, an electrical current across the heart but no contraction of the heart muscle in response."

"Open his IV and start a dopamine drip. Maybe his pressure is just too low to register."

A nurse shot an amp of medicine into a small IV bag, plugged it into the primary IV line, and snapped the line into an IV pump. "What rate Doctor?"

"Start at ten micrograms per kilogram per minute. Have X-ray send ultrasound in here stat." His first order, directed to the med nurse, was followed by a second order, directed to no one in particular, but one of the nurses picked up the wall phone and called radiology.

The nurse punched the rate command into the IV pump, and the dopamine flowed into Mr. Simon's IV. Jeff waited, then shook his head.

"Go to forty mics," Jason said. He snapped the main IV line out of the pump and squeezed the IV bag, forcing saline into his patient, trying to raise a nonexistent blood pressure.

The nurse entered the new command into the second IV pump, and they listened to the pump increase its speed. Jeff continued searching for a pulse but shook his head. "I got nothin', Doc."

"Go to sixty mics and give me an amp of bicarb. He's got to be acidotic by now."

The pump increased its speed again, while another nurse popped the cap off a large syringe of sodium bicarbonate and pushed the plunger with both hands, shooting the solution through the IV.

They waited, but Jeff shook his head again.

"Give me one milligram of atropine. Maybe we can break a beta blockade."

The med nurse popped a syringe of atropine and pushed it into the IV line. "Nothing," Jeff volunteered.

"Defib at three hundred sixty, and where the hell's that ultrasound machine?" Jason said. The *feeling* was driving him to desperation, and it came through in his voice.

"He's in EMD, Doc," Jeff answered. "A shock's not gonna do anything."

"Just do it," Jason snapped. His judgment was blurred by the *feeling*, and his mind moved in and out of focus.

Bonnie stood ready at the defibrillator. She flipped the switch to defib mode, and the machine emitted a high-pitched whine then held, indicating the charge was ready.

"Clear!" Bonnie yelled, and everyone stepped back from the patient. The machine discharged with a loud snap, sending Mr. Simon's body into a single convulsing spasm.

The ultrasound tech rolled her machine into the room and powered it up. She rubbed conduction jell over the transducer head and handed it to Jason. He slid the transducer across the patient's chest then angled it and directed the beam of sound waves down through the heart. The scattered lines, reflecting off the heart wall, appeared on the screen. There was no movement of the heart muscle.

"Asystole," Jeff said quietly.

The nurses recognized Jason's desperation, and he knew it. He took a slow, deep breath and tried to regain control. He knew it was over; there was nothing else left to do. The *feeling* contracted, centered at a spot behind his eyes, and sizzled like the fuse on a bomb. He wondered if he was having a stroke. *Is this what the end feels like?* He asked himself.

"Anyone have any suggestions?" Jason looked around the room, but there was no response; they all knew they had reached the extent of what they had to offer this patient. Medical science had just run out of miracles, foiled by a heart muscle that was too badly damaged to respond to anything they had to give.

"What's it gonna be, Doc?" Jeff asked.

"Continue CPR while I talk to the family."

Jason walked back to the quiet room. He dreaded these times. He had no control here and nothing to offer a family other than aphorisms. This case was even worse. The patient wasn't dead, but there was nothing else he could do, and they couldn't keep doing CPR indefinitely. Should he bring the family in to say goodbye? Should he stop CPR first or let the family see the patient awake and alive? He wondered which would be harder for the family? Should he tell the patient they were stopping? Christ, they didn't teach this in med school, and he sure as hell had never encountered it before. There was no time for a consultation from the ethics committee. The decision was his, and he made it quickly.

Several additional people had joined the family in the quiet room, and they simultaneously focused on Jason. The weight of the responsibility he carried showed in the faces of these people. Unfortunately, Jason knew failed responsibility often resulted in a sudden change to blame. One of the drawbacks of playing God was the ultimate lack of control — a regrettable disadvantage.

He spoke to Mrs. Simon. "We placed a pacer wire into his heart, but we were unable to get his heart started. We're going to have to stop CPR soon. There's nothing more I can do."

Mrs. Simon cried out, "No, I can't lose him!" One of her sons wrapped his arms around his mother and wept.

"I'm sorry. We've done everything we can do."

The feeling of blame and failure crashed down on Jason. He knew there were no magic words now.

"No, there has to be something!" the other son shouted, his voice charged with anger.

"Mrs. Simon, he's still awake. Would you and your sons like to come in before we stop? You can say goodbye, and I think he would like to know you're here."

"Yes, I want to see him," she answered. Her voice choked with tears and pain.

They entered the cardiac room, and it suddenly struck Jason how this must look to someone from the outside. Blood stained gauze, empty med syringes, and debris littered the floor. A second nurse had taken over chest compressions while a respiratory tech did respirations with the Ambu bag. The cardiac monitor still showed the pacer spikes, accentuated with a regular beep, but no cardiac complex. The C-arm stood in place over the patient like an enormous mantis, ready to attack. *This must look like something from a nightmare to the family*; he thought. Yet, it was so familiar to this staff and every ER staff in the country.

Mrs. Simon hurried to her husband's side and took his hand. She bent and kissed his forehead and his eyes opened wider in recognition, then filled with tears.

"Carl, honey, it's me." She was sobbing uncontrollably now. "The boys are here, too."

He looked past her and saw his sons. "We're here, Dad," they said in near unison, their voices filled with false bravado.

"Carl, we want you to know we love you. We'll always love you." She stroked his head as she spoke.

"We'll never forget you, Dad," one of the boys said. "We'll take good care of mom for you."

Mr. Simon moved his eyes to Jason as his face morphed into confusion. *God,* Jason thought. *He doesn't understand.* For the first time, real panic was evident on his patient's face. Jason couldn't take much more, and he could feel the stress of the rest of the staff around him.

"Mrs. Simon, we need to go," Jason whispered.

Her sobs increased. "I love you, Carl. I can't . . ." She broke off, unable to continue. Both sons bent and kissed their father goodbye, then walked their grieving mother back to the quiet room — to wait.

Jason leaned over to Mr. Simon's face and spoke softly. "Mr. Simon, we need to stop now. I'm sorry," was all he could say. Terror replaced the tears in his patient's eyes — a terror now matched in Jason's entire being. He knew the *feeling* was going to kill him.

Jason turned to the tech doing compressions. "Come off the chest."

Jeff followed suit and flipped the power switch on the pacer box to "off." Jason turned to the respiratory tech at the head of the gurney. "Stop respirations."

The room was completely silent except for the steady, high- pitched hum of the cardiac monitor where a straight line repeatedly floated across the screen. Mr. Simon's eyes closed in death. No one cried, but Jason knew there were some on the verge of tears, as they stood looking at the body of what only seconds before had been a living human being. Someone, who just like them, got out of bed this morning with plans and feelings. Someone who had a family and a life, and never thought he would end the day in the morgue. Rooster's words came back to him, "We get paid for what this job does to our souls."

Out of habit, Jason reached up and gently placed his fingers on his patient's neck over the carotid artery to confirm there was no pulse. At that moment, he identified the *feeling.* He remembered where and when he had first felt it and his childhood name for it. He had been close — extremely close.

"GOD!" Jason screamed, recoiling. He was thrown back by the jolt that instantaneously flashed through his body. Jeff barely caught him as he fell backward.

"You shocked me!" he yelled in reflex at Bonnie, who was standing at the defibrillator.

"The hell I did. I never touched it, Doc," Bonnie said incredulously.

Jason forced himself to stand, bent over from the bone-throbbing pain in his arm. He tried to hold on to consciousness, but his mind started to blur. He groaned and stumbled. Jeff held him up, but he wasn't looking at Jason any longer. All eyes in the room had shifted to the cardiac monitor still attached to the patient.

"We've got a complex," Jason heard the words through the fog that was quickly wrapping itself around his brain.

"Check for a pulse." Jason forced the words out.

Jeff reached up cautiously and placed his fingers on the patient's carotid artery. "We've got a good, strong pulse," he answered. "Helluva save, Doc," Jeff laughed, his offbeat humor intact.

Jason stood alone, still bent over in agony and staggering, his mind blurred in pain and confusion. His vision cleared briefly, and a floodgate of memories and cognizance swept over him like a vast rolling wave, then vanished as quickly as it had appeared. The *feeling* was gone. He uttered a single word, "Rachel," then fell into a silent world of darkness. The room remained quiet except for the cardiac monitor that announced his patient's resurrection. Beep. . . *beep* . . . *beep* . . . *beep* . . .

Four

Beep . . . beep . . . beep . . .

Jason awoke to the sound of the cardiac monitor still beating a steady rhythm. Something was wrong; nobody was doing anything. His mind swam in confused pain. What was happening? His training kicked in, and he went into autopilot. If no one else was going to do anything, he would. His partial words came in forced, broken slow motion. "Je—, we nee— to ge— him to Univers— Hosp— for emerg— angioplasty." He tried to get up, but someone held him down. "Le— me go. Nee— to ge— him transferred to University Hospital for an emergency angioplasty." His words cleared as he awoke and edged back to reality.

"Jason, it's okay. Just relax, you're all right." Jesse's words reassured him, and her grip on his arm relaxed.

"What the—? Where am I?" He groaned and reached for his head. The heart monitor continued to beep, and he realized the pounding in his head matched his own pulse.

"There was an accident in the ER. You got a shock from the defibrillator or something, and you blacked out. You hit your head on the floor." Jesse said, trying to ease him back into bed.

The feel of cold starched sheets and bright, anonymous lights mingled with the smell of antiseptic and some nurse's stupid cologne focused his mind. He was in ICU.

"Ah, Dr. Corey, I see you're awake. How are you feeling?" A nurse chirped as she entered his ICU room. Her name badge said *Rita.* She had a pleasant face, but something about her said, "don't push me too far." Maybe it was her extra mascara or her smile, which said she wasn't actually smiling.

With a professional air, Rita pushed a button on his monitor and the blood pressure cuff inflated on his arm. She pulled a pen light from her pocket and flashed it back and forth into his eyes.

"Ow, that hurts. What are you doing?" he complained as he shielded his eyes and pulled away.

She stretched each word of her response as if she were speaking to an imbecile. "I'm checking your pupils."

"You can't have anisocoria in a fully conscious patient," he snapped. "That much increase in intracranial pressure would put the patient into a coma."

"Oh God. I hoped you wouldn't be another typical doctor-patient."

"I'm not a patient. Where's my doctor? Who's my doctor?" he protested.

"That would be Dr. Kiley, the intensivist. They weren't sure whether to admit you to Neuro or Cardiology, so they fudged and put you on the Intensive Care Service." She nearly sang the words as she bounced from place to place in his room.

"Yeah, well that's all a moot point, because I'm leaving."

"Jason, you're not leaving because I'm not taking you home unless they release you." Jesse countered.

"Well, they can't keep me if I sign out against medical advice," he said as he pushed himself out of the bed. He didn't see Rita remove the syringe from her pocket and stab the needle into his IV port.

"Yeah, Dr. Kiley said you'd probably try the AMA thing. That's why he left the med order," Rita laughed.

Jason dropped back onto the bed. "Oh, you didn't."

"Oh, but I did." She twirled the empty syringe in front of his face.

Rita and Jesse eased him back against his pillow as a silky peace washed over his mind and body. The pain in his head eased, his breathing slowed, and his eyelids leisurely dropped him into darkness. He barely felt Jesse squeeze his hand.

"Jesse, I love you." He forced the words out and was gone.

The two nurses looked at each other across his bed.

"Men," Jesse said.

"Doctors," Rita countered.

Jason lost the rest of his day in a medicated cloud of CT scans, cardiac conduction tests, and sleep. He was more alert but still woozy when he saw his doctor at evening rounds. Jesse was still at his bedside.

"How are you doing Jason?" Jim Kiley asked.

"I'm okay and ready to go home. I'd be out of here now if nurse Ratchet didn't slip me a mickey."

"Yeah, sorry about that, but I didn't think you were in a clear state of mind. I'm sure you can understand if you look at it from a professional point of view."

"I know. I'd probably have done the same thing. You know how doctors are as patients," Jason admitted.

"I'd probably be the same way. Anyway, I thought you'd like to know all your tests are negative. You've got a concussion, and had a hell of an electric jolt, but we're not finding any major problems. We don't have to start drilling burr holes in your skull for now."

"Good, then I can go home?" Jason shot back.

"Tomorrow. You're still throwing some ectopy from the electric shock. If your heart rhythm is normal, I'll spring you in the morning."

Jason frowned, but Jesse spoke up before he could respond.

"That'll be fine, Dr. Kiley. I'll see to it that he behaves himself tonight. If he gives me too much trouble, I'm sure Rita will be happy to help me control him."

Dr. Kiley laughed. "Yeah, she can be rather convincing. I'll see you in the morning." He wrote something in Jason's chart and left.

Before Jason could say anything, Jesse poked a finger at his face. "Don't start."

The next morning Rooster knocked on his door. "You look like shit," he said, then spotted Jesse. "Oh, sorry Jesse. I didn't see you there. Have you been with this guy all night?"

Jesse ran her fingers through her hair. "I imagine we both look a little frazzled."

"No, you look beautiful, as usual." He tried to smooth over his entrance.

"If you can get me out of this place, I could be in the ER for the eleven o'clock shift," Jason offered.

"Yeah, I don't see that happening. I understand they're releasing you today, but Jim Kiley says you're on R&R for the next several days." Rooster turned a chair backward and sat down with his arms folded across the back of the chair.

"Did you find out what happened yesterday?" Jesse asked.

"Not yet. I've got BioMed working on it. They're running diagnostics on all the equipment, but they haven't found anything so far. Personally, I feel it was a defibrillator discharge. That was no minor shock from a short circuit. I've heard of people being knocked into cardiac arrest from this sort of thing."

"How'd the patient do?" Jason asked. "I haven't heard anything about him."

"Amazingly. He's doing fine. We transferred him out, and they took him straight to the cath lab for a rescue angioplasty. This case is one for the books."

Rooster stood and headed for the door. "I'll talk to Jim Kiley to see when he's going to clear you to work, and I'll give you a call. Jesse, good to see you again. Keep him down if you can."

Jason was restless, and Jesse finally got him up for a walk down the hallway. They had only gone a short distance when they ran into Dr. Kiley.

"Well, I see you're up and about today. Are you ready to go home?"

"I was ready to go home yesterday," Jason answered quickly, and Jesse elbowed him softly in the ribs.

"Okay, I'll write the discharge order, and they'll get you set. I want you to take it easy for at least the next few days though." He directed his comment toward Jesse.

"Don't worry, I'll tie him down if I have to," Jesse answered.

"I'd schedule him for a recheck in my office in about a week but I doubt he'd show up. Just let me know if he has any trouble."

They turned and walked back toward his room, when Jason noticed the patient board at the nurses' station, which listed room numbers and patient names.

"How come they have a picture of a flower next to my name?" he asked Jesse.

She hesitated briefly before she answered. "I think it's just their way of reminding everyone the patient in that room is a doctor. You know how political things can be in the hospital."

"So they put a picture of a lily by my name? Seems a little morbid."

Jesse led him down the hall. "That's not a lily dear; that's a snapdragon."

Jason touched the bruise on his forehead and winced. It had been four days since his accident in the ER, but his head still reminded him of the episode. He shifted his weight in the lounge chair, closed his book, and reached for the glass of wine on the table next to him. A warm breeze drifted off the sound and scrubbed him with salt air. His patio deck, high above the surface of the water, provided him a spectacular view of the bay, which extended from the marina below him to the main body of the Puget Sound. He watched several amateur sailors clad in jeans working on their boats below, while a dozen or more sails in the distance broke the seascape as they tacked their way across the open water. Jason was a sailor wannabe.

Jesse had finally returned to work today, and Jason was savoring his first taste of privacy in what seemed like weeks. He had slept in this morning, then made a quick trip to Starbuck's for chai tea and a muffin. Boredom was already stalking him, and he considered a walk along the marina.

The smooth sounds of Glen Yarborough drifted from the open deck door behind him, and despite the boredom, added to his sense of serenity. It was a unique sensation for him. Maybe it was the result of his mini electroshock treatment, or maybe he had just been burned out and needed a break. Whatever the reason, he was enjoying the almost euphoric feeling. He wondered if the average person, someone not in medicine, felt like this all of the time.

The sound of the phone echoed from inside the apartment and brought him back to reality. Jason, like most doctors, hated the sound of a telephone. He had known colleagues from residency who became physically ill at the sound of a ringing phone. He reluctantly lifted himself out of his chair after the fourth ring and checked the caller ID. The screen read COREY, ARTHUR.

"Dad, what are you up to today?" Jason asked.

"I was just wondering the same about you. How's the head?"

"I'm fine. I didn't hurt anything important. Besides, if you're going to get electrocuted, what better place than an ER?" Jason laughed.

"Did they find the source of the shock yet?"

"Not yet, but I think it was a defibrillator discharge to give that kind of a jolt."

"Well, I'm just glad it didn't do any permanent damage. I was wondering, if you're feeling up to it, would you and Jesse like to come over on Sunday for steaks on the barbecue?" Arthur asked.

"Sounds good to me. I'll check with Jesse, but I'm sure she'll be up for it. You know how she adores you."

"That only confirms her intelligence and good taste," Arthur quipped. "Don't forget your swimsuits and we'll have a soak in the Jacuzzi."

"You've got it Dad. We'll see you then."

A killer stroke had taken Jason's mother when he was eleven years old. After that, Jason had retreated into a sanctuary someplace deep within his mind, to survive. His father had fought for him, and eventually coaxed him back to reality. In doing so, Arthur had saved himself, as well. An unexplained distance, which had existed between them before their loss vanished, and over the years, they had remained devoted to each other.

Jason not only loved his father but admired and respected him. Arthur had been born on a farm in Minnesota and had grown up with nothing. From that background, he had earned a Ph.D. in both genetics and biochemistry. He had taught at the University of Washington, among other places, and had been one of the top people in his academic field. Now, at eighty, Arthur called himself "practically retired," but he was still as physically and mentally sharp as ever. He occasionally advised on research projects and gave a periodic emeritus lecture on his favorite topic of bioethics. Jason had learned not to debate his father on any of the topics in his field of expertise. Arthur had not only read all the articles but had written a number of them.

Jason and Jesse awoke on Saturday morning to a spectacular spring day, which portended the fast approaching summer. They packed their things into the BMW, dropped the top, and headed for one of their favorite spots. Gig Harbor was a small village, nestled between the sound and the surrounding mountains, across the Narrows Strait — a short distance from their home. The traffic was heavy, even for a weekend. It seemed most of the population shared their desire to enjoy this beautiful day. As they drove across the Narrows Bridge, Jason spotted a Cheoy Lee double master below them, laying over hard under the wind. When he looked back to the road, he glanced at Jesse, who had obviously been watching him.

"See something down there?" she asked, teasing.

"No, just looking."

"I know how much you want a sailboat. Why don't you check some out?"

He grinned. "I have been."

"Really? And when were you going to share this information?"

"I guess it just got lost in the excitement lately."

"Yeah, I'm sure that's it." She shook her head and smirked. "I never have to worry about you cheating on me. You're a terrible liar." Her smile betrayed her words.

Jason grew serious as he reached for her and squeezed her hand. "Jesse, you know you never have to worry about me hurting you by cheating or in any other way. I would never intentionally hurt you."

"Hey, I know that. I'm just teasing." She hugged his shoulders and kissed him on the cheek.

"It's just important to me that you really know it, though," he said, still serious.

"Is everything okay with you?" she asked.

"Yeah, everything's fine," he answered, dismissing the question.

He swung the car onto the Gig Harbor exit and slowed as he downshifted through the gears.

The affluent little community was only a few minutes away from Tacoma via the Narrows Bridge. The picturesque hamlet named for its small harbor was supposedly only large enough to accommodate a captain's gig. The town's natural beauty and ambiance made it a favorite getaway. The surrounding waters and towering evergreens, which seemed to grow to the very edge of the village, usually left the temperature a few degrees cooler than the nearby cities.

They parked the car, and, hand in hand, explored their way down the gently sloping shop-lined main street. When they reached the end of the street they were ready for lunch, and Jason pulled her into the Tides Tavern. The local landmark was famous for their burgers, seafood, and view. They found a table on the deck, outside over the water, and ordered Tide Burgers and Roslyn beers, without looking at the menu. The waitress brought their beers, and Jason lit a cigarette. Jesse didn't smoke and had learned it was useless to try and alter Jason's habit.

Another customer stood and flipped potato chips into the air to the flock of seagulls that frequented the deck, waiting for handouts. The graceful birds snatched the chips in midair amid a cacophony of cries and flapping wings. When the feeding was over, Jason and Jesse sat quietly, basking in the salt air, surrounded by the ambiance of the Sound.

Jason looked out over the water at the snow-covered mountains beyond and once again, was aware of the quietude within him. Something was changing in his life as if he were evolving into a new being. He didn't understand the process or the purpose, but it was genuine, nonetheless.

"Jesse, I've been thinking about something." He paused while she took a sip of her beer. "Will you marry me?"

Jesse jerked the mug away from her mouth, sputtering and choking through a spray of the dark beer. She glared at Jason and grabbed a stack of napkins. Jason's face reddened as several nearby customers stopped their conversations and looked their way.

"Geez, Jason, that's not funny." Her expression changed to disbelief when she saw his face. "God, you're serious, aren't you?"

"Yes, I'm serious. Do you really think I'd joke about something like that?"

"But . . ." She paused. "I thought you were the world's most confirmed bachelor."

"People change, Jess."

She looked at him in disbelief through eyes rapidly filling with tears, and the reality of his question took root in her mind.

"Is there an answer coming?" He smiled and reached for her hand.

"An answer? Yeah, ah, yes. The answer is yes. Absolutely yes," she screamed as she came around the table, threw her arms around his neck and kissed him. A small round of applause rippled through the surrounding tables, and Jason acknowledged them with a quick, dismissive wave. Jesse pulled her chair to his side of the table and sat down next to him. Their burgers came, but they barely touched them.

She finally regained her composure. "Do I get a ring?" she asked.

"It's not official until there's a ring," he replied.

"When can we go shopping?" She was giddy from the moment and could hardly contain herself. She had dreamed of this moment for years but had always feared it would never come.

"How about right now?" he answered.

They finished their beers, paid their bill, and walked, again hand in hand, back up the gently sloping street. Jesse found an upscale jewelry store they had passed with a large display of diamond rings. As they walked, Jesse's quick pace slowed slightly, as her mind processed what was happening. She cast an occasional sideways glance toward Jason while her mind worked, and finally formed the words in her mind, but before she could ask the question building inside her, they arrived at the jewelry store.

The salesman brought out a large tray of diamond rings in response to Jesse's description. "I know exactly what I want. I've dreamed about it since I was a little girl."
She only looked through the rings for a few moments before she made her initial choice. "There, just like this," Jesse said, selecting a ring with a larger marquis stone in the center, guarded by three smaller stones on either side. She slipped the ring onto her finger and held it out for inspection. "Perfect, this is the one."

Jason nodded and looked back at the salesman. "Do you have one with a larger center stone?" he asked.

"Jason, this is fine," she whispered.

"We do have some individual stones, sir," the jeweler offered."

He brought out a box of stones, each wrapped in a small, translucent envelope, and opened one.

"This one is very nice, sir," he said handing the stone, locked in a pair of jeweler's tweezers, to Jason.

"Bigger," Jason said. Jesse groaned.

"How about this one, sir?" The jeweler looked extremely happy.

"Bigger," Jason answered. Jesse looked pale.

"I'm certain you'll like this one," the jeweler said confidently.

Jason took the stone and held it out toward Jesse. "I think this one will be just about right. Jesse could only nod in stunned agreement."

"Can you place this stone in the ring today?" Jason asked as he handed the large diamond back to the jeweler. The jeweler hesitated only briefly. "For you, sir, absolutely! And how will you be paying for your purchase today?"

Jason laid his gold card on the counter. "Excellent, sir," he said as he picked up the card. "It will only take me a minute to clear this, and I'll have your ring ready in about an hour if that's acceptable."

"Great. We're going across the street for a cup of coffee, and we'll be back," Jason said and steered Jesse out the door.

They found an outdoor bistro table at a sidewalk coffee shop, and Jason ordered lattes for them both. He shook a cigarette out of his pack and lit it, aware of the look of uncertainty that had appeared on Jesse's face.

"Earth to Jesse." He brought her back to the present. "Are you okay with this?" he asked.

"Yeah, I'm okay," she answered. "It's just that I want to be sure it's what you want, too. It's kind of sudden, and after your fall and all that in the ER the other day . . ." Her voice trailed off.

He laughed louder than he meant to. "You think this is post-concussion syndrome?"

"I just want to be sure, Jason. I want this to be for the right reasons, and not something you'll regret in the future. You have to admit; it's a big change."

He took a long sip of his latte and flicked his ashes into the ashtray on their table, thinking before he finally answered. "There has been a change, Jesse. I just don't know if I can describe it."

She reached across the table and took his hand, barely containing it in both of hers. She had learned that Jason, like most men, tended to keep his feelings to himself. She didn't know if it was a risk of being perceived as weak or vulnerable, but she knew the subject of feelings, hopes, and fears, was taboo with most men. She hoped she was going to get a glimpse into his private thoughts.

"There have been a lot of things going on with me lately. I haven't been happy." She flinched at his words. "Don't worry," he said in response to her tension. "It has nothing to do with you. I've become one of those doctors who doesn't like what I do, and I've reached the point of resenting my patients. I'm tired of trying to live up to unrealistic expectations."

"What do you mean? You're an excellent doctor," she replied.

"It doesn't have anything to do with the quality of medicine I practice; it has more to do with the patients. They want too much from me, and I can't live up to those expectations anymore. Do you know a doctor's white coat is the second greatest symbol of power in this country? It's second only to the seal of the President of the United States. But, at the same time, the only profession that people trust less than doctors are garbage men."

"Oh, that's not true, is it?" she interrupted.

"Ninety percent of people think their own doctors are capable, but only ten percent of people think someone else's doctor is competent. People see patients saved by doctors on TV every night, and then they're angry when we can't perform the same miracles in real life. I'm tired of being the bad guy. If they're mad enough, they sue us. In some areas of the country, 50 percent of the practicing doctors have a lawsuit pending at any given time, most of which are frivolous. That's why most doctors hate their jobs, and we have one of the highest divorce and suicide rates of any profession. It's all topped off with 250,000 dollar's worth of school loans hanging over us before we ever go into practice." He shook his head and poured the rest of his latte down his throat.

Jesse was stunned. She hadn't known he was so unhappy or so angry. "Are you saying you want to quit? You want to stop being a doctor?" She could barely speak the words. She loved Jason, no matter what he did, but she had only known him as a doctor and couldn't imagine him as anything else. It defined who he was.

"I thought that's what I was going to have to do, Jess." He looked at her face and paused before he continued. "But something has changed."

Jesse waited, but Jason didn't continue. "And . . .?" she finally asked.

"And . . . that's all I know," he answered. "I don't know what has changed, or why. I just know it's changed. I've changed." He shrugged his shoulders.

"When did this happen?" she asked, frustrated.

"Since I came home from the hospital." He didn't elaborate.

"Okay, how do you feel?" she pressed.

"Good," he answered.

"Good? That's all you can tell me?" Her frustration edged higher.

"Yep, that's pretty much it, but it's an enormous change for sure."

"And you're good with us with all this going on?" she asked.

"Jesse, I know I love you and want to be with you. This only makes it better."

She smiled and squeezed his hand, triggering Jason's glance at his watch. "I think it's been about an hour. Shall we?"

She started to rise, and then stopped. "Jason, since we're talking about things, there's something I wanted to ask you about." She seemed reluctant, almost embarrassed to ask the question. "When I was sitting with you in the hospital, before you regained consciousness, you said something." She paused briefly. "You mumbled the name Rachel a few times. I was just wondering."

Her words focused in his mind and froze him. He remembered, like someone recalling a forgotten dream, brought back by a trigger word.

"Rachel Hanson," he said. "She was our neighbor and my babysitter when I was a kid in Minnesota." The memory of the day he had seen a change in her face, the foreshadowing of impending death, crystallized in his mind.

"That seems like an odd thing to remember. Have you seen her lately?"

"She's dead. She died when I was a kid," he answered, then finished his answer in his mind. "I saw her just a few days ago."

The little bell over the door tinkled their arrival, and the salesman came around the corner from the back workroom holding a blue, velvet ring box.

"Just in time," he said as he handed the box to Jason.

Without looking into the box, Jason turned it toward Jesse and opened it while he watched her face.

"Oh, Jason," was all she could say, but her face said a great deal more. He slid the ring onto her finger, lifted her chin, and kissed her.

They drove home talking about their future together, something they had never dared to explore before. Their dreams energized them and drew them closer. They came into view of the Seattle skyline, and the pale light of early evening highlighted the buildings of the city, eliciting a passing blush across the spires. Within a few minutes, darkness settled, and the city lights flickered awake. Jesse rested her head on his shoulder, her arm around his neck. The sounds of her favorite CD invited them to *sail away on an Oronoco breeze*, through the streets of the quiet city.

The intimacy of the day had captured Jesse, and now built inside her like a gentle, warm wind, which rose and engulfed her. As they neared home, she moved her hand to his leg and gently stroked his thigh.

Jesse came to him, needy and ready to consume him before Jason could switch on the lights inside their townhouse. He moved her through the apartment to their bedroom, where they undressed each other in the dim glow of the lights over their bed. Still standing, she unsnapped her bra and threw it aside, then stepped out of her jeans. Wearing only her panties, she strained to get at him, but he held her away.

He cupped her breasts in his hands, caressing. Her breaths quickened as he took her into his mouth. When her passion rose beyond what she could stand, he effortlessly picked her up, laid her on their bed, and kissed her lips. She reached for him, but he forced her hands away, over her head, and pinned her arms to the bed. Methodically, he worked his lips down her throat, again to her breasts and hardened nipples. She reached for him a second time, but again he pushed her arms to the bed above her. He watched the fire of her sex blush slowly grow and spread across her chest as her pleasure rose. He moved his lips across her slender belly, stopping only to tease her navel with his tongue. Her hips pushed upward, into him, and he slid her panties down, still tickling her with his tongue.

"You're making me crazy." Her voice was raspy from her passion. She started to reach for him yet again, but he easily rolled her onto her belly, then slowly slid her panties down and over her bottom as she arched, rising to him. He gently caressed her cheeks and moved his hand lower to feel the wetness between her thighs, and then rolled her to her back again. Unrelenting, he continued his journey over her

46

body with his mouth until he tasted her essence. He cupped her cheeks, savoring her, working her until she climaxed and exhaled in a hard, sustained, breathy groan. As her back arched, he felt her muscles contract, pulsing in the rhythm of her orgasm.

He went to her and kissed her deeply as she moved her hands over him. Still trembling from her zenith, she slid her nails down his back. Desperate for him, she brought him to her and opened to him.

He looked into her eyes as he penetrated her, and felt a shudder engulf her. Her eyes closed, driven by desire beyond her control.

They made love until they were spent. Exhausted and at ease, they lay in each other's arms in the quiet time of the night. A nearly empty bottle of wine sat on the nightstand, and the silky sounds of Johnny Mathis soothed them with "Misty." The balcony door was open to the night, and the room had cooled, driving them under their thick quilt, where they snuggled and drifted toward sleep, lullabied by the rhythm of the ocean.

Jason watched her blush fade, her skin still glistening from their passion. He placed his open palm flat against her chest and felt her heart beating in a soft double rhythm.

"Ummm, whatcha doing?" she purred, her eyes glassy from near sleep and fresh sex.

"Feeling your soul," he whispered.

She laid her hand over his. "And what do you feel in my soul?"

"I feel love and goodness."

"Yes, lots of love. I don't know about the goodness," she said smiling.

Jason gradually became aware of the ache in his hand, which slowly grew to a deep, heartbreaking agony. He looked into her face and grimaced. "Oh, Jesse. I never knew."

She was instantly alert at his words and looked at him questioning.

"The pain, so much pain for the children."

She knew at once what he meant. She had carried the anguish of the dead and dying children, from her time on the cancer ward, in her soul for years. Her eyes filled with tears, and she started to speak, but his face stopped her. He had become the embodiment of sorrow, and the awareness of his agony frightened her.

Suddenly, she gasped, and her shoulders convulsed back against the bed, then quieted. They had both changed when she opened her eyes. She looked at him and saw a tranquil serenity which matched the emotion within her. In a few moments, she was asleep, filled with a peace she had forgotten could exist.

Jason's thoughts cleared. He knew he hadn't been asleep, but the prior moments were imprinted on his mind like a fresh dream. He watched her sleep, a slight smile on her lips and breathing easy. He gently eased himself out of bed, poured the last of the wine, and walked out onto the balcony. He stood naked under the stars, and emptied the glass while he smoked a cigarette. A meteorite flared across the sky and was gone as if it had never existed, much like his glimpse of Jesse's soul. A voice reached him from the depths of his mind. "Jason, why didn't you warn me? Why didn't you save me?" Rachel's words morphed and became his mother's voice, repeating the same words. "Why didn't you warn me? Why didn't you save me?" He shivered slightly; the only visible sign his life was in chaos.

FIVE

The sound of waves splashed through his mind as he drifted alone on the vast ocean. Something was terribly wrong, and that knowledge drove his panic.

Seagulls, sailing above him on a gentle breeze, examined him through polished onyx eyes. He rose up on the same breeze, which held the birds aloft, and sailed lightly above the water, the sun warm on his extended arms. The underlying smell of seaweed and dead things in the tidal basins seasoned the sharp saltiness of the air.

A pool of pale pink flowers coalesced below him in the waves until he could make out the form of a little girl in a pink playsuit, her blond curls drifting in the surf. She watched him through large pastel-blue eyes and smiled as she extended her arms to him. Slowly, he forced himself down to her and reached for the tiny hands, just beyond his grasp. Her features twisted in fear, and a cloud of blood-red water billowed around her as she slowly disappeared into the depths. He willed himself toward her, desperate to reach her, desperate to save her. He peered across the water, and there, on a faraway sand spit he saw Rachel — watching him. She shaded her eyes against the bright sun and slowly shook her head, telling him he had failed yet again.

"I'm not God," he called to her. "I'm not God!"

The scene receded like a tide pulled back by some unseen force, and left him coughing and sputtering. He expected tainted seawater, sullied with awful, but instead only coughed up spit and ragged sounds.

Jason jerked awake in the sun brightened room, still frantically calling. The wind still carried the sound of gulls, leaving him briefly confused, unsure which world he was in. He moved across the apartment, working the stiffness from his muscles, and found Jesse sitting on the deck in a pink terry running suit. His dream flashed back to him, and he scowled.

"Good morning sleepyhead." Jesse smiled and handed him a cup of coffee.

"Morning. He bent and kissed her cheek sparing her his morning breath. "How long have you been up?" He pulled his chair closer to the table, positioned his face away from the sun, and lit a cigarette. He gulped down several swallows of the tepid coffee in an attempt to bring himself fully awake.

"For a couple of hours. Someone kept me up talking in his sleep again."

"I don't talk in my sleep. I stayed up once and listened."

She pulled a face. "Well, I wish you had been listening last night."

"Did I mention any names?" He grinned, then too late remembered Rachel, and gulped down more of his coffee.

"No, and you'd better not either." She punched his arm. "I couldn't understand a word you said last night. It wasn't your usual running monologue from the ER."

"Good, I'm safe then." He smirked and rubbed his arm.

She stood with her cup in her hand. "We've got time for one more cup of coffee before we have to get ready for your Dad's." He passed her his cup for a refill and lit another cigarette.

Jason gazed out across the water and recalled the events of last night. "Maybe it had all been a trick," he thought. His mind reacting to too much wine before approaching sleep. Maybe his endorphins, generated by their passion, had combined with everything else and worked as a hallucinogen. He heard Jesse behind him and dismissed his thoughts with a mind shrug. She handed him his cup and pecked his cheek. When she sat down, Jason noticed a slight grimace.

"You okay?" He asked in response to her pain.

"Just a little sore this morning."

"What from?" he asked as he automatically went into doctor mode.

"Why Doctor, I can't imagine why I could possibly be sore today," she replied in a Southern belle drawl." She touched her finger to her cheek and continued, "Perhaps it has to do with what some fine gentleman did to me in bed last night. Why yes, I remember now, you tried to screw my brains out," she twanged and broke into a laugh.

"Aren't we just full of ourselves today? I didn't hear any complaints last night."

"And no complaints today either," she countered and squeezed his arm. "In fact, I don't ever remember feeling this good."

He steeped in her happiness, knowing this remarkable woman was his and that he was in no small part responsible for her joy. He knew he loved her more than anyone in history had loved another person, and she felt the same way, as if the two of them had invented this feeling.

"Tell me something, will you?" he asked. "What's the last thing you remember last night?"

"Why?" she answered coyly.

"Just humor me."

She smiled and answered, "I remember falling asleep, safe and warm in the arms of the man I love, knowing that I will never be afraid; *knowing there's no more pain.*"

"That's beautiful." He took her hand. "I just hope I can live up to it."

"I'm not the least bit worried." She kissed him, laid her head against his chest, and nestled into him. She missed the brief cloud of concern that passed across his face as the words repeated in his mind: *knowing there's no more pain.* He held her facing him and placed his open palm on her chest. Her expression changed and became detached as if she were searching for a memory. Jason watched her eyes drift away, and his breath caught before she returned to him. He turned his head slightly, questioning her.

"Just a little déjà vu." She shrugged. "We're late, and I get a shower first." She bounded through the door, shedding her clothes as she went. He watched her naked silhouette disappear down the hall, and finally took a tentative breath. Something was happening to him — had already happened. He had no idea what, and while it seemed the overall effect was positive, more than one aspect of his apparent metamorphosis disturbed him.

Jason and Jesse made the hour-long drive to Arthur Corey's home on the Skykomish River. They pulled into the drive of the well-kept ranch home, and parked under the giant fir trees that stood sentry over the house. The high mountain peaks, which climbed sharply away, just beyond the river, dwarfed the giant firs around the house. The ranch home stood alone, ensuring Arthur's privacy, something he cherished since his retirement from teaching. Arthur liked people and liked the world, although he considered both confused, but not confusing.

Jason knocked on the front door as part of the protocol but knew there wouldn't be an answer. He led Jesse through the immaculate home to the tiered rear decks where they found Arthur sitting in the middle of a miniature forest of bonsai trees, carefully trimming a tiny branch. The miniature trees lined the deck in rows on perfectly aligned shelves; some covered with shade screening and others purposely placed in the direct rays of the sun.

"Hi Dad. I thought we'd find you back here." Jason threw his arms around the sturdy old man and greeted his father with a hug.

"Oh, Jason, I didn't hear you drive up. And Jesse," Arthur easily wrapped his arms around her and pecked her cheek. "How's my girl? Is he treating you well?"

Jesse held his embrace for an extra few seconds and inhaled the faint scent of his British Sterling cologne. "Let me look at you Arthur. You're looking very dapper," she said as she stepped back.

"Oh, my dear, you know I love you. You don't have to flatter me."

Jesse held up her left hand and flashed her new ring.

"I don't believe it. He's going to make an honest woman out of you at last." He laughed and hugged her again as if celebrating a victory. Jason stood back; his hands stuffed into his pockets and whistled while he looked up into the trees in mock neglect. When Jesse and Arthur finally finished their celebration and noticed him, he continued whistling and checked his shoes.

"Oh, Jason, are you still here?" Arthur played the game.

"No, no, that's okay, I understand. I'm just a minor character here." He held his hands up.

"See how bright he is? He's learned his place already." Arthur laughed and embraced his son. "I think this calls for something special. I'll be right back."

Arthur disappeared into the house and emerged a few minutes later with three champagne glasses and a dusty bottle of Dom Pérignon. "I've been saving this for a long time for a very special occasion." He passed the glasses to Jesse and started to open the bottle.

"Why don't you let me do that, Dad? I should be good for something around here."

Jason removed the wires, then to the applause of Jesse and Arthur, cautiously worked the cork until the bottle erupted with minimal loss of the precious contents. Arthur poured and raised his glass in a toast. "To my two favorite people in the entire world. May you always bring each other as much happiness through the years as you've brought this old man today. And, perhaps a grandchild or two, before I'm too old to enjoy them." They laughed, bumped glasses, and drank, savoring their happiness.

The day progressed through the champagne, drinks, and Arthur's famous barbecue, followed by an obligatory tour of his bonsai trees. The trees were changing rapidly with the new season; much as Jason's and Jesse's lives were changing. Jason appreciated the beauty of the little trees, but more so, the joy they brought his father.

Early evening began to settle, and the air gave the first warning of the crisp mountain night to follow. They moved to the deck, around an open fire pit, where they finished their drinks and fell into small talk, warmed by the flames and the alcohol.

Arthur stood to freshen his drink. "Jason, I meant to ask if they found any cause for your little episode in the ER."

"If you mean the shock that almost fried me, they haven't found anything yet."

"It seems very strange to have that significant of an electrical discharge and not be able to find a source." Arthur dropped several ice cubes into his glass.

"I think they'll find something, but it may take them another few days to finish the diagnostics on the equipment," Jason answered.

"I stopped into the ER while Jason was admitted to the hospital, and Rooster told me they were working on it," Jesse injected.

"The hospital should consider themselves lucky you came through all right, and that you're not the litigious type." Arthur filled his glass and started to turn back toward them.

"The nurses are calling the patient Jason's miracle save," Jesse laughed.

"Well, I hope — " Arthur stopped in mid-turn, his head cocked.

Jason and Jesse watched him and waited, but Arthur remained transfixed.

"Dad?" Jason finally asked, but Arthur didn't seem to hear.

"Dad?" Jason questioned louder. "Are you okay?"

Jason stood and touched his father's arm before Arthur finally startled and responded.

"Oh! Yes, I'm fine. Sorry, I was just thinking about something for a moment."

Jason glanced at Jesse, "I thought you vapor locked on us there." He guided Arthur back to his seat.

"No, I'm fine, just fine," he answered. "Just old thoughts in an old mind." He chortled and took a large gulp of his drink.

"I think Jesse and I are going to head home, if you're all right. I've got the early shift tomorrow." Jason watched his father.

Arthur rose, kissed Jesse and embraced his son. When their eyes met, Jason saw something he had never seen in his father eye's before. Fear.

SIX

"Dr. Corey, I need you in here now!" A nurse yelled from the door of cardiac room number two.

Her words triggered a small surge of adrenaline, and Jason felt his pulse jump. It was a black Monday, and he was getting slammed. Jason, like most ER doctors, studied patient visit patterns and knew Mondays were a problem. He had worked his way through the morning of weekend-warrior injuries, but now things were heating up. He had a couple of MVAs as well as the ongoing string of bread and butter patients. He also had two chest pains, one of them apparently hot, judging by the tone of the nurse who was demanding his presence.

The morning had started out badly when Jeff Noles started heckling him from the time he entered the department. "Hey, Doc, I've had this headache for a few days. Could you just touch me and give me one of those miracle cures? Minus the shock, of course."

It had unnerved Jason slightly at first, but now it was getting old, and Jeff was showing no signs of letting up.

Crystal Tyler, the team leader, swiveled by and caught Jason's attention. The petite, curvaceous brunette was hard to miss. He stopped and briefly watched her move away from him toward a waiting paramedic, one of many who would invent a reason to stop by the department today in search of fictitious missing equipment or paperwork. The rumors around the department said Crystal was quite a party girl, who shared more than just a few drinks with whichever medic was her current favorite. Jason didn't mind her admirers parading through the department because she was a capable nurse. Besides, he thought she was kind of cute himself. God forbid Jesse should ever read his thoughts.

Jason returned from the cardiac room, wrote several orders, and slid the chart into the nurse's rack. He looked up to see one of the ER techs push a patient past him in a wheelchair, headed for an exam room. An ancient black woman beamed him a toothless smile from her perch in the chair as she passed. A confluence of wrinkles and fissures covered her small round face, interrupted only by her gaping mouth and tiny, age-sunken eyes. Despite her apparent age, her face was animated, and her smile radiated an energy that belied her years. The material of the shapeless black dress, which covered her skeletal frame, looked as if it might have been silk, but time had left it faded and lifeless. A black, straw pillbox hat sitting squarely on top of her head caught Jason's attention. At first glance, he thought some type of fringed material covered the hat. On more careful examination, he saw the woman's hair had grown through the hat and held it permanently in place. Her smile followed him over her shoulder as she disappeared into an exam room. Jason found her completely fascinating. He had treated a few more patients before he pulled the old woman's chart from the rack:

"Washington, Rhea. Female. Age: 92."

He scanned down through the vital signs and found the chief complaint: "Vaginal Irritation." Not what he had expected.

Jason looked around the department for an available nurse and found Crystal leaning against the counter talking to a paramedic. "Hey, Crystal, I need a chaperone. You busy?"

She strolled his way. "Never too busy for you, Doc."

The paramedic scowled at him, and Jason shrugged in response.

They found Mrs. Washington sitting on the exam table wearing a paper gown, still smiling, still wearing her hat.

"Mrs. Washington, I'm Dr. Corey. How are you today?"

She considered his question before she answered. "I've got a pain in my privates," she answered softly, pronouncing the word "privets."

Jason nodded. "I see. How long have you had this pain?"

Her brow furrowed in thought before she slowly answered. "A good while." She nodded her head in confirmation.

Jason glanced at Crystal, who had become totally captivated by Mrs. Washington's straw hat. "How about if the nurse gets you ready and we'll check and see if we can find what's causing your pain."

She leisurely nodded her head again. "That would be fine."

Jason left the room for a few minutes while Crystal readied the old woman for the pelvic exam. When he returned, Mrs. Washington was draped and laying on her back. There was no way her arthritic hips would allow her feet to stay in the stirrups, so she lay slightly frog-legged on the table. Crystal flipped on the overhead exam light and slid the drape up, revealing Mrs. Washington.

Jason heard Crystal stifle a gasp at the sight of several pale green leaves protruding between Mrs. Washington's legs. It took him a moment before he could organize his thoughts enough to ask, "Mrs. Washington, have you put anything into your vagina?"

The old woman faltered before she answered. "Nothing but my pessry."

The answer didn't help Jason. "I don't understand," he said. "What did you put inside yourself?"

"You know, my pessry, like the doctor told me," she answered matter-of-factly.

"I'm sorry Mrs. Washington; I still don't understand what you're telling me."

Crystal gradually moved her head closer, peering at the leaves.

The old woman tried to explain again. "When my utrus dropped, the doctor back home told me to use a pessry. Oh, that was years ago," she said stretching the words.

"Wait, are you telling me you have a prolapsed uterus?"

She answered tentatively, "Yes, that's it."

Jason had never seen a pessary, except for pictures in old medical books. "So you use a pessary for your prolapsed uterus."

"Yes, that's what he said, and I've been doing it every since."

"Are you still using the pessary your doctor gave you?" Jason asked.

"Oh Lordy, no," she laughed. "I lost that thirty years ago."

"So what have you been using?"

"Well, my sister said I could use a potato, so I just been using one of them."

Jason bit his lip hard and tried to keep his composure. "Mrs. Washington, I'm going to have the OB/GYN doctor come and take care of this, but it's going to be just fine."

Crystal helped the old woman sit up and straighten her gown.

"Whatever you think is best, Doctor, but can I ask something first?" Mrs. Washington said.

Jason looked into the aged face. "Sure, Mrs. Washington. Do you have some questions?"

"No, I just wanted to ask if I could touch your hands."

Her request took him by surprise. "My hands? Why would you want to do that?" he replied patiently.

She reached out to take his hands and held them against her. "I thought so," she said smiling. "How long have you had the power? It's good that you're a doctor."

"I don't understand, Mrs. Washington. What are you talking about?"

"The power, child. I've never seen it this strong in anyone before."
She started to say more, but stopped and released his hands.
Confusion slowly crept across her face and replaced her broad smile.
"You need to go now," she said and pulled the gown tightly around
her. "I'll see the other doctor, but you need to go."

Jason glanced at Crystal, who seemed as confused as he was by the
old woman's transformation.

"Mrs. Washington, did I say something to upset you?" Jason asked.

"If you're not the Angel, you must be the Serpent." She wouldn't
say anything more.

Jason sat down at his desk and paged the chief OB/GYN resident on
call. Peter Loft called back in a few minutes, and Jason tried to explain.
"I've got a consult for you in the ER. I think you're going to have to
come and see this for yourself. I can't explain it on the phone."

Dr. Loft finished his exam, sat down at the desk, and shook his head.

"I've never even heard of anything like this before. I think I can
get this published as a case study," he said.

"Yeah, it's a little different all right. Did she give you any problems
in there?" Jason asked. "I think she's a little confused."

"No, she was fine. Seemed like she was with it to me." He stood
and headed out the door, the tails of his long white coat trailing
behind him.

Larry Todd, the double coverage doctor, came on duty at eleven a.m.
Five minutes later, Rooster emerged from his office and waved his
cigarette lighter toward Jason. "Meet me in my office," he called,
meaning the outside deck. Jason acknowledged with a nod and followed.

Rooster stretched his muscled arms and took a drag off his
cigarette. "How're things going?" he asked.

Jason lit his own cigarette and answered. "Just another day in
paradise."

"I wanted to get back to you with BioMed's results on your little
accident the other day."

Jason grimaced. "So who pushed which button and tried to sauté me?"

"I'm afraid all diagnostics were negative; we're never gonna know.
At least you can have the satisfaction the shock in all probability
saved the patient's life."

Jason paused in thought. "It's just all too strange. An electric
shock comes from nowhere, nearly kills me, but starts the patient's
heart from asystole, which shouldn't have had any effect at all."

"Maybe Jeff is right; it's a miracle," Rooster snorted.

"Geez, don't encourage him. He's already making me crazy with that," Jason shot back.

Rooster leaned against the railing and rubbed his neck.

"Okay, I won't mention it again. But, there's one more thing I need to talk to you about. I want you to keep an eye on Larry Todd."

"Larry, what's going on with him?" Jason asked surprised.

"His wife filed for divorce. Larry's taking it pretty hard."

"I heard they were having some trouble, but I didn't know it was that bad. What's the problem?"

"She's had problems with drugs and alcohol for some time. Larry has tried to work through it with her in counseling, and all, but hasn't had much success. He got home early from a swing shift a few weeks ago and found her drunk and high, in bed with some guy. It turns out she's been cheating on him for quite awhile."

Jason shook his head. "So he's working his ass off in the ER, and she takes the opportunity to have an affair."

"More like affairs," Rooster emphasized the word. "She's been spreading herself around, if you get my meaning," he added. "Larry threw the guy out and gave her a choice. Either get off the stuff or get out. Apparently she chose the latter."

"Don't they have kids?" Jason asked. "How can she throw that away?"

"They've got two little girls, but she's not throwing anything away, except Larry," Rooster countered.

"How's that?"

"This is Washington State. Larry will lose the house, the kids, everything."

"You can't be serious," Jason was incredulous. "The State would give the kids to a mother who's a druggie and is cheating on her husband?"

"Not only that, he'll pay up to 50 percent of his income for support. This state is too liberal thinking for alimony, so they hide it in inflated child support. He'll be lucky if he even gets to see his kids occasionally."

"That's just not right. What about the drugs and the cheating?"

Rooster responded with a cynical laugh. "This is a no-fault state. They don't care about cheating, unless it's the guy. As for the drugs, the courts are only interested in getting the case finished and making sure the mother doesn't need state support. Since Larry's a doctor, it'll be worse. In Washington State, Lady Justice peeks a little under her blindfold."

"No wonder Larry's taking it hard. Are you sure it's going to be that bad for him?"

"I'll tell you what a lawyer friend of mine told me. The family courts aren't controlled by judges, but rather by something they call a court commissioner. A lot of these guys are lawyers who couldn't make it in private practice, so they maneuver a position as a commissioner. Lawyers usually already dislike doctors, and it shows. If the wife files for divorce, the commissioner assumes the husband was cheating. If the husband files for divorce, they also assume it's because he's cheating and wants out. They don't care that research shows infidelity in marriage is split almost fifty-fifty. The commissioner can rule any way he wants, and other than an expensive appeal, there's no recourse for the husband. In a criminal case, either party can request a judge they consider biased be removed from the case, and it's pretty much mandatory. In family court, once a commissioner is assigned to a case, they can't remove him, so they know they can get away with a lot. A group of attorneys set child support schedules in the state. Are you getting the picture?"

Jason was stunned. "I had no idea it was that unfair."

"As unfair as it is, Larry is still better off without her. I knew Diana when she was a nurse. She was a gold-digging tramp who had her hooks out for any doctor she could snare. Unfortunately for Larry, he was the type of guy who bought her act hook, line and sinker."

"Geez, makes you think about getting married," Jason mumbled.

"By the way, congratulations on your engagement," Rooster chuckled.

Jason rolled his eyes. "Yeah, thanks."

"Anyway, keep your eye on Larry. The next few months are going to be hell for him."

"Will do. If there's anything else I can do to help, let me know."

"Hey, who knows, sometimes what goes around comes around, and these things work out," Rooster said with a smug smile and flipped his cigarette away.

Jason watched him leave. He knew Rooster well enough to know his comment wasn't idle chitchat.

Jason lit another cigarette, and his thoughts went to Jesse. He was suddenly aware of a tiny cloud of apprehension pushing at the periphery of his mind. He knew she would never cheat on him, but he also knew people change. People fall into love, and people fall out of love. He remembered a line from an old movie: "Love is what's left when the fire of being *in* love burns away." He wondered what they would have left when their fire was gone.

The pace inside the ER had picked up, and the chart rack was filling quickly. Larry was sitting at the desk thumbing through lab work.

Jason vacillated but finally decided to approach him. "Larry, I was talking with Rooster, and he told me about your wife. I just wanted to tell you, if there's anything I can do to help, all you have to do is let me know."

Larry's face revealed a hint of his pain. "That means a lot to me, Jason, I appreciate it. Right now, I feel pretty alone."

"I can't imagine how hard it must be for you, but remember we're all with you here."

"Sometimes the pain gets so bad, it just feels like I can't go on one more day. I even wake up in the middle of the night screaming. I can't believe this is happening to me and to my kids."

"Larry, I do know this will get better; it has to, and you'll be all right." Jason put his hand on Larry's shoulder.

"I'm going to try for custody of my kids, but my lawyer says Washington favors the mother when it comes to custody."

"Don't the drug and alcohol issues count at all?" Jason asked.

"It might if I had some proof, but her psychologist refuses to release her records, and the attorney says we can't get them, so it's her word against mine."

Crystal walked up behind them and leaned over with a chart. "We've got a lunger in trouble in room three."

Jason took the chart and picked up his stethoscope. "I'll take this. Why don't you take a break?"

Larry stood and rubbed his hands over his face. He looked like a man on the very brink of defeat — exhausted and beaten by something beyond his control. Jason hoped Larry had the strength to get through this and couldn't help but wonder how he would do in the same situation.

SEVEN

Old ghosts and new fears had haunted Arthur's night. He had almost forgotten what the fear was like, but now it roiled and twisted in his chest, revived by Jesse's words. He had lived with it for years before the fear had faded away and left him some peace. The experiment had failed, thank God, but now, maybe not.

Arthur appeared calm on the exterior, sitting at his desk, fidgeting with a pair of bonsai nippers. However, inside his mind, he was screaming into the phone he held in his other hand.

"Goddamn it, Harrison, answer your phone." His gaze rested on the Japanese tea rose sitting in front of him while he calculated the time on the East Coast once again. After four rings, the answering machine three thousand miles away picked up.

"You've reached the residence of Dr. Harrison Fellows. I am unable to take your call. Please leave a message. Thank You."

Dr. Harrison Fellows was recognized as one of the most accomplished genetics researchers in the world. Years earlier, he had left a successful and lucrative OB/GYN practice to focus on his research, and since then his work had been groundbreaking. Over the years, he and Arthur had shared a number of projects as well as a friendship of sorts. Fellows was currently the chair of the Department of Genetics at Harrington Hanover, the leading research university on the East Coast.

Arthur had tried his first call early this morning. Now, the frustration of not being able to reach Fellows was driving him mad, and he ran his hand through his thinning gray hair in irritation. He had resisted leaving a message on earlier calls, but now he blurted the words when the answering machine beeped. "Harry, this is Arthur. I need to talk to you as soon as possible. Jason has had . . . an occurrence and — "

The receiver picked up on the other end, cutting him off in mid-sentence.

"Arthur, what's happened?" Dr. Fellow's voice bristled with excitement.

"Thank God, Harry. I didn't think I'd ever reach you." His words were piqued.

"I just got back from a breakfast meeting with the chancellor of the university. Tell me, what's happening with Jason?"

Arthur spoke with a slight tremor in his voice. "He had something happen at the hospital. A patient he was resuscitating was revived after they had given up on him."

"That doesn't sound so unusual, Arthur." Dr. Fellow's voice changed from excitement to exasperation. "People are resuscitated out of cardiac arrest frequently, even after we've given up hope. You know that." His voice leveled to a reassuring tone.

"I know that Harry, but it wasn't like that. Listen to me, damn it. They had stopped efforts on the patient and were shutting down. The patient had been in refractive asystole — even failed a transvenous pacer. Jason checked the patient's carotid pulse, and there was a shock of some sort. It knocked Jason into an ICU bed, but it restarted the patient's heart." Arthur shifted to the edge of his chair.

"Still, Arthur, there could be a perfectly normal explanation. The pacer fired, the monitor discharged, or a short occurred in one of the instruments." Fellows rocked back in the deep leather chair behind his massive mahogany desk.

"They've checked all that. They can't find a thing that remotely suggests a source. Harry, the nurses who were there are calling it a miracle."

"Arthur, I think you're making too much of this, but you know how to answer your question. Perhaps it's time." He tried not to push his old friend too hard.

"I promised Helen, before she died, that I'd never do that. She made me swear it, and I have no intention of breaking my oath to my dead wife. I just thought you should know. You always said to contact you immediately if there were any questions; any occurrences."

"I know, Arthur, and I appreciate your call. If anything else happens let me know, but right now there's not much I can do without the test. Try to calm down and see if you can get any idea from Jason if he sensed anything. It's probably nothing. Remember, our evaluations of him when he was a child all were negative."

"Do you still have the original, Harry?" He asked, afraid of the answer.

"Yes, Arthur, I still have the original."

"You haven't used it again, have you?"

"No Arthur, that was the bargain. I haven't used it again."

"I wish we had never started this. You don't know what it has been like over these years; not knowing and always wondering if something's happening." The old man sounded frantic.

"Arthur, we've been through this before. You had plenty of chances to change your mind. Remember, you wanted the opportunity for the fame and power as much as I did."

"Not the power, Harry. Never the power. But I was wrong all the same. I know that now. I should never have involved Helen. I don't think she ever forgave me."

"I told you not to tell her. You were a fool for letting her know, Arthur."

"I suppose, but I could never lie to her. I had to tell her."

"Then you should have told her before instead of after, and let her make her own decision. You know why you didn't tell her, Arthur. You were afraid she would say no." All empathy had gone from Fellow's voice.

"I'm sorry, Harry. You're right. I shouldn't have bothered you. I've got to go." His voice echoed the pain and guilt he felt in his heart. He carefully placed the phone back on its stand.

Three thousand miles away, Dr. Fellows replaced his phone and rocked back in his chair. He thought about what he had just heard, as the words echoed in his mind. *Maybe,* he thought. *Just maybe.* Fellows had obtained the fame he had sought years ago, but his thirst for power was greater than it had ever been. His quest for power possessed him and drove his life. Now, the potential for that power was beyond imagination, even for him.

Arthur slumped in his chair, his body numb. His friend was right; he had been afraid. He had tried to tell his wife, but they had waited so long. He had wanted to adopt, but Helen wanted to keep trying for their own baby. Then, they were too old for adoption, and there were no options left. No options until his associate, Harrison Fellows, had approached him. Arthur had wanted a child for Helen, and maybe he had wanted the fame for himself. He could admit that now. He had planned to tell her all along, but yes, Harry was right; he had been afraid. Then, when Helen was pregnant, he was frightened that she would get upset and lose the baby. He tried later, but he saw the color in her cheeks, the changes in her body, and how happy she was. He couldn't force himself to tell her because he was afraid she would hate him.

After the baby was born, Arthur knew he couldn't wait any longer. He hoped her love for the baby would override her anger. Harry wanted to do the test then, but when Helen learned the truth, she had forbidden it.

Arthur remembered the day he told her. She refused to believe him and said he couldn't do such a thing, but his face said he wasn't lying. Helen had gone into the nursery, picked Jason up, and held him. She had rocked him for what seemed like hours, looking into his face with tears running down her cheeks while she sang to her son. Finally, late that night, she came to Arthur, her eyes red but her voice controlled. She said she forgave him, but he knew she never truly did — not completely. She wanted to know exactly how they had done it. He tried to explain the best he could, and she seemed to understand. She had asked a few questions, and Arthur had tried to simplify it for her.

When they were done, she demanded they call Harry to the house. He arrived disheveled, obviously from his bed. Then, she talked. She didn't talk about what they had done, only how the future was going to be. No tests, no special schools, no special anything. When Harry argued with her, she had become furious. She threatened to expose him, no matter what the cost to Arthur. When Harry still pressed his point, she grabbed a knife and buried the tip in the wood of the dining room table. The mark stayed there, a permanent reminder of her resolve.

Despite Helen's objections, but without her knowledge, Arthur and Harrison had studied Jason as a child. Simple little experiments they could do quickly and privately, but they had finally given up. They hadn't found anything, and Helen had become suspicious, making any further study impossible. All that remained were Arthur's observations at home. Jason, of course, never knew about any of it. Arthur had carried it with him all these years; what they had done and what might be. Now his fears were reborn.

Jason's alarm chirped softly and brought him into another day. He half rolled and reached to flip the alarm off, still enveloped in an early morning fog. He kept the volume of his alarm low, so it wouldn't wake Jesse when he had an early shift. His head cleared, and he realized something was wrong. Jesse wasn't there. He ran his hand across her side of the bed and found it rumpled, but cold. A twinge of panic scurried across his mind. Jesse was a sound sleeper, and never got up early, unless she had to. He pulled on his shorts and walked to the main room, where he found Jesse asleep on the couch, bundled in a blanket. Her head was skewed on the pillow, and Jason resisted the urge to tousle her hair. She looked as if she'd had a rough night.

A piece of paper on the coffee table caught his eye. He pulled the note out from under their cassette recorder and read the message written in Jesse's fluid hand. *Don't talk in your sleep? Listen to this, please. I'm getting ear plugs or separate rooms.* The note ended with a happy face with sagging eyelids and a string of tiny Z's trailing away.

Jason went through his morning routine as quietly as he could. Before he left, he slid the cassette into his pocket and left two cotton balls on Jesse's note. It was the best he could do for earplugs on short notice. He hoped the attempt at humor would help make up for her night. He was halfway out the door when he stopped, and went back to the table. He turned her note over and wrote, "Sorry about that. Let me see what I can do. I love you." He finished with a happy face with wide eyes and a string of small hearts.

Jason's morning commute took him in the opposite direction of the main flow of cars. One of Seattle's biggest problems was its traffic, and Jason watched the mass of stop-and-go vehicles across the median. He had decided to try his commute today with the top down on the roadster, but had quickly turned up the heat and flipped on the seat warmer. As he moved through the lanes, an occasional driver glanced at him questioning his sanity.

He remembered the tape in his pocket and pushed it into the car's cassette player. Jesse greeted him in an obviously sleep deprived voice. "Good morning. I hope you had a good night's sleep," she kidded, with a touch of resentment in her weary voice.

"I'm taping this at three a.m. I thought you might want to hear what you've been saying most nights for the last week or so. Maybe it means something to you, because I sure as heck can't make anything of it. Have a nice day, and I'll call you when I wake up *much later* today. Love you." He heard her lips smack a kiss, and smiled.

There was a pause, then a voice. For a brief instant, there was a flicker of familiarity, like the flash of a face in the crowd that resembles an old friend; then it was gone. It wasn't his voice. He fast-forwarded and hit the play button again, but the same foreign voice, speaking gibberish came through the speakers. He rewound and started over. Jesse's words were there again, followed by the same unfamiliar voice. Jason leaned forward, punched the eject button, and flipped the tape. The sound of the Beach Boys rolled from the speakers. He hit eject again, checked for a loop of snagged tape, and restarted it. The tape didn't sound like it was dragging. He listened closer but couldn't identify any particular words, even though the speech was clear and deliberate. The rise and fall of the inflection sounded like sentences, but that was all he could get. *This has to be some mistake*, he thought. Jesse had probably tried to record over something else — he didn't know what — and done something wrong. But her voice was there, loud and distinct. He shook his head, hit the eject button again, and slid the tape into his shirt pocket.

"What the hell's going on?" He mumbled to himself. His life had taken an oblique turn toward the bizarre. Little old ladies thought he was the Serpent; he was doing something peculiar in his sleep, and he couldn't forget Rachel. No, Rachel was too significant to ignore. The thought of her visits sent a cold surge through him, and he reached for the dash and turned the heater control to high.

EIGHT

It might have been appropriate if the air had become still, and the earth had slightly quaked, but that didn't happen. At eleven a.m., Dr. Steve "Wild Thing" Lubeck arrived at the ER for extra coverage. He crossed the department in paced, double-length strides, and unceremoniously deposited his bag behind the desk. He glanced up at the packed chart rack and growled, "Shit." Several of the nurses slowly gravitated away from the doctor's desk.

Jason looked up and smirked. "Hi Steve, good to see you."

"Bite me," Lubeck answered. Jason knew Steve had the driest sense of humor known to mankind and laughed in response.

The ward clerk answered the phone and turned in their direction. "Dr. Lubeck, there's a drug rep here. He wants to know if you'll talk to him."

Steve glared in her general direction but didn't answer.

"I'll just tell him you're busy," she mumbled.

It wasn't that Lubeck was a bad guy. Actually, he was a very likable guy, once you got to know him. It was just that medicine and the ER had taken their toll on him. Steve had been doing his job for twenty-five years and was the oldest physician in the department. Some said he had been doing it too long. He was one of the doctors who had practiced emergency medicine when it wasn't even a specialty, just various physicians filling in coverage for ERs. In those days, patients who weren't emergencies were sent away to follow up with their family doctors. Sometimes the ER doctors were young physicians, just starting their practices, who needed the extra income. That meant the doctor taking care of a heart attack in the middle of the night might be a pediatrician or a radiologist. Doctors like Steve Lubeck had stayed with it, and honed their skills to become the jack-of-all-trades that ER doctors had to be. When emergency medicine became a specialty, Lubeck had been grandfathered in, and became board certified by passing the specialty boards without formal residency training in emergency medicine. It was no small feat. Jason felt doctors like Steve deserved some degree of respect for what they had done for the specialty. Steve Lubeck was one of the doctors who had stayed current and remained a solid doc. He could quote the most recent research articles and knew what they meant, which was more than many of the younger, residency trained, doctors could do.

Unfortunately, Dr. Lubeck suffered from a common malady of long-experienced ER physicians: he was bitter. Within the profession, it was called burnout. It could happen to ER doctors of any age, but its frequency increased with time and experience. Steve's mindset manifested itself in his general attitude toward patients and hospital administration. He resented the increasing government interference in medicine, and what he called the decline of the profession. Steve Lubeck was one of a dying breed.

Steve was professional enough not to allow his pessimism to interfere with his practice and his interaction with his patients — most of the time. But, periodically he would let a word slip or his attitude would come through, which often resulted in a letter of complaint from a patient. Rooster kept Steve in the ER for one primary reason: he was the best clinician in the department. Rooster always said if he was lying on an ER gurney, he wanted to look up and see Steve Lubeck's face looking down at him; bedside manner be damned.

Jason thought about calling Jesse, but he still felt guilty and didn't want to risk waking her. Finally, around noon the ward clerk told him Jesse was on the line. He sat back in his chair and picked up the call.

"Good morning," she greeted him.

"You mean good afternoon."

"Maybe it's afternoon for someone with a good night's sleep, but for me, it's morning."

"Yeah, I know. I'm sorry about that. I played the tape you left for me, but you must have done something wrong when you recorded it. That definitely wasn't me."

Jesse answered defensively. "Oh yes, it was."

"Jesse, it wasn't my voice, and I don't have a clue as to what that language was."

"I listened to it after I recorded it, and that's exactly what I heard, and what I've heard almost every night." Jesse countered.

Jason could see it was better to drop this subject for the time being. "I'll tell you what I'll do. I'll have Rooster write a prescription for some sleeping pills for a few nights while we sort this out."

"Please do something. I go back to work tomorrow, and I need some sleep." She sounded almost desperate.

"Okay, listen, I've gotta run, but I'll give you a call later."

"Later." She closed with a kiss.

Jason rocked in his desk chair for a moment and chewed his lip. Jesse was sure the tape was of him. He'd check it with her tonight, but suppose she was right. How could he sound like that, and how could he speak some language he'd never heard? He'd seen things like this on TV, but never actually believed them. He was a scientist, and things like this always had a reasonable, rational explanation, or so he thought.

Steve stood in front of the chart rack and pulled out the next chart. His response brought Jason out of his reflection. Lubeck flipped the chart open and groaned, "God no, not Mrs. Arnt."

He slapped the chart closed in disgust. Mrs. Arnt and her family were well known in the Harborline ER, but every ER had many patients like them. They were called frequent flyers because they came to the ER repeatedly for not only non-emergency problems, but sometimes for no problem at all. They didn't go to their family doctors because they didn't want to make an appointment and wait. Often these were welfare patients, what the staff called U and I insurance, or Gold Card members.

"I'll see her, Steve," Jason offered.

"No, I'll see her. I don't believe in cherry picking the charts," he said, referring to the practice of going through charts and leaving the problem cases.

Lubeck dragged himself to exam room four, looking like a kid headed to the principal's office, and Jason couldn't suppress a grin. He knew how difficult patients like this could be, and how much Steve hated them.

"Mrs. Arnt, I'm Dr. Lubeck. What can I do for you today?" He tried to sound professional, and hide how he truly felt about the patient in front of him.

Mrs. Arnt sat fidgeting on the edge of the exam table. Her overdone makeup attempted to hide her age, but couldn't conceal her extra fifty pounds of weight. She shifted her bulk and pulled her skimpy skirt down around her generous derrière. Her stump legs dangled over the edge of the exam table and ended in a pair of shapeless white go-go boots.

"I've been waiting here for over an hour," she snapped in reply. "And I know very well who you are. You're the one who made the wrong diagnosis on me the last time I was here."

Steve clenched his jaw and tried to remain calm. "Well, let's check your chart here. Hmm. It says you signed in at triage fifteen minutes ago." His frustration came through in his voice.

"I know how long I've been here. That girl at the desk got the time wrong, too, just like she gets everything else wrong."

Steve felt the break coming, but tried to evade it. "Suppose you tell me why you're here, in the Emergency Department today," he said, stressing the word *emergency*.

"I've already answered that question twice since I've been here." She folded her arms across her chest and uncrossed her legs, giving Steve a view he would have preferred to avoid.

"Since you're convinced the registration clerk — and I'm sure the triage nurse — got your information wrong, I thought I should get it directly from you." He crossed his arms in response to her attitude and forced a smile.

"I don't know why I bother coming here," she said sarcastically. "All you people do is order a bunch of tests to run up my bill, and tell me something that isn't even right. I have to go to my own doctor to find out what's really wrong. Why don't you just refill my hydrocodone and let me get out of here?"

Steve had tried and failed. He could feel the eruption building deep inside his gut. It wouldn't be denied!

"That's a good question, Mrs. Arnt. Why do you come here, time after time after time, if we're all so bad?" he asked, throwing out the challenge and inviting her to push him farther.

"I can come here any time I want. That's what the law says, even if you are all a bunch of quacks," she snapped at him, taking the bait.

"Hmm. Quack? No, Mrs. Arnt, if I were a quack, I'd do something like this: QUACK, QUACK, QUACK," he shouted. He dropped into a duck walk, flapped his arms folded into wings, and darted toward her.

Mrs. Arnt screamed and jumped off the exam table, swung her purse at Steve, and fled for the door. Lubeck stayed in pursuit, wings flapping and his head bobbing. "QUACK, QUACK, QUACK . . ."

By the time she exited the exam room, a small crowd had gathered, then parted as Dr. Lubeck chased the purse-swinging patient through the department, still in his duck walk, still quacking like a barnyard terrorist. The reaction of the onlookers varied from confusion to laughter, but the commotion brought Rooster from his office.

"What the hell's going on out here?" Rooster demanded.

Mrs. Arnt and Steve came around the corner, looking like a scene from a demented fairy tale. Rooster's face showed a remarkable lack of emotion as he waited for Steve to pursue his patient out the ER doors. Lubeck stood, and when he turned back toward his desk, came face-to-face with Rooster.

"Excuse me, Dr. Lubeck, could I have a word with you in my office?" Rooster's words were slow and edged. The ER quieted as Lubeck followed Rooster into his office, and the door closed behind them.

Rooster sat down at his desk and tented his hands in front of his face.

"Do I even want to know what that was about, Steve?"

"You know what she's like, Rooster. She just pushed me over the edge today. I'm tired of being her convenience walk-in clinic and putting up with her rudeness and bullshit." Lubeck's arms gesticulated.

"I know what it's like dealing with patients like her as much as you do, Steve. But, the bottom line is that administration doesn't know and doesn't care, and I'm the one who has to answer to the CEO when the complaints come through. Believe me when I say that your little diatribe out there *will* generate a complaint. How, exactly, do I justify to administration that one of my ER doctors chased a patient out of the department quacking like a fucking duck?" Rooster's voice was glacial.

Steve hesitated before he answered. "I know, Rooster, and I don't mean to make trouble for you, but everybody has their limit." He wasn't backing down.

"Yeah, Steve, and your limit is a little shorter than everybody else. Medicine isn't like it was twenty years ago. Today, it's a competition for patients, and patient satisfaction is as important to this business as customer satisfaction is to any other business." Rooster's voice resonated with frustration.

"That's part of the problem, Rooster. The pencil pushers and politicians have made this just another business. I still happen to believe it's more than that. We deal with human lives, not hamburgers and deodorant. That should mean something. At least it should be worth a little respect from the people we take care of." He gestured toward the ER and leaned over Rooster's desk. "I'll be damned if I'll take attitude from trash like Mrs. Arnt. She wouldn't go into Walmart and treat them the way she treats us because they'd throw her out. But we have to take it because administration says we have to be *professional* with everyone, no matter what. The bottom line is that administration wants the revenue from her, and we can be damned." Lubeck's shouts had turned his face crimson.

Rooster took a deep breath. "Steve, calm down and sit down before you blow a gasket." He restrained his own anger.

Lubeck dropped into a chair.

"I'm sorry, Rooster, but this stuff just pisses me off." He sat massaging his temples and started to deflate.

"We all know this stuff, Steve, and we all put up with it, whether we like it or not. The more you let it get to you, the worse it is. You should know by now there's not a single thing you or I or anybody else can do to change the way things are. You're right. This is what medicine has become, and it's never going back. In fact, it will probably get a lot worse. We have two choices: accept it or find another profession. At least you're lucky enough to be looking at retirement not too far in the future. That's assuming you live that long." Rooster moved from his chair and sat on the corner of his desk. He looked down at Lubeck and watched him rub his temples.

"Steve, if you don't let go of this it'll kill you. Look at yourself. Shit, your BP must be through the roof. The other thing you need to consider is that administration could demand your removal. I would try to block that, but if it comes down to you or the contract here, I have the welfare of other doctors to consider."

Lubeck dropped his shoulders as Rooster's words sank in. "I know, you're right. My wife used to tell me the same thing. Sometimes it just . . ." Steve's voice started to raise again, and Rooster stopped him with a hand on his shoulder.

"Steve, you've got to do something about this. Get on meds or see a shrink. Take a vacation, but for your sake and everyone else's, do something."

"Don't you think I've tried? I tell myself every day not to let this stuff get to me. Then, in comes a Mrs. Arnt, or a family of welfare patients all wanting to be *checked*, and I just lose it. I know it's a problem. It makes my life hard, too, but it just won't go away." Steve began to sound more frustrated than angry.

"Okay, all I'm asking is that you do what you can. I don't want administration making the decision for us." Rooster watched Steve's face as he walked back around his desk and sat down.

"I'll do what I can, Rooster. I hope you know I appreciate the help and support you give me with administration. I consider you my friend, Rooster." Steve was back in control of himself.

"I am your friend, Steve. But I've also got a department to run."

Steve nodded, stood, and walked back to the ER. When Jason came out of an exam room, he spotted Steve, standing at the desk.

"Everything all right?" Jason asked.

"Yeah. Rooster's a little pissed, but it'll be okay. Can I ask you something, Jason?"

"Sure, what do you need?"

"Am I too much of a hard-ass with the patients?"

They both sat down, and Jason pulled a face while he considered his reply.

"I'm not exactly sure how to answer that question, considering you just chased a patient out of the ER quacking like a duck," he chuckled.

"I want an honest answer."

"Okay, but remember, you asked." Jason hesitated briefly then went on. "I don't think you're a hard-ass, Steve. I think you've never learned to accept things for what they are. We all get irritated by the same things that get to you: the welfare patients, the rude patients, the government rules. We all deal with them. The difference is, we don't allow them to take control of us. It's just the way things are. It doesn't do a damned bit of good to let it eat you up, and it won't change a single thing, except give you a heart attack or get you fired."

Steve's face almost stopped him, but Jason continued. "I suspect it goes deeper than just the patients, Steve. I suspect you carry that same level of anger and frustration through the rest of your life." Jason stopped and waited for the explosion, which never came.

"You're right. You're right, and I can't deny it. I'm sure my ex-wife would tell you the same thing." Steve exhaled. "But I don't think you fully understand, Jason. If you and the rest of the next generation of doctors don't take a stand, our profession is doomed. Medicine, as we know it, is doomed. We're the best in the world, Jason. Do you really want to lose that?"

"I'm afraid it's already gone," Jason replied.

Steve shook his head. "I care about my patients too much to accept that."

Jason didn't know what to say. "I'm not a psychiatrist, Steve. But, you asked me, and I've given you what I consider to be an honest answer. The question is, what are you going to do about this?"

"I appreciate it, Jason. And I'll work on it. I know this is eating me up, and it makes it hard for everyone around me. Thanks." He took Jason's hand and shook it briefly, a bit uncomfortable with the contact.

"It's not all bad. That duck thing was the funniest thing I've ever seen," Jason laughed.

"Yeah, but I don't think Rooster shares your appreciation."

As if on cue, Rooster called "J.C.," and held his cigarette lighter in the air. Jason pulled his cigarettes out of the pocket of his white coat hanging on the back of his chair and followed Rooster outside onto the concrete deck.

A cloud of smoke already rolled above Rooster by the time Jason came through the door. He extended his lighter and lit Jason's cigarette for him and asked, "Lubeck okay?"

"Define okay," Jason smirked. "The man just chased a patient out of the department doing a duck walk and quacking, for Christ's sake."

Rooster rolled his eyes then lost it in a fit of coughing laughter. "I have to admit that was one of the funniest damned things I've ever seen," he said trying to regain control.

"You're taking this awfully well, considering administration is going to throw a shit fit," Jason said, surprised at Rooster's response.

"Yeah, but it was funny," he chuckled. "I've wanted to do something like that to that old bat, Arnt, for years. Maybe not exactly that, but something like that." Rooster laughed again still trying to compose himself. "I'm not too worried about administration; I know where he lives," he finished with a knowing smile.

"Geez, Rooster, is there anybody in this city you don't hold a marker on?"

"No, and it's all part of the business, and no matter what Steve Lubeck says, it is a business."

"You don't hold a marker on me," Jason responded half joking. Rooster stopped and blew a cloud of smoke above his head. "Don't I?" He questioned. "You might think about that. But don't worry, I'm not going to ask you to kill anybody. Not yet anyway." His eyes fixed on Jason to the point of discomfort until he laughed again and took another drag from his cigarette. Jason followed suit, a little unnerved.

Rooster finally broke the awkward silence. "Have you seen Larry lately? He seems to be comfortable talking to you."

"Yeah, I talked to him a few days ago. He's actually anxious to get into court for the initial hearing. Somehow, he came up with a videotape of his wife using drugs. He says it just came in the mail. His attorney is even optimistic for a change."

"Good, I'm glad he's going to be able to use that tape. It didn't come cheap."

"You sent it?"

"Yeah, but that's between you and me. If Larry doesn't get some help with this, he's going to get screwed."

"I wouldn't have any idea how to go about getting something like that. How'd you do it?"

"Remember me? I hold a marker on everybody. And some of the people who owe me might surprise you." There was no humor in Rooster's voice.

Rooster flipped his cigarette away and turned to leave when Jason remembered his promise to Jesse.

"Ah, Rooster. I hate to ask you, but could I get you to write me a script for some sleeping pills?" he asked, somewhat reluctantly.

Rooster reached into his shirt pocket and withdrew a prescription pad. "No problem, but you've never struck me as the type who needed these things."

"They're partially for me and partially for Jesse. She claims I've been talking in my sleep lately. She's worn out, and a little pissed off. She taped me last night, but I think something's wrong with the tape. That couldn't be me."

Rooster smiled and wrote a prescription for Ambien®. "Incompatibility in bed. Doesn't sound good." He tore the script off the pad and handed it to Jason.

"Thanks, Rooster, I appreciate it."

"No problem, but remember, you owe me." He smirked and turned away.

Jason looked at the script in his hand and murmured to himself, "I guess I do," meaning for more than a prescription.

Larry Todd hated courtrooms. He disliked the way the entire system seemed to put everyone involved under scrutiny as if daring them to do or say something wrong. The family courtroom was only slightly less intimidating than the regular trial rooms in the austere county courthouse. Larry and his attorney, Princeton Marshal, sat at what would normally have been the defendant's table. Marshal could have been the poster child for all the middle- aged, distinguished attorneys in the country. Diana Todd and her attorney, Jennifer

76

Compton, sat opposite at what normally would have been the prosecution table. Ms. Compton was the antithesis of conservatism. She was young, attractive, and fiercely aggressive. The hem of her tailored suit stopped just short of the boundary of prudence, something that extended beyond her wardrobe. It seemed to Larry, the assignment of tables wasn't accidental, even though divorces were supposed to be no-fault in the State of Washington. He felt as if he were a criminal, despite the fact he hadn't done anything wrong. Somehow, the system seemed to have Larry Todd in its sights. The rest of the room was empty, except for a few attorneys who were killing time between their own cases.

Larry shifted uncomfortably in his chair and made small talk with his attorney while he tried to avoid looking toward Diana. It was hard. After several excruciating minutes, the court was called to order, and Commissioner Chris Dickum made his entrance. Larry wasn't sure whether the greasy little man had practiced his manner of arrogance and self-importance or whether it came to him naturally. The court commissioner marched into the courtroom in an entrance that would have made any supreme court justice burst with pride. Dickum climbed the single step to his bench, gathered his oversized, black robe around himself, and with one final flourish sat down. He peered out over the room through small wire half-frame glasses that rested on the end of his large weasel-like nose. Even though the court commissioner was staring at them, he avoided eye contact. The court came to order.

"We're here today to hear preliminary motions in the divorce case of Todd vs. Todd. Is council ready?" Commissioner Dickum asked without looking up.

Both attorneys replied in the affirmative.

"Mr. Marshal let's hear motions from your client first." An insincere smile briefly flashed across the commissioner's face.

"If it pleases the court, my client would like to set visitation with his children as every other weekend, alternating holidays and one month in the summer. This is a standard visitation schedule."

"Ms. Compton, do you have any objections?" Dickum asked.

"Yes. My client feels that the children, aged three and five, are too young for frequent or extended periods away from their mother, and we request to modify to one weekend a month with the father, no holidays, and one week in the summer." The female attorney finished with a smug smile directed at the court commissioner.

"It would seem that since this is a temporary visitation schedule, that sounds reasonable, with further adjustments to be made at the time of trial," Dickum said, shrugging.

Larry's lawyer stood. "This court is fully aware that initial visitation schedules frequently become permanent schedules at the time of the divorce. There is no reason my client should not be entitled to a standard visitation schedule."

Ms. Compton replied, "We had hoped to stay out of this area, but my client is concerned that the children might be exposed to Dr. Todd's female companions, with whom he had significant contact during the marriage."

Larry sprang to his feet and yelled, "That's a lie, and she knows it. The only cheating in our marriage was by her."

Dickum pounded his gavel. "Mr. Todd, this court will not allow such outbursts. Once more and I'll charge you with contempt. Is that understood?"

Larry sat down and nodded. His attorney whispered into his ear, "Let me do this."

"Judge, could I say something?" Diana Todd injected, smiling demurely.

"Go right ahead Mrs. Todd, but I'm a court commissioner, not a judge." He returned her smile and absentmindedly smoothed his pomaded comb-over.

"I understand that some of the topics in these proceedings might be difficult for my husband to hear, so in the interest of keeping peace and moving things along, I would like to strike any reference to his infidelity." Her smile was a mixture of masked pain and suffering, frosted with cutesiness.

Preston Marshal physically pushed Larry into his chair as he stood himself.
"Might I remind all parties that despite the fact that Ms. Todd has made totally unsubstantiated claims, which she is using to poison the court, this is a no-fault state and such subjects cannot even be brought up." His words camouflaged his anger.

"Believe it or not, Mr. Marshal, I am fully aware of the law, and what may or may not be considered." Dickum looked down briefly and cleared his throat as he prepared to make his proclamation. "Visitation will be set as one weekend a month, alternating holidays and two weeks in the summer. Does that make you happy, Mr. Marshal?"

Both faces glared back from Larry's table, but there was no other response.

"Ms. Compton . . ." The commissioner's demeanor changed as he turned to the other side of the room. "Do you have any motions for us today?" He asked smiling.

The attractive young female attorney stood again. "Yes, Your Honor. First, we would like to address a videotape that Dr. Todd has introduced into evidence. This tape is hearsay evidence; we cannot validate it and it bears no relevance to these proceedings."

"Mr. Marshal, I'm sure you have something to say in response."

"Yes. We have the private detective who took this video and who will testify as to its authenticity. We are also prepared to present an expert witness who will validate that the voice on the tape is indeed Mrs. Todd's."

Ms. Compton replied. "Mr. Marshal has already pointed out that this is a no-fault state, and such material cannot be entered into evidence," she responded smugly.

Preston Marshal replied, "this tape shows Mrs. Todd using illicit drugs. Its purpose is not for the divorce portion of the trial, but rather the child custody portion. This tape clearly establishes Mrs. Todd as an illegal drug abuser and an unfit mother."

"You set the stage counselor," Dickum said. "What's good for the goose is good for the gander."

"This is an entirely different issue, not related to no-fault. Might I remind the court that the welfare of the children is supposed to be paramount to all proceedings?"

Dickum slammed his hand on his desk. "Counselor, I am getting very tired of you telling me what my job is. The tape is excluded!"

"We have only one more thing this afternoon." Ms. Compton stood again. "That is to establish temporary spousal and child support during these proceedings. We are requesting two thousand dollars a month for each child, and four thousand dollars a month for Mrs. Todd, for a total of eight thousand dollars a month." Once again, the attorney smiled at the commissioner.

"Mr. Marshal?" Dickum asked, sarcasm oozing from his large pores.

"According to the state support guidelines for my client's income, support should be one thousand dollars a month per child. We maintain that Mrs. Todd was earning an income as a registered nurse before the marriage and is more than capable of doing the same now. She requires no spousal support."

The commissioner snorted. "Now counselor, you know all doctor's wives get spousal support."

"Might I point out that statement is prejudicial?" Marshal replied.

"Oh, I don't think so, Mr. Marshal," Dickum countered in a patronizing tone.

"So the statement that all blacks are guilty of rape would also not be prejudicial?"

Dickum sobered as he realized he had been caught. "I think that's an entirely different situation — "

"We don't." He spoke as he sat down, cutting off the commissioner's response.

Dickum glanced down at the papers in front of him briefly before he spoke. "Temporary support is set at eight thousand dollars a month. This hearing is over." He rapped his gavel and stood before anyone else could get up, and quickly scurried out of the courtroom.

Larry Todd remained in his seat, stunned. His attorney started to speak, but Larry interrupted."

"What the hell was that?" Larry stammered. "Is that this state's version of justice? To hell with the kids, screw the father and let the wife write her own ticket, rules be damned?"

Princeton Marshal leaned toward him. "Don't let them see this got to you. It'll all change in the actual divorce trial. Dickum has no say there, and we can readdress these things then."

"And in the meantime? I can't pay my bills or see my kids except for an occasional quick visit. That gold-digging, cheating, bitch walks away with my life."

Larry's voice rose eliciting a quick glance and whispers from the opposing table.

Larry's lawyer hustled him out of the courtroom ahead of the small group of people who had been observing the proceedings. At the end of the crowd, Diana Todd and her attorney followed at a leisurely pace, chatting and laughing. None of them noticed or paid any attention to a single visitor at the rear of the room, where Rooster sat quietly — waiting.

NINE

The bottle of sleeping pills in Jason's pocket drummed a cadence with each step, as he climbed the stairs to their town house. He was still too wired from his shift in the ER to take the elevator. He looked forward to seeing Jesse at the end of his day, but simultaneously dreaded dealing with the issue of the tape recording.

He unlocked the door and quietly entered the softly lit, silent rooms. The sliders to the deck were open, and a gentle breeze off the sound cooled the town house. He walked to the kitchen and found a vase for the bouquet of flowers he had brought for Jesse, added water, and placed the arrangement on the table.

Jason walked to the balcony and found it deserted except for the wind chimes Arthur had given them. He paused to listen to their chaotic oriental notes, accented by the sound of the waves below him before he moved on to the bedroom. He found Jesse there, asleep. He stood over her, watching, and gradually became aware that she looked somehow different. Her skin lacked its usual glow, and faint dark circles shaded her eyes. She looked tired, but he sensed more than he saw; something else was there. A vague heaviness spread across his chest, perhaps just his guilt from keeping her awake for the last few nights. He wanted to take her in his arms and comfort her, but knew that would awaken her, and right now he wanted what was best for Jesse.

He quietly slipped into the kitchen, filled a glass with ice, and added equal parts of gin and tonic — his summer drink of choice. He found a half empty bag of his favorite Tim's Potato Chips and returned to the balcony. He maneuvered himself onto a lounge chair, spilling part of his drink in the process, and reclined back against the cushion. He relaxed there, munching chips, and watched the sun drop into the Pacific Ocean. Jason had spent time on the East Coast, where the emptiness of the ocean at sunset had left him feeling unfilled, as if the sun were setting on the wrong side of the world. He preferred the West Coast evenings with the sun where it belonged.

Jason finished the chips and returned to the kitchen for another drink — his third — when he remembered Jesse's tape. He carried the recorder to the deck, retrieved the cassette from his pocket, and slid it into their machine, only to hear the same disembodied voice speaking the same foreign words. He reached to turn the recorder off when he felt a hand on the back of his neck. He jumped, spilling most of his drink, and spun around, only to find Jesse yawning behind him. She laughed as she leaned against him and kissed his cheek. He savored her touch and responded with a long kiss on her lips.

"Umm, potato chips and gin. My favorites," she teased.

They stood for several moments in each other's arms, reaffirming their love, just as couples had done since man moved out of the trees, and perhaps before.

Jesse spoke first, breaking the spell. "I see you've been listening to your tape."

She held his hand while she settled onto one of the lounge chairs and yawned again.

"Is this really what I've been doing at night? No jokes now. I feel bad enough as it is," he said taking his place next to her on the lounge chair, still holding her hand.

They listened together to the broken melodic words on the tape, in the voice neither of them knew as his. "That's you all right. I didn't notice in the middle of the night, but the voice really doesn't sound like you, does it?"

Jason reached over the table and clicked the recorder off. "At least you'll get some sleep tonight," he said as he produced the bottle of sleeping pills. "And just in case — " He pulled a small package of foam earplugs out of his pocket and opened the bag. "We'll just make sure you sleep like a baby," he said and gently pushed an earplug into each of her ears. "How's that?"

"What?" She feigned deafness.

"I said, I've got a date tonight but I'll see you tomorrow," he said, this time his voice louder.

"The only date you've got is right here." She pulled him to her and hugged him.

He settled in front of her on the lounger, back to front, and let his head rest against her breasts as he backed into her embrace.

"I'll even go for one of your favorite garlic specials from Boston Pizza if that'll keep you home," she offered while she massaged his neck.

"Mmm. How about if you just keep doing that all night." He arched his neck against her hand.

"Somebody has to order the pizza. I'll make you another drink and call for delivery."

She slid out of the lounger and let him drop the rest of the way onto the chair. As she stood and turned, he saw her wince in pain out of the corner of his eye. She hesitated briefly and glanced over her shoulder toward him as if to see if she had been caught. He rose out of his relaxed position, rolled onto his side, and held himself up on one elbow.

"What's that all about?"

"It's no big deal. Probably just sore muscles or getting ready for my period." She tried to brush him off, but he wasn't buying it. He knew she wasn't a complainer, and it took a lot to get a reaction from her. No matter how much she tried to deny it, he had seen real pain on her face when she got up.

"Is that the same pain you had several days ago? The day we went out to Dad's place?" He asked.

"I'm not sure." She started to walk away. "People get little pains. It's no big deal."

He bounded to his feet and held her by the shoulder. "Oh no, not so fast. Something's causing pain and has been for more than just a day or two. When was your last physical?"

"I had a physical and a PAP just before we left California," she answered still trying to move away from him, and the issue of her pain.

"Jesse, that was over two years ago," he said in disbelief. He had both of her shoulders now and held her facing him. "Who's been writing your prescription for birth control pills?"

"I just told the pharmacy that you had okayed it," she answered matter-of-factly. "Isn't that all right?"

"It's okay if you've had your annual PAP and physical."

"If I had that, I wouldn't need you to fill the prescription for me, now would I?" She tried to joke as she still tried to escape his grasp.

She looked up and finally faced both Jason and the issue of her pain. "I know I should have had my physical, but now I'm a little scared." She pushed into his chest and wrapped her arms around him, clinging to him for reassurance.

"It's all right," he said returning her hug. "We'll get an appointment and get it taken care of. I'm sure it's just an ovarian cyst or something like that. You're young and healthy. Besides, do you think I would ever let anything happen to you?" He squeezed her, trying to reassure himself as much as her. "Better?"

She smiled up at him. "I promise I'll get an appointment."

"Good. Then go order me some pizza." He kissed her cheek and released her.

When she came back to him, a few minutes later, he was back on the balcony, leaning against the rail, focused on the bright water below them. She handed him a fresh drink and asked, "So what did you think about your tape?" She edged against him, shoulder to shoulder.

"Well, if you're sure that's what you heard?"

"And I am!"

"I have no idea whatsoever. The voice is confusing enough, but the words almost sound like a language, with the inflection and all."

"Yeah, that's what I thought. Are you sure you've never heard it before?

"Positive. Foreign languages were never a strong point for me." He took a cigarette from his pocket and lit it.

"It might be fun to see if someone could identify it or translate it for you."

"I doubt there's anything to translate, but I'll think about it. Right now, I'm more concerned about you getting some sleep tonight." He picked up the bottle of sleeping pills, shook two out, and swallowed one with his drink. He held the other capsule out to her and offered his glass.

"I didn't think you were supposed to take these things with alcohol."

"One pill and a couple of drinks won't make a big difference," he answered.

She hesitated briefly, then took the other pill. "I'll try anything to get a good night's sleep."

The night air cooled, and pushed them indoors to eat their pizza and watch a movie. Before it was over, Jesse was nodding off, coerced into sleep by the sleeping pill. Jason undressed her and tucked her into bed, then returned to the main room. Despite the alcohol and the medication, his mind fought against sleep, as if there was something he needed to know or something he needed to do. A strange uneasiness stalked him. When he finally went to bed, the warmth of Jesse's body next to him and the lullaby of her paced breathing quickly eased him into sleep.

TEN

As the day faded and progressed into darkness, the creatures of the night began to emerge. Smart-ass gang bangers, desperate druggies, ill-tempered leather boys, Goths, psychos, hookers, drunks and familiar "players" were all regular late night visitors to the ER. These bizarre members of society were only part of what made night shifts difficult for Jason and other ER doctors. The repetitive flip-flopping between days and nights confused his circadian rhythm, and in time, could actually shorten his life span. At a minimum, it contributed to the chronic fatigue that plagued most ER physicians.

Ancillary services, such as ultrasound, were minimal or entirely absent at night. On the other hand, patients who sought out the services of the ER at three a.m. were often the sickest, and most in need of help. An occasional ER doctor preferred night shifts, but Jason wasn't one of them. He hated nights in the ER.

Rooster was working the second swing shift, five p.m. to one a.m., overlapping Jason's seven p.m. to seven a.m. shift. Rooster didn't work many clinical shifts, and Jason enjoyed the rare opportunity to work side by side with him. The first swing shift doctor, scheduled from eleven a.m. to eleven p.m., had already left for the night, and the ER volume started to dwindle as usual. Just after midnight Rooster gave Jason the cigarette lighter sign and they moved out to the rear deck for a quick smoke.

"Have you heard anything from Larry?" Rooster asked through a cloud of exhaled smoke.

"Nothing for a few days. Wasn't his custody hearing scheduled this week?"

Rooster scowled. "Yep. The almighty family court commissioner refused to take the videotape into evidence."

"How's Larry taking it?" Jason exhaled and shook his head in disgust.

"Worse than I had expected. The guy just doesn't understand the system. He keeps expecting justice from the American Judicial System," Rooster snorted.

"I'll see if I can reach him tomorrow and check on how he's doing."

"There's also a problem with Steve Lubeck," Rooster continued. "Administration is after him about his little duck attack in the ER the other day."

"I thought you said you could handle administration."

"Yeah, well it seems good old Mrs. Arnt has some shirttail connection with a member of the hospital board. The board member went to administration, and they want Lubeck's blood." Rooster's disgust came through in his voice. He inhaled deeply, shifted his weight, and rubbed the back of his neck. The pressure of having two of his doctors in crisis, and what it could mean for the ER, was taking its toll.

"You don't think he's going to lose his job over this, do you?" Jason asked.

"My experience has taught me that dealing with members of the hospital board of directors can be somewhat like dealing with a five-year-old with a gun. They know they can call the shots whether they have a good reason or not, and they like the power. Reasoning with them is completely nonproductive. If I can't stop this, it won't be the first doctor I've seen terminated at the insistence of a board member."

"So, if I understand, when it comes to the board, they don't care about patient care or who's in the right, only a chance to flex their political muscle."

"Not all board members, but there are more than a few who play that game," Rooster answered.

Jason flipped his cigarette butt over the railing and exhaled. "I'm beginning to think I should have gone into organized crime instead of medicine."

Rooster followed him back through the door. "Do you really think there's a difference?"

Rooster signed his patients off to Jason at one a.m. The ER was down to a reasonable pace, and the staff settled into night mode. Occasionally the ER doctor could get a few hours sleep, but more often, patients trickled in all night long. This was going to be one of the nights for trickle-ins. Jason saw a couple of patients with chest pain and admitted them to telemetry. Occasionally, talking to a patient's private attending physician in the middle of the night was a less than pleasant experience. Most of the doctors maintained their professionalism on the phone, but others felt compelled to take their fatigue and frustration out on the ER doctor who was calling them to admit their patient. Jason had learned a long time ago to ignore those doctors, and just get the patient taken care of and admitted. Still, it was another unpleasant part of night shifts in the ER.

The early morning hours brought out the usual night visitors: a leather boy with a broken hand from a *fall,* which Jason knew was a boxer's fracture from a fight; a drug addict in early withdrawals looking for narcotics for a *headache;* a psych patient in custody of the police, threatening suicide. Jason knew this was a common pattern for ERs everywhere. The scenarios encountered in most ERs on night shifts weren't a flattering commentary on American society.

Mr. Smith wandered through the doors of the hospital at four a.m. with a bloody rag over his arm. It was obvious he was a street person, one of the millions across the country who have no place to go at night, or any other time for that matter. Mr. Smith obviously appeared to be in this group.

Security found him wandering through the ground floor of the hospital holding his arm, and they reasonably brought him to the ER. At triage, he gave his name as Johnny Smith, but several of the medicine bottles he carried in his dirty army jacket pocket bore different names. The bottles were all psych medicines, written by several different doctors, from more than a few different community outpatient psychiatric clinics. Some of the prescriptions were duplicates, and some of the bottles contained a different medication from the label. Many of the bottles were old, and still filled with pills, verifying that the patient didn't take his medications. This was a typical problem among psych patients.

Mr. Smith, or whatever his real name was, spoke deliberately and softly, as if he had learned to carefully monitor each word. It was hard to tell how old he was, since living on the streets tended to prematurely age a person. A snagged toboggan covered his head, which looked too large for his gaunt frame, but it was hard to say whether it was the head or the body that was disproportionate. Several day's growth of beard shadowed his grimy face. His appearance was a result of existing without the benefits of running water, shower, or laundry. His sallow skin was covered with several layers of grime, and a worn, oversized army jacket draped over faded, baggy trousers. The pants were stacked over throwaway tennis shoes, sans socks. Jason watched him as the nursing staff placed him in an examination room, and tried to determine exactly where Mr. Smith ended, and his encrusted clothes began.

Jason's charge nurse tonight was Summer Knight. She was a thirty-year-old second-generation nouveau hippy, born and raised in Seattle. Summer wasn't unattractive, but she didn't wear makeup to help soften her rather prominent features. She traversed the ER in a long, swinging gait, more typical of a backpacker than a nurse. Each of her steps was accented by the flop of her Birkenstocks. The row of pierced earrings that lined each ear matched the one in the side of her nose. When she smiled, the stud in her tongue flashed. Jason had heard stories of other piercings, but he really didn't want to know. He knew she had tattoos, besides the intricately braided leaves around her right ankle. Several months earlier, she had asked him to check her new "tat" because she thought it might be infected. He was surprised when she dropped her scrub suit bottoms and flashed a fresh Betty Boop on her right butt cheek. Modesty wasn't one of Summer's strong points. He thought he had recovered nicely, despite the heat that flashed across his face. Pierced body parts and tattoos aside, Summer was a solid nurse, and Jason liked working with her.

Jason picked up Mr. Smith's chart and started toward the exam room, when the sensation emerged. It was like a familiar flavor that passed over his tongue and was gone before he could identify it. It wasn't the same feeling of impending doom he had experienced before his shock, but rather a diluted essence of the *feeling*. He stopped and waited, afraid it might be a harbinger of worse to come, but there was nothing more.

He examined Mr. Smith and found a fresh four-inch-long laceration on his right forearm. The linear edges still oozed bright blood; a typical knife wound.

"How'd this happen, Mr. Smith?" Jason asked while he cleaned the area with antiseptic.

"Somebody cut me, Doc. They cut me bad."

The answer was measured, in a voice that modulated abnormally, an indication that the patient was off his medication.

"Uh-huh. Who cut you, Mr. Smith?' Jason asked casually while he prepared to suture the wound.

"There was a whole bunch of them, Doc. I think they were Russians. Yeah, they were Russians all right."

"Yeah, the Russians can be very bad this time of year." Jason injected the wound with Lidocaine, a local anesthetic, and peeled open a suture packet.

"I know, Doc. I don't like Russians. They cut people with their knives for no reason at all."

"Well, I wouldn't worry too much. I understand they're only allowed to cut somebody once. After that they have to pay a tax, so they only do it once." Jason spoke while he quickly closed the laceration with several interrupted sutures of 4-0 nylon. He glanced up and saw Summer, who looked as intrigued as Mr. Smith, by his explanation of the Russian cutting tax.

"There you go, Mr. Smith. Now I want you to keep this clean and dry, and we'll take the stitches out for you in ten days, right here, okay?" Jason realized his instructions were absurd before he finished the sentence. He peeled off his gloves and rinsed his hands in the sink. "The nurse is going to get you cleaned up, Mr. Smith, and put a dressing on your cut. Would you like a sandwich before you go?"

"Yeah, that'd be great. The Russians took all my money too."

Jason pulled his wallet from the back pocket of his scrubs, removed a twenty-dollar bill and pushed it into Mr. Smith's hand. "You take care and stay away from those Russians," Jason said on his way out the door. He only heard part of Mr. Smith's response.

"I'll do just that, Doc, and you take care too." He waved the bill clutched in his hand.

Jason chuckled and sat down at his desk to finish the chart. A few minutes later, Summer rolled Mr. Smith, who cautiously guarded a wrapped turkey sandwich in his lap, past the desk in a wheelchair on his way to be discharged. Jason looked up and saw his patient already removing the fresh bandage from his arm.

"No, Mr. Smith!" Jason jumped up and made a grab for the bandaged arm just as the dressing dropped into Mr. Smith's lap, with several intact, neatly tied sutures stuck in the bandage. Jason lifted the arm to check the wound.

"It's okay, Doc. It's all better now," Mr. Smith reassured him.

Jason inspected the arm and found nothing but freshly washed skin.

"See, I told you, Doc. It's all better now." A large smile spread across Mr. Smith's face.

Summer leaned farther over the patient and saw the same thing Jason had found; no laceration. "Cool," she remarked and rolled the patient away to be discharged.

Jason couldn't move from the spot. He held the bandage in his hand and examined the sutures, still neatly tied and stuck in the gauze, as if they had been expelled from the wound.

There was a break in the patient flow and the ER remained empty, but Jason didn't sleep. His mind churned in a confused tempest that made him question his sanity. For the second time in his life, the usually crisp line between what was and what wasn't, began to slowly unwind, like a tattered truth.

Sheri Black crossed her long legs and slowly bounced her right foot, her shoe half off. Meetings like this were a regular occurrence with Carl Rich, her editor at the Seattle Tribune, but tonight her svelte frame seemed ready to spring from the chair. Carl liked to meet with all of his feature writers on a regular basis to "mind meld." That was his term for directing them toward stories he thought would sell newspapers. He didn't mind a writer coming up with their own story ideas, as long as he had a chance to contribute to the project, and maintain some control over the story's direction.

Sheri secretly welcomed his input today. She was experiencing a bit of a creative dry spell, partially because of a growing and well-earned reputation for taking stories in directions her sources had not intended. In other words, she dug up dirt.

She followed Carl with her large dark eyes as he walked around the office offering ideas. She chewed the end of her pen and periodically made a quick scribble on a notepad in her lap, more as a courtesy to Carl than any actual interest in a particular concept. She brushed her long dark hair off her right shoulder, jotted "fresh" on her pad, and surrounded the word with squiggles. They merged into the pattern already there, which framed the words "novel" and "distinctive." The words "sex sells" stood out in bold letters near the top edge of the pad.

Something Carl said caught her attention. "Maybe it's time for something along a medical line, something about doctors or nurses — blood and guts stuff. Reality shows are big right now. How about something like, 'A Day In the Life of a Surgeon'? No. Or . . . 'A Real Doctor's Life'? God, no."

"How about something from an ER?" Sheri offered.

"ER is good, but we need some singular line or approach." He paced around the room and polished his forehead.

"Maybe I can find something if I can get on the inside of an ER and nose around. Dozens of TV soap operas can't all be wrong," she offered.

Carl stopped and sat down at his desk chair. "That's not a bad idea. I think I can get you in on the pretext of some free PR for a hospital via a human interest story. Administrators love that stuff. How about University Hospital?"

It was Sheri's turn to pace. She walked to the full-length window overlooking the lights of the Seattle skyline. Despite his age, Carl couldn't resist a glance at her silhouette through her sheer dress. A pair of high heel mules accented her shapely legs, and her slender waist emphasized her full breasts. No matter what people said about Sheri, they couldn't deny she was an exceptionally beautiful woman. She wore her sexuality the way a leopard wore its claws: always barely hidden just below the surface, but ready to be used as a weapon without warning.

"No, not University." She rocked back on one heel and looked out over the city. "We don't want to be accused of doing an unseemly story about them. Besides, they tend to be a little too wholesome for my purposes. Let's go a little more uptown. How about Harborline?" She turned away from the window, her eyes fierce with anticipation. Like a great cat, she began the hunt. Carl almost felt sorry for her prey.

ELEVEN

A horn blared over Jason's left shoulder, and he shook himself awake as he swerved the roadster back into his lane. His body responded to the quick shot of adrenaline the near miss had injected into his bloodstream. The trip home after night shift was a blur of traffic that barely registered in his mind. His fatigue, as well as the phenomenon of the disappearing laceration, left him confused, and his brain struggled desperately to function at its normal capacity. The adrenaline fix, generated by the blast of the horn, helped him focus, but only briefly. Jason had learned from years of night shifts that it was difficult to make decisions or handle problems until he got some sleep. Every minor setback seemed an insurmountable obstacle to his sleep-deprived brain.

Jason walked into an empty apartment and dropped his bag behind the door. Jesse had already left for work, and he was only too happy to have the apartment to himself in his condition. He knew he could be more than a little irritable when he was this exhausted, and he didn't want to worry about picking his words today.

He wandered through the apartment and tried to focus his thoughts. He was worn out, but sleep was still several hours away, held at bay by the level of stress from his night shift in the ER. He made his way to the kitchen, found some bagels and cream cheese, and stuffed the bagel into the toaster. He filled a glass with gin and tonic — light on the tonic — before he realized he had forgotten the ice. He swore under his breath, chugged part of the warm drink, and threw several ice cubes into the glass. The toaster popped, signaling his breakfast was ready. The food did little for him. The liquor settled his nerves and allowed him some peace, but he was still too hyped to sleep. He checked the bathroom medicine cabinet and found the bottle of sleeping pills. He paused for a moment, then thought, *What the hell*, and downed a pill with his drink.

He mixed another gin and tonic then dropped into the worn spot on his favorite chair. He turned on Fox News, but he was too restless to listen to the seemingly endless litany of war and disaster around the world. He flipped through his stack of CDs, found a Bruce Springsteen disc, and slid it into his player. *Yeah, a little bit of The Boss suits me just fine this morning,* he thought

Jason carried his glass to the balcony and tried to clear his head, but the gin and sleeping pill had started to do their job. His mind finally shifted into low gear, assisted by the music and the sound of the ocean. After his third drink, he gave in to the sleep he needed so badly. An intense flu-like ache from sleep deprivation wracked his muscles. He curled into a blanket-wrapped ball in bed and drifted toward sleep. The music pulsed through his body while his nearly unconscious mind filled in the words *the Russians are coming, the Russians are coming.* The rest of the day was lost in sleep.

Sheri Black followed the signs to the Emergency Department. The hospital administrator had welcomed the opportunity for some free publicity, just as Carl had predicted. She waited at the registration desk while a nurse hurried a bloodied man away in a wheelchair, then stepped to the window.

"I have an appointment with Dr. Christianson," she informed the registration clerk and handed her one of her cards.

The clerk made a call and a nurse appeared a few minutes later to escort Sheri to Rooster's office. Sheri glanced into several open rooms and absorbed as much as she could as they made their way through the department.

"You guys seem to be pretty busy here." She made small talk with the nurse.

The nurse smiled and answered, "We have our moments, but it's pretty reasonable right now."

"You mean this is quiet?" She asked, taking in the rush of activity around her. A scream from one of the rooms partially covered her words.

The nurse winced. "We never say that word in the ER, it's a major jinx."

"What word?"

"That Q word you just said."

"You mean quiet?" Sheri asked confused.

The nurse pursed her lips. "Yeah, that word. Trust me on this. When you're in an ER never say that word, okay?"

"You're serious aren't you?" Sheri asked.

"Serious as a heart attack, honey. Here's Rooster's office. Good luck." She emphasized the part about luck and turned to leave.

"You think I'll need luck?"

The nurse paused and turned back to face Sheri. "You've never met Rooster, have you?"

"No, but I meet a lot of people in my line of work. I'm a newspaper reporter."

"Yeah, um, that's even worse. And yes, you'll need luck." The nurse left and double-timed it toward the source of the screams still resonating across the department.

Sheri paused for a moment, fluffed her hair, and made sure the top of her blouse was unbuttoned before she knocked. There was no answer. She knocked again, and after a brief delay, a voice yelled from the other side. "It's open!"

Rooster was sitting behind his desk, the phone to his ear. He motioned Sheri to a chair but continued his conversation.

"So you're telling me that's it; he goes. No way out." His words seethed with anger. "So, now you're doing the hiring and firing in this ER. Just so I've got it straight." He paused. "That's bullshit, and you know it. It can't be both ways. Either I run this ER or the board runs it." Rooster shifted forward in his chair and slapped his desk with his right hand.

Sheri sat quietly, wishing she could hear both ends of the conversation, and casually studied the man in front of her. He was a scrapper. She doubted he took crap from anyone, and obviously didn't like what he was being handed right now.

"I'll tell him all right. And when I do I'll suggest that he sue your ass off and name you personally, and the board, member by member." Rooster shifted back in his chair and folded one arm across his chest.

"Bob, do you remember what happened the last time you threatened me? Yeah, well you should keep it in mind. I don't take threats very well." He paused.

"Fuck you, too, Bob." He slammed the receiver down, eliciting a single chime from the phone.

"Jesus H. Christ!" Rooster pounded his desk again with his fist.

"If this is a bad time, I could come back later," Sheri offered with no intention whatsoever of leaving.

Rooster's blazing eyes peered up at her through his eyebrows. "This is probably as good as it's going to get for a while," he snorted.

She intentionally leaned down over his desk and handed him her card. "I'm Sheri Black, Dr. Christensen. I appreciate you taking the time to see me." She sat back down and crossed her legs, making sure her skirt rode up on her thigh.

"Miss Black, I apologize. I didn't intend for you to hear that." His voice calmed somewhat, but she could still feel bubbling lava just beneath the surface of his words.

"Please, call me Sheri." She beamed her most charming smile.

"And you can call me Rooster. Everyone else does."

"Rooster," she acknowledged him. "Don't worry about it. A newspaper isn't exactly a Sunday school either. I'm used to it."

He stood up, poured a cup of coffee into a Styrofoam cup, and offered it to her.

"Cream?"

"Black is fine, thank you." She took the cup, making sure she touched his hand in the exchange.

He poured a second cup for himself. "Let's go to my office."

She stood and followed him. "I thought this was your office."

"It's one of my offices." He walked the few steps outside onto the deck. "This is the other one," he said as he pulled a cigarette out of his pocket, cupped his lighter against the breeze, and lit up.

"A doctor who smokes?" She questioned.

"That's right, and you can get rid of a lot of your other stereotyped ideas while you're in the ER." He exhaled but didn't smile.

She was beginning to understand why the nurse, who had shown her in, had wished her luck. "I didn't mean to offend you. I'm just a little surprised." She tried her wayward little girl smile.

"Uh-huh," he acknowledged her response. "Suppose we cut to the chase, Sheri. Why are you in my ER? And, you can leave out the crap your editor gave hospital administration about the free PR. Your reputation has preceded you." He leaned back against the rail and exhaled a rolling cloud of smoke.

"Okay, bottom line. I'm looking for something a little more powerful than the typical day-In-the-life article. I'm hoping to find something here that won't put my readers to sleep. The ER seems like a promising place to start."

Rooster watched her through a cloud of vanishing smoke. He didn't like newspaper reporters and liked female reporters even less. He had been misquoted more times than he cared to remember. Now, he only talked to reporters under the duress of an order from administration. Somehow, administrators were less concerned with the potential damage from a negative article than the allure of the benefit from a little free press.

"Just so we understand each other, Sheri, if I had it my way, you and your paper wouldn't get past the front door. But, since administration wants to play your game, I have to go along . . . to a point."

She smiled, as much to herself as in response to his words. She liked having the upper hand, especially with someone as potent as Rooster.

"And what rules am I supposed to follow to stay on your good side?"

"It's not a matter of being on my good side. You're here to write your little article about my ER. Cross the line, make it anything more than that, and it will cost you."

Sheri had no doubt Rooster meant what he said, but she wasn't someone who was easily intimidated. "So, where do we go from here?"

Rooster lit another cigarette and took a swig of coffee. "Simple. I set you up with one of my doctors, Jason Corey. He's bright, and you can make an interesting, straightforward story around him and the ER. He's also smart enough not to give you anything else."

She started to answer when the door opened and Jason emerged in the act of shaking a cigarette out of his pack. He looked up and immediately focused on Sheri.

"Oh, sorry Rooster, I didn't mean to interrupt," he said as he turned back toward the ER.

Rooster stopped him. "No problem J.C. Let me introduce you to Sheri Black. Sheri, this is J.C., one of our ER doctors."

She reached for Jason's hand and even though she wasn't the blushing type, felt her face redden. She suddenly felt self- conscious, and couldn't believe she was reacting to him like a schoolgirl, but it was beyond her control. The warmth of her blush spread deep inside her, and she felt herself drawn to him. His eyes left her feeling vulnerable and exposed. It was a sensation she wasn't used to, but surprisingly liked.

"Nice to meet you. Sheri, was it?" He carefully shook her hand.

"Yes, very nice to meet you, Doctor." She held on to his hand, captured by his eyes and his touch. *Why couldn't he be the doctor she was interviewing*, she thought. Even if she couldn't find a sensational story, at least she would have a fantastic time trying.

Rooster hadn't missed her response. "We'll be done in a minute J.C.," he said.

Sheri followed Jason with her eyes until the door closed behind him, then reluctantly turned back to Rooster.

"So, when do I meet this Dr. Corey? I'd like to get started on the article as soon as possible." She glanced back toward the door, still distracted.

Rooster considered her reaction to Jason before he answered. "You just did. I'll give him your number, and he'll be in touch."

Sheri tried to conceal the thrill that came with Rooster's announcement. This was going to be an extremely interesting assignment after all. She was used to getting what she wanted, both professionally and personally. Not many men could resist her once she made up her mind she wanted them, and she definitely wanted Dr. Corey. She handed Rooster one of her personal cards with her home phone and cell numbers. "I'm looking forward to hearing from him." She started to turn towards the door.

"Oh, one more thing, Sheri. That business with the skirt and the touchy-feely thing with your hand doesn't really work." He gave her a roguish smile.

She stopped, tilted her head slightly to the side, and for a moment presented him with a slight pout. The look might have convinced someone else she was actually hurt. It disappeared quickly, and she laughed. "Oh, Rooster, you'd be so much fun."

Her laugh followed her through the door. Rooster liked her. She was intelligent, witty, and undeniably beautiful. Under different circumstances, she might be worth a try, but he had learned long ago that some women were just too risky, and Sheri Black was far beyond risky. She was dangerous.

TWELVE

Rooster needed help. He was fighting for Steve Lubeck's professional life and even though he didn't like being the one to ask for favors, right now, he didn't have a choice.

Barb Henry's door opened slowly under the pressure of Rooster's knock. The assistant administrator sat at her desk, glasses perched on her nose, focused on the stack of papers in front of her. She looked up as Rooster casually strolled into her office.

"Am I interrupting?" He asked.

The striking, middle-aged women carefully arranged the papers on her desk into a neat stack.

"Hello, Rooster, I've been expecting you," she said matter-of-factly.

"A guy's gotta have some port in a storm." He smiled warmly and eased himself onto the couch against the wall.

"Why is it that the only time you turn the charm on with me is when you want something?" She strolled across the room and took a seat in an overstuffed chair facing him. "Let me guess, you want to talk about Steve Lubeck."

"We can't let this happen, Barb. Lubeck is too high quality a doctor to be washed out by some dickhead board member with a hard-on." He shifted forward to the edge of the couch.

She watched his eyes as he spoke and noticed the familiar worry line between his eyebrows was deeper than usual.

"Sorry, Rooster, but there's not a thing I can do. And the board member you're talking about is Armen Polling, the chairman of the board and a huge contributor to this hospital." Her voice became slightly cautionary.

"That little prick? So, how much did he pay for Lubeck's head? Fifty thousand, a hundred thousand, a new wing? What's the going price for a doctor's career these days?"

"Rooster, you need to remember who your friends are here."

He sighed, slumped back in his seat, and rubbed his forehead.

"I know. I don't mean to take it out on you. Shit, I get more like Lubeck every day."

She leaned forward and spoke sympathetically. "No, Rooster, you're not like Lubeck, but your temper is not your friend. One of these days you're going to self-destruct, and then who'll run this ER?"

He made a face and tightened his lips. "Don't worry about that. I've already got my replacement picked out."

She looked surprised, but he continued before she could ask the obvious question. "Jason Corey. I've been grooming him, and he could probably do the job right now."

"He's an excellent doctor, and he's got a lot of potential, but I doubt he's got the grit it takes to hold this contract together — at least not yet." She was all business.

"He's got it all right, he just wears it a little more subtly than I do."

Rooster rose to his feet in front of her and waited. When she finally arose, they stood face-to-face, like partners on a dance floor. "I guess I'll tell Lubeck today," he conceded.

"Rooster, you know this has been coming for a long time. You can replace him without any trouble. What's the big deal?"

"The big deal is we owe him; we all owe him. He invested his life in medicine, and he's what he was supposed to be, a competent doctor. But somewhere along the way medicine turned into a popularity contest, and now he's out. It's not fair, Barb, especially over something like this, and you know it." Rooster's anger had burned out, but his frustration was still very much alive.

"Yeah, it's not fair, but guess what? That word does not appear in his contract, and he had many years to make the transition, just like everybody else. He chose his path and now he pays the price for that choice." She walked back to her desk and picked up her glasses. "Rooster, some fights aren't worth the cost and this is one of them."

Rooster avoided the ER and wandered through the hospital. The halls were crowded with people performing a myriad of jobs, most of them non-clinical: secretaries and billing clerks, maintenance and management, PR people and others he had no idea about. It was obvious Lubeck was right. Medicine had become a business, and that far overshadowed anything else now. Rooster remembered his years as a resident when he had spent more time in the hospital after hours. The only people left at night then were the clinical staff — doctors, nurses, and technicians, all doing patient care. Maybe that's what medicine needed to get back to: patient care. But he knew it would never happen, not with this much money at stake.

Rooster finally ran out of excuses and wandered back to the ER. It was near the end of Lubeck's shift, the best time to give a doctor the bad news. He wouldn't have to continue to see patients, and could slip away to nurse he ego.

Rooster walked to the desk where Steve was finishing a chart.

"How's it going?" Rooster asked.

Steve looked up, his face twisted in exasperation. "Just finishing my last chart. A two-year-old with a critical mosquito bite for a week," he replied sarcastically. "The parents just wanted it checked. Said they would have come in sooner, but they had to wait for their welfare card."

Rooster didn't respond. He started to turn away, then stopped. He knew he couldn't put this off.

"You got a minute before you go?" He asked Lubeck.

"Sure, Rooster."

Rooster had fired doctors before, but never one he had known as long, or respected as much as Steve Lubeck. And certainly never for what he considered a half-assed reason like this.

Rooster motioned Steve to the chair in his office, then moved behind his desk. He sat slowly rocking in his chair and tried to prepare himself, but nothing helped. Finally, Lubeck broke the silence.

"What's up, Rooster?"

"We've got a problem, Steve," he answered. "You know Armen Polling, the chairman of the board of directors of the hospital," he stated more than asked. "It seems our friend, Mrs. Arnt, has some connection to him."

"Oh Geez," Steve said, disgusted. "I see where this is going."

"No Steve, I don't think you do. Polling went to the hospital administrator and wants you gone. Unfortunately, administration is pushing it." Rooster exhaled and dropped his shoulders. It was out, and nothing he could say or do would undo it.

Rooster had expected an explosion from Lubeck, but instead Steve sat quietly and nodded his head as he digested the news. "So, I guess that's it then."

"Look, Steve, I know this seems bad, but you've got ninety days left on your contract. A lot of things can change in ninety days. I'll work on administration, and I know you have strong support from the medical staff. Worst case scenario, I know every ER director in the Pacific Northwest, and I 'm sure I can get you a good position."

"I don't think so, Rooster," Steve replied calmly. "I think I'm done with medicine." His face showed as little emotion as his voice.

"Are you in a financial position to retire? If you are, that's great. I wouldn't blame you for getting out, but remember, this isn't over yet."

"No, Rooster, I don't want you to pursue it. I don't want to be here because someone got administration to *let* me stay. I'm tired of fighting a system that doesn't care anymore. It's like being the only sane person in the asylum. After a while, you start to question who's really crazy." The irony brought a smirk to Steve's face.

"You've got a couple of days off," Rooster said. "Do me a favor and think about it, okay? You don't have to make any decisions right now." He stood and walked around his desk.

Lubeck got up, turned toward the door, and stopped.

"I just want you to know I appreciate everything you've done for me, Rooster. You've been a good friend."

Lubeck picked up his bag at the doctors' desk then walked through the ER without speaking. He started to leave through the ambulance doors, but stopped to remember the thousands of patients he had treated and the hundreds of lives he had saved here. He also saw the ghosts of those he hadn't been able to salvage. He slowly placed his bag on the floor beside him then clapped his hands. The applause was uncomfortably slow at first then built to a raucous, noisy ovation. The ER staff stopped what they were doing and watched him, uncertain what to do. Then, one by one, they began to applaud until the ER was filled with the sound of their mutual respect. The commotion brought Rooster from his office. A smile, laden with emotion, spread across his face as he watched the scene in front of him. Suddenly, Steve stopped in mid clap with his hands apart, picked up his bag and walked out. The applause behind him slowly died away.

Rooster spotted Jason across the ER and motioned with a head nod toward the rear deck. Jason acknowledged him, grabbed his cigarettes, and followed.

"What the hell was that all about?" Jason asked Rooster as he lit his own cigarette.

"I'm not exactly sure, but I just gave him the bad news."

"How'd he take it?"

"Actually, a lot better than I thought he would accept it. Says he's quitting medicine."

They both stood with one foot on the guardrail, each with their own thoughts, until Jason finally interrupted the stillness.

"You think he's going to be all right?"

"Yeah, he's got a couple of days off. I told him that we'd work on it, but he wasn't too interested. We'll see how things go over the next ninety days."

Jason changed the subject. "I got in touch with Larry. He sounded pretty rattled, but I think he'll be okay, too. He's due back on shift tomorrow. I'm off, so you may want to check with him," he suggested.

"Thanks. All we need now is for Larry to spring a leak in his dingy and we'd really be in a hard spot."

Jason wavered and then asked, "Do you think you could write me a script for some more sleeping pills, Rooster? They've really helped."

Rooster's eyebrows dipped slightly as he pulled his script pad out of his pocket and wrote the prescription.

"You know you can legally write these for Jesse yourself. You're not married yet."

He tore the sheet off the pad and handed it to Jason. "That is, unless you're taking them, too." He quick-checked Jason's face, looking for a reaction.

"Yeah, I know. I just want to keep things straight up." His voice rose slightly, and Rooster knew he was lying.

"Not a bad idea. The last thing you want is the feds knocking on your door and pulling your license for diversion of a controlled substance," Rooster inserted the veiled warning.

Jason folded the script and slid it into his pocket. "I wanted to ask you about something else. Have you ever heard of a patient doing a trick with a laceration?"

"I've heard of lots of patient tricks, but never one with a laceration. What kind of trick?" Rooster turned toward him and leaned against the railing.

"Well, like one minute it's there and the next minute it's not." He sounded embarrassed to ask the question.

Rooster laughed. "No, I can honestly say I haven't heard of that one." A question mark crossed his face. "Why, you seeing disappearing lacerations?"

"No, just something I read about. Maybe I misread it or something. No biggie." He flipped his cigarette away and headed inside.

Rooster watched him leave and shook his head. Steve Lubeck's words about the only sane person in the asylum came back to him.

The drive home was different tonight. Steve had made the same commute thousands of times, but never like this, knowing it was one-way. He noticed things he had taken for granted for years: the subtle movement of the trees and the sweet scent of the summer air. His car found its way home as if on autopilot, without thought or direction from him. It was a short trip.

Steve's house wasn't elaborate. He didn't own one of the majestic, sprawling homes that overlooked the sound, like so many other doctors. Still, the house was neat, comfortable and quiet. Yes, dreadfully quiet. Tonight the stillness struck him and underscored the bitter emptiness that filled his life. He had done all right financially, but he wasn't rich. A divorce and child support and restarting his life had all taken their toll. Retirement was an intangible concept for Steve. He had always assumed he would just go on forever in the ER, or maybe just collapse, clutching his chest one day in the middle of a shift. That was the scope of his plans for the future.

His house was empty, as it had been for years. There was no wife, no children, not even a dog to welcome him home. Better times drifted through his memory — times when his return home had been met with hugs from little arms and a kiss from someone he loved. He dumped his bag on the couch and turned on a single table lamp. It was the only warmth in the room.

In the kitchen, Steve poured three fingers of scotch, neat, then added an extra splash for good measure. He walked through the silent rooms, as if he were searching for something. Maybe it was what he had been pursuing his entire life. Maybe he thought he'd find it tonight.

He moved to his den, sat down at his desk, and opened the top drawer. He searched through the back of the drawer, pushing dead pens and crumpled pieces of paper aside until he finally found a small glass drug vial and a syringe. He inspected the vial and smiled with satisfaction, then carefully placed it beside the syringe in the center of the desktop.

He returned to the kitchen and refilled his glass. He didn't drink from thirst, but rather because the pale amber liquid dulled his pain and enforced his courage. He flipped through a few unopened envelopes on the kitchen table — junk mail, bills, and a letter from the IRS. "Figures," he mumbled. He stood and returned to his den.

The den was the only room in the house with any character. The wall on his right displayed several carefully hung, framed documents: his medical diploma, certificates of recognition, and a letter of thanks from a previous patient. He called it his hall of accomplishments. The wall on his left was filled with a smoke-blackened fireplace and a faux river rock chimney. Several books lined the shelves on either side of the fireplace — medical texts and a few novels he had meant to read, but somehow never did. The wall in front of him displayed the only photos in the house, the summation of his life's memories — the pleasurable ones at least. The unhappy memories would have required a significantly larger area. The animated faces of his children smiled at him, caught in time when they were growing and maturing; his share of their lives displayed on a single wall.

They were all adults now. They had gone their own ways with their own chances for success and happiness. He paused in front of each image and gently touched every face. The memories were crisp as if the scenes in front of him had happened yesterday — as if the children were still young, and would come running through the door any second yelling his name. He had never had a chance to be a significant part of their lives. Medicine and divorce weren't exactly daddy friendly, but he knew that was only part of the problem. He accepted that he was just never first-class father material. He shrugged and returned to his desk.

Steve slid out of his jacket and rolled up his left shirtsleeve. He unbuckled his belt and slid it out of his pants. He had never used a belt as a tourniquet before, but it looked straightforward enough on TV, even though it wasn't. The syringe felt natural in his hand as he withdrew the clear liquid from the vial and snapped the air bubbles to clear them, then chuckled at the unnecessary precaution. "Let's hope old doctors aren't like old habits," he said to the vacant room. He carefully placed the empty vial of potassium chloride in the center of the desk where it couldn't be missed.

He drank the remaining scotch in one swig, savoring the taste, and placed the glass next to the empty vial. He picked up his desk phone and dialed 911. When a stranger's voice asked him the nature of his emergency, he quietly laid the receiver aside without answering.

He hit the vein on the front of his elbow on the first try and withdrew a small billowing cloud of his own blood into the syringe, assuring him the drug would go straight to his heart. He took a last look around the room. Except for a brief burning in his arm, his death, unlike his life, was painless.

Jason and Jesse returned from dinner just after ten-thirty. He was off tomorrow, and they had plans for the day as well as tonight. Jesse came through the door to the sound of a ringing phone, made a dash, and answered without checking the caller ID. Her heart sank when she heard Rooster's voice. A call from Rooster at night usually meant he needed someone to cover a shift.

"Yeah, he's here, Rooster. Hang on."

Jesse passed the phone to Jason, but she was already objecting. "Tell him no, please."

Jason frowned and answered. "What's up, Rooster?"

Jesse continued mouthing "no" while she listened.

"Day shift tomorrow? Well, Jesse and I actually had plans." Jesse pumped her arm and mouthed "yes." "But, if it's an emergency? What's going on?" Jesse's face dropped, and she turned on her heel and marched toward the bedroom. Jason listened for several moments before he answered. "Yeah, I understand. I'll be there at seven. You can fill me in then." Jason hung up and went after Jesse, but she was already in the bathroom with the door closed. When she came out, she was ready for a fight.

"Why do you always have to be the one to go in and cover shifts?" She half shouted. "Why can't Larry or Steve, or Rooster cover a shift?"

Jason was caught in the middle, and he resented it.

"Rooster is working the night shift tonight to help Larry out. His divorce isn't going well, and he's not holding up."

"So what about Steve?" Jesse shot back. She stormed past him half-undressed and pulled her pajamas out of a drawer. Pajamas meant she was particularly upset.

"That's why he was calling." He paused. Rooster's words were still settling into his mind. "Steve committed suicide. The police found his body this evening. It looks as if he injected potassium chloride."

Jesse stopped with her pajama top half-buttoned, as the anger left her like air escaping a balloon. "Oh no." She wrapped her arms around him and squeezed. "I'm sorry Jason."

"Don't worry about it. Besides, it's Steve we should feel sorry for."

He hugged her and gently rubbed her back with his hand, soothing himself as much as her. "Why don't you go on to bed? I'd just like to be alone for a few minutes. I'm going to have a quick drink, and then I'll be in."

She kissed him, slid out of her pajamas, and crawled between the sheets on their bed. Jason flipped the lights off as he left the bedroom, then walked to the kitchen, his mind hastily vaulting from one surrealistic image to another. He poured a gin and tonic and walked to the deck. White-capped waves clapped below him on the pebbled beach, pushed by a warm summer's night breeze off the Sound. He lit a cigarette, leaned against the railing, and tried to grasp the reality of Lubeck's suicide. His mind gradually painted a picture of Steve sitting alone, while he injected himself with the instantly lethal drug, seizing, and collapsing in death — still alone. A boat cutting through the night broke Jason's concentration, its single point of light skimming across the shadowy water like a fleeing soul.

His last image of Steve, standing at the ER exit, applauding and being applauded by the staff, crept into Jason's awareness, and he wondered if Steve had already planned his death. Injectable potassium chloride was hardly a drug someone normally kept around the house. He must have had the idea, at least in mind, for some time. He wondered how hospital administration would react to the news. They would probably pay lip service to the loss of an excellent and valued physician whose career they had ended only a few hours earlier; a victim of modern medicine.

He finished his drink and had one more cigarette. The concept of his own mortality danced through the fringes of his conscious mind, then disappeared, pushed back to a dark, hidden place. He took two sleeping pills and slid next to Jesse's naked body. He was aware of a subtle rage smoldering in his mind just beyond exposure — a mania which whispered to him, *You should have known, you should have saved him.* The pills and alcohol finally triumphed, and he slept. His dreams were filled with a muddle of confusing images, as yet foreign to him.

THIRTEEN

The ER staff was used to dealing with death, but this was different. The murky oppression of personal death hung over the department. A hospital is similar to a small town, and few secrets last very long. The news of Lubeck's suicide was followed shortly by the rumor of his termination. As a result, administration had few friends in the ER. Small groups of staff separated themselves and talked in hushed tones, periodically glancing away to see who might be listening.

Rooster and the members of the ER staff, who could get away, had attended a memorial service, along with a few staff physicians who had known Steve for years. Barb Henry was the sole representative from administration. Apparently all the members of the board, including Armen Polling, were too busy to pay their respects.

Jason tried to focus on his work. Patients didn't care that the department was in mourning, and kept up a steady flow as usual. He picked up the next chart in the ready rack and checked the chief complaint: "Vaginal Foreign Body." He seemed to be having a run on things like this lately, but unlike the last one, this patient was only twenty-four years old. He browsed through the patient information sheet out of curiosity and noted she was a nurse at University Hospital. As he walked toward the exam room, he saw Rooster leave his office carrying a cardboard box. Rooster's expression and stride both testified to his passionate determination.

The patient was an attractive redhead whose flushed face matched her curls. "I'm Dr. Corey," he said. "I understand you're having a problem."

The crimson of her face deepened even more. "God, yes," she laughed awkwardly. "I'm afraid I have a lost condom. I know it's there, I just can't get it out."

Jason smiled and tried to act as nonchalant as possible, hoping his demeanor would put his patient at ease. "Well, I guess that explains why you didn't go to the ER at the U," he laughed.

She grimaced. "That's the last place I'd go with this. It would be all over the hospital before I left the ER."

He started to turn toward the door. "I'll get a nurse, and we'll do a check."

"I don't need a chaperone if you don't." She lay back on the table, apparently more at ease. "Let's just get this over with."

Jason usually used a chaperone for pelvic and breast exams, but he felt he had little risk with this patient. Chaperones were for the protection of the doctor, not the patient. He pulled on an exam glove and squeezed a dab of lubricating jelly into his hand. The patient had already let her knees fall apart, and he pulled the paper gown up over her belly. Her face contorted as he slid his gloved hand inside her and began his search.

"So where do you work at the U?"

She relaxed a little and answered. "I'm a nurse in dialysis."

"You've got a good program there. How do you like it?" He nabbed the edge of the fugitive condom between his index and middle fingers, but the added pressure brought another flinch from his patient.

"Oh . . .just . . . fine," she said through her clenched teeth.

He withdrew his hand and turned his glove inside out encasing the slippery article, then dropped the entire packet into the trash can.

"All done." He smiled. "You know, those things aren't the safest form of birth control."

"Apparently not. I just started having sex with my boyfriend, and it wasn't really planned," she said as she repositioned her gown.

"You can get dressed, and the nurse will bring your papers in a minute."

"I appreciate it, Dr. Corey, and thanks for not making me feel . . . you know."

"You're entirely welcome. You take care." An appreciative, pleasant patient was an all too rare of an occurrence in the ER. Despite the fact Jason hadn't exactly saved a life, he got a significant amount of satisfaction from the simple case.

Jason walked back to his desk and spotted Rooster coming down the hall. The cardboard box was gone, but he was still taking five-foot strides. He spotted Jason and gave him the lighter sign.

The deck was bathed in warm sunshine, a contrast to the somber, cool air-conditioned ER. Jason lit a cigarette and leaned on the railing as usual, but Rooster remained rail straight, his arms folded across his chest, puffing one draw after another in silence.

"You seemed to be on a mission this morning," Jason finally said.

"Yep, I took Steve's things up to administration. Bob was busy, of course, so I left the box and told his secretary I was sure somebody would want them for their trophy room," he said through steel-tight jaw muscles.

"I can't say that I blame you, Rooster, but are you sure you shouldn't just let this go?"

"Letting things go is what brought this on to begin with. Remember that, Jason. When you're in charge, be in charge. Besides, I anticipate this will bring good old Bob to my office for a little visit, and that's exactly what I want." The muscles in Rooster's face appeared ready to explode.

"It's your call, Rooster. But I'm not sure what this is going to accomplish." He exhaled slowly.

"Hang around and you'll see. It's time to get things — a lot of things — under control here."

Jason didn't answer. He wasn't sure what Rooster was up to, but he felt the less involved he was, the better. Rooster lit another cigarette and seemed to decompress slightly.

"By the way, you need to call this newspaper reporter. She's doing some sort of article on the ER, and you're the chosen one to be a celebrity. You met her briefly here on the deck a few days ago."

"Oh, great. Why am I the lucky one?" He asked, obviously unhappy.

"Because I haven't got a lot of people right now who are stable and smart enough not to screw this up. Obviously Steve is out, Larry's out, and I'm sure as hell not doing it."

"Other than the hassle, what's the big deal?" Jason turned toward Rooster.

"This reporter has a reputation for digging up dirt. All you need to do is tell her a little about the ER — census and stuff — and keep her away from anything we don't want to see in the papers — like Steve," he emphasized.

"Okay," Jason said reluctantly. "Is she going to call me or what?"

Rooster already had the card out of his pocket and passed it to him. "Knock yourself out. And be careful. She's a looker, and I suspect a player," he added.

"I'm sure that'll go over big with Jesse."

Rooster laughed. "Time to decide who's the boss, or has that already been established?"

Jason responded with a sardonic smile.

"If there are any skeletons in your closet, make sure she doesn't find them."

"Nope, I'm clean," he replied too quickly. Rooster threw him a quick sideways glance.

In the back of his mind, Jason wondered what kind of story could be made out of his current situation. He was certain an ER doctor who took sleeping pills to keep from speaking a foreign language, magically healed lacerations and was developing a close relationship with his long-dead babysitter would make good reading. He could see the story line now: *Harborline Physician Sent To Macadamia Ranch.*

"It's time to get ready for my visit from Bob." Rooster crushed his cigarette and left.

Jason lingered a few minutes longer, remembering the young woman he had met briefly with Rooster. Although he wished he could deny it, she had made a significant impression on him. There had been something about her eyes and the message they sent. Her dark sensuality teased him, and as much as he wished he could deny it, he realized he could be tempted.

Rooster was right. Ten minutes later the hospital administrator rolled his squat figure into the ER. His expensive suit bunched and pulled over his midsection, and Jason noticed his thighs rubbed together when he walked, giving his pants a sheen from the extra wear. His posh silk necktie was tied in a careless knot and rested to the side of his collar from repeated tugs. Bob appeared nonchalant as he walked through the department, but he never veered from a line toward Rooster's office.

"How are you today, Dr. Corey? Everything going well?" Bob offered in passing.

"Just fine Bob," was all Jason could offer in return.

The administrator pretended to inspect the department while he steadily made his way toward Rooster's closed office door. He tentatively turned the knob, without knocking, and walked in. Jason heard part of Rooster's greeting before the door closed firmly, like the snap of a closing trap.

"Well Bob, what a surprise to see you here," Rooster offered graciously.

Rooster returned to his desk and sat down, crossed his legs and tented his hands in front of his face. He smiled at Bob but didn't speak.

"Rooster, that comment to my secretary was out of line. No one's sorrier than the administration and board of this hospital about Steve

Lubeck's death." He remained standing, his arms hanging at his side. "There's no way you can blame us for this."

Rooster lost his smile and stared at him just long enough to maximize Bob's discomfort.

"Cut the crap, Bob. We both know you and your pal Armen Polling are relieved that Steve's dead. It saves you the risk of a wrongful dismissal suit and he's out of your hair. Now all you have to worry about is his family finding out and suing this hospital. There's a sister in Montana, but they weren't close. I sure hope nobody calls her," Rooster finished sarcastically.

"I don't have to take this from you, Rooster. I personally feel this hospital would be better off without you too. I'm the administrator of this hospital now, not your buddy who was here before. I think it's about time the board considers other options for our ER." He tried to control the tremor, but his voice quavered with uncertainty.

"Bob, why don't you sit down?" Rooster's manner was the paradigm of composure.

"I don't need to sit down with you, and you can't change my mind."

"Bob, I think you want to be sitting for what I have to show you." He waited while the hospital administrator tentatively settled his plump body onto a chair.

Rooster reached into his desk drawer and pulled out a large manila envelope. An amused smile danced across his face as he shook the contents out onto his empty desk, without touching the photos.

"I think you'll recognize these." He waited while Bob picked up the pictures and watched his face slowly turn pasty white.

"Where'd you get these?" Bob challenged.

"Those were taken at the Las Vegas Hilton about a year ago. The date is right there on the bottom, right next to the time," Rooster said with mock concern. "By the way, Bob, how's your lovely wife? Karen, isn't it? I keep meaning to take you two out for dinner."

Bob looked up from the pictures, still stunned. "I would never have done this if she hadn't come on to me."

"Yes, Candy can be very persuasive, can't she, Bob? I hear she's left Vegas and moved to the Mexican Riviera or the Caribbean or someplace like that, just in case you were thinking of having someone look her up. But don't worry, Bob. I'm sure your wife will understand. She struck me as a very understanding woman, and you've got how many kids? Is it three?" Rooster asked as if searching his memory.

His rage finally erupted, and Bob threw the stack of photos onto Rooster's desk. A thread of saliva trickled from the corner of his mouth and ran down his chin.

"Oh, you can keep those, Bob. I've got others. And I kept these nice and neat for you. No messy fingerprints or anything." He looked over at the photos and pointed to the top picture, being careful not to touch the surface with his finger.

"That's one of my favorites. I didn't think those arms of yours could reach that far, Bob. And that thing with your finger . . . " Rooster chuckled.

"All right, Rooster, what do you want?" Contrary to Rooster's suggestion, Bob knew his wife was not the understanding type, especially over something like this. He realized he had no way out.

Rooster sat back and laced his fingers behind his head. "Here's what you're going to do, Bob. It's quite simple, really. It will only take you a few months. You're going to resign your position here, and you're going to see to it that your buddy Armen leaves the board."

"That's ridiculous. I have no intention of being forced out of my job, and I have no control over Armen Polling," he answered indignantly.

"That's too bad, Bob. Then I guess you can explain Candy to your wife and the board. I can see the headlines now: *Local Hospital Administrator Caught With Finger In Candy.*" Rooster rolled his head back and his body shook with deep laughter.

"This is blackmail, Rooster. Plain and simple." His anger flared again.

Rooster paused and appeared lost in thought. "You're absolutely right, Bob. Let's see you prove it."

"You think you're so goddamned righteous, Rooster. Tell me this. If you're so chaste, why didn't you use these to save Steve Lubeck's job, and maybe his life?"

Rooster sprang like a coiled snake. He was on his feet, halfway over his desk, in a vicious attempt to seize Bob by the throat, but missed by an inch. The administrator dodged backward, saved by his reflexes.

"You get the fuck out of my office, Bob," Rooster bellowed. "I'll see you at your farewell banquet and not before."

Bob scurried out of the office just as a crash shook the door behind him. Every eye in the ER followed him as he retreated out of the department.

Rooster stood over his desk, shaking with rage. For the second time in his life, he realized that he could lose control to the point that murder was possible. The single thing that infuriated him the most was that he knew Bob was right.

Jason struggled through the last hours of his shift, before a four-day break. He and Jesse were headed for the San Juan Islands in the Sound for a badly needed escape. When seven p.m. finally crawled in, he packed up and threw his bag into the Z4, dropped the top, and headed home. The sun was high above the horizon, and a warm wind whipped his face, while the pulsing music of George Thorogood blasted from the car's speakers. He tried to clear his mind of recent events and simply relax. The throaty roar of the engine and the pounding music lulled him into a state of peace and his mind cleared from the stress of the day.

The epiphany struck him without warning. He hadn't even been thinking about the day he was electrocuted in the ER, but the picture was there nonetheless. He could see it as if it were an instant replay running through his brain; unquestionable proof of the event. The shock didn't run up his arm — it went down through his body and out to his patient. *He* was the source of
the power.

FOURTEEN

Jesse was a picture of femininity as she scurried through the apartment wearing only a pair of sheer panties. Jason was tempted but knew if he didn't let her finish packing they would miss their ferry. They had reservations at Rosario Resort on Orcas Island in the San Juans. The San Juan Islands were one of the best-kept secrets in the country, known well to the locals of the Pacific Northwest, but little beyond the area. Orcas Island, like most of the San Juans, was accessible only by ferryboat. Like many people traveling by ferry, they planned to take their car with them on the boat and spend at least part of their time touring the island.

Jason had finished packing and decided to check on Larry and contact Sheri Black while Jesse finished her preparations. He dialed Larry Todd's number and waited. On the fifth ring, just as he was about to hang up, the tone was interrupted mid-ring, but no one spoke.

" Larry, are you there?"

"Yeah, who's this?" The voice on the line was vacant and unsteady.

"It's Jason. I've been trying to get in touch with you. How are things going?" He already knew the answer.

"I'm not sure, Jason."

"Hey, Larry, you sound like shit. What's going on?" He pushed for an answer.

"Things are just falling apart, Jason. I haven't been able to see the kids, and my lawyer says I should get ready for the worst. I can't imagine it can get much worse than this." His answer resonated with defeat.

Jason recognized the sound of clinical depression when he heard it, and Larry's voice and words left little doubt in his mind that Larry was in trouble.

"Do you want me to come over? I can be there in twenty minutes."

Jesse stopped mid-stride and stared in disbelief at his words.

"No, I'm okay. I think I've got things figured out."

"What do you have figured out, Larry?"

"I've figured out that no matter what I do, the result is going to be the same, with me or without me."

"What do you mean by that, with you or without you?" The image of Steve Lubeck, lying dead on the floor of his home, materialized in Jason's mind. Jesse stood in front of him, listening, but Jason turned away and leaned back against the counter.

"Don't worry, Jason, I'm not going to pull a Lubeck. I'm too much of a coward."

Jason's anxiety level dropped. "Larry, don't give up yet. No matter what, I promise things will get better." Jason didn't sound convincing, even to himself. "I'm headed out of town for a few days, but I'll call you later. If you need me, call me on my cell phone. Deal?"

Jesse's face came back to life. He hung up and turned toward her and was met by a hug and a kiss.

"What's that for?" He asked.

"Just because I love you," she murmured looking up at him. "And, because you didn't let me down."

"I wouldn't do that unless I had to. You should know that."

"Sometimes, it just seems everything else is more important to you than I am." She held him at arm's length, a slight pout on her face.

Once more, Jason felt pulled in two directions. "What am I supposed to do, Jesse, leave town for a few days and come back to find Larry dead, when there might have been something I could have done to prevent it? That doesn't sound like you, Jess."

"I'm not saying that. It's just that it always seems you're the one who carries the burden, fills in the shifts, or takes the extra responsibility." She sounded discouraged.

"I have responsibilities, just like everyone else. Anyway, Larry is taken care of for now, so how about we get you packed and get going."

Jesse picked up an armful of clothes and walked toward the bedroom. Once she was gone, he retrieved the card Rooster had given him, and dialed the underlined number.

"Hello, this is Sheri."

Her voice surprised him. He had missed the slight raspy timbre of her words at their first meeting.

He hesitated, mesmerized by the voice. "Ms. Black, this is Jason Corey. Rooster, I mean Dr. Christensen, gave me your card and asked me to call you. He said something about an interview." He felt awkward calling her, and his voice reflected his uneasiness.

"Oh yes, Dr. Corey. Thank you so much for getting back to me." Her voice was enthusiastic. "I wasn't sure Rooster would pass my card on to you. I don't think he likes newspaper reporters." Her laugh put him at ease.

"Rooster's bark is worse than his bite . . . most of the time."

"I was hoping we could get together soon and discuss an article I'm doing on your ER." She tried not to sound too eager, but it was difficult. He had been in her mind since their first brief encounter.

Jesse walked past him as he started to answer. "Yes, that would be fine. I'm headed out of town for a few days, but I could meet with you when I get back." He saw Jesse glance over her shoulder in his direction as he spoke.

"That would be great. Would it be okay if I came to the ER for our first meeting?"

He was aware of Jesse's presence and knew she was listening. He knew he wasn't doing anything wrong, but somehow he felt guilty "Yeah, that would be fine. I'll call you in a few days." He tried to sound casual.

Jesse stopped, still gathering clothes. "Who was that?" She asked.

Jason involuntarily tensed. "That was a newspaper reporter that Rooster has given me the dubious honor of working with, for a story about the ER." He tried too hard to sound indifferent.

"Hey, that's great. You'll be famous," she teased. "What's his name?"

He paused and made his decision. "Ah, Black I think. Probably some no name doing scud work at the newspaper. Are you about packed? Remember we only have a small trunk in the BMW."

She dashed for the bedroom, still wearing only her panties. "Ten more minutes and I'm set."

Jason poured a glass of white wine and ambled out onto the deck. He knew that when Jesse was packing, her ten minutes could be more like a half an hour. He lit a cigarette, leaned back against the railing and rubbed his neck. It seemed his life had gone from ordered to pandemonium in only a few weeks. He tried to process the realization that the shock that knocked him unconscious had come *from* his body, but the growing list of unanswered questions only added to his frustration and confusion. He had no answers to explain the shock, the magically healing laceration, or his apparent new capacity for a foreign language. He felt responsible for Steve Lubeck's death and seemed powerless to stop Larry Todd's spin into desolation. He gradually became aware of an ominous presence pushing on the horizon of his conscience, building like distant, sinister thunderheads: guilt.

"Hey, let's go. I'm tired of waiting for you." Jesse's teasing brought him back abruptly from his thoughts. He looked at her intently, standing in the doorway, alive and beautiful. His expression caught her off guard.

"Are you still with me? You look like someone just walked on your grave."

He laughed. "I don't think I've ever heard you use that expression." He drained his glass and crushed his cigarette butt in the ashtray. "I was just thinking about things." He was thankful she didn't know what those things were.

"What am I going to do with you?" She came to him, looked into his eyes, and held his face in her hands. "You can't save the world; it's not your job. Besides, it's been tried before with minimal success."

The fir and hemlock-covered foothills north of Seattle gradually changed to level, windswept tide flats as they drove north to the ferry terminal at Anacortes. When they arrived, Jason pulled the Z4 into the auto line waiting for the ferry, bought their tickets, and confirmed the schedule. They had missed the ferry they had planned on, and had almost two hours before the next boat would leave for the Islands.

They left the car and walked hand in hand up the street to the small town perched on the bluffs, overlooking the ferry terminal and the ocean. A stiff breeze off the water pushed them up the hill to the tourist shops and restaurants that served the ferry patrons. They window shopped along the quaint street until they turned the corner at the top of the hill and ran out of shops. The last point of interest was a weatherworn bar and grill. The wooden sign fixed to the top of the restaurant announced *The Captain's Chest*.

"How about some lunch?" Jason asked.

Jesse checked out the bar and grill, then glanced back down the street. "This place looks pretty sleazy," she said. "There must be someplace else a little less earthy."

Jason stepped to the window and inspected the sun-bleached menu taped to the inside of the fly-specked glass. "Hey, they've got Rosalyn on tap. It can't be too bad."

Jesse still held back.

"Come' on." Jason tugged on her arm. "Don't let everybody know you're a city girl."

They pushed through the heavy door and waited while their eyes adjusted to the muted light. Country and western music trailed from the rear of the empty bar, along with the aroma of fresh seafood and stale beer. Jesse rolled her eyes and started back toward the door, but Jason hooked her arm and intercepted her. He steered her to a table covered with carved initials near the front of the restaurant and they sat down. After several minutes, the scruffy bartender shuffled over to take their order.

"What's the specialty of the house?" Jason asked.

The bartender slid two yellowed menus across the table in response.

"I'm not really hungry," Jesse offered.

Jason frowned. "We'll have two Rosalyns and two orders of clam strips." The bartender slid the menus under his belt and left.

"People get ptomaine poisoning in places like this, you know," Jesse badgered.

"The beer will kill anything that can hurt you," he countered and tickled her side.

She pulled away from his hand and slapped his arm. "I'll remember that when you're calling Ralph on the big phone tonight."

Jason flipped the ash from his cigarette, sipped his Rosalyn, and looked around the bar. Their food came quickly, and they ordered another round of the dark Rosalyn beer. Jesse relaxed while they ate and talked about the trip, but she was glad they were the only patrons in the bar. The place was actually much larger than it looked from the outside. Several telescoping rooms angled backward as if they had been added in a series of afterthoughts, and led into a maze of hidden corners and secret grottos.

"I've got to go to the bathroom. If I'm not back in five minutes, please come and rescue me," Jesse asked as she left their table. She returned a few minutes later looking confused and slid into their booth facing Jason.

"What's up?" Jason asked in response to her expression.

"I could swear I saw Rooster back there with some guy."

Jason looked over his shoulder toward the rear of the restaurant.

"This is a little off the beaten path, even for Rooster. Are you sure it was him?"

"I'm not positive, he was wearing sunglasses, but if it wasn't him, it was his twin. The guy with him was absolutely gorgeous," she gushed. "One of those dark Hispanic types."

Jason pulled a face as he stood and headed for the rear of the building. When he came to the doors marked "Captains" and "First Mates," he saw Rooster at a nearby table. He was halfway out of his booth in the rear corner of the pub, headed toward Jason.

"Jason, what are you doing here?" He sounded almost disapproving as he took Jason by the arm and led him away from the booth and the other man. Jason glanced back and had to admit, the guy could have been a male model.

"Jesse and I are catching the ferry to the islands." He looked at his watch. "And we really better get going."

It was obvious to Jason that Rooster wanted to keep his attention away from the booth and its occupant.

"Great. You guys have a good trip and I'll see you when you get back."

Rooster walked him back to Jesse but kept Jason's arm in his grasp.

"Hi, Jesse. It's good to see you," Rooster said, still looking and sounding like a teenager caught leering at a Penthouse magazine.

"Hey, Rooster, good to see you too. Who's your friend back there?" She couldn't resist the question.

Rooster faltered then replied with a smile. "Oh, he's just an old friend. He was passing through the area, and we stopped in for lunch."

"If he needs a guide, you let me know, Rooster," Jesse kidded.

"Ah, he's married, and I think you're almost married, too." He picked up Jesse's hand and admired the large diamond.

Jason grinned and reached for the bar check on the table, but Rooster's hand shot out and grabbed the bill. "I'll get that. You two better get going." His words were stressed with underlying urgency.

"Okay, Rooster, but I'll remember this." Jesse stood on her toes looking past him to the rear booth.

Her words impacted Rooster like a slap in the face, and his expression became a scowl, focused on her.

"That wouldn't be a good idea, Jesse." He shifted his gaze to Jason as he spoke to emphasize his words.

Jesse started to speak, but Jason cut her off.

"No problem, Rooster. Hey, we gotta get going."

Jason practically dragged Jesse out of the restaurant. He stopped and waved back at Rooster as they went through the door, and their eyes met briefly. Rooster returned Jason's thumbs up.

Jason started down the hill toward the docks taking long strides, still holding Jesse's hand, who tried to keep up as best she could.

"What the hell was that all about?" She asked indignantly.

"Don't talk right now." His voice was relaxed, and he pointed to the incoming ferry below them. "Our boat's here."

They got back to the car just as the ferry finished unloading. Jesse had remained silent the rest of the way back, but that was about to end.

"Okay, I've been a quiet little girl. Now I want some answers," she said angrily.

Jason started the car when he saw the vehicles ahead of him start to load. "I don't have a clue." His unruffled voice deflated her anger.

"So, you're not mad at me about something?"

"No, honey, not in the least," he answered.

"Then what was the no talking bit all about?" She still sounded defensive.

"I didn't want Rooster to see us doing anything but strolling back to the car."

"Huh? Rooster was inside the restaurant," she responded confused.

"Not necessarily. He could have been watching us from up the hill, or his mysterious friend could have been around," Jason said as he pulled forward and followed the car in front of him toward the ferry.

"Why would he do that?" She was unconvinced.

Jason came to the entrance ramp onto the ferry where a worker directed him to the upper car deck. He slowly drove up the ramp where another worker directed him to the front corner of the parking area. He turned off the engine and set the parking brake, then turned to her.

"Look, Jesse, I don't have any idea what that whole thing in the bar was about, but I do know that whatever it was, we weren't supposed to see it." He leaned back against his door and put his right hand on her shoulder. "When you called attention to the guy with Rooster, his response told me you were close — way too close."

"Do you think Rooster's gay?" She asked.

Jason laughed. "Rooster may be a lot of things, but gay isn't one of them. There's a very dark side to Rooster, a side I've learned to stay away from and don't want to know about. I think doing anything else could be dangerous."

"Maybe he's just plain nuts," she offered.

"Jesse, do you understand what Rooster was saying back there?"

She thought for a moment. "Jason, I don't understand anything about what happened back there."

He smiled at her response. "Rooster was saying one thing and making it exceedingly clear. Forget about the whole meeting! Don't talk about it, don't think about it and don't ever mention it again. Okay?"

She took a breath and exhaled in frustration. "Okay. It doesn't make sense to me, but he's your boss. The guy with Rooster was sure good looking though. I'll bet he could get any woman he wanted."

They carefully opened their doors and squeezed out between the cars parked closely around them. They headed for the lounge on the top deck of the ferry to enjoy the cruise, but Jesse's words stuck in Jason's mind. A tiny buzzing gnat of a thought skipped through the periphery of his brain, then disappeared.

Rooster peered through the grimy window of the bar and watched Jason and Jesse walk down the hill toward the docks. He knew he had overreacted to Jesse's comment, but he also knew it was essential to his plan that their chance encounter today be forgotten. He was too far into his plot to have something like this — something that might be remembered at a later time — put the whole thing at risk. He knew from experience that simple mistakes could cause serious problems later. He trusted Jason to keep his mouth shut, but Jesse was a whole other matter.

Rooster returned to his table.

"You seem to have a lot of friends here. Maybe too many friends." The stranger's words were flavored with a slight Spanish accent.

Rooster glanced back toward the front of the restaurant. "You let me worry about my friends. You just worry about your end," he said unwaveringly.

The man ran his hand through his glistening black hair. "I worry about everything. You seem to forget, I have the most to lose if there's trouble." He crushed his cigarette in the ashtray and picked up his beer.

Rooster scowled and tried to control his anger. "If you don't like the way things are, you can walk out right now. I'm sure I can find another pretty-looking tough guy who would like some extra cash." Rooster was bluffing. He knew the brutishly handsome young man sitting across from him was perfect for the job.

The Mexican put his glass down harder than he meant to, splashing beer over the tabletop. "I'll take the job. You just make fucking sure you do your part."

Rooster fixed him with his eyes as he reached inside his jacket and withdrew a bulky envelope. He glanced over his shoulder and quickly passed the packet across the table.

The young Hispanic man casually slid the envelope inside his shirt. "I know I can count on the rest when it's done."

"Just get it done fast, and get it done right." Rooster was not about to be intimidated.

The Mexican slid out of the booth and left without looking back. Rooster lit a cigarette and finished the last of his beer. He didn't like the idea of Jason and Jesse knowing he had any involvement with this man, but there was nothing he could do about it now. Hopefully, there would never be a reason for them to make a connection between the two of them, but if they did, he would deal with it.

FIFTEEN

Jason embraced her with his entire being and felt the slight pressure of her breasts against his arm. The fragrance of Jesse's hair teased his senses as they stood back to front on the bow of the colossal ferry. A warm breeze swathed the deck and carried an occasional wash of ocean spray, which startled them with icy fingers. The warm summer sun reflecting off the waves belied the frigid water beneath them. Jason forgot about everything except the moment and Jesse. The only message his senses telegraphed to his mind was that Jesse was alive, standing next to him. Nothing else in the world mattered, for now.

The ship vibrated from its powerful engines, which pushed them through the seascape of the San Juan Islands. Scattered groups of gulls hung effortlessly in the air, suspended in the breeze, then suddenly dove to capture an unseen prize. The two lovers swayed in unison as the ship rocked and pitched through the waves.

The bluffs of Anacortes disappeared in the land-bound mists as they moved toward open water. Jason and Jesse searched the waters for killer whales, the namesakes of their destination, but the orcas were evasive. Their ship traversed the Rosario Strait and a number of small islands came into view, followed by the larger mass of Lopez Island. The tree-lined shore trailed away to the south in layers of green muted by the haze and finally vanished in the mist. The ferry nosed into the pier at Thatcher, on the north point of Lopez Island, and quickly offloaded several passengers, before continuing on their last leg to Orcas Island.

By the time they docked, they were both ripe with anticipation. Jason drove them off the multi-story car carrier with several other autos and they were absorbed onto the island like rivulets of rain disappearing into the desert sand. They slowly passed through the little town of white clapboard buildings perched along the cliff above the pier, and joked about the sign, which boasted the population of 378. Below them, they could see the ferryboat, which had brought them, moving off to its next stop, leaving them abandoned to each other.

Jason pushed the sleek sports car along the narrow, twisting roads and followed the signs that directed them to Rosario Resort, on the opposite arm of the horseshoe-shaped island. The pulsing sound of The Doors shook the speakers of the topless roadster as they shot through a straightaway that paralleled a surf-washed beach, littered with giant twisted driftwood corpses. The sun moved low in the sky, heralding the approaching dusk and the cool fog-touched evening.

The majestic, long-standing great house of Rosario appeared, nestled in the trees between the bay and the surrounding hills. They checked in then drove to one of the new buildings perched high above the bay, and quickly explored their room. They both tried to appear blasé rather than on the brink of a sexual frenzy.

They stood together on the balcony immersed in the beauty and ambiance of this pristine paradise. In the distance, they could see the setting sun reflect off one of the great mountains, Rainier or Hood; they weren't sure which. Below them, the lights came on in a double-masted sailboat resting at anchor in the bay.

Jason opened a bottle of wine they had brought with them, and they toasted to each other. Finally, the intimacy freed them. Jesse burrowed against him, lifted her lips to his and probed his mouth with her tongue. He enfolded her in his arms, pulled her to him, and they began to merge into each other's being. They each radiated a scent that only the other could identify — a scent that drove their passion beyond the boundaries of mere sexual response.

He slid his hand down her back under her waistband and felt the gentle slope of bare skin against his fingers. They separated long enough to move inside, then hurriedly, almost frantically, undressed each other. Still standing, they moved over each other's bodies, kissing and caressing.

At last, the pair stood naked in each other's arms. The fireplace cast pale shadows over the two lovers, its heat adding to their glow and illuminating the subtle sheen, which covered them. She reached behind him, kneading his cheek with the palm of her hand and stroked with her fingertips. She dropped to one knee, cupped him with her other hand, and gently squeezed. She took him into her mouth gently and caressed him with her lips, working him as he neared his point of surrender. He pulled her to her feet, turned her and gently pushed her forward over the edge of their bed. The muscles of her shapely legs turned taut as she lifted herself onto her toes and arched her back. He lifted her firmly, spreading and revealing, then entered her. Her muscles grasped in response and held him.

They moved in a lovers' ballet, sharing not only each other's bodies but also each other's essence. Their dance approached its crescendo and he stimulated her, encouraging her. At last, the sensation drove her over the edge, and she fell crashing through the waves of her orgasm. At each pinnacle, she fell back to him, only to be lifted again and driven to the next peak. A frantic cry escaped her lips, clenched in ecstasy. Her response released a primitive reflex deep within him, and they finished their dance in an amalgam of two bodies, two lives, and two souls merged into a single being.

They were both too exhausted to dress for dinner, and opted to spend the night by the fire with room service. They talked, held each other, and spent the night as lovers do after special times. They shared a second bottle of wine and finally fell asleep after making love again. This time, unlike the frenzied act of passion they had shared earlier, their lovemaking was filled with warmth and reassurance — a more exceptional thing to be cherished. They fell asleep entwined in each other's arms.

Jason slept fitfully, his mind besieged by thoughts of recent happenings and the fear of waking Jesse with his nocturnal ramblings. He had finally decided he needed to talk to someone about what had been happening to him, but he didn't have any practical options. He didn't want to worry Jesse or Arthur, and Rooster wasn't the type you went to with this kind of problem. He didn't like the idea of a psychiatrist, but he was running out of alternatives.

Jason finally gave up on sleep just before dawn, and made a pot of coffee in the room, then wrapped himself in a quilt and moved to the balcony. The nights on the islands were typically cool and damp, and this was no exception. He lit a cigarette, sipped his coffee, and gazed out over the water at the hills across the bay. Rolling banks of mist-laden fog drifted low above the inlet and up the valleys, like the fingers of some fantastic wraithlike spirit reaching from the depths. The chilly dampness permeated the blanket, and he wrapped himself tighter in the quilt. He stood looking at the distant hills as they faded away in layers — white on green, each one veiled deeper in clouds of mist than the one before.

Something stirred behind him, and he turned just as Jesse came onto the deck. She slid her naked body in front of him, squirmed under the blanket, and leaned back against his form. He wrapped his arms around her and enfolded her into the quilt and his body. They stood sharing their warmth and watching the shadowed vista below them.

Finally, she spoke. "You're up early. Couldn't sleep?"

"Just restless. I didn't want to wake you."

"You've seemed distracted lately. Is something bothering you?" She asked. She half turned to see his face. "I worry about you."

He wanted to tell her. This was the perfect chance, and she was asking. He wavered, and the words started to form in his mouth, but he stopped. He didn't want to worry her, but he knew that was only part of it. The reality was, he didn't want to be less in her eyes. He was afraid she would think he was crazy.

"It's just work and all this stuff with Steve and Larry. I'll be fine when things settle down." He lied, and the moment passed.

They stood wrapped together, sharing coffee and the ocean. She sensed there was something more, but she respected his retreat. Still, she wanted to know what was happening to the man she loved, and on some level, his silence hurt her.

They had an early breakfast in the main lodge, then headed out in the car to explore the island. Other than a few streets in the tiny community, the only road on the island was a single paved drive, which looped and traversed the countryside. They had taken part of the road from the ferry to the lodge, but today they were off to explore the rest of the area. The fog burned off, leaving a clear, crisp day for sightseeing. Their pace was much slower than their frantic race to the hotel the evening before. They dropped the top of the roadster and leisurely cruised the gently winding road to the soft sounds of Enya.

It seemed as if there was a shop or inn at every bend in the road, and Jesse wanted to explore them all. She gradually filled every extra inch of space in the car with treasures, until Jason cut her off.

"Don't even think about it," he said as she inspected a hand-turned piece of pottery.

"But this would look great on the end table," she protested.

"Jesse, we're out of room in the car. We'll be lucky to get the suitcase in as it is."

"I could hold it on my lap," she countered.

"What makes you think there's any room for you?" He placed the pot back on its shelf.

"Okay," she relented. "In that case, let's eat."

They found a hippy restaurant along the beach for lunch. Jason would have preferred a burger and a Rosalyn but settled for mushroom soup and herbal tea. They finished and headed out again.

The road wound through rolling pastureland, then skirted the water before it turned inland and climbed steeply through towering evergreens. They stopped along the way to absorb the view and enjoy each other. Each hiatus offered a different experience.

"Oh, look, Jason," Jesse said as they rounded a corner. "There's a fawn." She pointed to the spotted baby standing near the road.

Jason eased them to a stop at a wide spot, and they slowly climbed out of the car.

"Here, Jess, see if you can coax him over with these," he whispered and handed her a small bag of peppermint candies.

Jesse carefully moved to a log and edged herself onto a seat. She held one of the candies out and softly called to the deer. "Come on, you want this?" She coaxed.
The fawn scampered to her and without hesitation jumped into her lap and confiscated the candy.

"Ah, I think he's done this before," Jason offered. "See if he'll sit still for a picture." He bent down and snapped several shots.

"Oh, honey, we could sneak him home in the trunk of the car, and no one would ever know," Jesse said as she petted the fragile creature.

"Remember, fawns grow into adult deer very quickly. Besides, he's a wild animal," he reminded her.

Jason became uneasy. The *feeling* was back. Not like the first time, but it was unquestionably there. *Why here? Why now?* He wondered. Was this just free-floating anxiety or was it driven by some impending event?

"Are you a wild animal?" Jesse quizzed the fawn in baby talk. The deer responded with a succession of wet licks across her face. The fawn skipped to the side when she fell off her log, only to return immediately to continue its barrage of kisses. Jesse finally escaped to her feet with Jason's help.

"Oh, he's a killer all right," she sputtered through her tears of laughter and wiped her face.

Jason's uneasiness was growing. "Let's get going, Jesse. We need to go." He was adamant.

Jesse was reluctant to leave the baby, but Jason insisted. They finally escaped the fawn on their third attempt by leaving a small pile of peppermints several feet away and retreated to the car. Jason's anxiety decreased as they drove away.

At the parking area on top of the mountain, they climbed the old stone lookout and were rewarded with an astonishing view. Across the expanse of the sound, they could see the three famous snow-capped mountains of the Pacific Northwest. They were accustomed to grandeur and beauty, but this view left them without words.

The two poked around the area for an hour, laughing and sharing before they finally started the drive back down the mountain to the lodge. The view heading down the mountain was even more impressive than it had been climbing the peak. Jesse rested her hand on his shoulder and massaged his neck as they pointed out sights they had missed on the trip up as they saw things from a different perspective.

They approached the spot where they had stopped for the fawn, and Jason again became aware of the *feeling* of discomfort inside him. He slowed the car despite his need to escape, and glanced at Jesse and smiled. She was leaning forward, straining to spot the baby again. He brought his gaze forward, just as the patch of white-spotted fur flashed in front of the car. In the same instant, his eyes picked out the movement, he felt a dull thud against the bumper. Jason's foot reacted instinctively, and the brakes locked, throwing them both forward against their seatbelts. A sick feeling swept over him in the same instant Jesse's scream struck him like a second impact.

Jesse bolted and ran to the front of the car, deaf to Jason's shouts.

"Jesse, we've got to get out of the road before another car comes around the corner and kills us both."

Jason ran to the front of the car where she was kneeling over the body of the fawn. The animal was crumpled under the front fender, its neck crooked at an unnatural angle, and a trickle of fresh blood at the corner of its mouth. Jesse was crying hysterically. The *feeling* was pushing in on him and growing rapidly. He pulled at Jesse's arm, but she wouldn't move. In desperation, he scooped the fawn up and carried the broken body to the side of the road, with Jesse in tow. He was surprised the animal weighed almost nothing in his arms. He left them both on the shoulder of the road, then ran back to the car. He could see brief flashes of color through the trees where the road snaked around the curve above them. A car was coming, and it was coming fast. He punched the accelerator and squealed forward onto the shoulder out of the way, just as the SUV rounded the corner and swerved away, its horn blaring.

Jason climbed out of the car and walked back to Jesse where she was still kneeling over the body of the fawn.

"Jess, I'm sorry. It just came out of nowhere."

Jason knew his words wouldn't help. He knelt beside her and put his arm around her shoulders, intensely aware of the *feeling,* roiling inside his chest. It was growing by the second, driving his mind toward panic.

"It's not fair. Why does God let things like this happen? Little kids die of cancer, baby animals die for no reason at all." She choked the words out through her sobs.

"Jess, I don't think God does things like this. He just — "

"Then he doesn't care!" She turned her tear-stained face to him and shouted angrily.

"I wish there was something I could say or do," he stammered as he reached down to stroke the animal's neck. The broken body was still warm to his touch, and he flashed back to the little girl in the ER.

The shock was a mere echo of what it had been the first time. He may even have been prepared for it on some level of his consciousness. It still jolted him, but he was able to keep his hand in place on the fawn's neck. The animal jerked upright, wobbled a moment, then stood normally. It appeared stunned at first, but shook itself off, licked Jesse's face and scampered away. The *feeling,* which moments earlier had raged through him, was gone.

Jesse turned her confused gaze to Jason. She opened her mouth to speak, but no words came. He didn't know what to say, but knew he had to offer some explanation. It was in the open now; she had seen it with her own eyes.

"Jesse, we need to talk."

Sixteen

It was the kind of night the ER staff hated, and loved. The department was fueled on adrenaline, nerve, and black coffee. The nurses' power walked through the department and tried to keep up with doctors' orders and their patients' needs. Life and death decisions were made every few minutes in an atmosphere that didn't allow time for deliberation or second-guessing.

The ER was filled to far beyond capacity, and extra gurneys lined the halls. Rooster, Jason, and Larry were working at top speed, with ten RNs and a few ER techs. They needed at least another five RNs just to have the minimum staff they needed, but that wasn't going to happen tonight. Jeff Noles, the charge nurse, moved his staff and their patients like a conductor orchestrating a symphony. Despite orders and responses shouted over the din, there was no perceivable panic. Rooster ran a tight ER and didn't tolerate any break from the expected level of professionalism. Panic led to mistakes, and mistakes could kill people very quickly on a night like this.

The strobe light over the communications desk gave the first warning. It was followed in a few seconds by an unmistakable hammering gong, announcing a level one trauma. In a few seconds, the radio settled any doubt as to what was about to happen.

"Harborline, Harborline, this is Medic One. Stand by for report on a level one trauma."

Jeff slid into the chair at the communications desk and flipped the radio receiver open, allowing the ER staff to hear the report at the same time he talked to the medic unit.

"This is Harborline. Go Medic One." Jeff's voice was two tones higher than usual and gave a clue to the stress that the alarm had ignited.

"We are two minutes out with an approximately twenty-five year-old white male. Patient is a police officer with a GSW to the left chest. Weapon was reportedly a large caliber handgun at close range. Patient is currently decreased LOC, but awake. BP is eighty over sixty and falling. Pulse 140 and irregular. Respirations are rapid and labored, absent on the left. We have two large bore IVs running normal saline wide open. We are arriving at your location now."

"Harborline copies," Jeff said almost as an afterthought as he vaulted out of the chair. They could already hear the siren at the far end of the hospital parking lot. One of the nurses had rolled the patient from Trauma One into the hallway. Another gurney was coming back to the department, empty from a patient who had just been admitted.

"Move that gurney into Trauma One," Jeff signaled to the nurse pushing the bed.

Overhead, the hospital-wide page repeated, "Code Trauma ER, Code Trauma ER, Code Trauma ER." Rooster and Jason simultaneously moved toward the trauma room. A police officer with a gunshot wound to the chest called for the full court press. At the door, Jason paused and waited for Rooster to go in first. He knew Rooster was running this trauma code.

"Jason, get set up to intubate. I'll get the chest tube, and we'll go from there." The nursing staff was already tearing open the equipment trays they needed for both procedures.

"Jeff, get the thoracotomy tray and a rib spreader, just in case we need to crack his chest." Rooster mentally ran through anything he might need when the patient arrived.

The words triggered an adrenaline rush that surged through Jason's body. Was it the *feeling?* He wasn't certain, but he would know soon enough. "God, no," he said to himself. "Don't let it be happening again."

"Where's the lab tech?" Rooster asked.

A frightened young woman raised her hand. Rooster looked straight at her as he checked her name tag, and recognized the kid was scared. "This is just like any other case, Angie. Someone will pass the blood tubes off to you. Just label them and run for the lab. I'll tell you whether I want type specific or type O blood. Whichever I order, you get it fast, okay?" Rooster smiled, and she shook her head up and down. "That's my girl." He patted her arm as he walked away. Rooster was a pro at instilling confidence and calming his staff.

The doors to the trauma room imploded as the medics blasted through them with their gurney. Both medics had one hand on the gurney while they squeezed a bag of IV fluid with their other hand. They were both covered in sweat, more from the stress than the physical labor of what they were doing. Rooster moved to the head of the ambulance cot while they prepared to transfer the patient onto the ER gurney. The young officer's face was ashen, and his eyes were half closed, like a child fighting sleep. His shirt was torn open revealing a blood-soaked bulky dressing, which had been hastily taped to his left chest. His torso was smeared red, and his uniform shirt was soaked bloody black.

"Shit, no vest," Rooster said.

"Yeah, some of the guys don't wear them in the summer," the medic replied.

Jeff called the numbers, and they lifted the young officer to the ER gurney. The nurses moved quickly through their routine, connected the patient to the monitor, and moved IV bags. Rooster wedged in between two nurses at the side of the gurney and listened for breath sounds with his stethoscope; there was nothing on the left. He lifted the blood-saturated dressing and found what he didn't want to see: a bullet entrance wound over the heart. "Have lab get me ten units of type O blood." Rooster gave the knee-jerk order. The young cop watched him through eyes rapidly blurring toward unconsciousness.

Rooster nodded to Jason, standing at the head of the gurney. "Do it," he said.

Rooster started to turn away when he heard the muffled words from the cop. "Time for payback."

Rooster stopped and leaned closer to hear the words. "Lloyd said you'd pay me back someday if I didn't write that ticket."

Rooster looked at the cop's name badge: "Hughes." It took a few seconds before the name registered. "Well, Officer Hughes, that's exactly the way it works. Today I get to save your life." Rooster smiled.

"I'm counting on you, Doc. I've got a wife and a new baby at home." Rooster could barely hear the words.

"A deal's a deal. Time for me to go to work. You get some rest, and we'll talk later." Rooster couldn't have sounded calmer if he were chatting about the weather.

Jeff spoke up. "BP forty over nothing, we're losing him."

Rooster turned to the surgical stand behind him and pulled on sterile gloves. "Jason, get him tubed. His entrance wound is directly over the heart. We're going to crack him right now or we'll never have a chance."

A nurse responded to the order and pushed 100 mg of succinylcholine into the IV line to paralyze the patient. Jason slid the laryngoscope blade into the young cop's mouth and down his throat until he could see the vocal cords. He suctioned out the airway and spotted the gap between the cords, slid the ET tube home, and inflated the balloon to secure the airway. The respiratory tech fitted the Ambu bag into place and started breathing for the now unconscious and chemically paralyzed patient. The process took less than thirty seconds.

"He's all yours, Rooster." Jason signaled the intubation was done. He could feel the familiar adrenaline rush, but nothing more. He prayed it stayed that way.

Rooster was ready. A splash of antiseptic solution trickled down the side of the cop's exposed chest and Rooster quickly picked out his landmarks. He slid the scalpel over the chest, just under the fifth rib, and opened a gash that extended around the cop's chest. The second arc of the scalpel penetrated into the chest cavity and released a flood of dark blood which rolled over Rooster's scrub pants and shoes. "Tell lab to get me that blood right the fuck now." His voice was still calm but the blood splashing around his feet emphasized his urgency.

"Jason, see if you can get a central line in his femoral vein," Rooster ordered, more than asked.

"Spreader!" Rooster's commands became precise. He slid the rib spreader inside the gaping hole in his patient's chest and ratcheted it open, wide enough for him to reach the heart.

"Rooster, we've got no BP and his beats are stretching out to an agonal rhythm," Jason said from his position across the table.

"I've got his heart in my hand. I'm doing internal compressions, but it's flaccid. I need some blood." Rooster's voice was physically labored as he spoke from his position, bent over with his right arm buried almost to his elbow in the young cop's chest.

A nurse hurried into the trauma room with two bags of blood. Jeff spiked an IV line into the first bag and slid it into a pressure transfuser while a second nurse repeated the process with the second bag.

"I can feel the hole in his ventricle. Get me some 3-0 Tevdek on a long needle driver. And tell the lab to send me the rest of the blood now!"

"The lab says they can only release two units at a time," the nurse who had brought the blood answered.

Rooster took the loaded needle driver and guided it into the chest. This was almost a blind procedure, over sewing a hole in the barely beating heart. "You tell the lab that Rooster says to send the rest of that blood right now, or else." There was no need for him to finish the threat.

Jason finished threading a large bore IV into the right femoral vein in the patient's groin, and Jeff spiked another bag of normal saline and squeezed, forcing IV fluid through the tubing.

"We're in V-fib," one of the nurses called out.

Rooster strained, still working blindly. "I've got it." He tightened a second knot in his suture and then a third. "Okay, I've got the hole in the heart closed, but it's still flaccid."

A nurse ran into the room with what seemed like an armful of blood bags. Three nurses grabbed the bags and locked them into pressure transfusers.

"Apparently the lab knows you, Rooster," Jeff joked.

Rooster ignored him. "Push an amp of Epi and give me the internal paddles. We're running out of time."

The med nurse pushed the drug into the IV line while Rooster slid the internal defibrillator paddles into the chest and held them against the heart. The mini shock from the paddles placed directly on the heart muscle had no effect except on the cardiac monitor. The tracer line jumped across the screen but returned to the bizarre, saw-toothed fibrillation pattern. Rooster continued compressing the heart inside the open chest of his patient, but felt no blood inside the empty bag of muscle.

"You've got six units of blood and three liters of fluid on board, Rooster. Are you seeing any change in the heart?" Jason asked.

"I've still got nothing. Something's wrong."

"Rooster, we've got a lot of fresh blood still coming out of the chest." Jeff pointed to the growing pool of crimson fluid around Rooster's feet.

"Swing a light down and let me see what's going on inside the chest."

Rooster withdrew his arm and stepped back. Jeff brought the overhead surgical light down and pointed the beam through the gaping incision. Rooster lifted the lung aside and revealed the human heart hidden deep inside the gaping chest. The surface was glistening wet with blood, but the hole in the front of the heart was dry around his stitches.

"There," Rooster said defeated. "He's bleeding behind the heart. The bullet must have gone through." He lifted the heart exposing a large ragged hole on the hidden back side of the organ. "We can't fix that," Rooster said, his voice detached. They stood for a moment, staring at the dead heart.

"We're done folks. Call the code at 21:18," Rooster glanced up at the wall clock.

The room became quiet and started to clear as the nurses moved back to the care of other patients. Rooster stepped back and peeled off his surgical gloves.

"He should have given me a ticket."

Jason stood looking at the face of the young cop, distracted. "You say something, Rooster?"

"Yeah. He should have given me the ticket. I didn't keep my end of the deal." His voice modulated between anger and grief.

Jason returned his gaze to the young cop's face, which was now passive and without expression. He was aware of an inner peace, far removed from the dread he had experienced earlier.

"Rooster, you mind if I put on some gloves and get the feel of his heart? It's been awhile since I cracked a chest on a GSW to the heart."

"Be my guest. I don't think he'll mind," he said as he turned to his paperwork on the counter.

Jason slid his gloved hand into the still warm chest cavity and gently squeezed the heart. It remained still and flaccid in his hand. He withdrew his hand, glanced over his shoulder at Rooster, who was still writing in the chart, and placed his hand against the cop's neck. Nothing happened. He closed his eyes and concentrated his energy on the body in front of him. The *feeling* wasn't there.

"You okay?" Rooster was watching him now. "You looked like you were praying or something."

Jason pulled his hand away, startled. "Yeah, just trying to picture some anatomy."

"I'm going to find the family. This should be fun. We've got a heck of a life," Rooster said sarcastically.

"What?" Jason answered, still preoccupied.

"I said, I'm having sex with your wife. Are you okay?" Rooster sounded irritated.

Jason tried to focus. "Yeah, fine."

Rooster left the trauma room without looking back.

Jason started to reach for the dead cop again but stopped. *What the hell am I doing?* He asked himself.

He peeled his bloody gloves, tossed them toward the trash can, and walked away from the young cop's body, leaving it alone in the empty room. This death, like most, was permanent.

SEVENTEEN

The blood pooling behind Jason's eardrums threatened to explode with each spike-driven beat of the song. "In-A-Gadda-Da-Vida" jackhammered through the car. The lurid opus suited his mood perfectly. His shift had run long, and it was after midnight. He should have been exhausted, but his adrenaline-saturated brain pushed him into the night. Jason could still feel the young cop's heart in his hand and could almost imagine the organ beating to the pulse of the music.

Sometimes, death was an incredibly abstract entity, something vague and without form. But sometimes it was more tangible. It could be nearly palpable in the air around him as if he could see it and grasp it in his hands. Death was the ever-present enemy to be battled and conquered. Other times, Jason felt he could more subtly outsmart death, and cheat the specter of a victim. He liked the sensation of defeating death, but he knew any victory, no matter how hard-fought or dramatic, was only a temporary reprieve for anyone. Nonetheless, that feeling of victory was a power trip, which left him heady and swaggering like a teenager who had just won the big game. Unfortunately, the reverse was also true. Losing left him feeling conquered, and no amount of rationalization or excuses could take away the feeling of losing to death. It was a sensation that had to wear itself out like a windstorm, leaving him to try again. Jason took losing personally. Technically, this was Rooster's loss, not his, but he felt it just as much.

Different doctors took a patient's death in different ways. Some grieved with the family, then some shrugged it off, as if it were some insignificant part of their job. Some physicians got angry about a fatal outcome. Rooster unquestionably fell into this group and took each lost patient as a professional affront, an insult that demanded satisfaction.

Jesse was doing a night shift as a favor to a friend, and Jason didn't feel like going back to their empty town house. It was just as well. Things had been uneasy since their trip to the San Juans. After the incident with the fawn, they had talked for hours. He had tried to explain, and she tried to understand, but without much success. She had an excuse, a rationalization, for everything that had happened before that day: he had been stressed, overtired, burned out — things weren't what they seemed. She assured him everything would return to normal, and he would understand. She was even sure the fawn had been stunned and not actually dead. He wasn't sure whether she was trying to convince him or herself, but he knew he wasn't satisfied. Now she was treating him as if he was more than slightly unstable — just what he hadn't wanted. Hell, he couldn't be sure he wasn't delusional, but he knew he didn't like Jesse thinking he was crazy.

Jason went to his phone's contacts list and called Jesse's floor at the hospital. Another nurse told him she was busy in a delivery, and he left a message that he was going out for a while. He turned the music up, accelerated quickly, and savored the feeling of power at his demand. The wind rushed through the topless roadster, aiding his escape. He exited the interstate and slowed slightly as he rolled down the exit ramp. The light at the bottom of the ramp turned green ahead of him, and he accelerated again, the engine responded immediately to the pressure of his foot on the accelerator. He shifted up a gear, settled back into his seat, and turned onto a winding street, headed for the beach area near the outskirts of the city. The muffled skyline fell away behind him, and the brisk night air from the sound met him, enticing him toward the water like the promise of a lover. He drove like this for almost an hour, pushing the sports car and decompressing until he felt the tension drain from his mind and body. His grip on the steering wheel relaxed as his psyche calmed.

By the time he took notice of his surroundings, he realized he was lost. The lights behind him told him he was on one of the points that jutted into the Sound, but he had no idea which one. In the distance ahead, he saw neon lights, which announced The Safe House. He had heard of the nightspot, a favorite place for the young, affluent set to network, but he and Jesse had never been there.

Jason pulled into the nearly empty parking lot and walked inside. The décor was a mixture of a seventeenth-century office theme, and a scene from a *Twilight Zone* knockoff. Thankfully, the dimly lit bar area was almost empty. He found a stool at the far end of the bar, ordered a Pimm's Cup, and asked for a menu. He lit a cigarette, gazed at the reflections on the waters of the Sound, and tried to relax.

"Excuse me, Dr. Corey?" A vaguely familiar voice accompanied a hand on his shoulder, and a pleasing sensation enveloped him as he recognized the source.

"Miss Black. I wasn't expecting to see you out this late." He blushed at the inanity of his response.

"Believe it or not, Doctor, I'm a big girl and get to stay out as late as I want," she teased, letting him off the hook.

She purposefully stepped into full view in front of him, revealing her short black dress, cut low across her breasts. Her stiletto heels accentuated her entire figure, especially her legs. The outfit left little doubt about her motives in a place like this.

"I can see that," he stumbled again. "I just meant that I assume most normal people are home in bed by the time I finish a swing shift." He grimaced and bit his lip. "Not that you're not a normal person because you're not in bed, I mean at home . . ." he stammered and shook his head. "I'm sorry Miss Black, I seem to be a little flustered tonight." He felt an intense blush spread across his face.

She sat down on the stool next to him. "Please, it's Sheri. Do you mind if I join you?" Her smile was captivating, but he had to concentrate to keep his attention on her face rather than her cleavage.

"Please. Can I get you a drink? And it's Jason."

"Jason, that would be great. I'll have a dry martini, neat." She shifted on the stool and moved closer to him. Her dress slid a few inches higher, exposing more of her thighs.

"So, what brings you to The Safe House at this hour?" She turned towards him and touched his leg with her knee.

"I just finished a very long shift and needed some air. I kind of wandered in this direction and got lost."

"I heard about the shooting. News travels fast in my business. Things like that must be hard on a doctor." She held the long-stemmed glass cupped in her hand and sipped her drink.

He hesitated. "Is this on or off the record?" He asked cautiously.

"I'm not all business, Jason. If I'm on the record, I'll tell you. I promise I'm not the monster that I'm sure Rooster made me out to be." She toyed with her olive and watched him through deep, dark eyes.

Jason had met many women, but none as blatantly seductive as the one in front of him now. Every movement of her body, every inflection of her voice, exuded a sultry sensuality, which he knew was directed at him at this moment. He watched her slide the olive off the stir stick from her drink, hold it in her lips, and slowly bite it in half while she stared directly into his eyes.

Jason cleared his throat. "You have to know Rooster to understand him. He just has very strong feelings about some things," he laughed. "Actually, about a lot of things."

"So tell me, is there a Mrs. Corey at home?" She asked as she took his left hand and rubbed her thumb over his ring finger.

He liked her touch. He liked a lot of things about her; things that made him feel at ease and appreciated. "Not yet, but I am engaged."

She tilted her head slightly to the side. "Let me guess, a perky blonde pediatrics nurse who was your high school sweetheart." Her smile taunted him, but she kept his hand, slowly rubbing it with her thumb.

Her words made his love for Jesse sound less than what it was — stereotyped and common. He shifted slightly and took a drink. "Actually, she's an OB nurse, and we met during my residency."

She nodded, and her lips formed a slight smirk, but she didn't respond.

"And you? I assume there isn't a Mr. Black."

"No. I'm looking for something very special." She emptied her glass and twirled it toward him by the stem.

Jason signaled the bartender and pointed to her empty glass.

"Let me guess, you want a real go-getter, an aggressive, strong, take-charge kind of guy on the fast track. Somebody who says what he means and means what he says. Nerves of steel, quick thinker who makes important decisions all day long without breaking a sweat." He grinned and lit a cigarette.

"Mmm. You are very perceptive." She emphasized each measured word. "Know anybody who meets the bill?" She took a sip, watching him over the rim of her fresh martini.

This was moving too far, too fast. "So when would you like to do your story?" He moved back slightly in his chair.

"You name the time, and I'll be there."

"I work day shift on Wednesday. Why don't you come down, and I'll see if I can get some material for you?"

"Sounds good to me," she answered coyly.

She finished her drink and started to stand. "This has been great, but I'd better find my ride." She stood and leaned toward him, her breath warm on the side of his face. "Wednesday it is," she whispered into his ear, brushing his face with her lips, and leaving her perfume on his collar. As she turned away, her purse dropped to the floor beside his chair. He was too stunned by her intimacy to think fast enough to pick it up for her, and by the time it registered, she had already crouched beside him to retrieve the bag. She paused and looked up, presenting an unavoidable view down the front of her dress and her exposed, bare breasts. He pulled his head back, surprised, but she had already looked up into his eyes. She smiled and slowly stood. He watched her leave, aware that his body was responding to her. She walked away from him, one foot precisely in front of the other, her legs and rump high-heel taught. Her motions were slow and graceful, like a predatory cat in her jungle.

Jason lit another cigarette and sat back to finish his drink. She was in his head, and they both knew it. Thoughts of Jesse prodded from the edge of his mind, but he chose not to allow her in right now. He crushed out his cigarette and started to stand when he became aware of her perfume again, and felt her at his side.

"I'm truly sorry, but it seems my ride left without me. Could I possibly bother you for a lift back to the city? If you're headed that way?" She added.

He knew he didn't have a choice, but he also knew he was glad she was back. Her warmth beside him was almost more than he could take. "I'd be happy to drop you off." This time he locked onto her eyes.

He escorted her through the club and noticed her glance toward a table where three attractive young women watched them pass. He thought he detected a knowing look pass between them, but he didn't care. She held his arm as he walked her to his car and watched her slide into the seat, making no attempt to hold down the hem of her dress. She kicked her shoes off and tucked her legs beneath her.

"Very nice." She slid her hand across the back of the leather seat. "I took you for the foreign sports car type of guy."

"Would you like the top up or down?" He reached for the control panel.

She took his hand. "No, down is just fine. Where's your CD case?"

He reached under her seat and handed her the leather case. He started the car and pulled out of the parking lot while she flipped through the CDs, made her choice, and slipped a disc into the player. George Thorogood's "Bad to the Bone" exploded from the speakers. She directed him to the highway, and he pushed the car through the night. He watched her immerse herself in the sound and the wind. Her long dark hair blowing behind her as she laid her head back and closed her eyes, her face turned to the night sky. He had never experienced a woman like this — this wild child. And he liked what he saw.

He pulled to a stop in front of her apartment and left the engine running.

"Oh no," she scolded. "Let me at least pay you back with a drink." She turned the key off and pulled him from the car, then led him to her apartment. The warmth of her home surprised him. It wasn't the ultra modern, stainless steel coldness he had expected. She dropped her shoes and directed him to the bar. "You know what I'm drinking," she said and disappeared into her bedroom.

He mixed her drink, made a gin and tonic for himself, then wandered to her balcony and looked out at the view of downtown Seattle and the Space Needle. From this location, the city looked like an immense backdrop of lights and life, full of activity even at this time of night. He stood there, immersed in the excitement of the city, smoked a cigarette, and nursed his drink until he heard her return and pick up her glass. The little black dress was gone, replaced by a black, silk sleep-shirt that barely covered her bottom. He briefly wondered if she was wearing anything beneath it. His question was answered when she walked to the stereo and bent from the waist to turn on the music, exposing her toned cheeks accented by a black thong.

The sultry sounds of a lamenting tenor saxophone oozed through the room. She dimmed the lights and walked to him slowly, stalking him. He dropped onto the couch and sat back, watching, unable to stop her or himself. She came to him, straddled his lap, and moved her hands over him, her nails clawing softly under his shirt. Her perfumed hair fell across his face as she kissed him with full, soft lips, her tongue penetrating. She methodically unbuttoned the silk top and let her breasts fall to him. Any remaining resistance vanished, and he lost all resolve as he responded to her. His fingertips swept across her silken skin, and she shuddered at his touch. She rolled back onto the couch, brought her knees to her chest and discarded the thong in a single fluid motion. As his body pressed against her, lightning flashed in his mind and left the afterimage of Jesse's face burning in his brain.

EIGHTEEN

Jason's guilt accused him and tortured his sleep. He stirred when Jesse, home from her night shift, snuggled against him, her bare skin next to his. He wrapped his arms around her but felt uneasy. Somehow, she felt different, almost foreign to him. At last, he gave in and eased himself out of bed. He glanced out the slider window at the sun, nearly at the zenith of its arc in the sky. The day was half-gone.

He brewed a pot of coffee and moved to the balcony, his body and mind stressed from a night of broken half-sleep. But the coffee and cigarettes did little to calm his nerves. He had decided it was time to get some answers.

Jason found the tape recorder in the desk and checked to make sure the tape hadn't been erased. He looked in on Jesse before he left, and found her curled up in her blankets, holding her pillow like a lover. He stood and watched her, his emotions roiling in his gut. She looked more than tired; she looked pale and exhausted. He left a note saying he'd be back in a few hours and left.

The day was warm and sunny, but he sensed the earliest hint of crispness in the air — a forewarning of things to come. Their summer was like an outgoing tide, and his thoughts hung briefly on the bleak winter ahead. There was no way he could have known the extent of the darkness before of him.

Traffic was light for Seattle. He threaded his way to the campus of the University of Washington and found the Foreign Language Building. Parking was always a problem at the U, but he finally found a visitors' parking area and walked several blocks back to the Language Building. Jason hadn't taken a foreign language in college, but he had gotten the name of the chairman of the language department. He climbed the three flights of stairs and hunted for the room number he had found listed on the directory at the building's entrance. The hike to the building and the stair climbing left him winded. He stopped to look out over Lake Washington through the glass front building, and watched several sailboats while he rested. He worked to catch his breath, and told himself again he should give up cigarettes. *Yeah, right*, he thought.

It felt strange to be back on campus at the U. He hadn't been in any of the campus buildings for years. Surprisingly for someone who had spent half his life in school, he had never truly liked college. He liked learning, but the extra stress of worrying about grades — not just passing, but grades which would get him into medical school — had been a constant presence looming over him. College had not been an enjoyable time for Jason.

The plaque on the door read, "Dr. James Perry, Ph.D." Jason's knock was answered by a low voice, which invited him inside.

"Dr. Perry, I'm Jason Corey. I spoke with you recently about a tape I have."

Jason extended his hand and was surprised by the strength in the grip of the slight, middle-aged man.

"Yes, Dr. Corey, it's very nice to meet you. Please have a seat." He motioned Jason toward a high-backed leather chair in front of his tidy desk. "So, tell me about this tape of yours."

Jason had decided to reveal as little information as possible about his recording. "There really isn't much to tell. A family member recorded it while he was traveling abroad on a trip through several countries. It was mixed in with several other tracks, and they couldn't remember where it was made or what it was from. I was curious and decided to see if someone could identify it for me."

Dr. Perry looked somewhat dubious about the explanation, but finally spoke. "Well let's hear it and see." The professor sat back in his chair, ran his hand through his thinning hair, and waited.

Jason placed the recorder on the desk and pushed the play button. There were the words and sounds he had heard the first time he listened to the tape, in a voice still completely foreign to him. The tape played through and ended in a static hiss.

"Yes, it's a language all right. You can tell that by the voice inflection. Almost like the person is reading or speaking from memory. I can recognize some words, which are similar to a few Near Eastern languages, but that's about it. I think I know who may be able to help you though." He picked up his phone and dialed. "One of the world's experts on Eastern and ancient dialects is on staff here. He only works a few days a month now, but I heard someone say he might be around this week."

The phone rang on the other end without answer, but Dr. Perry seemed unconcerned with the delay. "Sometimes Sol only answers if he thinks you won't go away otherwise," he said, smirking. After what seemed minutes, he finally connected. "Sol, this is Jim Perry. How are you?" He spoke loudly. "Good. Listen, Sol, I have a doctor here who has an interesting tape he's trying to decipher. It sounds like a dialect that's up your alley. Do you have a few minutes?" He listened and rolled his eyes. "I'll tell him that you're rushed, Sol, but I'm sure it won't take you long. I'll send him right up."

Jason raised his eyebrows, questioning. "He doesn't seem too happy about it."

"No, he's fine. Sol just likes people to think he's always busy. Actually he's a wonderful man."

Jason followed directions to the sixth floor and found the office door marked, "Dr. Solomon Rosenthal, Ph.D.," and knocked. A strong voice from the other side answered, "What is it?"

Jason opened the door and started to introduce himself to the professor.

"Dr. Rosenthal, I'm — "

"I don't have time for student meetings today," he said, cutting Jason off. The portly man was dwarfed behind a huge desk piled with papers and open books. Several tufts of white hair stuck out at oblique angles, partially pushed awry by a pair of reading glasses jammed on top of his head. He briefly glanced up at Jason, then motioned him away with his hand. "Maybe tomorrow, but I'm too busy today. Good-bye."

"Ah, Dr. Rosenthal, I'm Dr. Corey. Dr. Perry called about me a few minutes ago."

The man stopped bustling for a moment, trying to remember. "You're a doctor? A doctor of what? You're too young to be a doctor."

Jason suppressed a smile and eased into the office, which was as messy in its entirety as the desk. "I'm a medical doctor, sir."

"And what does a medical doctor want to know about languages?" He slowed his activity only slightly.

Jason repeated the story he had given earlier, and tried to find a place for the tape recorder on the desk. Dr. Rosenthal finally pushed a stack of papers aside. "Well, let's hear what you have." The old man sat back and folded his arms.

Jason ran the tape again, slightly louder this time for the benefit of the aged professor. The old teacher moved to a corner of his desk and sat as he listened intently. "Ah-huh," he injected and laughed. "Yeah. Yeah." He pointed at the recorder.

Jason started to speak and received an immediate and stern "SHHHSH" from the professor. He hadn't been shushed in an awfully long time but decided to take the directive.

The tape finished, but the old man didn't look up or speak except to say, "Again please." Jason rewound the tape and started it over.

"You see, right there, that's not right." He continued to listen. "And there," he laughed. "Or maybe . . ." He furrowed his bushy white eyebrows as he climbed a small ladder to the top of his bookshelf, and pulled down a heavy dust-covered volume. The reading glasses dropped into place unaided, and he thumbed through several pages until he found what he was searching for. "Interesting," he half mumbled and snapped the book shut. The tape finished again, and Jason flipped the player off and waited.

"Young man, either you are playing a joke on me or someone is playing a joke on you. Either way, I don't have time for such nonsense. Please close the door behind you." He returned to his desk and started searching through a stack of papers.

"Dr. Rosenthal, I assure you this is no joke. My father is a retired professor from this very university, and I would no more waste your time with a joke than I would waste his time."

The old man looked up. "Corey, Corey. Arthur Corey is your father?"

"Yes, sir."

He looked Jason over, measuring him. "All right Dr. Corey, suppose you start by telling me the truth about this tape. Where and when was it made and by whom?" He asked tersely.

"I'll answer that question on the condition the information never leaves this office." Jason waited for a reply.

"I'm not certain I can agree to that, Dr. Corey. The source of this tape, if authentic, could have enormous significance and value. I can assure you that any information will not be released to the public or the news media. I'm not after publicity."

Jason considered his options. He felt he could trust the old man, but he still wasn't certain. "I'll trust you, doctor, and I hope you won't let me down."

Dr. Rosenthal waited, chewing on one of the temples of his glasses.

"That recording was made a few weeks ago in my home. That's me speaking," Jason explained.

The old linguist pulled a face. "Then you know exactly what you were reading, and what the language is. This is a joke after all! I will admit that your pronunciation is excellent. Where did you study?"

"I didn't study anyplace, and I've never heard that language before. I was talking in my sleep."

The professor erupted. "You take me for a fool, an old fool? I assure you, young man, I am no fool." He stood over his desk shouting. "Now take your joke tape and get out before I call campus security." His white hair seemed to stand more on end, as if electrically charged, and his body trembled.

Defeated, Jason stood to leave. As he turned to go, the old man turned pale, clutched his chest, and dropped heavily back into his chair. Jason moved through the office clutter to the professor's side and felt the old man's irregular, thready pulse. "I'll call an ambulance."

Dr. Rosenthal protested weakly. "No, there's nitroglycerin in my jacket pocket." He pointed toward his office door.

Jason dug through the worn jacket pockets, and finally, beneath a pipe and several pieces of scrap paper, found the small brown glass bottle of nitroglycerin pills. He shook one into his hand, returned to the desk and pushed the pill under the professor's tongue. Color slowly returned to the old man's face, and his pulse became regular and strengthened, as the crisis passed.

"Are you sure you don't want me to call an ambulance?" Jason asked.

The old man pulled himself straighter in his chair and made an attempt to smooth his hair into place, without success. "No, I'm all right. I have these spells sometimes. My wife warns me about losing control of my temper, but I have yet to listen."

Jason gathered the tape recorder. "I'll be leaving then if you're sure you'll be all right." He turned to go.

"Wait, please. Jason was it? I may have been hasty. You don't behave like someone here to play jokes on an old man." His voice had softened. "I've known your father for a long time. Not well, unfortunately, but everything I know of him tells me that he would raise a good boy. I should have known better." He motioned Jason back to his chair. "Let's listen to that tape again."

"Are you sure you're all right, sir? Maybe another day would be better?" Jason offered, still not sure if he should call an ambulance.

The old man nodded and motioned to the tape recorder. Jason played the entire tape again while the old man listened intently and periodically nodded. When it had finished, he looked at Jason, his eyes probing as if he were seeking a solution. He watched Jason for a reaction, then finally spoke.

"The language on this tape is Aramaic," he said. "Do you know what that is?"

"No, sir, not to the best of my knowledge."

"It's an ancient language that goes back approximately three thousand years, one of the Semitic languages. Today it's spoken in some form by small pockets of the population, mainly in Syria, Turkey, Iraq, and Iran. But it hasn't been spoken in the form on your tape for over two thousand years. Now, it's used in the form of Syrian Aramaic. The form on this tape, called Old Aramaic, was in use between about 975 B.C. and 700 B.C. We know this from ancient scrolls that have been translated." He paused, waiting for some reaction from Jason.

"Dr. Rosenthal, this sounds pretty far-fetched. You're telling me that I'm speaking an ancient dead language in my sleep?" He asked skeptically. "Doctor, I didn't even take a foreign language in college, and I've certainly never studied anything even close to this. As a matter of fact, if doctors were still required to learn Latin, I'd be in another line of work."

"The mind is a very complex thing, Jason. I would suppose that in certain sleep states, people might remember things much as they would under hypnosis," he said more as a question than a statement.

"This just doesn't seem possible to me. What am I saying on this tape, anyway?"

"The tape starts at about the middle of the Lord's Prayer. The pause is at the beginning of a fable, the story of Belshazzar's feast and the handwriting on the wall."

"I'm sorry, Doctor. I was raised Lutheran and know the Lord's Prayer, of course, but I'm afraid my Sunday school days are a bit far back."

"Here, listen to this and see if it sounds at all familiar." He flipped the tape on and they listened. *"El-a-lum all-meen. A-men."* He looked at Jason expectantly.

Jason shrugged. "Nothing. Gibberish."

"It means forever and ever, amen."

They sat quietly without a word between them. Finally, Jason stood and gathered up the tape recorder.

"What are you going to do now, Jason?" The old man's voice was benevolent.

"I don't know, Dr. Rosenthal. I don't know."

"Perhaps hypnosis could provide some answers, or possibly a psychiatrist could help you sort some of this out. You have several channels open to you."

Jason extended his hand. "I'll think about it. There are a few other things I need to settle right now. Thank you for your help, Doctor. You're sure you're all right?"

"Yes, yes, I'll be fine. However, I might ask the same question of you," he said as he shook Jason's hand. "Just one more thing. Is there any chance I could convince you to leave that tape with me? I assure you, it won't leave my possession."

Jason snapped the recorder open and handed the tape over. "I'll trust you, Doctor."

"I'll be extremely careful with it. It's not every day an old professor has the opportunity to hear the language of Jesus of Nazareth in its natural and original form." He held the tape up.

Jason stopped. "Jesus? I thought Jesus spoke Hebrew."

"Oh, no, young man. Jesus spoke Aramaic."

Jason walked back to his car in a state of bewilderment, barely aware of the world around him. He didn't see the parking ticket on his windshield blow away when he drove off, narrowly missing another car as he pulled out of the parking lot. A young man in a small pickup truck yelled something at him and gestured with his middle finger, but Jason was unaware.

Dr. Rosenthal sat rocking slowly in his leather chair, and tapped the tape against his chin. After several minutes, he decisively leaned forward, picked up the phone, and dialed the department secretary.

"Hazel, this is Dr. Rosenthal. Would you check with the faculty office and see if you can find the home number of a Dr. Arthur Corey, please? You can call me back when you have it. Thank you, Hazel."

NINETEEN

Pain comes in many flavors: sharp, burning, cramping, and a dozen others. Jesse's pain was menacing. Her pain, while not her friend, had become her constant companion, and greeted her in the same instant she opened her eyes every morning. She slid her hand to Jason's side of the bed and felt only the coldness of being alone. The bedroom, washed in the cool colors of twilight, did little to comfort her as she forced herself from the bed and walked sleepily to the bathroom, her eyes half-closed against the light. She sat down on the commode and winced as she relaxed her muscles to empty her bladder.

She stood and reached for her terry robe hanging on the door as she turned on the light switch. The brightness revealed her reflection in the bathroom mirror, but the face that looked back at her was pale with lifeless, hollow eyes. She looked away as she slid into her robe and flipped the handle of the commode. She looked down just in time to see the flash of bright bloody water disappear, and in the same instant became aware of a warm sensation inside her thigh. She opened her robe and watched the trickle become a stream of bright blood running down her leg. She grabbed the towel hanging over the shower and pushed it between her legs as a wave of dizziness whirled through her head. She sat down hard on the floor and called out for Jason, but the only response was the stabbing pain deep in her belly. There was no other answer from the empty apartment.

Jason was still reeling from his meeting yesterday with Dr. Rosenthal. The contents of the empty cup of Starbucks on his desk had done little to clear his sleep-deprived mind. He had driven for hours after leaving the University until he finally ended up in a roadside bar for a greasy burger and several drinks. Jesse was in bed, asleep when he had finally arrived home. He had still been too agitated to sleep and had spent the next few hours alone on the balcony, drinking and trying to make some sense out of the madness that had overtaken his life. He had not found any reasonable answers. Sometime after two in the morning, his mind had shut down from the alcohol and fatigue. He washed down two sleeping pills with the gin flavored melted ice from his last drink and stumbled into bed. Jesse hadn't stirred and was still sleeping soundly when he got up at five a.m. for his day shift.

Jason's hangover and fatigue were seasoned with a heavy dose of guilt. He hadn't called Jesse last night to let her know he was going to be late or even to let her know he was all right. He knew she was going to be pissed, and rightfully so. He reminded himself to call her later. His mood and physical condition left him less than empathetic to his patients this morning. He hoped the caffeine and Tylenol he had taken would kick in soon and improve matters, but so far, he was still waiting.

A hand on his shoulder interrupted his thoughts.

"I see you're working hard today." Peter Loft, the chief OB/GYN resident, said as he pulled up a stool and rolled over to the desk.

"Geez, an OB doctor in the ER. What's the occasion?" Jason sparred in return.

Peter smirked. "I heard there was an ER doc down here near death who needed someone to cover his back. You look like shit."

Jason rubbed his left temple and shook his head. "Don't go there."

"Oh, this younger generation. When will they learn?" Peter laughed.

"Isn't there a vaginal bleed somewhere that needs a stat D&C, or a postpartum depression who needs to cry on her OB doctor's shoulder?" Jason countered.

"Ouch," Peter responded in mock injury. "Actually, I stopped down to send a message home with you for Jesse." Jason's mind focused quickly. "Tell her that I do exams on patients on their periods all the time, and to please keep her appointment."

Jason's face twisted in confusion. "What the hell are you talking about?" He answered, his voice touched with impatience.

"No big deal, but Jesse called this morning and canceled another appointment. She said she was on her period."

"Wait, how many appointments has she canceled?"

"Ah, today was her third. I assumed you knew about this." Peter backed off slightly.

Jason shook his head in disbelief. "No, I had no idea." He paused and tried to concentrate. "And she said she was on her period? I'm sure she's in the middle of a pill pack. She shouldn't be on her period now."

"Hey, I'm just telling you what she told the clinic secretary when she called this morning. Anyway, I thought it was sort of strange, her being a nurse and all." The senior resident shrugged.

Jason started to answer, when something pulled his attention to the desk behind Peter. Sheri Black stood there quietly, looking demure in a teal sweater dress that did little to hide her figure. Her presence jolted his memory, not only about her interview scheduled for today, but also about their last encounter. He found himself smiling at her, warmed by her presence. Peter realized he had lost his audience, and glanced backward over his shoulder at the target of Jason's attention. He brought his focus back to Jason and raised his eyebrows. "Uh-huh." He emphasized the last syllable.

Jason scowled. "I'll talk to Jesse. I guarantee she'll be at her next appointment."

"Well, I can see you're busy, so I'll get going," he said through a grin.

Jason ignored him and headed toward Sheri. "I see you made it." He pretended he hadn't forgotten their appointment.

She patted the valise hanging over her shoulder. "I'm all set for work."

"Let's take a break outside and we'll decide how we're going to do this."

They headed toward the back deck, and she threaded her arm through his. A wave of exhilaration instantly washed over him in response to her touch and left a warmth in its wake. Jason was unaware of the heads that turned their way as they passed through the department.

They emerged onto the deck, and he freed himself from her grip to light a cigarette. She stood on her toes and kissed his cheek. "I've missed you," she whispered, and hugged his shoulder. Her intimacy surprised him, but his body responded, remembering their tryst only two nights earlier. He fought for control as he created a few inches of breathing room between them.

"So, how would you like to do this today . . . the interview I mean?"

She smiled knowingly and allowed him his space. "Suppose you tell me what you'd like."

He cleared his throat and slowly inhaled his cigarette. "How about if you observe what we do and I'll try and fill in the gaps. Of course, you can't have any patient contact, and I can't discuss any specific patient cases."

She nodded. "That would be fine. Am I allowed to talk to the nurses, or has Rooster made them off limits?"

"I'm sure that would be okay, again without asking for specific patient information."

"I'm ready whenever you are." She reached inside her bag and brought out a yellow legal pad and a tape recorder.

He flipped his cigarette away and smiled. "Let's do it."

Rooster looked up from his desk when they passed his partially open door and met Jason's gaze. Rooster raised his eyebrows, and Jason nodded his confirmation in response.

The morning passed like most days in the ER. Sheri watched, asked questions, and made notes. She attempted to corner any available nurse and get whatever general information she could about the workings of the ER, when Jason was busy. Attempts to go any deeper, especially about Jason or Rooster were fruitless. Whenever her questions became too invasive, the particular nurse seemed to find an excuse to cut things off and hurry off into a patient's room.

Larry Todd came on duty at eleven a.m. Rooster had warned him about Sheri, and he avoided her like his soon-to-be ex-wife's divorce lawyer. The pace gradually built until the ER was running at full capacity, leaving Sheri lost. She could barely make sense out of the apparent chaos, much less understand any method. Jason tried to maintain contact with her and show her what was happening, but before long, he had to leave her to fend for herself. By late afternoon, she was overwhelmed and exhausted. She parked herself at a desk, out of the way, and watched. She was developing a whole new level of respect for what these people did, as well as the pure stamina the job required.

Sheri tried to spend a few minutes alone with Jason through the day, mostly without success. After the night in her apartment, she was confused and more than a little frustrated. She sensed something within him that responded to her on some level, and the more she was around him, the more she knew she wanted him. She sensed something — an element of his being hidden deep below the surface. She was attracted to that quality in a way she had never experienced with any other man. She appreciated his personality, his character, and intellect, but she perceived that somewhere just beyond her reach, something much more cryptic was secreted.

Sheri was thinking about the end of her day, when the trauma code alarm sounded. She recoiled from the sound and her adrenaline level involuntarily surged. She focused on Jason as he moved to the radio desk.

"Harborline, this is Medic One. How do you copy?"

Jason slid behind the desk, opened the mic and responded. "Medic One, this is Harborline. We copy. Go."

"Harborline, we are en route to you with an approximately eighteen-year-old white female, victim of a gunshot wound."

Sheri was aware of a breach in the sudden quiet behind her, as several nurses moved to the main trauma room.

The radio continued. "Patient was a bystander at the site of a gang-related shooting. She has a single wound to the neck, reported by police to be from a 9mm handgun."

Jason's face showed no emotion while he listened to the continuing report. "There was significant blood loss at the scene. Bleeding now controlled. We are unable to intubate patient and currently have bagged respirations. We have two large bore IVs running normal saline."

Jason's lips tightened almost imperceptibly in response to the rest of the report. "Vitals: BP 80/40, pulse 120 with bagged ventilations. Glasgow Coma Score is 1, 1, 4. Our ETA is ten minutes. Do you have any questions?"

Jason's response was immediate. "That's a copy, Medic One. No questions. We'll be ready for you in Trauma One. Harborline clear."

Jason slid from behind the radio desk and headed to the trauma room. Sheri scurried behind him at a distance, unsure what to do, but certain she didn't want to miss the excitement. A surgical gown, protective mask, and gloves were already open and waiting for Jason in the trauma room. Larry peered in briefly from the door. "You okay here, J.C.?"

"Yeah, I've got this, Larry, if you can manage the rest of the department."

"Gotcha covered," Larry said and disappeared through the door, only too happy to be out of the hot seat. Jason spotted Sheri standing out of the way just inside the door.

"Ms. Black, I think you can stay for this if you want." He pointed to the far corner of the trauma room. "Just stay back there and lean against a wall if you feel sick."

She already felt the effect of the adrenaline rush on her body, and she wasn't going to miss this for anything. This was the kind of stuff that sold newspapers.

The team was ready when the ambulance gurney rolled through the doors. The girl was just a kid, but her bloodied face and blood-matted hair hid her age. When the medics lifted her lifeless body onto the ER trauma table, they could see the quarter sized hole, ragged and bruised, on the left side of her neck. The 9mm slug had done an obscene amount of damage, and the rest of her neck was swollen and purple. The nurses went through their routine and hooked the young girl to their monitors and machines while Jason moved to the head of the table. The medic turned his Ambu bag over to a respiratory tech.

"We need to tube her now." Jason's words started a series of actions by nurses and another respiratory tech. In a few seconds, someone slapped a laryngeal scope and Yankauer suction catheter into his hands. The respiratory tech held the endotracheal tube in easy reach of Jason's right hand, while he slid the scope through the young girl's mouth and suctioned the airway. One of the medics spoke up. "I couldn't get a tube in her, Doc. Her airway was just mush."

Jason peered down his patient's throat, suctioned, and muttered an obscenity under his breath. "Nah. This is FUBAR."

He withdrew the scope and suction catheter. "We need to do a crich before she goes T.U." Again, his order triggered a flurry of activity as the nurses set up for a surgical cricothyroidotomy.

Sheri leaned toward a nearby nurse and asked, "What's tea you?"

The nurse smiled. "That's capital T, capital U. Tits Up, honey. You know, like your goldfish?"

"What's our BP?" Jason asked.

"We're at ninety over fifty with two liters of saline in," a nurse replied.

"Get lab in and give me a trauma panel. Type and match six units of packed cells, but give me the first four units type specific as soon as they've got 'em."

Jason shifted to the side of the table near the patient's head. The respiratory tech was still trying to bag the patient, but a fine mist of blood erupted from the hole in the girl's neck with each squeeze of the Ambu bag, like surf against shore rocks.

"Doctor, her pulse-ox is down to 70 percent." The tech called Jason's attention to the pulse oximeter monitoring the patient's oxygen. It was critically below the nearly 100 percent it should have been. Jason knew if the oxygen dropped much lower or stayed down for very long, the patient would have a high risk of brain damage.

Jason pulled on sterile gloves while a nurse rolled a stand with the crich tray next to him, and another nurse quickly swabbed the young girl's throat with antiseptic. Jason held the gleaming scalpel poised in his right hand, felt for his landmarks, then made his incision over the cricothyroid membrane. A thin, bloody line, two inches long, appeared down the center of the young girl's throat. The room had become surprisingly quiet, and Jason heard a faint groan from Sheri where she stood in the corner. He glanced up briefly and saw her leaning against the wall, her face pasty white.

"Would someone get Ms. Black a chair please?" Jason cracked a faint smile and continued his work. He dissected through the bloody, swollen tissue of the neck and finally felt the firm resistance of the thyroid cartilage. He pushed the scalpel into the membrane and turned the blade, opening a hole into his patient's airway. He held the gap in her throat open with a pair of forceps and without looking up, reached out as someone slapped a trach tube into his hand. He slid the tube through the opening and held it in place while the respiratory tech switched the Ambu bag to the trach tube and started ventilating the patient. Jason looked up and watched the numbers on the pulse oximeter slowly start to climb: 80, 84, 89, 94. The tension, which had gripped the room, dropped with each rise in the number and finally broke as the young girl's body responded to the oxygen reaching her lungs and brain.

"Alert the on-call vascular surgeon. She's going to have to go to the OR for an exploration of her neck. What's our BP?" The pressure was off Jason, but his patient was still critical.

"BP is up a little to ninety-five over seventy, Doctor."

"Okay, let's go to X-ray and see where that bullet's hiding. Call the lab and find out where my first unit of blood is," he said as he moved to the patient's head.

He lifted her eyelids and checked to see if her pupils responded to light; they didn't. Maybe she had just gone too long without enough oxygen to her brain. They might not know the answer to that question for days. He was all too aware he might have saved the patient's life, only for her body to survive without a functioning brain. He paused and looked at the blood-spattered face. If it weren't for the blood and the hole in her neck, she would have looked like any other sleeping teenager. But this teenager had just had her childhood abruptly destroyed by a stray bullet from the gun of some punk gangster. Now, she and her family, would pay for that moment for the rest of their lives. He hoped the little piece of street trash who pulled the trigger paid as well. But Jason knew that in the American court system, the shooter would, in all probability, be on the street long before his victim had her life back; if she ever did.

The on-call surgeon hurried into the trauma room and looked at the young girl's neck. "I see the natives are restless tonight," he said.

Jason gave the surgeon a report on the patient while the nursing staff readied her for her trip to X-ray. "I'll take it from here, Jason. Good job. I'll let you know how it turns out." The surgeon spoke over his shoulder as he followed the gurney out the door.

It was over almost as abruptly as it had started. Jason checked in with Larry and headed for the back deck for a cigarette. He was almost out the door when he remembered Sheri and returned to the trauma room. She was still sitting in the chair next to the wall while people cleaned up around her. Some color had returned to her face, but her expression hadn't changed.

Jason leaned over and asked, "I'm headed out for a cigarette. You want some fresh air?"

She nodded, stood, and followed him outside without speaking. The early evening air felt like fall. He remembered the smell of burning leaves from autumns past. His memory was clear enough that he was sure he could actually smell smoldering leaves in the distance, despite the fact that such things were banned in the city now. He lit a cigarette and leaned against the railing.

"You're very quiet," he said through a cloud of exhaled smoke. She looked up at him through her tears.

"My little sister is sixteen," she half-whispered. "That could have been her."

"Life is a very fickle thing, Sheri. One minute you're a healthy teenager, enjoying life, the next minute you're on a gurney in an ER fighting for that same life." He spoke matter-of-factly, unaware of the effect his words.

She pushed into his arms and embraced him, holding on like a frightened child.

"Hey, you're a big girl. None of this should be a problem for you, Ms. Big Time Reporter." He tried to step back, but she held on, still clinging to him.

After a full minute, she spoke, her arms still wrapped around his body. "Writing about it is different from smelling the blood and watching you cut into a girl's throat."

"I suppose you're right. We tend to get a little cavalier in the business." He looked down at her and inhaled the scent of her hair as he had done in her apartment. She lifted her eyes to meet him, and suddenly he was overwhelmed by the warmth of her embrace. His passion, fueled by the intensity of what they had just experienced in the ER, impelled him. He felt his body respond to her as she yielded to his kiss, and eagerly pulled herself against him. She became more frantic and reached for him as he pulled her closer, his hands on the curves of her flanks.

He finally regained enough willpower to release her. She resisted, but he held her away, his hands around her waist.

"I'm sorry," he said. "I know this isn't right."

"No, Jason, it's very right. I know what I feel, and I think you feel it too. Why shouldn't we be together? I want you more than I've ever wanted anyone in my life." She was breathless, her face flushed with passion.

"And what do I say to Jesse? Remember, I'm engaged."

"Jesse's a big girl. Is it fair to her to stay in a relationship out of guilt?"

"It's more than that, Sheri. I love Jesse. I can't lie."

"And what about me, Jason? What do you feel for me?" The frustration in her voice spilled out.

"I know I feel different about you than I do about Jesse. It's just different with you, Sheri. I don't know if it's better or worse, or just more intense. I don't know," he said shaking his head in frustration.

"Maybe it's the real thing with me, Jason. Did you ever think of that?" Anger started to creep into her words.

"Yeah, I've thought about that, and it doesn't make it any easier."

"You know you can't have it both ways, Jason. I won't wait on the sideline forever. How long do you think you can live a lie?"

"I can't do this right now." He dropped his arms to his side. "I need some time. Can you understand that?"

She moved toward him and took his hands. "Jason, I love you. Do you know what this is like, waiting for you to decide, knowing there's another woman and there's nothing I can do but wait?" She spoke through her tears. "I envy Jesse. At least she doesn't know, doesn't lay in bed alone at night and wonder who you're going to choose."

"I'm sorry, Sheri. I never meant for this to happen. I never meant to hurt you or Jesse. It just happened."

"That's not true, Jason. It doesn't just happen. You only find someone else if you're looking. Maybe you should ask yourself *why* you were looking."

"I've got to get back inside." He kissed her cheek softly, dropped her hands, and walked away.

She stood alone and looked up at the infinite night sky, the stars blurred by the tears still slowly running down her cheeks. She held herself against the chill of the early night and felt the pain and fear inside her trying to break out. She had never known feelings like these before, and she realized for the first time in her life the meaning of the word heartache. She didn't like it.

The door behind her opened, and she turned, hoping it was Jason returning to her. She started to say his name, but stopped when she found Rooster standing behind her.

"Oh, Rooster," she said as she turned away and wiped the tears from her face.

"Sheri," he answered and lit a cigarette. "How's the story going?"

"Good, Rooster." She tried to sound unemotional as she mopped her tears with the heel of her hand.

"I understand you folks had a hot case tonight." He spoke evenly as he moved to her side and rested a foot on the railing. He looked off into the night, avoiding her face and the tears.

"Yeah. Should make first-rate material for my story."

"So, what do you think of our Dr. Corey?"

"He's wonderful. The readers are going to love him. I'd better get going. I've got a long day tomorrow." She turned to leave, but her sobs broke through.

"Sheri, if I could say something?"

She stopped with her back to him and her face hidden.

"This is a different world, here in the ER, from what most people are used to. Everything and everybody seems bigger than life. Things that most people seldom think about, like life and death, grief and pain, are magnified. It distorts things and scrambles your judgment. Sometimes, it's better to make important decisions about ourselves under more normal circumstances. Does any of that make sense?" His voice was gentle and colored with compassion.

"Yeah, Rooster. I'll try and remember that." She left without turning around.

Rooster looked up at the stars, exhaled and scrubbed his face with his hands. He had never been especially adept at giving that kind of advice.

Jason swung the Z4 through traffic, his mind galloping erratically from image to image. He thought about Jesse — thoughts of simultaneous worry and resentment — but he couldn't think about Jesse for long before his mind vaulted to Sheri. He could almost feel her body beside him in the car, and the memory of her perfume flickered through his senses. He pushed her away mentally, just as he had pushed her away physically, and now as he did then, he wanted her back.

The apartment was dark, and there was no sign of Jesse. He flipped on the backlights in the living room and made a drink. He made his way down the hall to the bedroom, looked in, and found her there asleep, curled into a ball under a pile of covers. Sheri's words came back to him; Jesse was lucky she didn't know what was going on in his mind.

Jason gulped his first drink and made another. The dark molasses sounds of The Cowboy Junkies floated onto the deck where he stood watching the night and struggling with his soul. Halfway through his third drink, he still felt uneasy. He made his way quietly into the bathroom, opened the bottle of sleeping pills, and shook one, then a second, into his hand. He washed them down his throat with what was left in his glass, but the pills and booze didn't embrace him until he finished his fifth drink.

Jason undressed in the dark, slid into bed, and reached for Jesse. His arm brushed her pajamas, and he suddenly remembered he had forgotten to call her. She had every right to be to be angry. She didn't stir when he rolled against her and formed his body to hers.

The dampness under him slowly registered on his mind and he pushed his hand under the covers, exploring the endless area of sticky wetness. In an ER flashback, he recognized the feel and the smell immediately. He threw the blankets off and jumped for the light switch. The brightness revealed a bright red, billowing stain of blood that soaked the entire lower half of their bed. Stunned, he moved to her side.

"Jesse, can you hear me?" He shouted then shook her, but she didn't respond.

He felt her wrist and found a rapid, thready pulse, then turned her hand over and pinched her hard across one of her fingernails. She groaned and barely pulled away. He knew she was alive but in shock. He pulled her pajama top up over her belly looking for some kind of injury. A barrage of questions rushed through his mind. Had she been stabbed or shot? There was no evidence of an injury to her abdomen. He pulled her pajama bottoms down and found the blood-soaked towel between her legs, covered with a large meaty blood clot. He lifted the towel away and revealed the steady trickle of blood. He grabbed the pillows from the head of the bed, lifted her legs and slid the pillows under her, then covered her again and ran to the living room.

The operator answered on the fourth ring. "This is 911. What is the nature of your emergency?"

"This is Dr. Jason Corey. I have a thirty-two-year-old female in hemorrhagic shock from a vaginal bleed. I need an ambulance right away." The panic in his voice reminded him of one of his patients.

He ran back to the bedroom and unlocked the door to the apartment on the way. He realized he wasn't dressed and pulled on a pair of jeans and a T-shirt from the bedroom floor, then returned to Jesse, and checked her pulse again. It seemed to be racing faster, but he wasn't wearing a watch to count the beats. He sat next to her on the bed and cradled her head in his lap. Her skin was pale, all signs of her summer tan already gone. She was far enough into shock that her skin was dry, past the point of being sweaty. He talked to her, unsure whether she could hear him, but he spoke nonetheless, and hoped he was reaching her on some level.

"I'm right here Jesse. It's going to be okay. Everything is going to be okay now." He prayed he was right.

His time with critical patients in the ER flew by. An hour disappeared in a few minutes, but the time he spent holding Jesse, powerless to do anything but wait, dragged by at the pace of a funeral dirge. *Shit, did EMS get the address wrong, or had he given it wrong?* His usual calm in a crisis was gone, and he felt the panic slowly twisting and tightening in his chest. Jesse remained still, her head in his lap, her breathing rapid and shallow, her pulse too fast and weak.

The warbling rise and fall of a siren materialized in the quiet night. He wasn't sure it was there at first, then a blasting tone told him the sound was real. The siren came closer and stopped, just as the panicked thought flashed through his mind that it was going to continue on its way into the night, leaving Jesse to bleed to death in his arms. Moments later, he heard pounding at the open door.

"Hello, Medic One here. Somebody call for help?"

"In here. I've got a patient in shock. Hurry!" His voice had lost its professional composure, but he didn't care.

The medics moved quickly. The IV needle somehow looked bigger than the same sized needles in the ER. Jesse winced when the medic pushed the gleaming steel tip into her arm, and Jason started to reach for her. "It's okay, Doc, we've got it," the medic tried to reassure him while he squeezed the IV bag forcing fluid through the clear plastic line. The second medic checked her blood pressure then repeated the process as he started a second IV. Nothing seemed to change, but Jesse's blood pressure slowly started to climb.

"Okay, Doc, we're going to roll. It's best if you follow in your car. We're going to Renton Memorial," the first medic said as they lifted Jesse onto the ambulance gurney, still squeezing the IV bag.

"Yeah, that's closest. I'll follow." Jason's voice seemed foreign, like someone else's words coming from his mouth.

Jason walked behind them to the ambulance and watched them load Jesse. They accelerated away and the sound of the siren sliced open the night, jolting him. He stood for several moments and watched the darkness swallow the lights and siren, leaving him alone in the night. His mind flashed back to another night, many years ago, when he watched another ambulance disappear into the night with Rachel. He had failed again.

He went inside, quickly changed clothes, and hunted for his wallet and keys. He tried to keep his eyes away from the bed, but as he reached for the light switch, he couldn't evade the bloodstain any longer. The thing stalked him and accused him. Like something alive, it seemed to have grown to cover more of the bed. The size of the stain drove home the realization that this wasn't just another patient, this was Jesse — his Jesse — and he might be losing her. His own guilt drove the fear into his brain like a skewer. He hadn't cried since he was a kid at his mother's funeral. He had always been able to distance himself from his feelings, but now he closed his eyes against the burning tears that came beyond his control. For a moment, he shuddered, and a wave of fear erupted up through his body.

He fought for control of his emotions as he drove to the hospital. He knew the significance of Jesse's condition and knew she was in mortal danger. In his mind, he questioned if this was God's way of punishing him. If it was, he deserved it, but not Jesse.

In their empty apartment, the phone rang four times before the answering machine picked up. "Jason, this is Dad. I was hoping we could all get together this weekend. Give me a call."

161

TWENTY

It was true then; it had to be. What other possible explanation could there be? It was Occam's razor: The most *obvious* answer was the correct answer. Arthur wondered if the principle applied even if that answer was beyond comprehension.

Arthur had hardly known Solomon Rosenthal from his time at the university and considered him more of an associate than a friend. His phone call had taken him by complete surprise.

"Dr. Corey, Dr. Arthur Corey?"

"Yes, this is Arthur Corey. Can I help you?"

"Arthur, this is Solomon Rosenthal from the university. Do you remember me?"

Arthur faltered while he searched his memory. "Yes, yes. Sol, how are you? What can I do for an old colleague?"

"I want you to know, Arthur, I'm calling as an old friend and a father myself. I thought you should know I just met with your son, Jason."

"Jason?" Arthur answered surprised. "What's he up to?"

"He brought me a tape recording he wanted interpreted. He said it was of himself talking in his sleep. I was doubtful at first, but I think he was telling me the truth."

"If Jason said the recording was of him, you can believe him, Sol. But I'm confused. Jason doesn't speak any foreign languages. He's sort of foreign language impaired," Arthur chuckled.

"That's what he said. It's especially confusing since he was speaking Aramaic. It's an ancient language . . ."

Arthur cut him off. "Yes, Sol, I know what Aramaic is, but I don't see how that's possible." His voice was filled with reservation.

"That seems to be the 64,000-dollar question. Jason seemed quite upset when he left here, and I thought you should know."

"I'm glad you called me, Sol. I'll see what I can find out."

Arthur had run every possible scenario in his mind since the call, but he still had no other answer. He almost called Harrison Fellows but decided against it. He knew what Harrison would say, and perhaps he would be correct. Perhaps the time had come to do the test.

Now, a day after the call, he had no further insights. He thought about talking to Jason directly, but wasn't sure if he would consider it an intrusion or if he would be upset about the call from Dr. Rosenthal. At last, he came to a decision, one he should have thought of before. He would talk to Jesse.

He tried to reach her all day without success, and finally, late in the evening he gave up and left a message on their machine.

Jason pulled into the visitors' parking lot at Renton Memorial and spotted the ambulance, which had brought Jesse, still parked in the ambulance bay. He considered going in through the ambulance entrance, but decided to play by the rules and go through the registration desk.

"I'm Jason Corey. My fiancé, Jessica Noble, was just brought in by ambulance. I'd like to see her please."

"I'm sorry, Mr. Corey, but the doctor is still with her. If you'll have a seat, I'll let them know you're here." The receptionist spoke politely but without eye contact.

Jason hated to play the doctor card, but he couldn't stand sitting in the waiting room and not knowing.

"Actually, it's Dr. Corey. I'm an ER doctor at Harborline. I'd appreciate it if you would let your ER doctor know."

The receptionist flashed a contemptuous smile, but picked up the phone and passed the message on. "Dr. Darien will be with you in just a minute," she replied with a little less attitude.

Jason found a place in the waiting area and fidgeted. There were only a few other people there — typical late-night ER patrons. He could feel their occasional glances, but for the most part, they ignored him. He realized he looked like one of them; no scrub suit or stethoscope around his neck. The ER looked different from this side of the desk.

After a half hour, Jason was ready to go back to the receptionist and start making demands, but restrained himself. A few minutes later, a middle-aged doctor appeared and called his name. He looked familiar to Jason, but he didn't know him personally.

"Dr. Corey?" His words brought immediate stares from several people around the waiting room. "I'm Dave Darian. Nice to meet you."

When he shook his hand, Jason noticed a slight pause. Something that said there was a problem. "Let's go back here."

Dr. Darian pointed him toward the ER.

As they walked to Jesse's room, Dr. Darian asked Jason about Jesse's medical history, just as Jason had done thousands of times with his own patients. He knew it was necessary, but right now, it wasn't important to him.

"Dr. Corey, has Jesse had any medical problems?"

"No, nothing significant. Her only medications are birth control pills and a vitamin. And please, call me Jason." He flipped back and forth in his mind between doctor mode and patient mode.

"Has she been feeling ill lately? Any recent complaints?"

"Actually, she's been complaining of some intermittent lower abdominal pain for the last few weeks. She was supposed to have seen her OB/GYN about it, but I found out today she had cancelled her appointments." (doctor mode)

"That might be connected with what's going on tonight, but we'll have a better idea once we get labs back."

"How's she doing? She looked pretty serious when the ambulance loaded her." (patient mode)

"She's doing better. Her bleeding has slowed down, and her BP is up from the IV fluids, but she's still unresponsive. Is there any chance she could be pregnant?"

"Pregnant? She's on the pill, but that's no guarantee of course." (doctor mode)

"We can go in and see her for a minute, but then she's headed for ultrasound."

Jason walked to her bed and reached for Jesse's hand. She still looked pale, but her face had a bit more color. "Jesse, can you hear me, baby?" (patient mode) Jesse didn't respond to his voice or his touch.

"Jason, I'm going to put you in our doctors' call room while we do some more work on Jesse. Can I get you a cup of coffee?"

Jason followed him to a small room just off the ER, coffee in hand, where he waited alone. It was like the doctors' call room in any one of thousands of ERs across the country: a desk, a few books, a small TV, and a single bed, which was rarely used. He paced, flipped through a few journals, and finally turned on the TV. He wished he had a drink. Jason was on the verge of going out to check on Jesse again when the door opened.

"Are you moonlighting on me now?" Rooster asked.

"Rooster, what are you doing here?" Jason's speech was slow.

"Dave Darian called me. He said you were here with Jesse."

"Yeah, I was just going out to check on her. It's been quite awhile."

"Sit down, J.C," Rooster said in a somber tone.

"What's going on, Rooster, is it Jesse?" Jason started out of the chair.

"Jesse's fine. Dave will be in to talk to you in a minute. Right now, you're the problem." Rooster pushed him back into his seat.

"Me? I'm fine. What are you talking about?" Jason's words slurred together.

"Shit, you're drunk. How much have you had to drink tonight?" Rooster's words broke over him like the crack of a whip. "And what else have you got in you?"

"I had a drink or two when I got home, and took a sleeping pill. I was just going to bed when I found Jesse." He sounded more defensive than he intended.

Rooster was in his face. "You're a lying piece of shit. Who do you think you're talking to, some intern who hasn't spent the last twenty years of his life in an ER taking care of drunks and druggies? Two drinks, my ass. Let's get a BA on you right now, and how about a drug screen, while we're at it. Dave will run it for me off the books. Let's find out." Rooster stepped back seething, his face blood red.

"That's right. Dave and everybody else will do anything you want, Rooster. Everybody owes you," he sneered.

"And it's a damned good thing for you that they do. Do you know what happens to a doctor who gets arrested for DUI?"

Jason's face hardened in response to Rooster's words, and he looked away.

"Let me remind you. You lose your medical license immediately for a minimum of ninety days, while you do an in-patient detox program. Then, *if* you get your license back, you're on probation while the state monitors you, while you go to meetings for five years. All of that looks damned shitty on a resume. Is that what you want for your career?"

"All right. I had a few drinks and took two sleeping pills. You make it sound like I'm hard core."

"Come on, Jason, we've all seen good docs go down this road. Let me tell you, my friend, they all start out just like this." Rooster didn't pull any punches.

A knock on the door stopped them, and Dr. Darian came halfway into the room. "Am I interrupting?" he asked.

Rooster stepped aside and clenched his jaw like a coiled steel spring.

"No, it's nothing. How's Jesse?" Jason asked.

"Okay, here's what we've got so far. Her vital signs are stable, and she's starting to wake up. Her pregnancy test is positive. Her cervix is dilated about two centimeters, and she's still bleeding, but the Pitocin is slowing that down. Ultrasound confirms an incomplete AB. We're giving her some blood now, but we need to go to the O.R. for a D&C. The OB/GYN resident is getting ready to take her up."

"I want to see her before she goes," Jason said and pushed himself to his feet. He brushed past Rooster as he followed Dr. Darian to Jesse's room.

A wisp of blonde hair stuck out under the edge of Jesse's surgical hat, across her pale face, and he gently brushed it to the side. A bag of dark blood hung from her IV pole and slowly dripped into her IV line. Jason checked the monitor and saw that her pulse had slowed closer to normal.

Jesse's eyes slowly opened in response to his touch. The smile he loved appeared on her face, but the usual verve was gone from her eyes.

"How's my girl?" He asked softly.

"Better, now that my doctor's here," she answered in a drug-thickened voice.

"Did they tell you what's going on?" He asked as he picked up her hand.

"I guess I didn't do a very good job on my first try as a mom." Her lip quivered as she spoke, and tears pooled in the corners of her eyes. "I'm sorry, Jason."

"Shh. Nothing's your fault. It's going to be all right, and it'll be better next time." He squeezed her hand.

The nurse caught Jason's eye as she released the foot brake on the gurney. "They want her in the O.R. We've got to go now."

Jason leaned over, hugged Jesse, and kissed her forehead. "I'll be waiting right here. You be good." He squeezed her hand a final time, and the nurse rolled her away.

Jason walked outside into the chilly night air and lit a cigarette. A trace of early fall mist, the droplets detailed by the parking lot lights, swirled around him. This wasn't the true bleak rain of winter, but rather a whispered secret of what was to come. For now, the drizzly night air refreshed him.

Jason's skin flushed again as Rooster's words returned to him. They added their weight to the rest of his guilt; the guilt of not being there when Jesse had needed him and the guilt of not making sure she followed up with her OB/GYN doctor. His guilt about Sheri. And now, guilt that he was here with enough drugs and alcohol in his system that the ER doctor had called Rooster. His anger rose inside him, and he gritted his teeth against the pending eruption. His mind was clear enough to understand that most of his anger was with himself. He had failed Jesse this time, and he swore it wouldn't happen again.

Jason's cigarette burned to its end, and he lit a second off its ember. He paced near the entrance of the ER and let the night air finish clearing his head. When he couldn't stand the wait any longer, he found the O.R. waiting room and settled in. He hadn't been there long, when a young doctor dressed in surgical scrubs found him. Jason couldn't believe he had ever been that young as a resident.

"Ah, Dr. Corey? I'm Dr. Early," he said and shook Jason's hand. "I'm the resident taking care of Jesse." He sounded as if he was trying to convince Jason of his credentials, and Jason couldn't help but be amused by the young man's discomfort, talking to an *older* physician.

He tried to put the young doctor at ease as he shook his hand and introduced himself. "I really appreciate what you've done for Jesse tonight. How's she doing?"

Jason could feel the resident's stress level drop as he talked. "She's doing just fine. Her D&C went smoothly, and her bleeding has almost stopped. Her H&H dropped pretty low, but she's had a couple of units of blood, and we'll give her some more tonight. She should be ready to go home tomorrow or the next day, depending on her blood count and bleeding."

A weight dropped away from Jason as Dr. Early spoke. He remembered an old adage among medical people, which said if there is going to be a complication, it usually happens to one of their own. Jason had seen it happen too many times to ignore the superstition.

"This may sound strange but could you by any chance tell the sex of the baby?" Jason asked.

Dr. Early hesitated before he answered. "It was a girl."

Jason nodded, and it registered on some level that his little girl had died tonight. The image of Jesse walking hand in hand with a petite version of herself burned itself into his heart.

"There is one other thing, Dr. Corey." The inflection in his voice froze Jason in his chair. "When we checked Jesse's ultrasound we found another problem. She has a six centimeter mass on her right ovary. I confirmed it on pelvic under anesthesia; it's a complex mass."

Jason's mind searched like a computer hunting for lost files and found the information buried with a thousand other esoteric facts from medical school.

"Complex ovarian mass in a young, otherwise healthy female; that's 95 percent benign with a 5 percent occurrence of malignancy," he said and looked at the OB/GYN doctor for confirmation.

"I'm impressed. I hope I can remember things like that when I get older."

Jason half smiled at the reference. "So, what's the next step?" He asked.

"We'll wait four or five weeks and repeat her ultrasound. That'll tell us if we need to biopsy, or more likely it'll be resolving."

Jason only nodded in response. "How long will she be in recovery?"

"She'll be out in about an hour, but she'll be pretty snowed all night. You might as well go home and get some sleep."

"I wouldn't leave her tonight for anything in the world. I'll be right here until she goes to her room. I'd appreciate it if you could have a nurse tell me when she's being moved."

"I understand, and can't say I blame you. It sounds like things were pretty hairy before she got here."

Jason settled into his chair, alone in the surgical waiting room, surrounded by the quiet of the late-night hospital. He tried to rest, but an old superstition slowly gnawed at his gut, and kept any chance of sleep at bay.

Twenty One

Diana Todd sprawled on her stomach, tanning on the lounge, with her top undone. Her thong bottom covered only what was absolutely necessary, and from the side, she looked as if she was totally nude. Her pose would have been extremely provocative on many of the younger women on the beach. However, Diana was a bit too old and a bit too generous in the thighs and butt to carry it off — details which she refused to accept. But then, Diana had a tendency to see herself as something a bit more exceptional than she actually was.

Hanging beads of moisture covered the metal bucket on the table next to her. The droplets mirrored the world around them a thousand times over, and periodically combined and casually trickled down the metal side to add to the small puddle on the plastic tabletop. Two Coronas sat chilling in the ice inside the bucket, and four empty bottles lay discarded in the sand, tossed aside without regard to esthetics or safety. Three filled shot glasses of tequila shooters remained among several empties on a tray which sat nearby on the table. Two bodies reclined under the cabana, much like the bucket of ice, sweating in the tropical heat.

They had been in Ixtapa for five days and had spent their time in an endless binge of sex, drinking, and excursions to the beach. Diana knew she deserved the good life and a beautiful man, and now, she finally had those things. Yes, she thought beautiful was a far more appropriate term than handsome for Carlos. God knew she had worked for this. Five years of marriage to that fool Larry Todd had been more of an ordeal than even she had anticipated. Ensnaring him had been the easy part. A few smiles, a little attention, and she had her first date. Doctors were so gullible if an attractive, young nurse knew how to play them — at least Larry had been. On their first date, she had fawned over him, smiled, and stared into his eyes as if she adored him. She thought she was going to puke before her plan came together. It would have been easier if he hadn't been so . . . unattractive, and that was being kind. Oh, he was a pleasant enough guy, but far beneath her in every way except one: money.

On the way back to her apartment, she had sat close to him and rested her hand on his thigh. The poor jerk could barely drive. Once inside her apartment, she took the lead and had him in bed before he knew what was happening. She knew she had him the moment he climaxed inside her. Three months later she missed her period. Larry Todd was not the kind of man to abandon a pregnant woman. Besides, the poor schmuck loved her. They were married a few months before their daughter was born. That wasn't quite enough financial security for Diana, but two years later a second daughter arrived and that was enough. Then, all she had to do was sit back and ignore him until their fifth anniversary. She had done her homework and knew the return on her investment would be maximized under Washington State law after five years of marriage. One week after their anniversary, she had divorce papers served to him at the hospital. She moved his belongings into storage before he got home.

And now, she had Carlos. Umm, Carlos. She had only known him a few weeks, but she wasn't going to let this one get away. When he suggested a trip to Mexico, she sent the brats off to their grandmother and packed her most seductive dainties.

Diana reached out and drew the letter C in the droplets on the ice bucket, setting off a small stream of rivulets down the side of the cold metal. He was exactly what she deserved. He was a god. She was sure she had seen him on TV, even though he denied it. He was young, muscled, charming and beautiful. God he was beautiful. She had lost count of the number of their sexual encounters since they had been at the resort. He was wearing her out but not enough to stop her, of course. He didn't talk about his work, but his Rolex, his way with money, and his clothes told her all she needed to know.

She heard him move to her side, then felt his hand slowly slide down her back. His fingers skimmed between her cheeks, eliciting a schoolgirl giggle from the grown woman.

"How's my love?" He murmured, his words seasoned with a slight Hispanic accent. He leaned over and kissed the small of her back.

She rolled over and grabbed her bikini top a moment too late to keep one breast from fortuitously falling into view as she turned over. The show was wasted on everyone except the elderly couple two cabanas down.

She ignored the glare from her neighbors and giggled again in response. "Your love is just fine, and I should know."

He sprinkled salt on the back of his hand and squeezed a wedge of lime over her exposed belly. He licked the salt from his hand and knocked back another tequila shooter. She squealed as he moved his tongue over her lime-flavored navel and down. The elderly couple packed up and moved down the beach.

"I think we've offended our neighbors," he laughed, looking over his shoulder at the retreating pair.

"Fuck 'em," Diana sneered, momentarily forgetting Hispanic men prefer their women demure.

He hid his reaction to her well. "We've got to get going if we're going to make the sunset at the Villa de Silva."

"Are you sure you wouldn't rather do room service? I'll make the view well worthwhile."

"Not tonight. Tonight, I'm going to show you one of the most beautiful places in the world. Besides, I want to see you in the dress I bought for you. But, I will give you a little appetizer before we leave if you hurry."

The Villa de Silva was the former summer residence of the Presidente. The contemporary building sat high on the cliffs overlooking Ixtapa Bay, every room open to the sea and the sky. Now a restaurant, it was the premier place to watch the spectacular sunsets of the resort city.

When they arrived, the sun was already dropping low toward the ocean horizon. Diana, still warm from a sex blush, wore Carlos on her arm like an expensive piece of jewelry, accented by the too- tight dress he had bought her. The maitre d' ushered them to a table near the back of the restaurant, away from the cliffs.

"Senior," Carlos stopped him. "We would like the table at the point."

"I'm sorry, Senior, that table has been reserved" The maitre d' sincerely apologized.

Carlos palmed a bill into the man's hand and smiled. "Surely they would be here by now if they were coming."

"I'm sorry, Senior, they are very important people."

Carlos raised his eyebrows and glanced down at the maitre d's hand. The man quickly glanced at his palm, just long enough to see the corner of the hundred-dollar bill. The man smiled graciously. "That's a no-show," he said and guided them to the table farthest out on the point of the restaurant. They sat suspended past the cliffs, over the surf and the rocks far below.

Diana had to admit, she had never seen anything as spectacular as this place, highlighted by the setting sun before them. They had just taken the first sip of their drinks when the bottom edge of the massive molten sphere touched the water. On cue, the maitre d' stepped to the front of the restaurant and called everyone's attention to the vista — as if his direction was necessary. Suddenly, the clouds, which moments earlier had been barely noticeable wisps across the sky, exploded in a backlit kaleidoscope of electric orange and red. The usually slow moving sun began to move faster than Diana had ever imagined possible. The diners sat in awe, awaiting the immense creaking groan that had to accompany the impact of heaven moving against Earth. In a few seconds, it was over, and the final shard of light disappeared. The stillness of early dusk materialized across their world, and the maitre d' led the diners in applause.

They ate leisurely, savoring the food, drink and ambiance. The tropical night remained balmy, despite the slightest whisper of breeze off the ocean. The restaurant was almost empty by the time they finished eating.

"I want to show you something before we go." Carlos's eyes flickered with excitement.

He led her to the side of the restaurant and a secret exit. She held his hand as he escorted her along the hidden path to the edge of the cliffs. Far below them, lights from a single fishing boat stood out against the night sky, overflowing with stars. He turned her toward the ocean and wrapped his arms around her.

"Tell me Diana, has this been good for you?"

She rested back against him, tranquil in his arms. "More than I can tell you."

She turned toward him. "Carlos, I love you. I want you to know that. I never want this to end."

He held her in his arms and smiled as he slowly rocked her backward until she was off balance. She tensed, then relaxed in his arms, when he asked, "Do you trust me?"

"Yes," she answered as she looked into his eyes. "I would trust you with my life."

"I want you to know something, too, Diana. Rooster says good-bye."

Confusion momentarily clouded her face, before her eyes opened wide in terror as he released her. Her scream disappeared into the darkness below.

"Jason, wake up." The resolve in Jesse's voice grabbed him like a pair of hands around his throat and yanked him toward consciousness.

"What's wrong?" He bolted upright in bed and instantly cleared his mind.

She pushed an open newspaper in front of him. "Read this." Her voice was insistent.

" Jesse," he started to protest.

"Read this! I'll get you some coffee."

Jason had planned on sleeping in this Sunday morning. Arthur was coming over later for brunch and a trip to Pike Place Market on the waterfront, but he still had a few hours he had reserved for sleep. He was relieved Jesse was okay, but now he was more than a little irritated at being awakened. His annoyance passed quickly as he focused on a story in the front section of the newspaper. The headline read *Seattle Woman Killed in Fall*. He quickly continued to the story.

A 37-year-old Seattle woman died Friday night in the resort town of Ixtapa, Mexico. Mexican authorities report that Diana Todd plunged to her death when she lost her footing while walking with a companion on the cliffs near a local restaurant. Mrs. Todd had been staying at the Las Brisas Resort there with her companion, who was not available for comment. Authorities have ruled the death an accident. Sources say the body has been released and will be returned to the United States within the next few days. Mrs. Todd was the estranged wife of Dr. Larry Todd, a Seattle physician. Photos taken at the scene at the time of recovery of the body show the victim fell several hundred feet to her death.

Below the story, a grainy photo showed high vertical cliffs that dropped onto a rocky shoreline. Near the edge of the picture, a man with what looked like a rescue crew, glanced back over his shoulder, as if surprised by the camera.

Jason was studying the picture when Jesse returned with his coffee.

"Well?" she asked as she sat on the bed. "What do you think?"

He reached for the coffee and shook his head. "I think Larry has to be pretty shaken up. Divorce or not, this will hit him hard."

Jesse leaned over and tapped the paper with her finger. "No, I mean what do you think about the picture?"

"I think it must have been a hell of a fall," he said staring at the photo.

"No, I mean the picture. The picture!" She hammered the paper with her forefinger for emphasis.

Jason looked again but responded with a confused expression. "Okay, I see cliffs, rocks, water and some Mexican guys." He shrugged and pulled a face.

"Argh." Jesse sprang off the bed, jogged out of the bedroom and returned a few seconds later with a magnifying glass. "Look!" she ordered and shoved the glass into his hand.

He started from the top of the picture, but Jesse positioned the glass over the man's partially turned face. He took the cue and studied the man carefully. Gradually, a tiny light flickered in his mind, like a cold fluorescent bulb coming to life, then caught.

"No! It can't be." He laid the glass down on the paper.

"Oh yes!" Jesse responded passionately. "I'm positive!"

He picked the glass up again and re-examined the face. "Jesus Christ."

"Not by a long shot," she countered. "That's Rooster's mysterious companion from the ferry docks. That's not a face a girl forgets."

Jason met her gaze but remained silent. Finally, she raised her eyebrows and asked, "What are we going to do about it?"

"What do you mean, do about it?"

"Jason, Rooster had her murdered."

He leaned back. "Jesse, we don't know that. The paper said it's been ruled an accident. Besides, what would I do? Accuse Rooster to his face, or call the police and say we saw them together, so he must have had her killed? I don't think so. Plus, I kind of like my career."

"So we just let him get away with murder?"

"Why would Rooster even want her dead?" Jason asked.

"You said he has a dark side. Who knows? Maybe he wanted to protect Larry, or maybe he just hates women."

"Jesse, I don't believe Rooster is a murderer." He tried to sound convincing.

"Okay," she said as she stood up. "Just don't ever let him get the idea you're not happy with me. I might find myself taking a somersault off the Space Needle." She headed for the kitchen.

Jason started to laugh, then stopped.

TWENTY TWO

It was time. Arthur wasn't happy about it, but that fact was irrelevant now. The sequence of events had dictated it, and his mind was made up.

His watch said it was eleven o'clock sharp. He prided himself on his punctuality, even now in his retirement years, when time was an insignificant thing to most people his age — something that merely marked the proximity of their mortality. He smoothed the front of his three-piece suit and straightened his coordinated silk tie. Arthur was not the kind of retiree to show up in a striped shirt and checkered pants. As usual, he was perfectly groomed and gave off just the slightest scent of his favorite British Sterling cologne. Despite his years, he presented himself with pride and an unmistakable air of dignity. He took a deep breath to strengthen his resolve, and knocked on the door.

Jesse answered and greeted Arthur with her usual kiss and hug, which he absorbed with distinct pleasure.

"Jesse dear," he chortled, "You are a bright spot in an old man's life. If I were a few years younger, I'd take you away from that son of mine and treat you like a queen."

Jesse hugged him again. "And what makes you think you need to be a few years younger?"

"All right you two," Jason injected himself and hugged his father. "If I can pry you two apart, I'm ready to eat."

"He always was a party pooper, even as a child," Arthur replied, offering his arm to Jesse. "But since he's buying lunch I suppose we should humor him. I'll just use the facilities and we can all be off."

"And who said I was buying?" Jason called after his father.

The three of them strolled the crowded streets of Pike Street Market, basking in the quintessence of the district. The sidewalks were crowded with locals and tourists, all looking like children at a carnival. In many ways, the market was a carnival — a pageant of regional and international sights, smells, and sounds that taunted onlookers and beckoned to them like sideshow hucksters.

Jason walked behind Arthur and Jesse as the three of them shared a giant cinnamon roll. They had planned on lunch first, but a storefront bakery, which blew the aroma of their wares onto the sidewalk, had changed their plans.

Jesse looked well. She had been out of the hospital for three weeks and was almost back to her old self. Her color was vibrant, and she felt renewed. She tried not to think about the miscarriage, but at times, especially at night lying in bed next to Jason, thoughts of the lost baby haunted her, creeping into her mind like a silent specter. On those nights, her dreams took her searching for her lost child, and she often woke franticly sobbing in Jason's arms. She gave little thought to the cyst on her ovary, even though she still had the pain from time to time. The lingering shadow of grief was the only scar she carried.

Jason had become entirely focused on Jesse, to the point she sometimes wished she had a few minutes to herself. He had cut back on shifts so he could spend more time with her. When she first came home from the hospital, he had pampered her mercilessly. Thankfully, that had passed in response to her protests. Jason had stopped talking in his sleep, perhaps because his sleep had become lighter. Most nights, he lingered just below consciousness, as he listened for Jesse's cries when she awoke, hysterically looking for their lost daughter. A colleague in psychiatry had assured Jason this was expected and would pass with time, and he hoped that was the case. Each time it happened, her pain stabbed at his heart and revived his guilt.

Jason had virtually no contact with Sheri, outside of an initial few calls with questions about the article, which she tried to expand to questions about him. He had stopped the sleeping pills and cut back on alcohol. After some thought, he had decided Rooster might just be right. When he first returned to work, things had been uneasy with Rooster, but this also had resolved with time. Thankfully, there hadn't been any more occurrences in the ER, and Jason had been spared further episodes of what he had written off as panic attacks. His preoccupation with Jesse allowed him to force his mind away from those things — almost.

They wandered through the fish market and watched the sellers throwing salmon across the counter to fill their customers' orders. Jason elbowed Jesse when he spotted a little boy staring into the mouth of a great toothed fish. Jason knew what was coming. One of the fish men reached out unseen, yanked the tail of the huge fish, and sent the boy darting away.

They slowly ambled down the length of the street through the marketplace, stopping periodically to listen to street musicians and add a few dollars to their collection of coins. Many of these performers were accomplished musicians who played as much for fun as the money they brought in.

At the end of the block, where the shops thinned, they stopped in a grassy area and looked at the panorama across the Sound stretching away beneath them. This small park was a favorite spot for street people who populated the area, especially at night. During the day, they seemed to disappear, absorbed back into the alleyways and hidey-holes of the city, except for the few who ignored the law and openly panhandled and drank in public.

The trio watched a ferryboat slowly pull away from the dock, headed for its next stop on the Sound or the San Juans. Suddenly, amid the peaceful scene, Jason became aware of the *feeling*. It emerged like a sinister mist from the distant horizon and grew, becoming more powerful with each breath he forced into his lungs. He started to sweat, and a wave of nausea rolled up from his stomach, nearly gagging him. He didn't see the disheveled man heave himself from a nearby bench and weave his way toward them. The transient pulled a drink from a bottle, poorly camouflaged in a brown paper bag, and stuffed it back into the pocket of his stained overcoat.

Jason turned as the man hailed them. "Hey, folks. How are you fine folks doin' today?" The words were thick with alcohol.

Jason found himself looking into the man's stubbled, dirt-smudged face, and instinctively stepped forward to block his access to Jesse and Arthur. "We're doing just fine," he answered as he started to steer them away.

The man half walked, half stumbled the rest of the distance to Jason. "Aw, you don't have to be afraid of me. I ain't gonna get you dirty er nothing, but I sure could use a couple of bucks to get something to eat." The man stopped well inside Jason's personal space and sneered.

"I can probably help you out with that," Jason said as he reached for his wallet and extracted several one-dollar bills while he kept his eyes fixed on the panhandler. The smell of alcohol mixed with stale sweat pushed Jason back a step. "There you go." Jason handed him the bills and started to turn away

The panhandler took the bills, then grabbed Jason's arm. "Hey, buddy, by the looks of you folks, I bet you could spare more cash than that." He pushed the bills into his torn coat pocket and withdrew the hilt of a knife. Jason froze, immediately thinking about Jesse and Arthur standing behind him. Jason started to open his wallet again when he heard a voice from the street.

"Is there a problem here?"

Two police officers on bicycles pulled up and stepped off their bikes. The young, shorts-clad officers were obviously more than a match for the panhandler.

"Are you bothering these folks, Jimmy?" The first officer asked as he moved toward them while the second officer flanked the panhandler.

"No way, man," he replied flashing a quick smile. The knife disappeared, and he released Jason's arm. "I was just giving these nice folks some directions. Ain't that right?" He flashed a menacing glance at Jason.

Jason took the opportunity to step away and shoved his wallet into his pocket. He hesitated then answered. "Everything's okay here, officer."

Jason ushered Jesse and Arthur to the street and away. Behind him, he heard one of the cops. "Not so fast, Jimmy. Let's have a little talk."

"What was that all about?" Jesse took his arm as they crossed the street while Arthur hurried to keep up as they walked away.

"It was no big deal. The guy was just a little aggressive."

"And quite intoxicated," Arthur added. "You can never be too careful with some of these street people."

Jason glanced back at the cops and Jimmy, who was now spread-eagled with his hands behind his head, while one of the cops emptied the pockets of the long coat. The flashing blue and red lights of a police car appeared down the street, and Jason had no doubt Jimmy wouldn't be bothering anyone else, at least today.

Jason guided them across the street and started back in the opposite direction. They still strolled casually but were a little less comfortable after their meeting with Jimmy. Their topic of conversation changed to a destination for lunch, motivated by the smells from the street-front restaurants. Jason stole several covert glances back to the site of their encounter with Jimmy, until the police car left with their guest in the back seat.

The encounter was over, and they were all safe and well — except Jason. The *feeling*, which had begun before he was aware of Jimmy, persisted. It wasn't fear, and it wasn't adrenaline. Jason knew both of those feelings well. This was something else. The *feeling* was an overwhelming power, devouring his spirit and his will, leaving him to fight for control of his own mind.

They worked their way through the crowds, and Jesse gradually drifted away from Arthur and moved to Jason's side, leaving Arthur to pick his own way and stop whenever something caught his interest. They paused in front of an art gallery and studied several impressionist paintings. Jesse and Arthur had a far greater appreciation for this type of art than Jason, who stood back waiting, still struggling against the force that was trying to overpower him. The power was overwhelming, well beyond Jason's control. It moved him; drawing him to the edge of the building and the alley. He peered down the narrow passage, strewn with empty cardboard boxes and trash. He fought back and turned to rejoin Jesse and Arthur, when something out of place caught his eye. He stopped and leaned backward, allowing another inspection of the alley. The narrow, brick paved passage was guarded by tall buildings on either side, which left it shaded most of the day. The fetid dampness carried the smell of urine, and several broken bottles littered the ground, reminders of the night inhabitants of this place. A few steps took Jason deep into the haunt of the nighttime denizens of Pike Street.

Jason's eyes searched the alley for whatever had caught his attention. At last, he spotted a tattered shoe protruding from behind the edge of a box, stained and ruined like the rest of the litter around it. He would have ignored it, but the shoe stood on end on its heel, held in place by a foot. He started toward it but stopped when he heard his name.

"Jason, what are you doing back there?" Jesse called, her voice edged with concern.

"Nothing. I'll be right out. You stay with Dad." Her concern reminded him of his recent encounter with Jimmy and his knife, but he didn't have a choice. The power inside him swelled and pulsed with each step, drawing him forward. He moved cautiously toward the shoe, barely aware that Jesse had followed him.

"I thought I told you to stay with Dad." He spoke without looking back. She didn't respond but instead reached for his hand.

"What are you doing back here?" She asked, in a loud whisper. Jason took her hand, knowing she wasn't going to listen to him and stay behind.

"There's somebody back here. I just want to make sure they're all right."

"What, are you crazy? People get killed doing stuff like this."

This time it was his turn to ignore her. They hung near the middle of the alley as they moved ahead to see who was attached to the tattered shoe. Their question was answered when they cleared the end of the battered, cardboard box, and found an elderly woman, barely conscious, laying on her back with the other discarded debris.

Dried blood smeared one side of her badly bruised cheek, and Jason noticed immediately, the left side of her soiled face drooped unnaturally. He knelt beside her and removed a tattered, hand knit hat, covering a tangle of dirty gray, hair. He reached for her hand, the only other part of her body not covered in layers of shabby clothes, and spoke to her.

"Ma'am, can you hear me?" He asked loudly.

She moved to the sound of his voice and tried to talk, but her left side remained motionless from a stroke. He checked her pulse, then lifted her eyelids and found her pupils were grossly unequal. He turned to Jesse, hovering behind him.

"Call an ambulance, then wait by the entrance of the alley to show them where we are. This woman is hurt and has had a stroke." Jesse whirled and disappeared toward the street.

Jason held the woman's frail hand and talked to her, reassuring her. "Everything's going to be all right. We're getting some help."

She was obviously homeless, but not like Jimmy. This was a person, like your best friend's mother, a victim of bad luck or poor choices, rather than a life thrown away on drugs or alcohol. She might be alone in the world, or she might have a family someplace, but they either didn't know about her condition or didn't care about her anymore. As Jason spoke to her, a tear formed in one eye and slowly bled down her dirt-stained face.

The power inside Jason reacted to the woman's pain. It roared and swelled, transforming his soul, perhaps in response to the injustice of life. He cautiously reached across her and laid his hand on her disfigured face. He closed his eyes and focused the Power inside him on her pain. Nothing happened. He squeezed his eyes tighter and concentrated, trying to force a power that he didn't know if he could control, or even possessed, but received nothing in response.

Jason's hope faded with his concentration, when he heard a movement behind him. Someone was there. He opened his eyes and started to turn, when the pain struck him. A jolt which unquestionably moved from him to the woman lying in the trash at his feet. He jerked away and came eye to eye with his father standing in the alley behind him.

"Is everything all right, Jason?" Arthur questioned.

Jason had been taken unawares and fumbled for a rational answer. "Ah, yeah, Dad," he answered rubbing his hand. "I just sent Jesse for some help. I think this woman has had a stroke."

Movement drew their attention back to the woman, and they watched as she sat up. Her smile was robust and equal across her strong, almost vibrant face. She straightened her tattered clothes with her hands, which now both functioned normally. They looked on in amazement as the transformation progressed like the rays of a cloud-veiled sun emerging across a landscape. Finally, the resurrection completed, and the woman rose to her feet, all signs of her paralysis gone.

"Jason? What?" Arthur faltered as his voice conveyed the confusion displayed on his face.

Jason turned back to Arthur, and as his mind processed what they had just seen, his brain frantically searched for an explanation to offer his father. None came. He was rescued by the sound of sirens from the arriving Ambulance and police. Jesse led the medics and two police officers down the alley to the three of them then stopped at the sight of the woman who now didn't appear as if she needed any help at all. All eyes turned to Jason, who still had no words of explanation. He broke from the group, quickly walked to the entrance of the alley, then made his way through the growing crowd of onlookers. Jesse turned to Arthur, whose only reply was a look of uncertainty. Her mind leaped to the only possible explanation and she jogged after Jason, who had already vanished into the crowd.

Arthur watched her disappear, past the shoulder of an approaching policeman.

"Excuse me, sir, but can you tell me what the hell is going on here?"

"Oh, I'm sorry, officer, but I don't really know," he answered politely. He walked away as he reached into his coat pocket for the small plastic bag that contained several hairs he had taken from Jason's hairbrush, earlier at the apartment.

"Yes," he said to himself. "It's time for some answers."

It had taken years to reach this point and he prayed his wife would forgive him for breaking his promise to her. If she didn't, he would have to live with that along with the many other mistakes, which had brought him to this place and time in his life. He slowly shook his head and once again, wondered at the arrogance of man.

TWENTY THREE

Jason drove through a silvery early morning fog that foretold of darker times. The chilly dampness of autumn had replaced the warmth of summer.

The thing, whatever it was, still possessed him, and the idea of that chiseled at his mind this morning as he drove to the hospital. It wasn't over. His encounter with the bag lady at Pike Street Market had confirmed that, and the knowledge left him on edge.

Jason had spent several hours with Arthur after the episode at Pike Street, trying to explain what had happened that day and what had led up to it. He was surprised at how easily Arthur had accepted and processed the whole story. He was relieved when Arthur agreed, over Jesse's protests, that a psychiatrist wasn't necessarily the answer. Unfortunately, Arthur didn't have any other suggestions. The whole interaction left Jason with a feeling that his father had some insight into the events that he wasn't sharing.

Today, Jason was also troubled for another reason. Jesse had an appointment for her repeat ultrasound this morning, and Jason was worried. He wouldn't fully believe that Jesse was well until he saw the negative ultrasound himself, and a growing fear of disaster hung over him. She seemed well, but Jason had learned that didn't always mean the patient was in good health.

He sat at his desk, nursed a cup of Starbucks coffee and read the paper between scattered patients who presented to the ER early in the day. So far, he had seen the typical non-emergencies that frequented the hospital at the beginning of day shift, but his respite was brief this morning.

The sound of the trauma bell and strobe light jarred the ER, announcing a level one trauma. The Medic One radio followed with their report.

"Harborline, this is Medic One. How do you copy?" The voice on the radio pulsated with controlled urgency.

Jeff Noles answered the call and left the radio speaker on, as usual. "Medic One, this is Harborline. We read you loud and clear. Go."

"Harborline, we are en route to you with an approximately twenty-year-old white male, victim of a truck versus motorcycle MVA."

As Jason moved to Jeff's side, he heard a muffled groan from one of the nurses behind him. Motorcycle accidents were notoriously brutal, hence the ER nickname of donor-cycles. The victims were usually a reliable source of kidneys, livers, and other vital organs, assuming there was enough left to harvest.

Medic One continued their report. "The victim was thrown approximately sixty feet from the point of impact. He has significant trauma to head and chest as well as both lower extremities. Victim was not wearing a helmet. Current BP is 60/40 with pulse 125. Glasgow Coma Score is 2, 3, 4. We have two large bore IVs running NS and patient is in full spinal immobilization. Our ETA is five minutes. Any questions or orders?"

Jeff shrugged. "No questions or orders. We'll go to Trauma One with your patient. Harborline clear." The nursing staff immediately moved into their routine in the main trauma room.

"Call the trauma code and alert the trauma captain," Jason called to Jeff as he headed to the room to set up. Almost simultaneously, he heard the overhead page: "Code Trauma, ER, ETA five minutes." The shrill broadcast repeated three times to make sure it was heard throughout the hospital.

In the trauma room, Jason's gear was waiting for him. These cases were usually bloody, so he donned a surgical gown, gloves, and a plastic face guard. In the process, Rooster strolled into the room, roused from his office by the page for the trauma code. He looked around the room briefly, totally at ease. His demeanor helped lower the level of stress in the room.

"Whatcha got?" He asked to no one in particular.

"A motorcycle versus truck," Bonnie answered.

"I assume we're not getting the truck driver," Rooster quipped. "You want some help?" He directed his question to Jason.

"Sure Rooster, if you're looking for something to do," Jason answered casually, in keeping with Rooster's demeanor. He knew Rooster probably had plenty to do, but he also knew an ER doctor was drawn to a trauma code like a pothead was drawn to the Twinkie aisle at a convenience store.

A nurse pushed a gown and face guard at Rooster. He had just finished dressing and was reaching for a pair of gloves when the ambulance arrived. The medics rolled the gurney into the trauma room, and the ER crew proceeded with their routine. It was immediately apparent the patient had deteriorated since the initial ambulance report and the medic was bagging the apparently lifeless patient.

"What's your status?" Jason asked.

"No respiratory effort and a falling level of consciousness. His BP hasn't changed much, even with two liters of saline in."

They lifted the patient, still on the backboard, to the ER gurney, and Jason quickly listened to his lungs. "Absent on the left and diminished on the right," he said. "I'm going to intubate. Rooster, you want to drop chest tubes for me?"

The respiratory tech took over the task of bagging the patient from the paramedic while Jason arranged his equipment for intubation. He had to be sure there was no movement of the patient's neck during the procedure. Done incorrectly, he could leave the patient paralyzed or dead. Rooster moved to the patient's side and changed to sterile gloves while a nurse opened a chest tube tray next to him.

"Give me ten milligrams of Vecuronium IV," Jason ordered then waited for the nurse to inject the medication into the IV line, which would chemically paralyze the patient. In a few seconds, the medicine left the patient flaccid and without any muscle tone or gag reflex.

"Stabilize the head for me," Jason directed the nurse to his side.

He carefully slid the laryngoscope blade to the back of his patient's throat and lifted the epiglottis, revealing the vocal cords. Luckily, this patient had a short neck and a high epiglottis. Jason effortlessly slid the endotracheal tube into the patient's trachea and started breathing for him. Just as he finished at the head of the gurney, he heard a distinct rush of air from Rooster's incision into the chest where he had relieved a tension pneumothorax.

"Very little blood on this side," Rooster said. "We're lucky so far. You want me to drop the tube on the other side?"

"Yeah, go ahead," Jason answered as he finished his initial quick exam of the rest of the patient's battered body.

Lab had drawn several tubes of blood, and X-ray was rolling a portable machine into position beside the gurney.

"What's our BP?" Jason asked as he stepped out of the way of the X-ray machine.

"We just lost our BP," Jeff answered.

"Shit," Roost responded. "He must have tension on the other side, too, and we've lost the stabilizing pressure from the side I just decompressed. He's kinked his vena cava, and we're not getting any blood back to the heart."

"Lab, give me six units of type O negative blood right now. X-ray, I need all seven cervical vertebrae on your first shot," Jason directed the tech aligning the portable X-ray machine next to the patient's neck.

Both techs responded and acknowledged his orders.

"Jeff, give me that large bore needle you keep in your pack," Rooster said as he moved to the patient's opposite side.

Jeff pulled a face and reluctantly withdrew a packet from the kit he kept in his side cargo pocket. "I hope you're going to replace this for me," he said as he slapped the packet into Rooster's hand.

Rooster peeled the packet open, revealing the giant needle. "Jesus Christ, what were you going to do with this thing? Sometimes you scare me, Noles."

"It's saving your ass isn't it?" Jeff shot back.

Rooster turned to the patient's chest and counted down to the space between the second and third ribs.

"I think it must be a Freudian thing," Bonnie offered. "You know, big needle, little . . ." She squeezed a small space between her thumb and forefinger.

Rooster chuckled and pushed the needle into the chest, releasing a geyser of air-propelled blood from the hub of the huge needle.

"Damn it, Rooster. You're spraying that shit everyplace," Bonnie yelled.

"Hey, I just said I was efficient. I never said anything about being neat," Rooster responded as he shielded the spray with his gloved hand until the eruption gradually diminished.

"We've got a BP back," a nurse at the head of the table announced.

"Okay, let's do it right and put a chest tube in on this side," Rooster answered.

"Set up for a central line and have X-ray send over an ultrasound machine. Have we heard from the trauma captain yet?" Jason spoke as he switched to sterile gloves and moved into position to place the central line.

Jeff trotted to the door and called to the ward clerk. "Page trauma again and tell them to get their butts down here."

Jason swabbed the patient's right groin with antiseptic and looked across to Rooster. "Are you about done there?" His answer came in the form of a surge of blood from the young patient's chest.

"Yep, just about done," Rooster responded as he took a reflex jump backward from the flow of blood, still holding his hand in the fresh hole in the chest.

"How about moving down and giving me a second femoral line when you're done?"

"I'm on my way," Rooster answered without looking up as he passed the end of the chest tube to one of the nurses, to be sutured into place.

Another central line kit appeared while Rooster felt for his landmarks in the young man's exposed groin. "Pulses are pretty weak."

"BP sixty palp." The reply came from behind him.

"I've got my line ready," Jason said. "Give me a bag on a pressure infuser," he ordered and pushed an IV line into the hub of the IV catheter he had positioned in the patient's femoral vein.

A nurse ran into the room carrying two bags of blood and handed them off to be spiked into the IV lines. The ultrasound tech rolled her portable machine into place right behind her and positioned it beside the patient. Jason listened with his stethoscope and rechecked lung sounds.

"Much better," he said. He moved to the patient's head, lifted his eyelids, and flashed a light in both eyes. "Left pupil is dilated. Where's my C-spine X-ray?"

"Right here, Dr. Corey." The tech hurried into the room and handed Jason an X-ray. He held the picture up to the light and quickly checked it while he shifted to examine the patient's abdomen. He marched his finger down the X-ray and counted out loud, numbers one through seven. "C-spine is clear on lateral — all seven," he said and flashed a quick wink at the X-ray tech, in recognition of her work.

Jason moved to the patient's abdomen and reexamined the area again. "Belly's getting hard with left flank bruising since our initial exam."

"There's a big surprise," Rooster offered. He knew all too well that accident victims like this often had internal injuries. "This guy's got a ruptured spleen."

Someone dimmed the lights and the ultrasound tech started her FAST scan of the patient looking for blood in the abdominal cavity. She moved the transducer from her machine over the patient's abdomen while Jason and Rooster watched the lines move on the monitor screen, giving an image of the contents of the belly.

Jason pointed to the viewer. "Yeah, he's got a large amount of free blood there." He tapped the screen with his finger. "You can see the ruptured spleen and probably a lacerated liver."

They heard the voice of Dr. Dan Weeks, the trauma surgeon, behind them. He had slipped into the darkened room unseen. His usual attire was a three-piece suit, but today he wore a surgical scrub suit topped off with a paisley print surgical cap. It was Jason's experience that most trauma surgeons were, frankly, pricks. Dan Weeks was an exception to the rule. He was a true professional who never lost his composure. Other surgeons were known for throwing charts, screaming at their staff, and behaving like spoiled children. No one had ever seen Dan Weeks be anything but calm and courteous, even when things weren't going well. Jason assumed Dr. Weeks relieved his stress on the tennis court where he was reported to be merciless. His muscled arms testified to his constitution.

"Gentlemen, what have we here?" He spoke in a deep, agreeable voice.

"Hi, Dan, good to see you. I appreciate you coming down." Jason nodded.

"You must have something big to get the old man out of his office," he joked as he acknowledged Rooster's presence.

Jason motioned to the ultrasound screen. "We've got a motorcycle rider hit by a truck. He's got a belly full of blood, and he's blown one pupil — probably an acute epidural bleed. We've been doing an aggressive fluid resuscitation, and we've relieved bilateral pneumos, but I think he needs to go to the O.R. as soon as possible."

Dr. Weeks watched the screen, then moved to the gurney. He felt the patient's abdomen briefly, looked at the chest tubes, and checked the young man's pupils. There was no waiting for a decision. He opened his cell phone and dialed the O.R.

"Thelma, this is Dr. Weeks. Do you have an open room?"

There was a brief pause. "That's not going to work, Thelma. Tell Dr. Stewart he's just been bumped and set up for a laparotomy and a simultaneous craniotomy. We need to go right now on this. Thank you, Thelma."

He dialed again. "Craig, this is Dan. Are you busy?"

He gave the neurosurgeon a quick rundown of the case. "We'll stop in CT on our way to the O.R. and shoot for starting in about ten minutes. Thank you, Craig."

He turned to Jason. "We're a go after a quick head CT. Could you please give him an additional four units of O negative, or whatever you can get into him quickly, and tell the lab to have twelve units on call for the O.R.? Nice work, gentlemen. As usual, it's been a pleasure." The door to the trauma room closed on his words.

Jeff called the lab while two other nurses readied the patient to be moved. They switched his IVs and the Pleur-evacs, which were attached to his chest tubes, to the IV poles on the gurney. In less than two minutes, they were rolling the patient out of the ER headed for CT, and then the O.R. They were well inside the "golden hour" that was touted for saving trauma victims, but this patient was still critical and had more than one life-threatening injury. The truth was, despite the efforts of the ER crew, he would be lucky to survive.

Jason and Rooster stood and looked at the empty room, now strewn with bloody litter and medical waste. They both peeled off their gloves, face guards and gowns, all splatter-painted with bright blood, and added these to the general debris of the room.

"Well, that was fun, now what should we do?" Rooster asked as he reached into his pocket. He flicked his cigarette lighter in Jason's direction.

"Sounds good to me," Jason answered.

Outside, they didn't talk about the trauma code or the patient while they smoked in silence. They still didn't even know the kid's name, and the young man merely remained *a case*, rather than a patient. There had been no family here, so they had no person-to-person contact with anyone conscious. They stood savoring the adrenaline rush as the last of the chemical washed from their systems.

No one in emergency medicine would deny that adrenaline was as addictive as any street drug, nor that it was even more compelling when combined with a power rush. What these doctors and nurses *would* deny was that the fleeting exhilaration was the same whether the patient lived or died. Nonetheless, it was true.

Rooster finished his cigarette and flicked the butt away. "Time to go back to the office."

"I'm going to have one more before I go in," Jason answered.

Rooster headed through the door and almost ran into Peter Loft, the chief OB/GYN resident.

"Hi, Rooster. Is Jason out here?" He voice was hesitant.

Rooster motioned to Jason with his head and walked away.

189

Jason turned but remained silent. He had already picked up on Peter's tone.

"Jason, I need to talk to you. I'm afraid there's a problem with Jesse's ultrasound." He gave him the news directly because there was no other way to say this to his friend.

Jason stood silently focused on Peter, fearing his acknowledgment of the words would make them real. He was barely aware of the pressure growing in his chest and the tightness around his heart, squeezing his breath away.

"I'm afraid the mass has gotten bigger," he paused. "And it's looking more like ovarian cancer."

Suddenly, Jason's world came to a halt. His pain gradually receded, and his breathing eased, but no words would come. But then, in reality, he didn't have anything to say. He knew all the specifics and all the statistics. Ovarian cancer was one of the most feared killers in all of medicine. Perhaps not at the top of the list, but certainly not far removed. Peter was talking, explaining more, but Jason didn't hear him. All he was aware of, was that the words honed a double-bladed fear within him; fear for Jesse's life, and fear of his own failure to save her.

TWENTY FOUR

The news came in short, measured doses, and although there was no intent, the progression maximized their suffering and dread. Jesse, as well as Jason, had been in constant pain since the diagnosis and the first surgery. The words had followed a dismal sequence: class 4, metastatic, and finally the term Jason had feared the most, but in some way had foreseen — terminal. Initial therapies had failed, leaving their hope hanging on a single experimental drug. Jesse's doctors said it was the one remaining chance she had, short of a miracle. Jesse was dying.

Arthur had seen them briefly the day after her diagnosis while Jesse was undergoing more tests and being readied for surgery. He had been so choked by grief he could barely speak. When he realized he was more of a hindrance than help, he leaned over Jesse's bed, kissed her, and forced out the words "God bless you," and left.

Arthur felt as if he were dying too. He leaned forward over his worktable and slowly unwound a wire from the branch of one of his bonsai trees, his favorite shimpaku juniper. A bulky sweater and crushed wool hat did little to protect him from the late autumn cold. A lifeless, veiled November sun hung in the sky, but did little to warm him.

Arthur's attention was not on his work today, and in fact, he was afraid he was going mad. He had finally gravitated to his trees out of a need to occupy his mind. Jesse's disease and his concern over Jason was almost more than he could bear. Usually, working on his trees relaxed him and wholly occupied his thoughts. Today, however, he was barely aware of what he was doing until the snap of a breaking branch pulled his attention. He dropped his arthritic hands to the table, still holding the tiny branch, and looked at the newly dead object in his palm. Tears welled in his eyes, then streamed down his face as he began to tremble. He sat like this, under the dull autumn sky, for several minutes. His body shook in silence, except for the occasional, barely discernible word burning in his mind: *Jesse*.

Arthur laid the broken branch on the table and slowly hobbled to the house. In the last few weeks, he had lost his vigor as well as much of his strength, and now seemed suddenly old. His usual energetic gait had become a shuffle, more typical of a man his age. Inside the house, he poured a small glass of brandy, sat down at the table in his darkened kitchen, and took a few sips of the warming liquid. He sat quietly, trying to regain control of his life, and stared through the window at the fading daylight. He rolled the glass in his hand as if it might thaw his soul.

The shrill sound of his telephone intruded on the stark quiet of the house. Arthur stifled his first reflex to pick up the phone immediately, afraid it might be Jason calling with news of Jesse. Finally, after several rings, he reasoned his denial wouldn't change what was waiting on the other end of the line, and he succumbed to his fear of the unknown. He stood and picked up the receiver.

"Hello." He barely recognized his own feeble voice.

"Arthur, is that you? This is Harrison Fellows." The words were charged with excitement.

Arthur answered, relieved, "Hello, Harrison. I've been expecting your call." His voice was subdued and reflected none of the excitement he heard from his friend.

"Arthur, I have the results of the test. They're a match to the original sample."

The words simultaneously stunned and relieved him. "Are you certain, Harry?"

"Absolutely. We ran the test here in my own lab as well as two others. There's no doubt, they're a match. And, Arthur, as we suspected, I've confirmed it's a genotype female, just like Jason."

Arthur reached for a chair and sat down heavily as the news worked its way into his mind.

"Arthur, have there been any more incidents like the earlier one you called me about?"

"Yes, Harry. There have been more incidents." His voice was without emotion. "My God. My God," Arthur half muttered.

"Exactly, it would seem that way. I'm taking a flight tomorrow morning. I've got to meet with Jason, and we have to pursue this now." Fellows practically crawled through the phone line in his eagerness to get to Seattle.

"No," Arthur shouted. "The girl, Jesse, she's dying of ovarian cancer. You can't do this to him now. It will have to wait." His voice gradually lost its force.

"All right, Arthur, I'll wait for now. But nothing is going to stand in my way this time. Nothing!"

"Harry, I need you to send a copy of the lab reports as well as a printout of the karyotype. I need them as soon as possible."

This time the pause was on the other end of the line. "All right, Arthur. I'll FedEx them to you, but I want your word you won't try and stop me once this thing with the girl is over."

"I just hope Jason survives this nightmare and is able to proceed. No matter what the outcome with the girl, I won't be able to stop things then. It will have gone too far. Good-bye, Harrison."

Arthur returned to his seat at the table, poured a generous shot of brandy, and took it down in a single gulp. The liquid fire stoked his resolve.

TWENTY FIVE

It was their wedding day. Not surprisingly, Jason took little joy and even less satisfaction from that knowledge. He hauled himself out of bed, stopped in the bathroom, then lurched unsteadily toward the kitchen. Half a pot of cold, murky coffee, leftover from yesterday or maybe the day before, lurked in the coffeepot. Jason sorted through a pile of dirty dishes stacked on the kitchen counter and selected the least menacing mug. He poured a cup of coffee and pushed it into the microwave, hoping to salvage one more serving from the lifeless brew. He searched through the accumulation of general litter and found a crumpled pack with a few overlooked cigarettes. He lit one, only to find it was split just below the filter and unsmokable. He flipped the cigarette into the sink, onto a putrid heap of assorted garbage in varying stages of decomposition. "Shit." He dug to the back of the cigarette pack and found a single intact cigarette. The timer on the microwave beeped, signaling the expectant revival of the coffee. He answered the second set of beeps as he stumbled toward the microwave.

"Yeah, yeah, I heard you the first time."

Jason grimaced at the first disappointing sip of coffee and reached for a nearly empty bottle of Jack Daniels. He tasted the coffee again after the addition of a hefty splash of Jack and decided the addition made the brew potable, then just for safety, added a second splash. He didn't notice the slight tremor in his hands when he filled his cup or lit his cigarette, but it was undeniably there, nonetheless.

He moved toward the deck, pushed the slider back, and stepped halfway outside, where he was stopped by a curtain of wintry drizzle. A pale dead-gray sky hung over the Sound, shrouding the mountains in a veil of shifting fog. He stood partially inside, still protected from the wind-driven rain, swigged the coffee, and took several deep drags off his cigarette.

His focus shifted from the mountains and spread over the surface of the Sound as if he were searching for something lost. His lifeless expression seemed as dead as the Seattle sky, but a more careful examination revealed something hidden in his eyes — a fierceness that hinted at hatred spiced with bitterness and betrayal. It occurred to him that his life had changed abruptly, like the simple seasons of a Celtic year, from bright summer to dark winter.

It had been almost three months since Jesse had been diagnosed with ovarian cancer. The initial shock and following few days had left him wandering in a state of disbelief, not wholly aware of the world around him, other than Jesse. The findings at the first surgery had, in fact, foretold the whole story.

The course of her illness had been harder for Jesse because of her knowledge of cancer. This was a different type of cancer from what she had dealt with in pediatrics, but she was all too cognizant of the significance of the findings. The day they made the diagnosis and again at each step backward, each failed treatment, Jesse's face had revealed her failing hope.

The first surgery had gone well enough . . . at first, but complications followed, supporting the old superstition about doctors and their families. A pulmonary embolus, a frequent complication experienced by cancer patients, had nearly killed her. Then, a post-op infection raised havoc with her body — a body already ravaged by radiation and chemotherapy. She had been transferred to ICU on three separate occasions, and each time Jason had feared it was a final event.

They had tried to support each other, but their bravery gradually gave away, extinguished by the ever-growing specter of death. At last, all vestige of hope was lost, leaving them only with each other. Something they both knew would also soon be gone.

After each crisis, they had tried to convince each other Jesse would get to come home soon, and they would get married. But each crisis was followed by yet another setback as her condition worsened. Now, they both knew there would be no homecoming and no wedding, at least not as they had dreamed. As a final option, Jason had arranged for them to be married in the hospital — a deathbed wedding.

The recent months had been a downhill, destructive spiral for Jason, as well as Jesse. The return to alcohol and pills had been an early escape then became a general anesthetic to ease the pain in his soul. Finally, when there was no longer any shelter from the pain, he drank out of habit. It did little to dull his rage.

Jason was still drinking this morning, even though he felt little effect from the alcohol he had become so accustomed to. He hadn't worked in weeks. He had lost weight, his body ravaged by a wasting disease of his soul, not unlike the wasting disease, which was slowly destroying Jesse's body. He had traded his usual neat appearance for the who-gives-a-damn look. The apartment had fared even worse.

He had been with Jesse until late last night when she made him leave, insisting it was bad luck to see the bride before the wedding on their wedding day. He laughed at the time, but as he left the hospital, he asked God just how much more bad luck he could possibly have. It was one of a number of one-sided conversations with God, the substance of which had deteriorated from bargains to pleas, and finally to desperate threats. God had not responded.

Jesse's parents arrived a few days ago. They had made several trips from California and were now prepared to stay until the end. Thankfully, they had refused Jason's offer to stay at the town house and had gone to a hotel near the hospital. Jason got along well enough with them, but right now he preferred the anesthesia of alcohol and drugs over companionship.

Jason finished the bottle of Jack Daniels and found his reserve bottle of Jim Beam. There was nothing left to eat in the apartment other than a half-empty jar of chunky peanut butter and a box of mac and cheese. He briefly toyed with the idea of walking to the nearest Starbucks for a muffin and a latte, but in the end settled for another drink and a few Ativan. By eleven a.m., he was feeling better and decided it was time to shower and get dressed. Jesse had insisted he wear a tuxedo for the wedding, even though her gown was more of a "hospital motif," as she put it.

Jason chugged his drink before his shower and swore it was his last until after the ceremony. Jesse deserved better for her wedding than a drunken, staggering groom, and he vowed he would be as sober as possible for her sake. He hoped the shower would clear his mind.

He shaved, brushed his teeth and combed his hair. He hadn't looked in a mirror for days, maybe weeks, and one glance into the mirror over his bathroom sink told him why. A stranger peered back at him, and try as he might, Jason couldn't recognize the face. He ran his fingers over his features, and pulled his old Doogie Howser face from his childhood, which almost struck a note of familiarity. In the end, he gave up and accepted that the image must be his own, only because of his knowledge of light and physics. The experience almost sent him running for the bourbon, but he called upon his last measure of strength and dressed in his tuxedo instead.

The doorbell rang just as he finished. Arthur had called him yesterday, adamant that he talk to Jason today before they went to the hospital. His arrival was uncharacteristically early.

Arthur stood in the doorway with his tattered brown leather secretary under his arm. Jason answered the door and stepped back, his eyebrows raised, asking, "How do I look?"

"Jason, you look good, Son. Better than I've seen you look in a while."

Jason ignored both the compliment and what he was sure was an unintentional dig.

"You're early."

"I wanted to be certain we have time to talk before we leave," Arthur said and stepped inside. He looked around the apartment, moved some clutter off a chair, and sat down, but immediately stood again and started to pace. "We haven't had much time to talk lately."

Jason looked at his watch. "Can I get you something to drink?" He offered, hoping Arthur would accept and give him an excuse to join him.

"Not for me, Son."

Jason vacillated, then reluctantly sat down without a drink and lit a cigarette. "So what did you want to talk about?"

Arthur found a place opposite Jason. "Son, you know I don't like to meddle, but I love you and Jesse too much not to say something now. I've waited a long time, but I can't wait any longer, or it will be too late."

Jason slumped back in his chair and sighed. "Look, Dad, I know I've been drinking a lot lately, but I have it under control. It'll stop after . . ." His words trailed off.

Arthur offered a slight smile. "Yes, you're right. You have been drinking too much, but I have enough confidence in you to know you won't let it become a problem. I'm afraid what I have to say is a bit more difficult than that."

They sat facing each other, neither speaking while Arthur bolstered his courage. At last, he began. "Jason, I need to know if you've tried to heal Jesse."

Jason looked confused. "That's it? Dad you scared the hell out of me. You know we've done everything — the whole course of treatments including experimental drugs. Yes, Dad. We've tried, but you know that."

Arthur's expression didn't change. "I didn't ask if you've attempted to treat her. I asked you if you've tried to *heal* her, and I think you know what I mean."

197

Jason stood, walked to the kitchen, and poured a generous shot of bourbon into a dirty glass. He took a long drink, then leaned against the counter and swirled the remaining dark liquid along the sides of the glass. His mind, frozen by his father's words, slowly fought for an answer. After several minutes, he returned to his chair and sat down.

"Dad," he began slowly. "I can't heal Jesse. I can't heal anyone. I'm a doctor and I treat patients, but I'm just like any other man. Some guys get up in the morning and go to work and sell cars or pump gas or fix air conditioners or a million other things. It's their job. I get up in the morning, go to work, and prescribe medicines, sew up cuts and all the other things doctors do. In the end, I'm no different than all those other guys out there making a living. Sometimes I make some difficult and pretty important decisions, but that doesn't make me anything holy. M.D. doesn't stand for Minor Deity, despite what television and the AMA would like people to think." He stopped and took another drink, then gave in. "No, Dad, I haven't tried to heal Jesse because I couldn't stand to fail." His voice broke as he spoke Jesse's name.

"I think you're wrong, Son. I promised your mother I would never tell you this, but I think she would want me to do this now — for Jesse. Perhaps I should have told you a long time ago, or maybe I shouldn't tell you now." He sat forward and watched his son's face. "Before I go on though, I want you to know that I love you. I also want you to know how sorry I am." Arthur's voice wavered and cracked.

"Dad — " Jason started to speak, but Arthur cut him off.

"This will probably be easier, at least for me, if you let me get this out without interruption." Arthur fought for control of his emotions.

Jason put his drink on the table and sat back in his chair.

"I'm sure you remember your genetics from college and medical school, but there are a couple of terms I need to refresh for you." He continued, anticipating his son's objections. "I hope you'll indulge me a little here, Jason."

Jason looked down at the glass beside him but resisted the temptation.

"You remember that a person's genetic pattern is called a genotype and what an individual looks like is their phenotype. In other words, the genotype is a distinct pattern of genes that says blue eyes, and the phenotype is the actual presence of blue eyes on the individual." He paused to make sure he still had Jason's attention. "A karyotype is an actual picture of an individual's chromosomes laid out in order and numbered, sort of like a Rosetta Stone translation of hieroglyphics. Of course, you remember that a single set of genes, one from each parent, determines an individual's sex. The mother can only give an X from her XX pattern, and the father can give an X or a Y from his XY pattern; thus the father ultimately determines the sex of their offspring."

"Dad, this is all basic genetics from undergrad, but I don't see what it has to do with Jesse," he said impatiently.

"I know, Jason, but I have to make sure we're speaking the same language. I think you'll understand in a few minutes." Arthur stood, walked to the window, and waited briefly while he carefully chose his words and arranged his thoughts.

"Have you ever thought about the conception of Christ? It's a very intriguing topic from a geneticist's point of view." He looked out across the Sound, avoiding Jason's gaze. "Since there was no true exchange of genetic material, Christ could only have the genes he received from Mary, XX, yet he was a phenotype male. There has been more than a little speculation in recent years that Christ had a child with Mary Magdalene; St. Sarah, a female, which of course makes sense since there was no Y chromosome to be passed on."

Jason gave in to temptation, picked up his glass, and took a gulp. He lit another cigarette and sat back again in his chair still holding the glass of bourbon.

"I suppose you could argue genetics like religion, by the hour and never have any definite answers. After all, science really can't resolve questions like that, and that's probably a good thing. I'm not sure mankind could handle that kind of reality, whichever way it came out," Jason said.

Arthur partially turned and smiled. "I hadn't thought about it in those terms, but you may be right. Nonetheless, I think science and religion can be reconciled in some areas, and this may well be one of them." He turned and faced Jason. "I believe I have scientific proof of Christ's genetic makeup."

Arthur's announcement took Jason by surprise, but the initial shock quickly faded to skepticism. "Dad, that's a pretty incredible statement. I think the scientific community, hell, the entire world, would have trouble accepting it. If you published something like that, I'm afraid you'd be called crazy, among other things. What kind of proof do you have?"

"Oh, I have no intention of publishing this. In fact, there are only three people who know about it, and I intend to keep it that way, if I can."

"Who knows about this besides us?"

"Unfortunately, Harrison Fellows."

"Uncle Harry? And why is that a problem? I can't believe he would do anything to harm your reputation."

"I'm not worried about that. I'm worried Harrison would use that kind of power to benefit himself." He returned to his chair and sat down heavily.

Jason walked into the kitchen and returned with two partially filled glasses. Arthur took a sip, and watched Jason's face as he reflected on what he had said.

"But I don't understand. How would putting a theory like this out to the public give him or anyone else any power? A lot of attention maybe, but not power."

Arthur looked somewhat baffled. "Anyone with control or even influence over this individual would have tremendous power, just like the individual himself."

"Wait, Dad. Who are you talking about?"

"Oh, I'm sorry, I've gotten a little ahead of myself." He took another drink and continued.

"Years ago, when Harrison Fellows and I were still doing active research, Harrison came by some cells, human red blood cells, taken from the Sudarium Christi."

"Wait, what? What exactly is the Sudarium Christi?" Jason stumbled through the words.

"I'm not surprised you haven't heard of this. Actually, very few people have. It was Jewish tradition that a separate piece of cloth, besides the shroud that covered the body be used to cover the face of the deceased at the time of death. Unlike the Shroud of Turin, which has received so much attention over the years, the Sudarium Christi has received exceedingly little publicity."

"Shroud of Turin? Dad, are you talking about the burial wrap of Jesus Christ?"

Before Arthur could answer, Jason continued. "Then you're talking about red blood cells from Christ!"

"Yes, Jason. That's exactly what I'm talking about. They were the only cells present, but based on their location and other factors, Harrison felt there was a good chance they may have actually come from Christ. The history of the crucifixion, as told in the Bible, tells us that there was a great deal of blood on the cloth used to cover Christ's face-the Sudarium Christi. Of course, that's assuming you believe the rest of the history of the Shroud and the Sudarium, and Harrison did. You need to understand, Harrison was an important researcher even in those days and had studied in several places around the world, including China. Most people aren't aware that China was one of the earliest countries to do serious research on cloning, and Harrison was significantly involved with that work."

"Cloning?" Jason sat forward on the edge of his chair. "You're not trying to tell me . . ."

Arthur interrupted him again. "The first problem, of course, was the fact that the cells were an XX genotype. That's when I came up with the explanation that there was no exchange of genetic material at the conception. The second problem was a host for a cloned embryo. Unfortunately, I also assisted with that solution."

Arthur placed his glass on the table, leaned forward, and withdrew several sheets of paper from the worn leather secretary sitting at his feet. He fumbled briefly with his glasses, then handed the sheets to Jason. "This is your karyotype, Son."

Jason took the sheets from his father and examined the fuzzy stick-figure photos of his own genes. He had just started to study the pictures when he stopped.

"Dad, this can't be my karyotype. This shows the XX pattern of a female."

"It's yours. It was confirmed by three different labs, including Harrison Fellow's, one of the best labs in the world."

"Again, Dad, this is a female karyotype." His words were now edged with frustration.

"That's right. The genotype is also a perfect match to the cells Harrison harvested from the Sudarium Christi. The baby Jesse miscarried, was it a female?" He braced himself for Jason's response.

The meaning of his father's words bored into Jason's consciousness, and all emotion drained from his face. The neurons in his mind fired, one connection after another, and grew to a cascading avalanche of understanding, as insanity and reality consumed each other, leaving the papers he held in his hand the only reality in his life.

At last, he looked up. "How? Why? Mom?" Jason forced the tortured words out.

Arthur maintained his composure, trying to remember this was all leading to Jesse. "Your mother and I wanted children very much, and

Harrison offered us a last hope. Your mother never knew until after you were born."

Jason slowly nodded his understanding. "So you think this explains the talking in my sleep and all the things that have happened in the last few months."

"Yes, I believe it does. But Jason, remember it also gives Jesse another chance. You have the power to heal her."

"And if it doesn't work, if I fail her again? You want me to play God, for Christ's sake." He failed to recognize the irony of his words.

"I don't know how to answer that, Jason. But I believe you have the courage and the strength to attempt to heal Jesse. Do you actually have another option? Can you live with yourself if you don't even try? You have some power, Jason. You're not the empowered Son of God, but you share something with him. That gives you a limited power that you can't fully control, but it might be enough to save Jesse."

Neither of them spoke. Jason lit a cigarette and walked onto the deck where a cold wind off the Sound washed him in thick fog. He finished the cigarette, flicked it away, and returned to his father.

"It's okay, Dad, but I need to process this. Can you drive to the hospital yourself and I'll follow in a few minutes?" He asked.

Arthur tried to read his son as they stood facing each other. "I love you, Jason." He spoke tentatively then hugged him.

"Its all right, Dad. I love you too."

Jason fought unsuccessfully for control of his emotions. He poured another drink, lit a cigarette, and tried desperately to comprehend what was happening to his life. He walked to the bedroom, Jesse's bedroom, and fumbled under some clothes in the bottom drawer of their dresser. He found what he was searching for, hidden far in the back under some old T-shirts. He had bought the .38 revolver for Jesse for the nights she was by herself, but she refused to have anything to do with the weapon. He opened the cylinder, shook the bullets into his hand, and laid them on the dresser. He liked the feel of the gun; the solid weight in his hand. He opened the cylinder again, and one by one, reloaded the shells. The pistol slowly absorbed the heat from his body and began to feel warm against his skin as if it were taking on a life of its own. The feel of it overwhelmed Jason's spirit. He slowly pulled the top drawer open and slid the revolver inside, assured that no matter what happened, he had an escape from what had become an unendurable life.

Jason's entire world had betrayed him; his father, medicine, even Jesse, though it wasn't her fault. No, more than that, God had betrayed him.

He groped for his sanity as the panic and anguish that burned in his chest gradually subsided. Arthur had been right. He had the courage to hold on and try, for Jesse's sake, but the reality of his life reminded him that his fate was tied to hers.

TWENTY SIX

Jesse's fear of death and the unknown was balanced against her desire to escape her pain. Death still frightened her, but she had made her own peace with the Specter. Since she actually didn't have any choice in the matter, she accepted it as a push, but it was a shitty hand.

The hospital room, that had been her home for the past several weeks, still seemed as if it were a foreign place. It seemed she should have been prepared for this, being a nurse and all, but that actually made it worse. Hospitals were for patients, those others who were sick or dying, but not for her. The alien sounds and smells she had taken for granted as a nurse, now permeated her world and threatened her. She watched the constant drip of her IV, connected to the port that had been surgically implanted in her chest. She shifted in her bed and tried unsuccessfully to find a position that wasn't bed sore. Her movements only snarled her more in her hospital gown, and left her, she was sure, exposed.

The hardest part of the last few months had been watching the effects of her illness on the people she loved. Her parents had never been ones to show their feelings, but she could see how hard this had been for them. Jason had suffered the most drastically, and it showed. She was sure he was hurting inside, but that seemed to pale when compared to the more obvious outward destruction. She knew the drugs and alcohol were destroying him, and it broke her heart to think she was to blame, or so she believed. She had not been able to deal with the other facets of Jason's problems on any level.

Arthur's transformation had also been difficult. Jesse had watched him wither and age unimaginably in the past few months. She wanted to reach out to him, to console him, but it seemed he could barely stand more than a few minutes with her before his grief overwhelmed him and drove him away from her. She was afraid he would follow her into death by his own will, if his grief did not destroy him first.

The pain in Jesse's belly slowly pulsed and intensified like a living, growing beast, beyond her control. Her doctor had decreased her pain medication today at Jesse's request. Now, she wondered if it had been the right decision. She wanted to see Jason and her wedding through lucid eyes, but as the pain increased she became more aware of how difficult it was to breathe. The sensation of suffocating frightened her more than the looming presence of her own death.

Jennifer Noble knocked softly and came into the room.

"Well, are we set to get ready for the big day?" Her mother asked.

Jesse smiled and nodded. Speaking had become extremely difficult as her breathing worsened, and she tried to save her breath.

Her mother laid a hand mirror on the small stand that extended across the bed, then turned to search for her makeup bottles in the bulky bag she had brought with her. Reluctantly, Jesse picked up the mirror and faced her own gaunt, pallid reflection. Murky eyes gazed back at her from deep, shadowy sockets. She pulled the scarf away from her head, revealing a few thin, wispy strands of blonde hair. She was overwhelmed by the image, and by the thought that Jason couldn't possibly want to marry anyone who looked like this. Her will to fight was gone, and she started to cry.

Her mother sat down on the bed, took the mirror from her hand and laid it face down on the table.

"I'm sorry Jesse, that was inconsiderate of me."

"It's okay, Mom. I should be used to it by now." The few words left her breathing heavily. "I guess I won't be the blushing bride."

"Jesse, you know how much Jason loves you. To him, you're the same beautiful woman he's loved for years, and nothing can change that."

"It doesn't seem fair." She fought for breath. "He shouldn't have to be a widower so soon."

Her mother held her and felt death rattle through her daughter's body with each labored gasp for air. Finally, Jesse settled, and her breathing slowed.

"Let's see what we can do with a little makeup and a few special things I brought. I'll bet you can still bring a great big smile to Jason's face when he sees you come down the aisle."

Jesse squeezed her mother's hand and wiped the tears off her cheeks. "Mom, I want you and Daddy to know, I wish I would have been a better daughter."

Her mother bit her lip to hold back the tears. "Oh, hush with nonsense like that. We've got work to do."

She started to smooth makeup across Jesse's cheek, then stopped. She smiled at the young woman and saw the child she had given birth to, raised, and watched grow into a woman. She leaned forward and kissed her forehead, then continued to apply the makeup. She held her feelings inside yet again and wished she had been a better mother.

Jason moved Jesse's Mercedes through the busy midday traffic, barely aware of the vehicles around him. He tried to make sense of what Arthur had told him a few minutes earlier, but his mind struggled and remained in standby mode. Thankfully, his body had gone numb, except for the awareness of suppressed panic churning deep within him. On some level, he had known for months that he possessed the power, but he never imagined its origin. Now, he couldn't deny it any longer, and worse, he couldn't avoid using it, trying to control it, to save Jesse. The terror escaped his control, gripped him again, and he screamed out loud. His mind grasped for a life preserver, and the image of the waiting gun rescued him.

Jason parked in the doctor's lot and walked toward the ambulance doors out of habit. He noticed where he was just in time and detoured to the main hospital entrance. He didn't have the strength to face his friends and co-workers in the ER today. He had more than enough good wishes and condolences. He knew they meant well, but today he simply couldn't do it; couldn't smile and say thank you.

He moved toward the bank of elevators, oblivious to the occasional glance in his direction. Men in tuxedos were conspicuous in a hospital. He pushed the button and looked at the floor indicator while he waited for the chime that announced the arrival of his elevator. When the door opened, he looked up into the glowing, beautiful face of Sherri Black.

Jason couldn't help but make a brief mental comparison to Jesse's appearance, waiting for him a few floors above them.

"Jason!" She was as surprised as he was. "How are you?" The timbre of her voice changed, and she placed a consoling hand on his arm.

"Hello, Sherri."

She half smiled. "Well, I love the tux, but you look like shit. What's the occasion?"

"I'm getting married. I've got to run, people are waiting for me."

She held his arm. "Jason, I want you to know how sorry I am about Jesse." Her voice was sincere. "I know you may not believe me, but I am truly sorry."

"Thank you, Sherri. And yes, I do believe you." He took her hand and squeezed. "I want you to know, I don't have any regrets about us."

"I have one big regret, Jason." She paused. "I'm sorry we never made love."

"I just couldn't, Sherri. I couldn't do that to Jesse. And now, that's one less thing I have on my conscience."

"I don't know a lot about Jesse, and I suppose this sounds strange under the circumstances, but she's a very lucky girl. I still envy her."

He leaned over and kissed her cheek. "You take care."

She released his hand, and he stepped into the elevator. The doors closed, and she knew he had left her life forever.

The now familiar sign reading "10th floor Oncology" greeted Jason. He remembered the first day he brought Jesse to the hospital and the impact of that sign. They didn't belong on an oncology floor. Jesse was too young and too full of life to be there. Now, he was afraid she would never leave again.

He walked down the hall to Jesse's room but found the door closed with a sign which read "DO NOT DISTURB" taped below her room number. He considered going in, but instead walked back to the nursing station.

"Hi, Dr. Corey. Are you ready for the big day?" A staff nurse he had seen many times before greeted him. "You look pretty sharp."

He smiled and rolled his eyes. "What's up with the closed door and the sign on Jesse's room?"

"Oh, that's to keep you out — strict orders from the bride. You're supposed to go ahead to the chapel."

Jason smiled, stuffed his hands into his pockets, and slowly walked down the hall to the small chapel, provided for patients and their families. It was designed to be consoling, and he doubted the room had ever been used for a wedding. He opened the stained glass doors and found the few rows of pews filled with people from the ER and the hospital. Rooster met him just inside, dressed in his own tuxedo.

Rooster shook Jason's hand. "We were beginning to think you backed out on us. Where have you been?"

"I was delayed a little. You didn't need to go to all of this trouble Rooster, and what's with the tux?" Jason stepped back to take in the full view.

"Well, I thought every groom needs a best man. That is if it's okay with you?"

207

"It's just fine with me, Rooster. I really appreciate it. I know how nervous weddings make you."

"Yeah, well as long as I'm not the groom, I'll be okay."

Jason felt a hand on his shoulder and turned to find Jesse's doctor at his side. Dr. Kelly Canter was acclaimed as the best oncologist in the Northwest, and many claimed the best in the country. She had made a name for herself not only by her skill as a physician, but also by her relationship with her patients. It wasn't uncommon to find her spending the whole night at a patient's bedside at the end. She actually cared for the people she treated.

"Jason, can we talk for a minute?"

He followed her into the hallway, away from the group in the chapel.

"How's Jesse doing today? I haven't seen her yet," he asked.

"Jason, I'm afraid all of this might be too much for Jesse. I tried to talk her into having the ceremony in her room so she could stay in bed, but she absolutely refused. We finally compromised on her staying in a wheelchair and wearing her oxygen." She waited for Jason to process her words before she continued. "We haven't talked about a time frame so far because I just wasn't certain, but I think we're getting very close to the end. Her breathing has gotten much worse, and she's extremely weak."

"I understand. How much time do you think we have?" His voice quivered slightly.

"No one can say precisely; a day or two, maybe hours."

"Hours." He nodded and looked down, his hands still stuffed into his pockets.

"Keep the ceremony short and get her back to bed as soon as you can. We're walking a fine line with her pain medication, but we let it wear off a little for the wedding, so she could be awake."

The door to the chapel opened behind them, and the minister leaned out into the hallway. "I just got the call that we're ready to go whenever you are."

"Then I guess we better get going." He started to turn toward the front of the chapel when Dr. Canter stopped him.

"Jason, she really needs you to be strong right now."

"Strong." He nodded again and walked away.

Jason took his place between the minister and Rooster, at the front of the chapel. The guests took their cue and found a place either in the pews or along the wall and quieted. One of the male nurses walked to the front corner of the chapel with a violin and softly started to play Pachelbel's Canon. The rich notes of the music seemed somehow to underscore the absurdity that was now Jason's life, and he fought to choke back the scream struggling to escape his body.

Jesse's mother entered, walked to the front of the chapel, and took a seat next to Arthur. The twisted handkerchief in her hand was already damp from her tears. The chapel doors opened again, and the violin made a seamless transition into the wedding march as Jesse emerged in a wheelchair, pushed slowly by her father. Her face was veiled with a small white, lace scarf, and a white afghan that draped over her robe, hid her frail body. Someone, probably her mother, had helped Jesse with her makeup; a little blush, some lipstick and a touch of eye shadow.

Jason could see the pain hiding behind her smile. She struggled to breathe, and the effort of the day was already draining her strength. Her father stopped the wheelchair next to Jason, kissed his daughter's cheek, and took his seat in the front row with his wife and Arthur. Jason took his bride's hand and turned to face the minister.

"Dearly beloved . . ."

Jason's mind escaped to another place and time. He remembered the years he and Jesse had shared, their first months together and their trips to the beach. Times exploring, cruising in the topless BMW with the wind in her hair, and nights they had spent talking for hours and making love. He had taken those times for granted, and now he would do anything to have them back, to have her back. He realized now that she was his life.

"Jason," the minister had finished. "Do you have something you want to say to Jesse?"

Jason turned and dropped to one knee. He looked into her face and spoke softly to the woman he loved.

"I have always believed that each one of us has one chance for true love in our lifetime. I thank God I have you. You have brought more love and more happiness to me than any man has a right to expect. No matter what, you will always be in my heart and entwined in my soul. I love you, Jesse."

The minister turned to Jesse. "And I believe Jesse has something she wants to say to Jason."

She spoke breathlessly in short bursts of words. "There are a million . . . things . . . I wish I . . . could say to you. So many things . . . I want to tell you. I know . . . some people . . . would say I'm crazy, but I'm the

luckiest . . . woman . . . in the world. You've given me . . .
a lifetime of love. Please know . . . that I love you . . . and I'm sorry."
Her final words were choked and nearly lost in her tears.

Jason bit his lip and the coppery taste of blood filled his mouth. He refused to break, and fought to clear his burning eyes. He would remain strong as long as he could, but at this moment, all he wanted to do was carry Jesse away, wipe away her pain, and make everything the way it had been.

Jason could see Jesse's strength was nearly spent. He retrieved her ring from his jacket pocket and slipped it onto her fragile finger, then placed his ring in her hand and helped her slide it into place. The smile he loved so much appeared on her face, and he leaned forward and gently kissed her lips. Jason held her in his arms while the minister introduced them.

"Ladies and gentlemen, may I introduce for the first time, Dr. and Mrs. Jason Corey."

Jason wheeled her out of the chapel past their guests, many of them in tears, and hurried her back to her room. He lifted her into bed, and two nurses reattached her IV, and injected morphine into the line. He sat on the side of her bed, held her hand and watched as the drug took effect. Jesse's breathing gradually slowed, and he felt her relax.

"Not a very exciting . . . wedding night."

He smiled. "The night's not over yet."

"Will you stay . . . here with me?"

"I'll be right here." He shifted closer to her on the bed. "Jesse, about what you said during the wedding. You don't have anything to be sorry for. I couldn't stand it if I thought you believed that."

"You deserve . . . so much more."

"Believe me Jess, no one could ever be more than you."

A soft knock on the door interrupted them, and Jesse's parents along with Arthur peeked into the room.

"We just wanted to stop in and say goodbye," Arthur said. "We're going to let you two have a little peace and quiet."

The three of them kissed Jesse, shook Jason's hand, and promised to return later. Arthur caught Jason's attention, his eyes questioning. They didn't have a chance to talk, but Jason knew what Arthur was asking.

Alone again, Jesse sleepily patted the bed next to her, and Jason half laid, half sat beside her, balancing himself with one foot on the floor. He put his arm around her shoulders and watched the morphine wrap her in its power. She was asleep in a few minutes.

Jason watched the rapid rise and fall of her chest. He waited, trying to collect his courage and focus his power. The only thing greater than his fear of failure was his fear of losing Jesse, and he knew he had to try to save her. He slowly reached across her sleeping form and placed his palm flat against the frail warmth of her chest. He waited, hoping to feel something which said whatever power he had inside him, was working to save Jesse's life. He willed it. He searched deep inside himself and concentrated, trying to command whatever might be there. Finally, just as he felt the last fiber of hope slip away, he felt it. The ache in his arm surged down through his hand, an ache he had felt before, and Jesse's face reacted. Her expression hardened in response to his pain, then changed and became serene. She opened her eyes and looked at Jason, then took his hand and smiled.

"I think it has to be this way." The words slipped from her lips.

Her eyes drifted shut, and she exhaled slowly and sighed. Her face softened, and a cloak of tranquility replaced the pain that had been there for so long.

"Jesse, I need — " Her hand released and dropped to the bed, cutting off his words. She did not take another breath, and he watched as the spectral shroud of death slowly crept across her face.

"Jesse. Jesse!" He called her name, but he knew there would never be an answer. He softly kissed her lips then stood beside her bed.

The sound started from a place in the infinite depths of his soul. It rose, drawing strength from the pain of broken promises, betrayal, and lost love; a loss he had been forbidden to mourn until this moment. It fed on his own guilt until it howled like a wind-driven inferno, and finally erupted in an anguished scream, which none of the nurses who responded to his cries understood.

"E-li, E-li, la'-ma Sa-bach'-than-ni"?

TWENTY SEVEN

Jason opened his eyes, and the memory of her scent instantly flooded his mind. The throbbing pain in his head paled next to the anguish of his soul. His sleep this night had been ravaged, as it had been every night since Jesse's death; haunted by his failed attempts to save her.

He heaved himself off the couch, still wearing Tuesday's clothes; it was Friday. He staggered toward the bathroom, clutched at the doorframe, then dropped to his knees and spewed blood stained bile into the commode — almost. He forced his sweat-drenched body to the sink and rinsed his mouth with cold tap water, then ran his wet hands through his hair. When he peered into the mirror, the face, which gazed back at him, was flushed with insanity.

Jason scuffed toward the kitchen, avoiding the bedroom on his way. He hadn't entered their bedroom since the day of Jesse's funeral. At times, the gun called to him with a siren's song, like the memory of a lost lover, offering respite from his surreal existence. The gun wasn't going anyplace, and he took some comfort knowing he could answer its siren's call whenever he chose.

He found the empty remains of a crumpled pack of cigarettes and tossed it aside. He shoved a stack of papers off the kitchen table and uncovered a nearly empty bottle of bourbon. He lifted it to his lips and drained the remaining amber liquid. The empty bottle hit the table with a dull thud and fell over. He searched the cabinets for cigarettes and found another half bottle of bourbon, but little else. He moved toward the balcony, through what remained of the apartment, now littered with empty liquor bottles, overflowing ashtrays, and discarded pill bottles. The apartment, which Jesse had kept so neat, now resembled a back street flophouse more than it did the home of someone respectable. No one would ever have guessed it was the residence of a physician.

He pulled the drapes back and raised his eyebrows, surprised it was still dark, or already dark, he wasn't sure which. The days since Jesse's death had bled together into an inseparable haze of booze and pills, days and nights, all to the cadence of the drumming ache in his chest. He checked his watch. He assumed it was ten-thirty p.m. since he hadn't heard of an upcoming solar eclipse. He moved outside onto the deck and sat down in the cold, night air, oblivious to the misty fog that surrounded him and permeated his clothes. He lit a cigarette and took a long pull from the bottle; his head felt better already. The sound of a single night gull rode the breeze over the water. The bird's cry, like everything else in his world, brought Jesse's memory screaming back to the surface of his conscious mind. The knowledge he had failed her made the pain all the more poignant.

Jason inhaled the smoke of another cigarette deep into his lungs and let the wave of alcohol push his head backward against his chair. At first, he thought the pounding was inside his head until it became more vigorous and intrusive. A visitor was the last thing he wanted. He took another pull from the bottle and tried to ignore the sound, but the knocking continued, louder and more invasive, demanding his attention.

"Go the fuck away," he yelled.

The uninvited guest stopped knocking and started pounding on the door with their fist. Whoever it was, they weren't going to leave.

"There's no fucking body home," he bellowed. "Go away."

The pounding stopped but was followed by Rooster's voice.

"You sure make a lot of noise for not being home."

Jason sighed and dropped his chin onto his chest. He knew Rooster wouldn't give up. He found his footing and staggered to the door.

"Welcome to my abode," he slurred and gestured Rooster inside with a grand, swooping arc of his arm.

"Well, it lives," Rooster mocked as he walked into the apartment. "I see the maid hasn't been here . . . this year," he said as he looked around the town house.

"Why, Rooster, are you impugning my skills as a domestic engineer?" Jason stumbled over the words.

"I was going to ask how you're doing, but I think I can see for myself." Rooster strolled through the apartment. "So, this is it, huh?" He picked up an empty pill bottle and read the label. "This stuff will kill you, you know that, don't you?" He put the bottle back on the table.

"Must be true. It's some of Jesse's leftover meds, and we all know what happened to her."

Rooster ignored the remark and moved to the kitchen. He opened the refrigerator door and found a light, but not much else. He turned to the table and picked up an empty liquor bottle and sniffed. "Well, I guess this answers the question of what wine goes well with Percocet."

"Wine? Now that stuff will kill you. Give me bourbon every time." Jason emphasized his words with a long swig from the bottle dangling at his side.

Rooster walked back to Jason. "So, I guess your goal is to drink yourself to death. And what the booze doesn't do, the pills will take care of. Is that it?"

Jason laughed and took a staggering half-step. "Die, me die? No, no, no." He wagged a finger in Rooster's direction. "I'm a God. I can't die. I just go on and on, bestowing my healing powers on the sick. I'm a doctor!" He shouted and pounded his chest. The movement knocked him off balance, and he half fell onto a nearby chair.

"So, this is what you became a doctor for?" Rooster asked.

"Ah, be careful of the dreams you're dreaming, or your dreams will be dreaming you; Willie Nelson." Jason toasted and emptied the bottle in a final gulp.

Rooster's face revealed little emotion. "Ah, I see. This is all about self-pity. You couldn't be the great healer, so just fuck the world, and be sure and pity me while you're at it."

Jason launched himself into a stumbling swing at Rooster, who quickly sidestepped the punch and pushed him backward onto the couch.

"Look, Jason, I know it hurts, and I know it's hard, but this isn't your fault. This is just one of those shitty things that happen. Now, you can throw your life away, sit here, and drink yourself to death, or you can be a man and deal with it. What do you think Jesse would have wanted?"

"A man, a man? Oh, how wrong you are, sir. I'm the Second Son of God, cloned from Jesus H. Christ himself." He grabbed Arthur's papers from the end table and threw them at Rooster.

"What the hell are you talking about?" Rooster picked up the papers and scanned them, shuffling from one sheet to another. "This doesn't tell me much. Suppose you explain it to me."

"Well, Rooster, that's my genetic karyotype — and the other one, well that's a karyotype of the cells from a famous religious relic. Supposedly cells from the big J.C. himself. If you go over them v-e-r-y carefully, you'll find they're identical, right down to the two X chromosomes. I'm cloned from Jesus Christ," he sneered.

"I'm not a geneticist, but this sounds like bullshit to me."

"Au contraire, Dr. Rooster. This explains everything; the mysterious shock and miracle in the ER, magically healing lacerations, and a little old lady healed of her stroke. Hell, I can even bring little fawns back to life. Yes-sir-ee, I can do it all. Well, almost all," he added sarcastically. "Right up to the one that counts, and then I'm just flat out of tricks." He accentuated his words with an attempted draw from the now empty bottle.

"Jason, I haven't — "

He cut Rooster off and continued. "You know, Rooster, it's a lot like being a doctor. We play the game; we have all the answers, right up to when it counts. Then, with the family in the waiting room, it comes to the real crunch time. Time to pull a miracle out of our hats, but *poof*, nothing." He flipped his hands into the air. "Who says God doesn't have a sense of humor?" He laughed until his body shook with a racking cough.

"That's right, Jason, we don't heal. We do what we can to help out, but the final decision is always out of our hands. We don't give life, and we don't take it away. Despite the TV shows, we're just mere mortals like everybody else."

"Oh, but that's not entirely true, is it, Rooster?" Jason wagged his finger in the air. "Sometimes we cheat a little and take a life, don't we? Like the patient we don't think should be coded so we do a *slow code*, or the cardiac arrest we cut short because we're too backed up in the ER, or maybe the person we arrange to have pushed off a cliff." He thrust the last slurred words at Rooster with his finger.

"You really think you've got all the answers, don't you?" Rooster's words were a mixture of anger and disgust. "You sit back and watch the world go by from your smug little niche and see what you want to see. You get handed the whole package, money, cars, and prestige, without so much as a bump in the road, but let the first jolt come along and it's all over. So long, fellas, time to bail, it's too tough for me. Before you start judging people and handing down your pronouncements to the rest of us mere mortals, maybe you should talk to Larry Todd. You see Jason, everything's not black and white. Everything's not a clear line in the sand. Sometimes you have to actually search to find the answer. And, sometimes the answer isn't popular with everyone. You may not always like what I do, but remember, when you need me, and I save your ass, some people may not like that either."

Rooster's anger ebbed away, its energy spent on his words. He waited for a response, but there was no sign Jason had even heard him, as he lit a cigarette and weaved toward the kitchen in search of another bottle.

Rooster shook his head. "So what's the long-term plan here, Jason? Are you planning on coming back to work, or do your plans only extend as far as the bottom of your next bottle?"

"You're right on the second count, Rooster." He turned the empty bottle over in his hand and shook it for emphasis, then tossed it toward the trash. He missed the can and the bottle banged against the floor and spun in a half-circle.

"So, I guess that's it then. I'll leave you to your self-pity. If you change your mind and want some help, let me know." Rooster slammed the door behind him. He had seen men beaten by life before. Some of them had been good men, but he couldn't accept Jason had been so utterly destroyed by Jesse's death. He wasn't sure what to make of his ramblings about being cloned, so he chalked it up to the effects of the booze and the pills. He hoped there was still a chance for Jason, even though the prognosis didn't look promising now. Maybe time would help if the drugs didn't destroy him first.

Jason wandered through the apartment looking for another bottle, and rolled Rooster's words in his mind. What did Rooster know about it anyway? "Yes, I hear you," he shouted toward the bedroom. No one could understand what his life had become in the last months; almost no one. "You understand, don't you?" He stumbled closer to the door of the room he had shared with Jesse. "I won't stay here alone, not like this. You can't make me!" The doorknob felt invitingly warm to his touch. "Jesse, is that you? Are you here, baby?" He pushed the door open and switched on the light. "Oh, Jesse, you don't know how much I've missed you." The gun was right where he had left it, in the middle of their bed. He picked it up and turned it over slowly in his hands as if it were a fragile living thing, and looked down into the eternal darkness of the barrel. The bullets stood lined up in a neat row, on the dresser behind him. He turned as he snapped the cylinder of the gun open, and reached for the first gleaming bullet. He looked back over his shoulder at the bed and smiled. "Jesse," he said tenderly. "I'm coming, baby."

Rooster stepped into his pajama bottoms. His mind still raced from his meeting with Jason, and he thought about the things Jason had said. Maybe he did make his own rules, but so did everyone else; to a degree. And, he tried to do what benefited other people, not just himself. Over the years, he had done things he wasn't necessarily proud of, but he had saved a lot of people a tremendous amount of grief and pain. Who was Jason to judge him? He slid between crisp, fresh sheets, reached for the light, and stopped. "Oh hell, I'll call him tomorrow." He turned the light out, lay back on his pillow, exhaled and closed his eyes.

The phone next to his bed rang as if it had been waiting for him to settle in. "Shit," he grumbled and reached for the phone. "Yeah," he answered informally. He knew only a select few had his number.

"Rooster, this is Dave Darian.ˆ Are you up?"

"I am now," he answered. "Actually I just laid down." His tone softened. "What's up, Dave?"

"I've got your boy Jason Corey in my ER. They brought him in by ambulance from an MVC awhile ago. I thought you'd want to know."

Rooster's mind lurched forward as the importance of what he heard registered. "How's he doing? Any significant injuries?"

"No, some contusions and skid marks. His CTs are negative. God watches over fools and drunks, and I think Jason's covered on both points tonight."

"Yeah, I saw him earlier, and he was pretty well blasted, but I thought he knew better than to drive."

"His B.A. is 375, and his tox screen lit up like a Christmas tree. I guess he believes in better living through pharmacology," Darian laughed.

"Have the police been there yet?" Rooster dreaded the answer.

"They stopped by briefly, but the kid was in X-ray. They had us pull a legal B.A. and said they'd be back for the blood later. We're just getting ready to admit him for observation for the night. Cops said he totaled his car. Luckily for him, there was no one else involved."

"Listen, Dave. Keep him there in the ER, and if the cops come back for that B.A., stall them until I get there."

Rooster raced through the late-night Seattle traffic, praying he wouldn't get stopped by the police. He pulled into the ER parking lot at Renton General Hospital thirty minutes later, found Dave Darian, and pulled him aside.

"Did the cops come back for his lab work yet?" He pressed.

"Not yet, but I'm sure they will. What difference does it make?"

The words were barely out of his mouth, when he realized where Rooster was going. "Oh no, Rooster. Tampering with evidence is a felony."

"You're not going to tamper with anything. Tell your nurses to get Jason ready to leave and show me your evidence lockup."

Darian clenched his jaw and stood his ground.

"Don't make me remind you of what you owe me, Dave."

Reluctantly, Darian withdrew a small key from his pocket. "Okay, Rooster, but this makes us even. Do you understand me? Even!"

"Okay, Dave, we're even. Now let's get going before the cops come back."

They walked into a small room off the ER filled with cupboards, and a small metal cabinet anchored to the wall. Rooster pulled a pair of vinyl gloves from a box on the counter while
Dave Darian unlocked the metal locker. Rooster withdrew a large white envelope with his gloved hand. The typed label on the envelope bore Jason's name, and Dave Darian nodded his confirmation. Rooster took a penknife from his pocket, attached to his key ring, and slid the blade through the seal of the envelope, splitting the words *Evidence. Do not open,* and replaced the packet back into the locker.

"There, so much for the chain of evidence. Now, let's get Jason the hell out of here."

Rooster pulled his Lexus SUV to the front of the ER, and within minutes, an unconscious Jason was loaded and strapped into the backseat. When they pulled away, they attracted a look of interest from the officer at the wheel of a police cruiser who was pulling into the lot. Rooster smiled and waved, but elicited no response.

"Lucky, lucky, lucky, my friend. This is your lucky day," he whispered to an unhearing Jason in the back seat.

Rooster drove south on Interstate 5, pushing the speed limit, but not enough to attract attention. What he was doing could easily be construed as kidnapping. If he were stopped in Seattle, he could probably talk himself out of the situation. An unknown state trooper in Oregon, across state lines, would present a much more challenging predicament. He pulled his cell phone out of his pocket and called information for the number of Rising Sun Retreat. He had Jason's admission to the exclusive detox center arranged before they left the state.

They drove through the still night of rural Southwest Washington. Two and one-half hours later, they crossed the bridge on the edge of Portland, skirted the sleeping city, and continued due south into Southern Oregon. Rooster counted off the familiar exits to the beach towns of Lincoln City, Newport, and finally, Coos Bay.

Shortly before dawn, Jason started to stir in the backseat. Rooster pulled off an exit ramp in the middle of nowhere and riffled through an emergency kit he kept in the back of his Lexus. It wasn't the run-of-the-mill emergency equipment, but he found what he was searching for. He helped Jason pee on the side of the road, pushed him back into the car, and injected him with 50 mg of Thorazine. Jason was unconscious again in a few minutes.

A bright Northern California sunrise emerged over Rooster's left shoulder, and a few hours later, he spotted his exit. They had made good time. He followed a number of turns through the countryside and finally ended up at a set of gates attended by a guard.

"Dr. Ian Christanson with an admission," he announced to the guard who checked his list and cleared them through. They followed the shaded drive another mile to the front of the hospital. Rooster stopped in front of the vast Victorian mansion where he was met by several hospital attendants. They carried a half-conscious Jason inside and directly to a detox room, while Rooster continued on to the office of the hospital director. The door was open when he arrived.

"Rooster, it's good to see you again. I see you've brought us another customer."

Rooster extended his hand only to have it engulfed and lost in the massive grip of the huge man. The only thing larger than Dr. Sheldon Sizemore's frame was his smile.

"It's good to see you again, Sheldon. How have you been?" The man eased himself into the oversized chair behind his desk, motioned Rooster to a seat, and rocked backwards.

Rooster sat down and suppressed a grin. Since their last meeting, Sheldon had dyed his long curly hair bright red. The color did little to assuage his freckled face.

"I see you've gone for the Howdy Doody look, Sheldon." Rooster finally chuckled.

The man behind the desk rolled with laughter. "Yes, well, I figured if I couldn't stun them with my handsome good looks, I would at least hold their attention while they tried to place the face. So, what have you brought me this time? Another one of your strays?"

"No, Shelton. This one's special, and I'm afraid you have your work cut out for you."

"You never did pick the simple ones, Rooster."

"This kid's one of my ER doctors, or at least he was. He had it all — smart, ambitious, engaged to a great girl — the authentic American dream. Several months ago, he began drinking a little too much, then started with some pills; nothing serious, just something light for sleep. He probably would have been all right, but the girl gets diagnosed with ovarian cancer. It turns out to be a wild type CA, unresponsive to treatment, and she died a few months later." Rooster raised his eyebrows and shrugged.

"Well, that can certainly be a recipe for disaster, but it's certainly not a given. Did anything else push him over the edge?" Sheldon asked.

"I think he's had a complete psychotic break. I was in his apartment last night, and through his drunken ramblings, he started yelling about being cloned from Christ. Says he's the second Son of God. He even had some sort of printout of his DNA."

"Do you have any idea where that might have come from?"

Rooster rubbed his neck and stretched. "Yeah, he's had some funny things happen in the ER. It started with some sort of electric shock. It knocked Jason out but ended up restarting the heart of the patient he was working on."

"Funny things happen, Rooster. Doesn't sound too mystical to me."

"The patient was in asystole, Sheldon. It shouldn't have done anything. But there were some other things, too. Some patient convinced Jason, and the nurse who was on duty, that his laceration was magically healed. There were just some crazy things like that, and they must have gotten into his head."

Dr. Sizemore crossed his arms in front of his massive frame. "Well, you really know how to pick 'em, Rooster, delusional, addicted to drugs and alcohol, a recent catastrophic life experience, and probably suicidal. This one may not have a good outcome."

Rooster smiled. "That's why I brought him to you, Sheldon, so you could work your magic."

His laugh shook his whole body. "We'll see. So, how have *you* been, Rooster?"

"Good, can't complain."

"No, I mean how have you *been?*"

"Ooh. I've been good, Sheldon." He held out both arms and showed the inside of his elbows.

"Please, Rooster, don't insult me. Just tell me that you're clean, and I'll believe you."

"I never could lie to you, Sheldon," he said through a smile. "Yes, I'm clean."

"Good. And Lori and the kids?" Sheldon asked.

"I decided it was best to leave it the way it was," Rooster answered, suddenly somber.

"I'm sorry to hear that, Rooster. Maybe someday?"

"Maybe someday."

Rooster stood. "I've got to get back. You'll keep me posted?"

"As always, Rooster. How many does this make now?"

"I'm not counting," he laughed and walked away.

Rooster drove north. After a few hours, his body ached from lack of sleep, and he caught himself nodding off at the wheel. The second time the sound of his tires on the warning strips at the edge of the highway jolted him awake, he realized he couldn't physically stay on the road any longer. He pulled into a small, nameless town, found some food and checked into an empty ten-room motel. His sleep was restless, haunted by oozing memories and the pain of nearly forgotten wounds.

TWENTY EIGHT

The human mind and body are resilient; to a point. Even so, Jason had a tougher time than most patients in detox, and the initial reports had not been encouraging. He was furious when his head cleared enough to understand where he was. He demanded to leave, until Sheldon presented him with the commitment papers Rooster had provided the hospital. They were, of course, bogus. Once Jason resigned himself to the fact he wasn't leaving, he rode a roller coaster of depression, anger and hatred. For the first month, Sheldon feared that his initial reservations had been correct, and this young man would not recover, but instead plunge into the bottomless abyss of insanity. But as time passed, Sheldon had worked his miracles as Rooster had predicted, and Jason slowly crawled out of his personal nightmare, back to a version of reality. The only residual of the prior months that he still embraced were his memories of Jesse, and his insistence that certain unexplainable happenings had been real. He kept the information he had received from Arthur to himself. Although he didn't discuss it with anyone, he knew what Arthur had told him was true, no matter how bizarre it sounded. Rooster kept up with Jason's progress and had even talked with him a few times once Jason's desire to kill him passed.

Jason had been gone four months, and things had changed at Harborline. Barb Henry was the new hospital administrator. Rooster had, as promised, attended Bob's farewell banquet, and was the picture of sincerity when he wished Bob well. He gave him an envelope at the dinner, which contained a best wishes card, signed "Steve Lubeck" with the negatives of certain sensitive pictures. Armen Polling announced his resignation from his position on the board of directors for proverbial "personal reasons." Rooster didn't know how Bob had done it, and he actually didn't care, just as long as it was done. He suspected Bob may have held certain leverage over Polling, just as Rooster had held over Bob. The following week Rooster signed a new five-year contract with the ER group and the hospital, with a significant increase in salary for himself and his physician staff.

Rooster filled Steve Lubeck's position with a fledgling doctor just out of his residency, and the young physician was coming along nicely under Rooster's tutelage. Larry Todd had moved on with his life. He and his children had moved into a new home and hired a nanny who cared for them all. She was sixty years old.

Another long, wet Seattle winter was over. The bright yellow Scotch broom was in full blossom and blanketed the roadsides, punctuated by the startling purple of thousands of flowering crab trees, which announced the arrival of spring in the Pacific Northwest. Summer wasn't here yet, but the rain had stopped, and on some days, the wind off the Sound carried the scent of promised sunny days and near balmy nights. The Great Mountain had even occasionally emerged, for brief visits, as if to assure the world it still existed, floating above them all, like a benevolent sovereign.

Rooster relaxed with a cup of coffee and a newspaper at the doctors' desk in the lazy morning ER. He became aware of someone standing over him, folded the paper down, and peered over the edge.

"Geez, sure is *quiet* around here," Jason said, emphasizing the forbidden word.

"Well, I'll be damned. The prodigal son returns," Rooster said as he stood up.

Jason shook Rooster's extended hand, then flipped his cigarette lighter. "I'll buy you one."

"Let's do it," Rooster answered smiling.

They walked through the door onto the rear deck, lit up and took their old bar-rail stance.

"So, how are you? You look a hell of a lot better than the last time I saw you."

"Yeah. You know, I can hardly remember that night. The whole thing seems like it happened a lifetime ago. I remember that when I left the apartment and went after another bottle I was trying to get drunk enough to come back home and . . . well let's just say I wasn't making any long-term plans." He inhaled deeply from his cigarette.

"J.C., if it makes any difference, I think you should know I've been at that same point in my life. I know how much it hurts."

"It's hard to believe anyone has ever been through what I have, Rooster."

"We've all lost someone we love, Jason. Some of us have even counted the bullets in the gun." Rooster smiled hesitantly.

Jason looked at him and truly saw Rooster for the first time since he had known him.

"Yeah, I went back to your apartment after I left you with Sheldon to make sure you didn't have a cat or something, and found the gun. Five bullets lined up on the dresser, and one in the chamber. It brought back old memories."

"I owe you, Rooster. I don't want to think where I'd be if you hadn't helped me."

"You're goddamned right you owe me, and I plan on collecting, and don't you forget it." Rooster smiled as he exhaled a column of smoke above them. "So, what's the greatest risk population for cardiac disease?"

Jason laughed, "What?"

"You heard me, answer the question."

"The greatest risk population for cardiac disease is that population that presents to the ER complaining of chest pain," Jason replied smugly.

"Sounds good to me, I think you're mentally crisp. So when are you coming back to work?"

Jason shook his head. "I don't know, Rooster. It's been awhile. It's pretty intimidating right now."

"You fall off a horse, you need to get back on."

"I'm not sure I can do it anymore, Rooster."

"Sure you can. An old cowboy friend of mine says only the dead stay down." Rooster bit his lip the second the words were out.

Jason looked down at his feet and nodded. "Okay. You call it."

"Tomorrow night. The new kid is scheduled for night shift, but he wants it off for a concert or some damned thing. Kids! I'll cover until . . . midnight; you got it until seven a.m. You all right with that?"

"I'll be here at midnight," Jason answered, surprised by his own words.

The door from the ER opened and Bonnie stuck her head outside. "Damn it, Rooster, we've got a hot one. Get in here! I shouldn't have to come looking for you like your blessed mother." She fired the words at Rooster before she saw Jason beside him. "Jason, darlin'," her voice softened, and she smiled. "I knew you'd be comin' back to us."

Jason unlocked the door to their . . . his apartment. He stepped inside and immediately felt the simultaneous, familiar, and foreign memories of a past life. The rooms had been cleaned, the bottles and pills gone, clothes picked up and trash removed. He knew Rooster's work when he saw it. He dropped his bag inside the door and waited, uncertain what to do next. The stark emptiness struck him, and he knew the rooms would never be as they had been when Jesse was alive. God, he wanted a drink. He walked to the deck, separated the curtains and slid the door open. The familiar view of the sound brought back even more memories. He stalled as long as he could, then walked to their bedroom.

The room felt like Jesse. He walked to their closet and tentatively opened the door. He was relieved to find her things still there, hanging neatly as if she would be home from work in a few hours. He needed to give her up a little at a time. He walked to their dresser, opened her drawer, and found the clothes neatly folded as she had left them. He picked up a camisole and held it to his face. Her scent was still there after all this time, or maybe it only persisted as a memory in his soul. He opened the top drawer but found the gun was gone. He smiled.

Jason worked his way through the day, one hour at a time, trying to reclaim his life. At noon, he checked his watch again and thought, thirty-six hours more until he started back at the ER. He called Arthur and made a date for dinner the evening after his shift. He tried to read, but his mind kept drifting to other places and other times, and to Jesse. He finally gave up and went out for a walk.

A warm breeze off the Sound re-energized him. He tried to jog for a while but found he was too out of shape and gave up. He dragged himself past a couple of small beachfront bars, after debating the harm in one beer with his conscience. He finally stopped at Starbucks for an iced coffee and rested until his nervous energy moved him again. He finished his trip with a stop at Boston Pizza and a large garlic special to go. Several hours after he left, he returned home in the early dusk with his pizza. He had survived his first day home.

Jason walked through the ambulance doors, wearing scrubs, and his bag slung over his shoulder. He tried to hide his apprehension. He was scared to death, and he knew it showed. He passed Summer on his way into the ER, hurrying on her way to a patient's room.

"Hey, Dr. Corey. Good to see you back." She flashed him a broad smile and disappeared. He could only raise his eyebrows in acknowledgement.

Rooster was sitting at the desk scribbling on a chart. He spotted Jason and pushed the clipboard into the discharge rack.

"I love to see my relief man coming through the door. Its been a pretty good night so far. I don't have any patients to turn over, so you can start fresh."

"Sounds good to me," Jason answered and dropped his bag on the floor behind the desk.

Rooster sensed Jason's level of anxiety but didn't comment. He knew Jason had to make it on his own now, or he never would.

Summer walked up behind them as Rooster got up from the desk. "Rooster, did you forget about the patient in room two?"

"Shit. I'll take care of it."

"Don't worry about it, Rooster, I'll pick it up. Whatcha got?"

Rooster hesitated. "No biggie. I just need to pronounce a DOA they dropped off. I'll get it, J.C."

Rooster's voice said volumes.

"Rooster, I can handle it! Go home."

Rooster met Jason's eyes. "It might be best if I did this one. Hell of a way to start your first shift back."

"Rooster, I'm okay. I'll take care of it." He was more insistent this time.

Rooster relented and handed him the chart. "It's a young female. Looks like an O.D."

Jason faltered slightly. "No problem."

Rooster gathered his things and left without looking back. Jason pulled his stethoscope out of his bag, picked up the chart, and headed for room two, ignoring the cup of coffee Summer had placed on his desk. He wanted to get this over with quickly.

The lights were out in room two, except for the spotlight over the gurney. The girl was covered entirely with a sheet which outlined the shape of her young body. Jason laid the chart on the side counter and approached the gurney. He braced himself and lifted the sheet away from her face. A beautiful twenty-something girl stared up from the table. Her long dyed-black hair fell over her shoulders and wisped across her thick, Goth makeup. The neckline of her black dress plunged to her waist, interrupted only by the metal studded collar around her neck. An ornate tattoo of three intertwined 6's contained in a pentagram stood out in the center of her chest. There were no signs of trauma, and he assumed Rooster's diagnosis of an O.D. was probably correct, but that would be for the medical examiner to determine. Jason's only job was to pronounce her dead, and forward the body to the morgue.

It didn't require years of medical training to confirm she was dead. Jason flashed a light into her unresponsive eyes. Her skin was the dusky cyanotic-blue, typical of a fresh corpse. He wanted to be thorough and go by the book. He held his stethoscope to her chest and listened for a pulse that he knew wasn't there. He looked at his watch and noted the official time for his paperwork. He paused and looked at her as he started to pull the sheet back into place over her face. He couldn't help but think about her parents, her family and friends, and all that she would never have; a husband, children, the joy and tears that make up a life. He thought about Jesse.

Jason looked back over his shoulder to make sure he was alone, then laid his hand on her chest, closed his eyes and waited. Once again, nothing happened. He pulled the sheet into place and walked away. He couldn't afford this, not now.

Jason walked to the counter, leaned over the chart and started to fill in the blanks on the death certificate, his back to the girl's body. Time of death. Date of death. Place of death. Certifying physician. He was lost in his thoughts as he worked. Otherwise he might have heard the faint rustle of the sheet when she rose from the table and shook off the veil of death. She slowly stood, took in her surroundings then riveted her gaze on Jason, like a hunter stalking her prey. She moved toward him in silent measured steps, her eyes unwavering. She stopped, inches away from Jason, and reached into her knee-high boot for the switchblade secreted there. Jason tensed briefly when he heard the blade snap into place. She paused momentarily, her breath on his neck, then plunged the stiletto blade into his back, through his right kidney, and twisted. Jason dropped to the floor without a sound, where he died in a swirling pool of his own bright red blood. The girl smiled with the satisfaction of an evil assassin who had accomplished her mission, then slowly walked away and disappeared into the misty, darkness of the night.

TWENTY NINE

It seemed as if it should be over. What else was there? What else could there possibly be? It had been Jason and Jesse's time, and now it had passed.

The world continued for those left behind, just as it always had. Individual stories might end, but the saga of life goes on, and as is often the case, endings are sometimes actually beginnings.

The days in the wake of Jason's death had been complicated. The police had no leads as to Jason's killer or the whereabouts of the body of the mysterious Goth girl. Her identity remained an enigma.

The ER staff wrestled with the actuality of this final tragedy. Some found solace in their belief that Jason and Jesse were together, but most only tried to work through their grief and anger, just as they had with so many needless deaths in the past. After all, death was an omnipresent part of their lives.

Rooster took advantage of the late-night calm in the ER to have a cup of coffee and read an early edition newspaper. He gravitated to the solitude of his office, rocked back in his chair and propped his feet on his desk. He sipped his coffee and began perusing the paper when a small article at the bottom of the front page caught his attention. The first few lines brought him lunging forward in his chair, dumping his coffee in his lap as his feet hit the floor. "What the hell?"

Body of Seattle Doctor Reported Missing

Minneapolis - Police have reported the disappearance of the body of Dr. Jason Corey. The body of the Seattle physician was sent to Minneapolis by plane for planned burial in the family plot near Elk River. Funeral home staff reported the body missing when they claimed the coffin from Sky Arrow Airlines but found it empty. Evergreen Lake Funeral Home, the Seattle mortuary that processed the body, confirmed all protocols were followed, and the body was in the casket at the time it was placed on the air transport. Dr. Corey was the victim of a bizarre murder in the ER at Harborline Hospital three days ago. Police are still without a suspect in that murder case. Minneapolis police are investigating the disappearance, but at this time are without a lead or motive.

This was as senseless as Jason's murder. No, this was worse. Who could possibly have any motive for such a theft, any possible use for the body? Rooster sat back and started to mop his scrubs with a napkin when he remembered his visit with Jason the night of the accident. Jason's words came back to him and rang in his mind with the clarity of the strike of a bell. *Cloned from Jesus Christ.*

What if Jason had been right? Was it actually so impossible? If not, then it wasn't a colossal leap of imagination or faith that, like Christ, there wouldn't be a body. Rooster had little faith but had always been blessed with imagination.

Dr. Harrison Fellows fidgeted at his desk and considered his options. Jason's death had severely limited his choices. At least he knew now, Jason's genes were a match for the original sample, and he believed the reports from Arthur gave strong evidence that Jason had possessed powers. The two genotype printouts laying side by side on the top of his desk taunted him.

"Damn it," he yelled and pounded his fist on the papers. He had it right in front of him all those years; had the opportunity to influence — no, control — the greatest power in the world.

Now, only one option remained open to him. He had done it once, and he could do it again. He still had the original cell line, and this time he wouldn't take any chances. He wouldn't leave his opportunity to be ruined by fools. No, he would control every step himself. His phone interrupted his thoughts.

"Dad, I need you to come down to the cryo area right away." His son's voice was adamant.

"What's wrong?"

"I think you'd better come down and see for yourself."

The elevator opened to the ultramodern cryo-storage unit. Several lab techs busied themselves, trying to avoid the row of stainless steel tanks that held frozen cell specimens. Harry junior, looking too much like his father, stood in front of a tank labeled "JC1."

"What's going on?" Harrison demanded.

"Feel it." Harry motioned toward the tank.

The senior Fellows eyes opened wide in disbelief as he placed his open palm against the tank.

"It's warm!" He shouted. "How the hell did this happen? Did you check the internal temperature?"

"I've checked the temperature and the time recorder," Harry answered. "The cells are ruined."

"Damn it! Why didn't the alarm system go off?" Harrison yelled.

"I don't know. We've checked the systems, and they all seem to be working. The tank just warmed, and the alarm didn't go off." Harry chewed his lower lip.

Harrison Fellows took a deep breath, exhaled, and shook his head. "That's it then. There won't be any more."

Dr. Robert Gurnert, Chief of Pathology at Renton General Hospital, sat at the table in his office peering through a microscope. Every few minutes he jotted a note on his pad then returned to his work. He didn't seem to notice the knock on his office door, but answered without looking up from his work.

"Come in."

The chief lab tech entered the office carrying a clipboard under his arm.

"Sorry to bother you, Dr. Gurnert, but I was doing an inventory and getting rid of some lab specimens and I have a question."

The pathologist looked up, removed his glasses, and rubbed his eyes.

"Oh, what's the problem, Roger?" He asked.

"I have a frozen specimen labeled 'products of conception' from a patient named Jessica Noble. I'm not sure why the specimen is frozen instead of preserved in formalin, like we usually do, but no one ever got a consent signed for disposal of the tissue after the miscarriage. I understand the patient is deceased, and I was wondering what you want me to do with it."

"I suppose with all the stir associated with that case the form got missed. You say the specimen was frozen?"

"Yes, sir. I checked, and the tissue looks like it's intact," the tech answered.

"Well, it doesn't make any difference. You might as well destroy it. Here, I'll sign the disposal slip." He reached for the clipboard his tech held out for his signature and scribbled his name.

"Thank you, sir. I've got a shipment going out to the disposal company today, and we need the room for storage." Roger closed the door behind him, and Dr. Gurnert returned to his microscope.

The lab was busy, filled with techs and semi-noxious smells. Roger Xeroxed the form on his clipboard, filed the original and attached the copy to the still-frozen specimen container with a rubber band. He stacked it in a cardboard box labeled "BIOHAZARD," with several dozen other containers, sealed the box with bright red tape and placed it with two other boxes near the lab door. A half hour later a burly man, wearing a brown uniform from the bio-disposal company, rolled a hand truck into the lab and parked it near the stacked boxes.

"These the ones to go?" He yelled toward Roger.

"Yeah, Frank. The paperwork's all there."

Frank stacked the boxes on his hand truck, propped the door open with his foot, and maneuvered the dolly toward the hall.

"Roger, do you still have that specimen you asked me about a while ago?" Dr. Gurnert called from his office.

"Hold it, Frank," Roger yelled toward the closing door. "It's just going out the door, Doctor. Is there a problem?"

"No problem, but pull it out for me, will you? I had a thought." the pathologist answered.

Frank pulled a face and unloaded his cargo. They found the specimen container in the second box, and Roger carried it to Dr. Gurnert's office.

"You wanted this?" Roger held the container out.

Dr. Gurnert chewed his glasses and nodded. "Yes. I was just thinking that maybe we can create some good from that disaster. I know someone doing some new work in stem cell research, and he's looking for new cell lines. I'll call him and see if he's interested. Who knows, someday those cells may be used to cure thousands of people. Put the specimen back in the freezer, will you, Roger, and bring me the paperwork with the mother and father's information."

Dr. Gurnert thumbed through his Rolodex and found the number he was searching for. He dialed as Roger laid the paperwork in front of him and listened to the phone ring three thousand miles away. The phone picked up on the fourth ring.

"Hello. This is Harrison Fellows."

ABOUT THE AUTHOR

Dr. Paul W. Nielsen lives with his wife, Deborah, on a 236 acre ranch near the Appalachian Mountains where he balances his time between work as an ER physician and writing his next novels. His hobbies include bonsai horticulture, horses and hunting. Nielsen released his first book, *The Cambion*, in 2014 from Morehead Publishing. This medical suspense/paranormal book earned a 5 star rating on Amazon and glowing reviews from readers. *The Cambion* was a Silver Medal winner in the Fiction Horror genre for the 2015 Global Ebook Awards.

Paul released his next book, *The Second Son,* the following year and it won a Gold Medal in the Fiction Paranormal category for the 2015 Global Ebook Awards. He has other projects in the works.

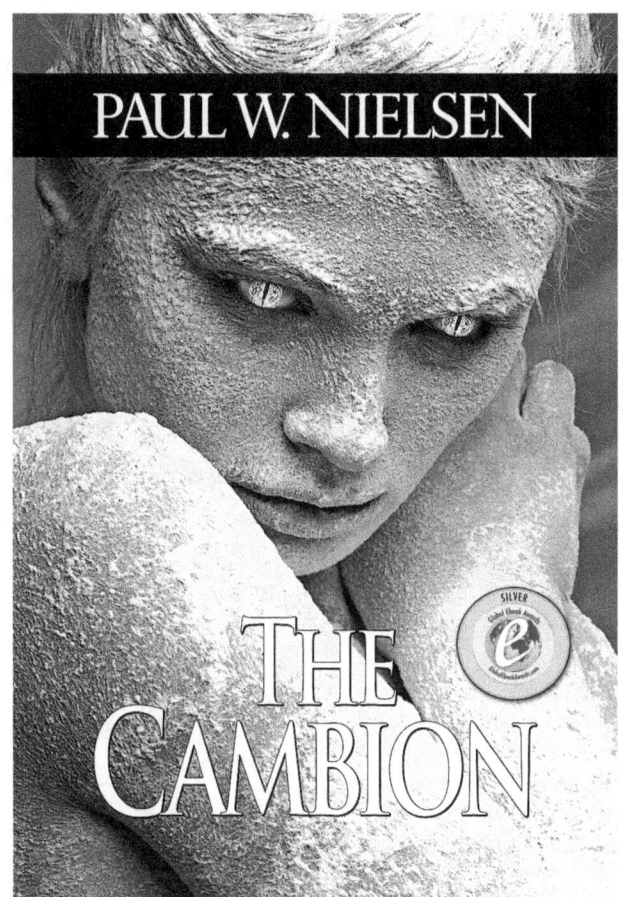

PAUL W. NIELSEN

THE CAMBION

"Just finished The Cambion and WOW! Have not read a book in a long time that kept me on the edge of my seat for the entire book. I found it a great mixture of history, modern day medicine, demons and things that go bump in the night. Not that I am a big believer of things that go bump in the night, but hey, what's so bad about sleeping with the night light on? Sweet dreams." — Mrs. B.K.

An Exerpt From
THE CAMBION
PAUL W. NIELSEN

Beth dressed quickly, ran down the stairs and found the Witch Board where Cynthia had left it. She turned it in her hands and absorbed its energy. *Could a single person use this thing?* She wondered. There was only one way to find out. She paused as Geri's words came back to her: "You can end up dead with your soul trapped inside the board."

If she had another way, any other way, she would have walked away from the board and tried to contact Bethlehem. But the stark reality was that the board was her only chance, and Beth needed that option.

She placed the board on the table, and through her sobs, positioned the pointer on its surface. She quickly rubbed her eyes and nose with her sleeve then placed her trembling fingers on the edge of the planchette.

"Bethlehem, talk to me. How do I free him? What do I need to do?"

The piece of ancient wood didn't move.

"Please, Bethlehem, help me," she screamed.

Initially, she couldn't tell whether the planchette was moving or whether her trembling hands shook it across the board, until it gradually gained strength and a purpose. She spelled the letters out loud.

"R-E-D-T-H-R-E-A-D."

"Red thread. What red thread? Help me Bethlehem."

"P-O-W-E-R-O-F-2-L-I-V-E-S."

The planchette stopped.

"I need to know, Bethlehem. What does it mean?"

The planchette remained still, its animation gone.

"Beth dropped her head, overwhelmed by the encounter with her own past soul, and tried to think. There was something there, lost in the dark corners of her mind. She tried to concentrate and search for the recollection just beyond her reach. The lost memory was there. The words written on a piece of paper started to emerge into her conscious mind, "A thread between two lives."

The noise above her snapped her attention. A second and third sound pounded across the floor overhead, moving toward the head of the stairs. For a moment, Beth sat transfixed, uncertain what to do, until the unmistakable sound of claws on the wooden floor, scraping between the heavy steps, brought a scream from her throat. Suddenly, she realized if she didn't get away she was going to die. She ran for the door, grabbed her purse, and snatched Tank in a single movement. She could hear the beast on the stairs when she slammed the door behind her and ran for her car. The sound was unlike anything Beth had ever heard or imagined, a sound that could only come from someplace in hell.

www.ingramcontent.com/pod-product-compliance
Lightning Source LLC
Chambersburg PA
CBHW070609130626
46556CB00001B/312